UNDER DARK WATERS

Also by Bernadette Calonego
The Zurich Conspiracy

UNDER DARK WATERS

BERNADETTE CALONEGO

Translated by Gerald Chapple

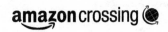

Text copyright © 2010 Bernadette Calonego
Translation copyright © 2015 Gerald Chapple
All rights reserved.

Previously published as *Unter dunklen Wassern* by Bloomsbury Publishing in Germany in 2010. Translated from the German by Gerald Chapple. First published in English by AmazonCrossing in 2015.

Quotations from the writings of Else Seel cited by generous permission of the author's estate and Professor Rodney Symington.

Published by AmazonCrossing, Seattle

www.apub.com

Amazon, the Amazon logo, and AmazonCrossing are trademarks of Amazon.com, Inc., or its affiliates.

ISBN-13: 9781477828526
ISBN-10: 1477828524

Cover design by Cyanotype Book Architects

Library of Congress Control Number: 2014919182

Printed in the United States of America

For Maria and Jean-Claude

PROLOGUE

Now he was in the thick of it. His Beaver had suddenly lost altitude, like it took on a load of lead—fast. Then it reared up like a frantic mustang, shaking, rocking violently. And then came the rain. A gray wall, with nothing behind it.

The ocean was much too close.

Just don't crash in that shit!

He pulled the Beaver up higher, and the plane vibrated like a jackhammer.

He'd been through a lot, ridden out terrifying squalls, a hairbreadth away from disaster. But today—it was the worst of the worst, a nightmare.

His adrenaline shot up. *Just don't go down in this goddamn hell.*

Not him. He always escaped. He knew those infernal traps where crosswinds locked together like mad dogs. He knew the fogs that snuck up on you and swallowed everything up in a flash. But what he knew best was himself.

He could have aborted his flight. If he'd had to, he could have kept his plane on the ground. He would have listened to his feelings if they had told him: You're not going to land in this storm.

It's stronger than you. It'll wipe out you and your Beaver in two seconds.

A voice in his headphones: "GQC to JPX . . . it's a goddamn fucking merry-go-round, a goddamn merry-go-round, I'm telling you, nobody can get through. I'm going back through Otter Channel and then out around Pitt Island."

There was another Beaver out there. Another madman risking his life.

He looked at his GPS. Yellow, land—blue, water.

"JPX to GQC . . . OK . . . I'll try Grenville Channel, but from here it looks like lousy pea soup."

Jumpy static in his headphones. That voice again.

"Got a pretty strong ELT signal."

So he'd picked up the downed plane's emergency locator transmitter, too; it was weak but continuous.

"Where are you now?" he came in again.

"I'm halfway up McCauley Island, between Hevenor Inlet and Newcombe Harbour. Like a washing machine here, a fucking big wind."

"I couldn't make it through Grenville Channel, had to go back and follow you. Lemme know right away if you see anything."

" . . . 'K."

The Beaver was dancing. A dance with the devil. The plane wasn't gaining altitude. He gave it more throttle.

You don't want to go swimming, baby. Keep it level. Nice and level. The water down there is cold, like frozen steel. Two minutes, and your blood thickens. Ten minutes, and your heart screams for help. Ninety, and it's game over.

The other pilot's voice thundered words in his headphones.

"Getting close. The ELT's howling like a wildcat. My gut tells me it's down there somewhere. This hole is pulling everything down."

"OK."

He'd seen these kinds of wrecks before: Most of the passengers drowned, caught in the wreckage. Sometimes they broke a bone or their back—or had their skull crushed in, the blood pouring out.

"Got something!"

The shout made him flinch.

"The plane's in the water right in front of Captain's Cove. I'll see if I can land and work my way in."

"See anybody in the water?"

"I'm being fucking hammered—hard to say from here. I'll let you know if I can land."

His headphones crackled: another shout.

"Jesus Christ! What's that? Straight ahead!"

"Can you get any lower?"

"Already low, damn low."

"Listen, don't go too slow!"

He'd better watch it. Or he'll hit the water, too.

". . . there they are! Jesus! There they are! Hey, man, I can see them!"

"What do you see?"

". . . the plane . . . it's broken apart, all broken up. Man oh man!"

"See anybody?"

"Gotta get down, man, gotta get down."

"Is the sea too rough? I can see waves."

"I think I can do it."

"Be careful, eh! Careful!"

The voice was gone. He waited.

Hope he doesn't go nuts when he sees what's there, lose his nerve.

The other pilot was a good one—he knew that. Almost as good as he was. Logged seven thousand hours mostly between Alaska and Prince Rupert. That coast was a death trap, a death trap for lousy pilots.

"I'm down, man, down in Captain's Cove and getting pretty close. One pontoon's sticking straight up out of the water. I think somebody's hanging on to it."

The voice was softer now, as if the vocal cords had been in water too long.

"Good job! I'll be right there."

"Jeff's getting out and climbing up on it."

So he took a guy with him. Why didn't he say that before? Never mind. Every hand counts. Especially with a rolling sea like this. But *he* wouldn't take anybody along and put their life in danger.

". . . oh, my God!"

"What's the matter?"

"They're all dead, man, all dead!"

"Dead or unconscious? Can you see?"

"Dead as a doornail, man, stone dead."

He stayed calm. *Gotta keep calm.*

He looked at his GPS. Still a few minutes to the crash site.

"I'll be there right away. Wait'll I get there."

The wind suddenly let up, playing itself out at last. Then he saw it. His pal's Beaver, bouncing like a rubber ducky in a bathtub. There was a second plane beside it: broken wing, cockpit at a crazy angle. A body on the left pontoon—legs in the water, not moving.

He shouted into the mic.

"Can you see me? I'm coming down. Can you see me?"

No answer.

He began his approach. A voice shouted into his headphones.

"Good God! He's alive! One of them's moving! He's alive!"

He was concentrating on landing. He had the Beaver firmly under control. *C'mon, baby. C'mon, c'mon.*

He had to land in a light side wind, parallel to the waves. There was a calm spot ahead. The pontoons splashed down.

Taxiing toward the planes, he had but a single thought: *Let's hope it's the right guy who's still alive.*

CHAPTER 1

Drugs. She looked at the immigration officer and knew right away: *That's what he's thinking. Drugs.*

Her eyes were glazed over like a yuppie's on coke. It was always that way when her allergies hit. *One* of her allergies. Her face, her whole body was bathed in sweat; her head throbbed.

The young officer eyed her with obvious suspicion. She'd pumped herself so full of antihistamines—the little red pills—before the twelve-hour flight from Zurich to Vancouver that she swayed like a sumo wrestler. If only the officer would wave her through fast. An allergy attack was bad enough, but add the exhaustion, and it was a nightmare.

The officer looked through her Swiss passport, then at her flushed red face. He entered some data into his computer and waited. Then he quickly motioned her over to Immigration, pointing at a line of people waiting with their baggage.

So she looked suspicious. She really should have known; people always knew when she had a secret just by looking at her.

She was the only white person in the line. There were men with turbans, women in shimmering saris, Asian faces and black ones. A bevy of children who weren't, to her surprise, whining or trying to knock over the movable barriers. No need to tell those kids how serious the situation was.

Sonya sat down beside a woman wearing a sari as blue as the Pacific Ocean she'd seen from the plane. *They're never going to let me in*, she thought to herself. *They'll find out everything and send me back. Or arrest me on the spot.*

"Passengers from Europe?"

A female officer standing several feet away looked around. Sonya got up and followed her to the end of a corridor, pushing a cart with her backpack and suitcase on it.

"Wait here," the officer said. Her manner was friendly. Sonya obediently went up to a counter, and a short while later a man appeared.

"May I see your travel documents?"

He took her papers and studied her carefully.

He can smell my fear. Yessir, that's real fear you smell. Just look at me. I'm scared of this strange country, scared of what I'll discover here. Any more fear, and I mightn't find a single thing I'm looking for.

"Sonya Werner." Her name sounded odd in his Canadian accent. "So you're looking to work here, eh?"

"No, I don't want to work. I'm just doing research for a Swiss museum, for an exhibition," she said in a husky voice. "I'm a historian," she added hastily.

He must have gone through everything: the permission letters, the references. He was certainly out to test her, to catch her in a contradiction.

"So what are you researching?"

"A German writer, Else Lübcke Seel. She emigrated from Berlin to Canada in 1927. I want to interview people who knew her."

Her explanation rolled off her tongue—she'd rehearsed it in her mind dozens of times. She spoke English well after two years at a London university.

"Where did this writer live?" He seemed interested.

"In northern British Columbia near Burns Lake. She married a trapper and lived in a cabin in the bush."

"Burns Lake. Are you going there by yourself?"

Sonya wavered. Was this one of those trick questions she'd been warned about? Did traveling alone arouse suspicion?

"A person I know in Vancouver is going with me." She tried to sound natural despite the lie.

The officer gave her a piece of paper. "Give me that person's name, address, and phone number, please."

She dug her address book out of her backpack and wrote down Diane Kesowsky's information.

"So you're German, from Berlin?"

Why did he ask when he'd already been through her passport?

"No, I'm Swiss, but the museum I work for is on the German border. We get a lot of German visitors."

Could he pick up any nervousness in her voice? Didn't this young man have a detailed knowledge of the map of Europe? Surely he was testing her, watching her body language. She would definitely have to drill it into Diane's head that the authorities now thought she was her traveling companion. Not that she intended to go with Diane; that wasn't the point. She would never reveal her true intentions—not to Diane and not to this man, who didn't seem ready to stop asking her seemingly harmless questions.

Suddenly the officer thumped a stamp into her passport, scribbled something over it, and handed her papers back with a cheery smile.

"Good luck with your research. And welcome to Canada."

CHAPTER 2

Waiting in line at the taxi stand, Sonya turned her feverish head and took in the night air. Vancouver in September. Was it raining this gently when Tonio arrived back then? He surely had no idea that he'd never return. He'd already be looking forward to coming back here. Looking forward to those assignations.

He had probably driven along the same streets she was on now, on the way to downtown: past little stores with flat roofs and colorful neon lights, past signs in Chinese and open Laundromats. Everything was lit up, though it was past midnight.

The taxi crossed a magnificent bridge, and the sparkling water below reflected the lights of the apartment buildings on the shore. Sonya could see through the windows into well-lit rooms where people were sitting at computers. A woman was on a stationary bike. Fitness training—in the middle of the night!

Glass and lights were everywhere—in huge storefront windows and transparent buildings.

Vancouver was a city with no place to hide.

The taxi stopped in front of a large building complex. Sonya asked the driver to wait, not wanting to be stuck there alone. Anxiety crept up the back of her neck once again. She tapped in Diane's entry code on the keypad beside the main doorway. Clicks. Noise. Then a woman's voice: "Sonya!"

Minutes later she was given a tight, warm hug by a stranger.

"How nice you're here at last! Come in. Everything's ready for you." Diane beamed as she took Sonya's suitcase. Sonya was still awake enough to take in her large, dark eyes and her soft, full lips. Lips like Angelina Jolie's.

"Let me guess," Diane said. "You don't want to eat or talk; you just want to get to bed and sleep."

"Yes," Sonya said, smiling her gratitude.

She was wide-awake at four in the morning. The glare of streetlights penetrated her dark blue bedroom curtains. Sonya lay under heavy blankets. She'd pushed several pillows to the edge of the bed. Her throat was dry. She felt her way around in the en suite bathroom and had a drink of water, which had a chemical taste. She discovered a small bottle of mineral water on the bureau. Diane had thought of everything. Sonya went back to bed, but she could forget the idea of sleeping. She sighed, retrieved the book with the green linen binding from her backpack, and slid back under the covers. It consoled her to think about Else. Else was in the past, far away somewhere, and that was solid ground. As long as she thought about Else, she was spared from other menacing thoughts.

Else Lübcke had sailed from Hamburg to Montreal on the steamship *Empress of Australia*, and then she had taken a four-day train trip to Vancouver. Else had been a Berlin poet in the twenties; she was the daughter of the owner of a country estate. By night, she was a secret *bohémienne*. By day, she worked as a clerk in a bank archive.

Then she suddenly left her home and went to Vancouver to meet this man, a trapper, fur trader, and gold miner. George Seel was a rough-mannered man with animal instincts: thirty-seven, a native Bavarian. He had lived in British Columbia for fifteen years and was in search of a wife. Why, Sonya asked herself for the hundredth time, why George Seel, of all people?

Else still puzzled her, though she knew the facts inside out. At thirty-three, Else had a job sorting newspaper clippings in a bank. Then she saw George Seel's advertisement: a personal ad, *single seeks single*, as it were. Something must have clicked in Else. Was it the desire for adventure? Was it a longing for the outside world, for the exotic? The feeling of being tied down, wanting to flee a stagnant existence?

"There's something behind it," Sonya's colleague Inge said when she heard. "Something must have happened. You don't leave Berlin just like that and go to the end of the earth! No theater, no reading clubs. There's something behind it, believe me!"

Inge's sense of drama worked wonders for the museum. After Inge became the curator, visitors came to the museum shows in droves. Sonya was responsible for their historical accuracy, Inge for their imaginative, creative side. And Else Seel stimulated Inge's imagination. Inge stood firm in her belief that a deep dark secret in Else's life took her to Canada.

"Maybe she was just bored," Sonya argued. She saw it more mundanely. She'd read that with her job, Else could support herself, her mother, and her aged aunt. At the same time, she was a poet, a dreamer with an artist's sensibility. Perhaps she realized that Berlin would see different times. Berlin was a circus on the verge of cracking up, a noisy ballroom where fire was about to break out.

So Else left for Vancouver in 1927. At the Saint Francis Hotel, where George Seel had reserved a room for her, there had been a knock at the door. Else said to come in, and when the door opened, she saw, for the first time, the man she would marry the very next day. It pleased her that he was tall and powerfully built. She liked his wavy brown hair and intelligent face.

Sonya reread the passage in Else's *Canadian Diary* that she'd published in 1964. *"I looked at him. He smiled shyly."* Sonya was frustrated once again by those terse sentences. Else wrote not a word about her feelings. Was she thrilled? Was it love at first sight? Butterflies in her stomach? Weak at the knees?

Not a word.

Tonio popped into her mind, and she let the book slip away.

How long she had repressed the memory of that summer's day in the canton of Valais, in the village of Ruhetal! Of all places! Ruhetal was no idyllic spa town; it wanted tourism, but progressive tourism: soft-adventure tours, river rafting, mountain biking, everything "English," everything cool. The town was going to construct a big jump for mountain bikers on Saint Martin's Hill, a hill she knew very well, from a historical perspective, of course. For millennia, it had been a place that people believed was sacred. She'd written an essay on it. First it had been the site of a pagan cult, then of a Christian chapel, then of a large church that was destroyed during the Reformation. Later the church was replaced with a chapel. Now it was to become a jump for mountain bikes. This generated some opposition.

At a town hall meeting, Tonio had sat beside her. Tonio Vonlanden: tourism entrepreneur and expert on mountain climbing, bungee jumping, and canyoneering.

"A sacred site!" Tonio had laughed. "How's that for superstition!" But it was a friendly laugh, revealing white, shining teeth in his tanned face. Sonya looked at his muscular forearms, his strong, sinewy fingers. He was a sportsman through and through. Sonya hated sports.

"I'm not a stubborn man," Tonio Vonlanden said to the villagers in the hall. "I'm perfectly happy to be persuaded." And turning to Sonya, he said, "You can tell me all about sacred places. How about this evening?"

The audience laughed.

Sonya held him to his word, and so, in the gathering dusk they sat on the grass on Saint Martin's Hill. Sonya enlightened him about the large house of worship in the eleventh and twelfth centuries. Desperate parents brought embryos and stillborn infants there. It was their last chance to have their children baptized and saved from everlasting hell. The Catholic Church didn't baptize dead people. The priests would place the little corpse on a warm platter, put a feather in its mouth, and if the feather moved from the warmth, that was a vital sign, and the child was quickly christened. Thousands of infants lay buried around the hill, tiny skeletons in the earth.

They sat together, talking until the sun went down. Tonio told his friends afterward that indeed he felt the sacredness. And how! It was powerful—magnificent! He had fallen in love that night with a historian from St. Gallen who had never set foot on a ski lift in her life.

Maybe that should have alerted him. Then all this wouldn't have happened. Tonio wouldn't have died under mysterious circumstances. And she wouldn't be here, in this room, in Vancouver.

CHAPTER 3

From: yh6t9abeil@yahoo.com
Sent: September 2, 13:36
To: Inge Stollrath
Re: Enemy Territory

Dear Inge,

I arrived safely. You will be happy to know you're the first person I'm e-mailing. And you were afraid my allergy attack would wreck all your plans! I feel like a genuine hero.

I'm in an Internet café in the heart of downtown Vancouver. I never thought it would be so complicated to order a latte. They ask about everything: size, whole or skim, organic or not, decaf or regular . . .

Immigration didn't search my suitcase, so Diane will receive all the forbidden goodies her German relatives sent her, as they seemed to think there's nothing to buy in Canada. I haven't seen Diane today. She'd already left before I got up. (I was awake all night, then slept until noon—my biorhythms are completely screwed up.) You were right, by the way: she doesn't speak a word of German.

You should see Diane's apartment. My bedroom walls are orange; the solarium has a red sofa and a mustard-yellow wall. The bathroom is purple and silver. The living room has mud-gray walls, and there's a bright green three-piece upholstered couch with multicolored cushions. There's a lot of Asian and native art. The kitchen is a hall of mirrors: mirrors on the walls, the ceiling, shelves for glasses, on the doors— there are dark-tinted mirrors everywhere. I can't avoid seeing my red-rimmed eyes. An eccentric streak and a mania for collecting must run in your family! I'm amazed that these turn up in your most distant relatives who left for Canada generations ago. By the way, Diane is your cousin how many times removed?

I can see a corner of the Pacific from Diane's apartment. She lives near False Creek, an inlet in the center of the city. Open the door, and you breathe in the salt air. You can hear gulls screaming and smell the fish.

A lot of Asian faces here. Everybody runs around with coffee cups, and the elderly wear high-tech sneakers. There are lots of young faces—I haven't seen so many young people at one time for ages. I already feel like I'm at a ripe old age at thirty-six!

Yours ever,

Sonya

"I'm a bit confused," Diane said later that day, snuggling into the bright green divan. "What's your trip got to do with that exhibition?"

She brushed a hand over her short black hair.

"Women who emigrate, but by themselves, no husband or family, don't you see?" She thumped Else Seel's *Canadian Diary* down on the table for emphasis. "There's the German connection—a poet from Berlin."

But Sonya was still overwhelmed with fatigue. Oh, how she hated jet lag! Inge had gotten her into this Else Seel business, into traveling to Canada. Their last exhibition—on the history of underwear—had almost driven her crazy; not the historical aspect, of course, but the fact that Inge always had to exaggerate everything. She used to say that understatement was the kiss of death for a museum.

At the same time, Sonya had to admit she was was quite taken with Inge's most recent idea.

Inge always had the number of museum visitors in the back of her mind. For the next exhibit, she hit Sonya with her plan for a trip to Canada.

"I want photos of Else and things of hers to put on display—all possible evidence."

Sonya had tried to pass the buck back to Inge. Especially because she suspected this may not be just a coincidence. All of a sudden, she felt unsure of herself. Did Inge know about the tragic happenings in Canada? About Tonio and Nicky, maybe even Odette? But she dismissed the thought. Inge couldn't possibly have a clue. She had never let on about it. Never a hint or a question. And Inge was as transparent as a pane of glass.

"Why don't you go yourself? You're the globe-trotter of the two of us."

It was Sonya's last attempt to escape her fate. But Inge waved her off.

"You know I have those meetings with the Department of Culture. We need their grants. I've got to stay on it now or our hopes will go down the drain."

Of course she was right. Guiltily, Sonya thought about last year when she'd stuck Inge with all the work. How many times had she phoned in: "I can't do it today, it's the usual thing, you know. Can you do it yourself?"

The usual thing. Her panic attacks. But she never let on, just saying they were allergies.

It had started with nightmares—out of the blue, with no warning: She was on a plane, certain they were about to crash. She saw the surface of the water coming closer, but eerily slow—it was unending torture. Then there were bodies floating in the water. She swam through the ice-cold waves, swam up to a dead body floating facedown on the surface. If only she could see its face. *Your face. Show me your face!*

The doctor prescribed rest and gave her some little pink pills so she wouldn't be overcome by panic.

Sonya, who had always sworn by Dr. Bach's homeopathic drops, now had her pills on her at all times: her lifesaver was a psychotropic drug. She felt ashamed, ashamed that her well-ordered life had gone off the rails. Three years had passed since they found the bodies. Until then she had never had a nightmare. Not this panic or breaking out in a sweat, no heart flutters, no claustrophobia.

For a while, she had only felt a dull emptiness, pain, and anger. Especially anger, after she'd found the letters.

"My dearest Tonio, I miss you so much it hurts. My body is screaming with desire. My skin is still burning where we touched each other . . ."

Inge had never held all those sick days against Sonya. She always advised her to get a good rest, saying it would get better. Sonya owed Inge. She had to take that trip.

CHAPTER 4

"C'mon, let's get going!"

Sonya was a bit startled when she saw Diane in her plum-colored skin-tight jogging outfit. Diane bounced up and down in her running shoes as if they were equipped with hydraulics; a water bottle hung from her belt.

Would Sonya have to keep trotting along behind her down the False Creek harbor? The fresh air was burning in her inflamed nostrils. Was she allergic to sea salt? Diane marched on ahead, bursting with energy.

"Do you know who you look like?" Diane asked.

Sonya knew.

"You look like Cate Blanchett in *Lord of the Rings,*" Diane exclaimed.

Sonya was never sure whether that was meant as a compliment. Yes, she did resemble the Australian actress a bit: the fine blonde hair, the placement of her light blue eyes, the wide mouth, the pale skin, the fine facial features. "Ethereal," Diane called it. Cate Blanchett was beautiful, but Sonya thought of herself as a simple watercolor: without clear edges, everything flowing into pretty forms that somehow lacked meaning.

Tonio had never seen it that way. He liked that elflike, water-color air. Once when he saw an old photograph of her in makeup, tarted up for a university play, he was shocked. She looked disreputable, he said, and he was *not* pleased. Sonya was amused at his reaction and made a naughty face at him. After that, she put on makeup every day. She thought you had to offer resistance to a man like Tonio every now and then. She felt instinctively that he liked it. Resistance produced friction, friction emitted sparks, and sparks produced the flame between them.

"Look, a dragon boat!"

Diane pointed to a long canoe with a red, gold-tongued dragon on the bow. It shot like a streak of fire over the water, rowed by a dozen men and women pulling on their wooden oars to the shouts of a coxswain.

"What, they're training already?" Diane called out in surprise. "The dragon boat race always takes place in June on False Creek. It's a Chinese custom."

They walked along a wooden jetty. Boats and yachts rocked in the water. Glass towers sparkled on the opposite side of the bay. Sonya spotted a tree rising from a penthouse patio that looked like a relic of times long gone.

Gone but not forgotten.

What if Tonio suddenly came toward her? How would he react? Would he come and take her in his arms? Or just stand before her, embarrassed, his hands in his pockets like a stranger in this strange town.

Pull yourself together. He's dead, he doesn't exist. Not in Vancouver or anywhere else.

"You all right?"

Diane took her by the arm, and Sonya realized she was gripping the jetty's railing.

"No, no, just a bit dizzy. Probably just my allergies."

"You didn't have a proper breakfast. Come on, let's go get something to eat."

She pulled Sonya into the tumult of the Granville Island Public Market, past pyramids of apples and ice-filled buckets of fresh seafood. Minutes later they were sitting at one of the wooden tables in the middle of the noisy hall. Diane set some little bowls before them: shrimp in peanut-butter sauce, marinated meat, perfumed rice, and vegetables exuding the aroma of exotic spices.

"Eat as much as you can. We've got a lot to do today."

Sonya actually did feel hungry now. That must be a good sign! She stuffed herself on tidbits, though they weren't exactly the biodynamic diet she followed at home. After all, as a historian, she had to further her culinary education. Diane enthused about the advantages of living in Vancouver, but Sonya only half listened. She floated like a water lily on the flood of distant noises and the scents around her.

"Over here. We'll make room for you." Diane broke off to speak to a man with a tray who was wandering helplessly around the rows of fully occupied tables. She put their bowls closer together. The man thanked her and set his plates down on the table. Sausages, onions, sour cream, pierogies—it must have all come from the Ukrainian food stand behind them.

"It's pretty darn full around this time of day," the man said, smiling at Diane. He was wearing a blue sweatshirt and a vest with several pockets. Sonya eyed him surreptitiously. Midthirties, she guessed. So this was a Canadian male, *Homo canadensis*. He radiated good health. He had muscular arms and a broad head, with a friendly face, powerful teeth, and a blond mustache.

Diane crumpled up her paper napkin, tossing it into one of the empty bowls.

"You should be here in summer with all the tourists. It's impossible to find an empty table."

"I'm from Calgary," the man said. "My friends told me I absolutely had to see Granville Island. There are great shops and galleries here, I must say. I can buy a couple of presents right now. But most of all I'd like to take the ocean back with me."

"Yes, I'd like to, too." The words popped out of Sonya's mouth.

"I'm in the fish business, eh," the man said, looking at her with some curiosity.

"She's from Switzerland—no ocean there," Diane explained.

The man smiled, fixing his eyes on Sonya. His head was shaved and nearly bald, like a military cadet. Sonya thought his eyelashes were a little too thin and long.

"Switzerland's very beautiful, so I've heard. Are you here on vacation?"

He piled sour cream on his pierogies.

"Yes," she said, hoping his questioning would stop.

"How long are you staying?"

"I don't know exactly."

It was a nice, innocent conversation, but she was wary nonetheless.

"Sonya's a historian," Diane added. "She's interested in the history of immigrants to Canada."

It seemed as if the two of them were in cahoots. Sonya noticed another curious stare from under two sets of the thin, dark eyelashes.

"You should go to Calgary. Immigrants come there en masse. There's a lot of work in Calgary, even more than in the oil fields in the North."

Sonya nodded, excused herself, and took the cardboard dishes to the garbage can.

"It was nice to meet you," the man from Calgary said as he was leaving. Sonya repeated his words, glad to use that polite, nonbinding formula.

By the time she and Diane were crossing the strait in the Aquabus, she'd already forgotten about the stranger. The colorful little boat neatly dodged a huge barge and chugged past two kayaks. When they landed on the other shore of False Creek, in-line skaters and joggers came at them. "Flight animals" was Sonya's name for that species. But she saw herself as a tortoise: duck your head, flee inside yourself!

In the sales lot, Diane headed straight for the used cars, stopping at a rather long red truck.

"I think this is just right for you. What do you think?"

"I'll never drive anything like that. It's a truck, and I'm no cowboy."

Half an hour later, Sonya signed the bill of sale for a red Ford pickup, twelve years old, with new brake pads and windshield wipers, and a covered cargo area as big as the mouth of a humpback whale. She reached into her backpack to pay, but her wallet wasn't there.

Her wallet was missing!

Things moved very quickly. The car salesman drove her and Diane to the Aquabus pier, and this time the crossing seemed to last forever. They rushed to the Granville Island Market. The table was bare. Nothing on the floor, nothing beside the garbage can. Panicking, they raced from one food stand to another.

"Yes, yes, a wallet," said an elderly lady at an Asian food stand.

"A man with a blond mustache and a blue sweatshirt found it," she said. "He took it to the police station one street over. Yes, he told me that's what he was going to do."

The man from Calgary, Sonya realized.

CHAPTER 5

Sonya remembered afterward how quickly Diane put the incident out of her mind. She made no mention of it, as if nothing had happened. While Sonya was still shaking inside, Diane went on and on about the pickup and that great price, vowing that Sonya would never forget her purchase.

There actually had been no harm done. Her wallet really was at the police station, along with her credit cards, bank card, and checks. She filled out a form, and everything was handed over with only a few questions because she could show her passport.

For Diane, that was the end of it. Now they could turn to more important things: the pickup truck Sonya was getting the next day.

"Maybe you can sell it at a profit after your trip and make money back!"

They had walked to Canada Place, where the conference center's white tent roofs pointed into the pale sky like sails. They stood at the railing in front of the Pan Pacific Hotel, looking out at the ocean and the snowcapped mountains on the horizon. A monumental cruise ship was docked at the pier below them. They watched in amazement as tons of toilet paper and cartons of fruit juice and Corn Flakes were piled into the lower part of the ship.

Passengers chatted on the balconies of their cabins; crew members in blue shirts and white aprons put artificial flowers in the windows.

Diane took her farther ahead.

"Come on, I'll show you the train station where your German writer arrived. It's just around the corner."

Sonya saw the ornate building in the classical style, which was still standing.

"And the Saint Francis Hotel across the street, where they met?" Sonya looked around everywhere.

"Gone. Demolished. If I'm not mistaken, it was where this parking garage is."

Sonya was disappointed. But what did she expect? To inspect the room where Else saw her future husband for the first time?

"She knew him only a day before they got married."

Diane wasn't impressed. "Yes, that's often the way it was with European women. They had to get married right away so that everything was proper."

Sonya wanted to ask if there was a man in her life, but Diane would have surely asked her the same question, and that was to be avoided at all costs.

Diane took her arm playfully.

"Did she like him? What does it say in your book?"

Sonya opened Else's diary and translated as best she could.

I was unpacking my suitcases when Georg came in. I looked at him, and he smiled shyly. When I spoke to him in German, he apologized for his poor German because he'd spoken only English for fifteen years. Then he said nothing. There was a pause.

Sonya made a face. "Romantic, isn't it? And you know what they did later? Else saw he needed a new necktie, so they stepped out and bought one. They went to the movies that evening and had dinner."

"And then? Now it's really going to get sexy!"

"George told her that they were getting married the next day, and that's what they did."

Diane didn't let it go.

"What did he look like? Was he good-looking?"

"I think so. He was tall and slim, powerfully built. He had dark hair and . . . I'd say a masculine face."

"Well, then, she should have been happy with that."

"I don't know exactly. She doesn't disclose much personal information, at least not in this book."

Diane put an arm around her shoulder.

"I love your Swiss accent. Canadian men will adore you."

They both laughed.

Sonya's eyelids got heavy. Late-afternoon jet lag. Diane picked up on her exhaustion.

"Take a taxi back and go lie down for a bit. I'm going for a jog."

She shoved her apartment key into Sonya's hand and was off.

Sonya was in the taxi when an idea flashed through her mind.

"To the Lions Gate Hotel, please."

The hotel was bigger and more impersonal than she'd expected, with a bare, sober facade, but the pompous entrance made up for it.

She leaned forward to the driver.

"Can you wait here for a bit? I'll be back in two minutes."

"OK, OK," he said.

She went through the revolving door and found the reception desk. There were only three people there—she could chance it. The clerk smiled.

"My husband was here three years ago, from September the sixth to the tenth. Can you confirm that? Can you find him in the computer?"

The young woman shook her head.

"No, we can't give out that sort of information. For privacy reasons."

Of course. How stupid of her. She was about to go when she added hurriedly, "My husband was here on vacation, and then he was killed in an accident. I just wanted to see where he was before it happened."

The young woman hesitated, seemingly concerned.

"I'm so sorry," she said.

Sonya had seen the name of the hotel on his credit card statement. Had Tonio met Odette here? Had she come here and asked about him, the way she herself was doing now?

"Our general manager is in a meeting right now, perhaps . . ."

"My taxi's waiting. I can come back another time."

"Leave me your phone number. I'll let him know. We can give you a call."

Polite, empty words—and Sonya knew it. Still, she wrote down her cell phone number, as well as her name and Tonio's, and the dates. An act of desperation. Nothing would come of it.

She rushed out to the taxi. The pressure in her head had gotten worse.

If Odette had been sleeping with him back then, what had they done with Nicky? Did he know about it, or were they able to keep it from him? And what was it exactly that Nicky had paid for with his life?

CHAPTER 6

"How cruel!" Tonio had turned very angry that evening long ago on Saint Martin's Hill. "How cruel to make parents believe their stillborn child is damned to hell for all eternity just because it wasn't baptized."

She could see how red his clean-cut face had become despite his tan. She began to suspect at that moment that Tonio Vonlanden was *not* a one-dimensional outdoorsman, not merely an adrenaline junkie addicted to the thrill of extreme sports. What did she know about him anyway? Only what the organizers of the hall meeting in Valais told her. That Tonio was the co-owner of an alpine ski school and a free-climbing master; he'd apparently climbed several peaks in the Himalayas, or had at least attempted to. He was one of those suicidal maniacs, or so she'd thought.

"It's all about frightening people. Scaring the hell out of them. That way, you can manipulate them very nicely."

She was soon to discover that Tonio thought fear was totally unnecessary. *"There's no reason at all to be afraid."* She was to hear those words later, again and again. As for her, she thought fear was legitimate sometimes. And it wasn't as if she did everything out of fear. But for Tonio, fear was ridiculous, a complete waste of time, something that you could dismiss with a flick of the wrist.

Which is why, in the years that followed, she kept it to herself that she feared for his life whenever he left on one of his dangerous adventures.

Else Seel had been the same way. George was often out for weeks, either trapping in the mountains in the middle of the terrible Canadian winter, or else searching for gold and silver. Else could never be sure that he'd come back to their cabin alive. One time he returned badly burned. He had been asleep in his shelter when a kerosene lamp set it on fire; in this shed he'd built, there were explosives to mine for gold. He had just managed to get out before it blew up. Else screamed when she saw him get out of the boat. There wasn't a doctor anywhere, so she cared for her badly injured husband as best she could. He survived, but with large scars on his neck.

Diane spread out the map on the dining room table.

"British Columbia is over 360,000 square miles and has a population of just under five million."

She sounded rather proud. Sonya's travel guide told her that Canada's westernmost province was as big as Germany, France, and Switzerland put together. Diane traced a finger over the green and brown areas.

"There are stretches of land where nobody has ever set foot. Isn't that fascinating?"

Sonya rolled her eyes. "It's intimidating."

She never wanted to go where others hadn't. She didn't want to conquer virgin territory like a Canadian pioneer. George Seel might well have been that sort of person. What did that good man say to his newly married wife when she was hanging out the wash in front of their cabin on Ootsa Lake? *"Laundry is hanging here for the first time since the world began."*

Diane put her hand on Sonya's arm, as was her way.

"Everything's going to be all right, you'll see. Canadians are friendly and always willing to help. You'll enjoy yourself."

Sonya noticed the sparkling pendant on Diane's necklace. A transparent stone flashed in the morning light. It couldn't have been a genuine diamond—that would have cost a mint—but she didn't dare ask. Inge had informed her that Diane was involved with diamonds somehow; she was a jewelry designer or something like that.

Sonya's eyes drifted back to the map. How was she going to make that trip all by herself? Else Seel had at least had a new husband with her when she sailed to Prince Rupert a few days after her arrival in Vancouver.

"Where did it happen?"

"Near Prince Rupert."

"Prince Rupert? Where's that? I don't understand. What could Tonio have been doing there?"

"That's what we'd like you to tell us."

"Listen, Sonya, you'll take this highway. It's a good road." She folded up the map. "You can take this. Didn't you want to e-mail Inge? You can use my computer."

Sonya nodded. Inge had sent her a short e-mail saying she was *very* busy but was fervently thinking about her. "Fervently"— Sonya thought that was rather insincere, seeing that she was still fighting her allergies. Didn't Inge appreciate how much courage this venture took? Of course not—she didn't have a clue.

In a rotten mood, she pounded the keys of the computer.

From: yh6t9abeil@yahoo.com
Sent: September 4, 10:01
To: Inge Stollrath
Re: Else's Son

Dear Inge,

I'll be starting on my long journey in two days. You can imagine how nervous I am. Fortunately, I got a place on the Prince Rupert ferry. I'll have to postpone my trip to the Else Seel archive in Victoria; it's being reorganized and is shut down for a week.

But you'll be happy to know that I've tracked down Else's son, Rupert, near Vancouver and will pay him a visit.

Don't ask me what mood I'm in. When I get back from this trip—if I'm still alive!—I'll be prematurely gray. And it will make our museum bankrupt. Best if you apply right now for double the grant money.

So nice that you miss me. You haven't written, but I've come to the conclusion that you're drowning in work.

Best regards,

Sonya

She sent the e-mail off and was about to shut down, but she changed her mind; Sonya entered a name in the search engine. She felt a bit like a thief. She actually shouldn't have gotten hold of that man's name from the policewoman she dealt with yesterday. On impulse she'd gone back to the Granville Island police station after leaving the Lions Gate Hotel. She wanted to give the honest finder a reward. She'd been so discombobulated when she retrieved her wallet, it had never entered her head.

She explained her business to the policewoman, and everything seemed to go smoothly at first.

"Here, I'll write down his information for you," the young woman said. But when she was about to hand her the slip of paper, she immediately took it back, blushing.

"Oh, I'm not supposed to do that. We have to protect privacy. Sorry." She crumpled up the paper. "I see now there's a note in the file that the finder doesn't want to be contacted, and he doesn't want a reward."

But Sonya had been able to catch sight of two words and memorized them because they reminded her of the novel *La dame aux camélias*. Camelian Inc.

What she now saw on the screen was less than literary. *"Camelian. Your Security Service."* What was that?

Suspect economic espionage? Worried about the security of your transports/shipments? About protecting your firm's documents or buildings? Is your data safe from prying eyes? Do you feel threatened by outside interests? We take care of all security issues!

Sonya clicked on "Our Customers": *"Oil Industry, Mining Industry (Precious Metals and Diamonds)."*

That was odd. Didn't the man in the market say he was in the fish business? Wasn't that why he joked that he wanted to take the ocean to Calgary?

She must have read the words wrong before the policewoman took back the note.

Suddenly she heard voices. Visitors? She killed the screen and left the study. Diane was in the living room, talking with two women. She looked up when Sonya came into the room.

"Sonya, these are friends of mine, Holly and Suzy."

The women gave her a cheerful greeting.

"This is Sonya, from Switzerland, a historian. She's doing research on the life of a German woman writer, who immigrated to Canada in the twenties."

"Oh, how interesting! Is she well known in Canada?"

"No, she isn't. She mostly wrote in German," Sonya said, sliding into an armchair. "She never became famous. Mainly because she was too far away; she lived in the bush near Burns Lake."

"Burns Lake. Where's that anyway?" Suzy asked.

"Somewhere up north," Diane butted in. "She rotted away in a lonely log cabin, imagine that, and she used to live in Berlin!"

"Yes, Germans like the wilderness; they can't be too secluded," Holly said, shaking her red hair. "My uncle lives in the Yukon, and there's any number of Germans and Swiss there."

"It just occurs to me. There was a Swiss lady here once—when was it? She was at one of your parties, Diane?" Suzy asked.

"I can't remember, but she wanted to go and live alone in the bush for a year," Holly said.

Sonya pricked up her ears. Her heart beat faster.

Diane got up. "I can't possibly remember everybody at my parties. While we're on the subject, shall I send out for Thai food?"

"Good idea. Let's order the same thing as last time. It was so good," Suzy said.

Diane disappeared into her study to call it in. Sonya had some questions for Holly.

"Was that Swiss woman's name Odette? Was she slim and a bit boyish? Athletic? Did she have thick, dark hair longer than mine?"

Holly raised her eyebrows.

"Could be. But I'm not exactly sure now."

"Was it maybe three years ago?"

"Three years. That's very likely. It was here, in this apartment. I know she was Swiss because we talked about the Swiss Alps."

The Swiss Alps. The mountains. Maybe this was her first clue about Odette.

Sonya shuddered.

CHAPTER 7

It was raining buckets. Sonya crossed the Lions Gate Bridge on her way to West Vancouver. She thought it very lucky that her windshield wipers were new. Meticulous as she was, she'd gone the day before to check out the road to the Horseshoe Bay ferry. Tonio would have laughed. She'd set two alarm clocks that morning—as always before important appointments—thinking that such a practical measure would reduce her nervousness. Tonio always teased her about it: "*That's going to lead you to a terrible fate.*" And then, more seriously, "*Just give in to whatever life brings.*" She couldn't put up with that, of course, and reminded Tonio that he himself would take precautions: for instance, why didn't he let his bungee-jumping customers hop off the bridge without a rope? Then he'd really find out if "life" had a safety net. Tonio usually ended such discussions with a hug and a kiss, marveling at how clever she was.

While Sonya was waiting for the ferry in Horseshoe Bay, the rain subsided a little. All she saw of the bay from her truck were black rocks and a tiny bit of the ocean. She poured some decaf coffee from her thermos and closed her eyes.

How lucky she was to catch Rupert Seel just before he was going away for three weeks. He was willing to talk about his mother to an unknown historian from Switzerland. Had Else Seel named her son after the port town of Prince Rupert?

"Where?" was the first question she'd asked the detective. *"Where did it happen?"*

"Near Prince Rupert."

"Prince Rupert? Where's that?"

"It's a port town on the northwest coast of Canada."

Tonio had never mentioned Prince Rupert, not even when he phoned her the last time that September. He talked about Vancouver Island, about Long Beach near Tofino, a fantastic, endless beach. Maybe he'd hike the West Coast Trail if the weather cooperated; she'd read that it was a difficult hiking trail on a wild part of the coast. Tonio said that Nicky would love it—the boy needed a challenge. There had been no talk of Prince Rupert. Not a word about a plane trip farther northwest.

"Seaplane," she heard the detective say.

"A seaplane?"

"Yes, he was the pilot. He was doing the flying."

"Where did . . . I mean, he was licensed for small aircraft, but how did he . . . Why would he want to fly a seaplane in Canada?"

"That's what we'd like you to tell us. Apparently it was his."

"There must be some mistake. He didn't have the money for that! It's impossible. He didn't have that kind of money."

She felt like giving the detective a good shaking. He glanced at his documentation.

"Your husband bought the plane in Prince Rupert."

Sonya didn't understand any of this. His bank withdrawals, the statements from the investment company. Tonio didn't keep anything from her, didn't gloss over anything. They were always open with each other. There must have been a giant misunderstanding.

She'd searched their house one more time. Every drawer. Every file folder . . . Then she found the letters.

The cars in front of her turned on their engines. Sonya gave a start, put her truck in gear, and followed the vehicles into the belly of the ferry. After she and the other passengers went to the upper decks, she stood at the rail for a while, the hood of her Windbreaker tightly tied around her face. Horseshoe Bay slowly faded from view. The white steel sides of the ferry pushed masses of water aside. The ferry passed by small wooded islands. Some houses were perched close to the shore as if they were about to slide into the water, like spooked ducks. She noticed a weathered tree root jutting out of the slate-gray surface.

Gusts of wind drove the rain into her face.

Suddenly, she sensed a quick movement near her. A man was trying to grab a newspaper page sailing over the rail, but he came back empty-handed. The man looked disconcerted, and then he shrugged, and his lips curled up into a fleeting smile: Not to worry. Could be worse. She smiled back and returned to the warmth of the passenger areas, making herself comfortable on a seat covered with green synthetic cloth. She must have dozed off, because she almost missed the loudspeaker's announcement that the boat was approaching the Langdale dock. A half hour later she was driving uphill in a column of cars. She'd seen on the map that this was the only highway on this stretch of the coast, which was known as the Sunshine Coast. The rain continued. At first the road was lined with shopping malls, gas stations, and motels; then there were just woods and an occasional collection of houses. The ocean came very close at times, then disappeared behind trees and cottages. Turning onto a side road, a little later she came to the driveway of Rupert Seel's home. A dark alley between tall firs opened up to a view of the water. It must be the inlet she'd marked on her map.

She parked in front of an imposing wooden house and knocked on the door. An elderly bearded man with glasses opened it and asked her in. Sonya began to apologize for her early arrival, but by then he'd shown her into his paneled living room and offered her a chair. The still water outside the windows filled the room with light and calm.

"So you're putting on an exhibition in Berlin," Rupert Seel said, looking at her with curiosity.

"No, not in Berlin, in Switzerland," she said, afraid of disappointing him, "but our museum is on the German border, and we get a lot of German visitors."

"How did you ever light upon my mother?"

"It was the museum director's idea. She came across a reference to your mother's diary on the Internet."

He reflected for a moment.

"Come with me. I've got something to show you."

They went down into the basement. On some shelves on the walls, there were strange objects that Sonya couldn't identify. He led her into a smaller room and pointed to an oil portrait on the wall.

"That's her. I don't know how old she was, maybe eighteen."

Sonya moved closer.

Else had an intelligent, alert face with a decisive mouth; her eyes looked off into the distance. Dark hair framed her face over a white, girlish collar. *No raving beauty,* Sonya thought, *but impressive.*

"Perhaps you'd like to see what my mother took with her from Berlin," Rupert Seel said.

He led her through more rooms, digging out one thing after another: a brass grandfather clock, sconces, silver bowls, small black opera glasses, a chessboard, a table bell on a marble base, a barometer, an antique playing-card press, a hand-painted vase, a wooden plate with the inscription "Give Us This Day Our Daily Bread."

Sonya's eyes fell on a wonderful, artistically decorated chest.

"This is where she kept her correspondence," Seel explained.

Next he pointed to the most essential memento: an old Adler typewriter, the indispensable tool for a poet.

"My mother held on to these things," he said. "They were in the family before her father lost his land and his wealth."

Else's father. A big landowner in Pomerania. He had died when Else was seven. Sonya recalled what Else wrote about him later:

My father was a farmer and used to read travel accounts in order to cope with life. My mother was his best servant, and in his service, she lost her pride and the qualities of her old family.

Sonya pointed to her bag.

"May I take a video of all this?"

Rupert Seel had no objection.

"You've surely read my mother's book," he said after she put her camera away.

"Yes, and I've studied articles and other publications on her. I know that after high school she and her mother moved to Berlin. Tell me"—she rummaged around in her backpack for a pen and notebook—"she worked in the Deutsche Rentenbank archives, didn't she? Inflation had eaten away her fortune, and she had to provide for her mother as well as herself, correct? Every day, she read newspapers in three languages and helped prepare reports on the world economic situation for the bank's board of directors."

"You're obviously well informed."

"Well, you can expect that from a historian," she said with a smile. "She saw George Seel's advertisement in the paper, of course. Do you have that ad?"

Rupert Seel shook his head.

"No, I've never seen it, and I don't think it's in the archive in Victoria."

Sonya felt disappointment rise up within her. The one item Inge most wanted to exhibit didn't exist! When Sonya asked about Else's letter replying to the ad, he couldn't give a positive answer either.

"I'm certain they no longer exist," he said, as if it were his fault. He looked at his mother's portrait.

"She thought my father was a rich man. He had silver mines, you know, and his prospects were very good."

"Wasn't he a trapper?"

"Yes, he was a trapper. He did his best to feed our family. By the way, I still set traps along the same line he did."

"Are you a trapper, too?"

"I'm a professional surveyor, but I occasionally go up north and trap as a hobby."

He opened the door to a large workroom. About fifty skins were hanging by a cord on the wall.

"These are sables. I caught them last winter."

"In traps?"

"Yes, but not the old foot traps. Those are banned today."

He picked up a rusty piece of iron. Sonya didn't really want to look at it.

"The animals bleed or starve to death, don't they?"

"No. Now traps kill the animal immediately by breaking its neck."

Sonya went cold. Did Else know about this cruel aspect of George's business before she left for Canada? Did she even care? Or was it part of the romance of living in the bush—before brute reality caught up with her?

Else must have been euphoric in the beginning. A new country. A new husband. Her spouse was masculine, strong, bold. *"The country, trees, animals, a house, Georg and me, it's all for the first time!"* That was what she wrote. The sentence had stuck in Sonya's mind.

Else was an unusual phenomenon around Burns Lake and particularly in Wistaria, where George's cabin was. She attracted attention, with her Berlin elegance and distinctive face.

Sonya imagined how it was for them back then. George carrying Else in his strong arms over the threshold. The embrace. The cabin with only a bed, a table, and a stove. Else, about to unpack her steamer trunk with the linens, silver, porcelain, books, watercolors, colorful tablecloths, and curtains. And George stopping her short. *"That's way too genteel for out here."* Most of it staying in the trunk, except for Else's beloved books, of course.

"So she thought he was rich." She picked up the thread of their conversation after they returned to the living room.

"Yes. Unfortunately he didn't find any silver. But he was a good man. He worked hard."

Rupert Seel offered her a plate of German gingerbread.

"From relatives in Germany," he said proudly.

"But your mother was an intellectual, wasn't she?" Sonya ventured.

"My mother never wanted to be a housewife. She always called herself a poet." He leaned back in his chair. "She read a lot, always late into the night. She would let the fire in the stove go out. I had to make breakfast in the morning for me and my sister, because she slept in."

"Did she miss the cultural scene in Berlin?"

He looked out the window. Canada geese had settled on the meadow in front of the house.

"She certainly missed the intellectual side of it. That put a strain on their marriage."

"Is that why she wrote to Ezra Pound?"

"Probably. But Pound exploited her. He wanted her to write long letters about her life. He only replied in a few sentences."

Rupert paused.

"In her later years, my mother wanted to go back to the city; she wanted to go to concerts and the theater."

"Did your parents argue?"

"Sometimes." He hesitated.

"What about?"

"If my father was away longer than he told her . . ." He fell silent.

"But she must have loved him, didn't she?" Sonya knew she was skating on thin ice.

"My father was uncomplicated. He worked hard. He wasn't strict with us kids. Everybody in Wistaria liked him. He was a big man and rather sobersided."

"Did she know what he looked like before she came to Canada?"

"He had relatives in Flotzheim, in Bavaria. She visited them before she left. I assume she saw pictures of him there. But as a city person, she was taken aback by the provincial life in Flotzheim."

"So why did she go live with him in the bush anyway?"

Seel scratched his head.

"She was an adventurous person, I think." He got to his feet. "Excuse me, but I must be off soon. You may drop in later, when I come back, if you like."

Sonya stood up, too. She knew Else Lübcke Seel's secret couldn't be revealed here and now.

"Thank you so much. And some of those objects and photos—could we exhibit them? We talked about it on the phone. I'm hoping for some things she needed in their cabin—the kerosene lamp you showed me, for instance, for reading and writing at night; and the washboards and butter churn and the iron she'd warm up on the stove."

"It goes without saying. If you want, I know someone who can take them to Germany, and you can pick them up there." He gave her his hand. "I'm delighted that you're interested in my mother. She would have been, too."

She raised her video camera.

"Just a few quick shots of you."

Rupert Seel obliged good-naturedly and escorted her outside.

Sonya had already opened her truck door when he spoke again.

"When you're in the archive, in Victoria, when you see the documents, you will surely find what you're looking for."

Then he raised a hand in farewell and turned back to the house.

CHAPTER 8

A woman sat looking out the rear window of an RV. It had been blocking Sonya's view of the road for God knows how long. Sonya gave her dirty looks. It was impossible to pass that monster. She felt provoked by this tourist with her permed hair, who apparently had nothing better to do than watch her.

But she was even more annoyed by something else. How could she have screwed up the interview with Rupert Seel so badly? How could she have acted so unprofessionally? She should have told him that the exhibition was celebrating Else Seel as a romantic heroine, a courageous pioneer, a poet in exile. That would have loosened his tongue. Instead, she asked him intimate questions about his parents' emotional life. She couldn't have been more stupid. *Congrats, Sonya, you pulled it off brilliantly once again.*

"Did your parents ever argue?"

"But she must have loved him, didn't she?"

"After all, she was an intellectual and he was a trapper. How could that ever work?"

"What do you two really have in common?" Odette had asked her out of the blue one day. Sonya was rather bewildered. They were in a high-end sportswear store for women. Odette had recently made a television ad showing her in a bivouac on a steep rock face, saying with a wink, "I can still pee with dignity in a bivouac!" Sonya had gone to the store with her friend out of curiosity: she wanted to know what special fabrics let women pee with dignity on a steep slope. And Odette had been complaining that they saw each other so seldom.

Odette's point-blank question was embarrassing. She didn't like to discuss her relationship with Tonio, not even with her best friend. For her, a relationship wasn't a public matter. You had to protect it from prying eyes. Nonetheless, it would never have occurred to her not to give Odette an answer. She finally said: "We like to be together, for no particular reason, you know. We cook, talk a lot, go to the movies. We play cards—you've certainly seen us do that." She deliberated for a moment. "I'm helping him with the guidebook he's writing about traversing Swiss glaciers, and he . . . he always listens to me, takes an interest in my work . . . I can't explain it. We just like being together."

"But you hardly ever are. Tonio is always on the move, in the mountains, on tours, going abroad."

Sonya didn't say anything. She was a little put off by Odette's sticking her nose into their marriage, but she tried to hide it.

"It's really a matter of quality, not quantity" was her somewhat lame response.

She felt she was now on the defensive. Odette's remark had touched a nerve. In the beginning, when Tonio was courting her, Sonya asked why he wasn't chasing one of those brave, easygoing athletic women who flocked to his mountaineering school.

Tonio just said, "Tried it, don't want to anymore." When she looked at him quizzically, he added, "I'd be nothing to them if, say, I had an accident and couldn't perform more heroics."

Sonya knew what he meant. One of his friends had been paralyzed from the hips down and was in a wheelchair for the rest of his life. All because of one tiny mistake, a tactical error he'd made when mountain biking. His wife divorced him a year after the accident.

When Tonio saw the pensive look on her face, he winked.

"I'm forty-two, an old man in this business. To me, you're the fountain of youth."

Then he burst out laughing and rumpled her hair affectionately. For a long time, she hadn't been sure that Tonio, the fearless daredevil, was looking for security in a relationship. To be honest, their relationship was anything but chummy. She was not Tonio's intimate version of a fellow mountaineer. And when it came right down to it, they were always sort of strangers to each other. The contrast increased the tension—especially the erotic tension. But there was no way she would tell Odette *that*.

Her friend knew Tonio before Sonya met him. She always said that everybody knew everybody else on the extreme sport scene. Odette was a qualified mountain guide herself by the time she was twenty-three and one of the best mountain climbers in Switzerland two years later. She led trekking excursions to Alaska and Nepal, just like Tonio. She was his competition; Sonya thought so even back then.

She always admired her friend. Odette seemed so strong and courageous and tough. The best athlete in their school in St. Gallen.

But they weren't friends in those early years, even though they were in the same class. They were simply worlds apart. Odette was the daughter of a conservative Member of Parliament, Alex Kreyental. He was a well-known name in Swiss politics. Odette's mother was the daughter of a prominent politician and knew how to tread softly in the shadow of dominating males. And then there was Sonya, whose father was usually abroad installing turbines in hydroelectric stations and whose mother was a successful antiques dealer. Her mother had to go to the theater or out dancing without her husband—which other wives noted with either envy or disapproval. Sonya inherited her mother's aversion to any kind of sports, and she also inherited her slim figure. (Neither of them had ever had a weight problem despite their healthy appetites.)

Sonya did well in school, but gym was her own personal hell. The rings, the horizontal bar, and the horse were transformed in her eyes into instruments of torture. Volleyball felt life threatening, and the running track a *via dolorosa* for innocent victims of the universal mania for fitness. The one thing she liked was relaxation exercises to the ethereal meditation music that the gym teacher played. Gym class would fade away, and she would drift off in a second. Someone would occasionally yawn loudly, and she knew immediately it was Odette.

It was apparent one day that she and Odette were the only ones in the class who were to move on to high school. Sonya was amazed because Odette was an ambitious but mediocre student. A helpful teacher offered to assist the girls to prepare for the entrance exam, so the two of them sat in the classroom on the appointed day, waiting for their teacher. It was quiet, and the situation was somewhat embarrassing for them both. Then Odette blurted out: "Nobody asked me if I even wanted to go to high school. And you. Did anybody ask you?"

"Do you want to go?" Sonya asked.

"I'm a little scared," Odette said. And then she spontaneously burst into tears. She covered her face with her hands, and her whole body shook.

Sonya sat there dumbfounded. Odette was crying! Odette, who would dive headfirst off the five-meter board into the water. Odette, who would ski downhill straight over moguls. Odette, who would dare to do a double somersault on the trampoline.

"I'm so scared," she heard Odette say in a choked voice. "I'm so scared I won't pass the exam. My father . . ."

The rest was drowned in sobs.

The teacher did not appear that day; she'd simply forgotten the appointment. But Sonya had found her first real friend.

Twenty years later she read the letters.

"*Dearest Tonio, there's nothing that can tear us apart. Any obstacle makes the bonds between us stronger. Trust in my love. We are soul mates . . .*"

"It's not important that we share everything." Tonio said this en route to the train station in Appenzell, where she wanted to buy organic vegetables and eggs from happy hens. "But you should try a couple of moves on a rock face, if you want."

A rock face. It didn't sound so hard, so Sonya agreed. They went to one that didn't seem very high. Sonya got into a climbing harness and stood in front of the rock. Her first moves and steps were successful, and Tonio's compliments spurred her to climb higher. At some point, she made the mistake of looking down. Into the yawning depths. She couldn't breathe. Her legs turned to butter, and she clutched the notch in the rock, her knuckles going white.

Tonio was holding the safety rope down below.

"Do you see that handhold up on the right?" he shouted.

"Let me down!" she screamed.

"What's that?"

"Get me down, I want down, fast, *fast!*"

Panic overwhelmed her. The fear of death.

She was unable to rappel, but somehow Tonio managed to help her slide down safely. When her feet were on firm ground again, she was seized with rage. Rage at her helplessness, rage at Tonio. Rage over the whole humiliating experience. She didn't want to cry. She blew up.

"That's it! I don't want to hear another word about it! Why do I always have to look like an idiot! I've got my own life to live, that's good enough for me, thank you very much! . . . I don't need this crap! I've had it up to here, for good."

She ran off—but not far because she was still tied to Tonio by the rope. She stumbled and almost fell.

"What a goddamn fucking piece of shit!" she screamed. Tonio said nothing. He took off her harness and packed up the ropes and carabiners.

It was a fair distance to the car. Halfway there, she suddenly stopped.

"My backpack, I forgot my backpack. The car keys are in it."

Tonio dropped everything and ran back.

She waited. Two minutes. Five minutes. Ten minutes. It seemed like an eternity. Where the hell was he?

Then she saw him coming around a bend in the path, her backpack over his shoulder. He looked so handsome and strong and desirable in his mountaineer outfit that it almost hurt.

They fell into each other's arms, and Sonya burst into tears. Tonio smiled at her.

"My snarling little tigress," he said. "I want to get caught in your claws tonight."

They went up a deserted path to a large rock; behind it, they fell on each other. Their sex was always fantastic when the tension between them was released.

They were married six months later.

No one was at the RV's back window; the woman had vanished. Sonya looked up at the vast sky. She had reached the landing for the next ferry, which would take her to Powell River. She parked in the lane the attendant indicated and got out. A bay opened up before her with curving mountaintops rising up from the water like stony backs of whales. The air was fresh and tingly. The car ramp rested on thick, shell-encrusted wooden pilings. Starfish shimmered in the clear water, gleaming purple and orange against the black rocks on the shoreline. Birds clamored in the woods like wooden rattles.

Sonya entered a diner next to the ferry slip behind a young woman in a tank top and miniskirt. She ordered her sandwich and sat down at the window. A whir in front of the glass. Looking closely, she finally recognized what it was. A hummingbird. Two, three hummingbirds. They darted like tiny colorful propellers at a flower-shaped feeder, sticking their needle-thin bills into the openings. The feeder was probably filled with sugar water. Sonya watched them, fascinated, while eating her sandwich. The bread was soft as cotton wool, but she was hungry. Eventually, she noticed that the woman from the RV was at one of the tables, sitting across from an elderly gentleman.

Sonya imagined what it would be like to have someone sitting across from her. If Tonio were there! She still felt overwhelmed from time to time by a powerful longing and despair.

There must be a logic behind all this, she said to herself. All she had to do was to put all the pieces of the puzzle together properly. Back then, she had carefully taken notes despite being in shock. Taking notes, getting it down, documenting—that was a routine she could cling to. Now she felt she had to go through everything carefully, one more time. She took out her notebook.

"What was your husband doing in Prince Rupert?"

"You've already asked me that. I don't know."

"Mrs. Vonlanden . . ."

"My name is Werner. I kept my name after we married."

"So he didn't tell you he was going to Prince Rupert?"

"No, he said nothing like that."

"Why did he go to Canada?"

"He always wanted to go. He often talked about heli-skiing in the Rockies."

"Then why did he go in September and not in winter?"

"He wanted to take Nicky with him, to go with his son. And Nicky wasn't able to ski. He hurt his foot playing basketball."

"Why didn't you go with your husband?"

"I'd been working on a long-term project, a TV series about prehistoric locations in German-speaking regions. My husband wanted to focus his attention on Nicky, understand? Just father and son."

"Why wasn't he with him very often?"

"What do you mean?"

"You're implying he had little time for his son. Why?"

"Is this important?"

"Mrs. Werner, we want to know the psychological state the pilot was in before the crash. Was he worried about money?"

"Worried? Are you saying that he . . . But that's absurd!"

"He wanted to sell his company, right? Did he have financial problems?"

"Who told you that?"

"That's neither here nor there, Mrs. Werner. You can make it easier for us by simply answering our questions."

"He . . . he was thinking about selling his mountaineering school. It was running very well, but the expenses were increasing. Especially the cost of insurance. After the canyoneering incident . . . You must know about those tourists who were killed in Finsterloch-Bach—that was really bad."

"But he wasn't at fault. Didn't it happen to another operator?"

"Yes, it was another company. Tonio had nothing to do with it; it was a colleague, a competitor, actually. But it still hit him hard. He'd organized that sort of canyoneering adventure himself, even to Finsterloch-Bach. People wear neoprene suits because of the cold water. But Tonio would never go just after a thunderstorm. You never knew if the stream would suddenly turn into a raging torrent. Unfortunately, that's just what happened. A flash flood came through the gorge and dragged them all under water."

"What was your husband's reaction?"

"He was completely shocked when the proprietor of Kreysi Adventures was sentenced to prison for involuntary manslaughter."

"He didn't think the sentence was right? After all, twenty-one innocent youngsters died in ice-cold water."

"Like I said, the catastrophe hit him very hard. He was deeply affected by it. The whole sports scene was shocked."

"And then there was that mishap with the American who was bungee jumping. Didn't your husband's company also offer bungee jumping?"

"Yes, Tonio did, too. What accident are you talking about?"

"*The young American who was tied to a five-hundred-foot rope for a three-hundred-foot jump. He jumped out of a gondola and plummeted straight to his death.*"

"*Yes, I remember now. That was a year before the canyoneering incident. That was also a different company. Tonio had nothing to do with it. He had his customers jump from a bridge, not from a gondola. But overall . . . Tonio found it harder and harder to find good people who . . . who could calculate risk properly.*"

"*Did his company stop offering canyoneering? Or bungee jumping?*"

"*No. He'd still take tours to Finsterloch-Bach every now and then. The tragedy didn't slow down the demand one single bit.*"

"*The show must go on.*"

"*If you say so, sure. It was as if . . .*"

"*Yes?*"

"*As if the incident gave young people even more incentive. Apparently it's . . . about the kick, about the adrenaline rush.*"

"*Your husband couldn't get enough of it?*"

"*What are you saying?*"

"*Didn't he want to give up the company because he wanted more adventure and less responsibility?*"

"*I . . . I don't understand the question.*"

"*Did your husband have any debts?*"

"*Not that I knew of.*"

"*Did he take drugs?*"

"*Where'd you get that idea? What's that question about?*"

"*We need to look at all the possibilities.*"

"*No, of course not. He never took drugs. What's that got to do with Canada? Are you keeping something from me?*"

"We understand your reaction, Mrs. Werner, but we have to try to clear up everything."
     —Report by Kommissar Yvo Herelinger,
     written after the interrogation on October 5.

After the interrogation Sonya had gone straight from the police station to Wittwer & Heck, Real Estate Office. If anybody knew anything, it was Heiko Heck, Tonio's business partner for eleven years—and more or less his best friend. Heiko had suddenly turned his back on adventure sports and sold his company share to Tonio a year before Tonio died.

"Not here," Sonya said when Heiko offered her a seat in his office. She was afraid of eavesdroppers, even though the office door was closed.

They went and sat in Sonya's car. Heiko listened as she reported the detective's questions. His brow grew even more furrowed.

Sonya's fingers drummed on the steering wheel.

"Why did they ask me about drugs? And if he had any debts?"

She looked Heiko straight in the eye.

"Is there something I don't know about? What do they want to know? You've known Tonio for so damn long . . . What . . . What are they getting at?"

Heiko took a deep breath and looked away. He took his time answering.

"I don't know, Sonya. I . . ." He slowly rubbed his temples.

Sonya felt an urge to open the windows, but she let it be.

"Heiko, there's something more to it—I can sense it. Tell me what you know."

"I don't know a thing, Sonya, that's just it. I . . . I just had the feeling in the last two years we both owned the business, well . . . I mean, he was often flying abroad to wherever. He never told me why or where he flew or—"

"You mean in his Cessna?"

"Yes, he always left unannounced, and when I asked him about it, he was always very vague . . . I couldn't make head or tail of it."

"I thought he was flying clients somewhere."

"Did he tell you that?"

Sonya gave it some thought.

"I think I simply assumed it."

Heiko took her by the arm.

"Sonya, whatever he did, you had nothing to do with it. You should just leave it at that."

Sonya looked at him in bewilderment.

"What do you mean by that? *What* should I just leave?"

"You know nothing. The police probably know nothing. Don't ask any questions; just let it go."

His voice grew more urgent.

"My advice as a good friend is don't ask the police anything. Don't go digging for things it's better not to know about. Let sleeping dogs lie."

"But I just can't—"

"I'm telling you: keep your hands off."

His eyes seemed to burn that warning into her brain.

But she had one more question.

"Was that the reason Tonio went to Canada? Were things getting too hot for him here?"

"I know nothing about that, Sonya, nothing at all. And *you* know nothing, which is good. Don't stir the pot."

She sat there, thunderstruck.

"I've an important appointment. But you know I'm always here if you need me," he said.

Sonya felt that the seat beneath her was on fire.

Let sleeping dogs lie.

CHAPTER 9

In the warm sun that shone over Powell River harbor, Sonya stretched out like a languorous cat. She thought it was a great idea to have Dave, a fisherman, take her on a sightseeing tour of Desolation Sound. Dave earned a little on the side offering day-trips on a boat he'd built himself. His sister ran Sonya's B and B. Sonya discovered on the trip that Dave didn't only talk; he insisted on serving oysters from the galley—a treat impossible to refuse.

"Where were you a gold prospector?" Sonya asked, squeezing a slice of lemon onto her oysters.

Dave plopped into the plastic chair on the boat's deck.

"In the Northwest Territories, up around Yellowknife. Do you know Yellowknife?"

Sonya shook her head. She was relishing the oysters as she slurped them down.

"It's about a hundred and twenty miles from the Arctic Circle. Back then, Yellowknife was full of prospectors looking for gold and whatever. Now it's filled with diamond prospectors."

"Diamonds?"

"Yeah, there are two diamond mines up there already. In the middle of the tundra. I think they're building a third one. But when *I* was in Yellowknife, nobody ever mentioned diamonds.

Who'd have thought there were diamonds up there, eh! Not me, that's for sure. Nobody. There was nobody except Chuck Fipke."

"Who's he?"

"Chuck was the first to find the diamonds. He just knew those damn stones had to be there. But he told everybody in Yellowknife he was looking for gold. And when word got out, when it was all in the papers, nobody in Yellowknife believed it."

"You too?"

"Naw. I was about to scoot off to Alberta for a job in the tar sands."

Dave leaned forward, gazing off at the distant ocean; he propped up his elbows on his thighs.

"I looked for gold for four years. Four goddamn wasted years. I lived in a tent and a log cabin, hunted caribou and moose, and bagged a bear once. You mustn't tell anybody. It's illegal. But the animal came too near my tent."

He put his oyster knife down.

"They're good, eh?" he said. "I scraped them off the rocks this morning. I know a good spot for them."

Sonya would have liked some white wine with them, but Dave had only cold beer on ice. *When in Rome*, she thought to herself, picking up a glass.

"What a life it was," Dave continued. "Nobody trusted anyone, not a goddamn inch. Everybody tried to cheat you. It was like an addiction: you look and look, find a bit of gold but never enough. Just enough to cover your debts. Very few got rich, but Chuck Fipke is probably a billionaire by now. He sold his mine to a big corporation."

"Do you know Prince Rupert?" Sonya asked, a little woozy. She never drank beer.

"Know it well. Why?"

"I heard it's good for fishing."

"I worked for a year up there in shipbuilding. It rains a lot in Prince Rupert. But it's an important port. Important for the North, I mean. A lot's going on there. Also a lot of smuggling. People and goods."

"Human trafficking?"

"Yeah, illegal immigrants and whatnot. Where there's a port, there are criminals not far away. You hear what you hear."

"So what do you hear?" Sonya wiped her hand on her jeans. She'd seen Dave do it.

"Organized crime, the Mafia, get it?"

All of a sudden Sonya wasn't so relaxed.

Dave opened another can of beer.

"The big gangsters have their fingers in any place there's money. In diamond smuggling, too, so I hear. There are always people you can bribe. And what can the cops do? There are far too few men in too big an area. It's hopeless, if you ask me."

He cleared the plates off the table.

"I don't want to scare you, but you'd better watch out who you hook up with. All sorts of shady characters mucking around there."

Sonya had an uneasy feeling.

"I can take care of myself," she said, sounding less concerned than she felt. "Why should gangsters have it in for me of all people?"

Dave turned around in the galley doorway. His face darkened.

"I read your tarot cards yesterday. Sort of a hobby of mine. I wanted to know who I'm doing business with."

Sonya laughed.

"That's a medieval superstition."

Dave was serious.

"I don't know the reason, but the cards tell me you attract dangerous people."

He crushed the empty beer can with his foot.

CHAPTER 10

The ferryboat moved out onto the ocean like a steamroller as it made for Vancouver Island. Through the raindrops on the window, Sonya watched the houses of Powell River disappear. Lonesome Dave was probably on a boat in the harbor laying out his tarot cards. *Utter nonsense!*

What was that fisherman thinking anyway, saying he knew something about her—she who'd always stayed out of harm's way, who'd never gotten mixed up in shady ventures. Who'd rather bury herself in books. *"Dangerous people."* She was caution personified.

She sat down and opened her thermos. The ferry's rolling motion was making her dizzy.

Tonio loved danger, but he wasn't dangerous. At most, he was a danger to himself . . . But what about Nicky? He was dead. And Odette? Vanished from the face of the earth. And she herself? How come she'd never suspected that Tonio harbored dark secrets? She grimaced. The decaf tasted dreadful.

She could never keep Tonio from putting himself at risk: climbing icefalls, free climbing without a rope, white-water rafting in raging rivers. She had never reined him in.

"It's his passion," she explained to her worried mother, who always asked criticizing questions. "He has to be able to live it. He needs to."

That was her mantra. Her parents had never completely accepted Tonio. Sonya's choice was difficult for them to understand.

Hello, you dangerous people, where are you? She took a defiant look around the passenger area. A young couple with an infant was sitting diagonally across from her, and behind her . . . a man was eyeing her with some curiosity. She snapped her head away. She'd seen him once before. His wasn't an ordinary face: chiseled but relaxed, about her age, with intelligent eyes, with sharply etched, wide lips. Of course. The man on the Horseshoe Bay ferry who'd lost his newspaper overboard. His blond, slightly wavy hair wasn't windblown now. He had a high forehead, a thinking man's brow.

She absentmindedly picked up the stack of papers beside her: e-mails she'd printed out that morning in the B and B at Powell River. She skimmed through them until she came to Inge's message.

Dearest Sonya,

I got your report. You've been doing great!

Important: don't pass on any details about your trip, not even to Diane, or else everyone will soon know about it. There are enough parasites around stealing ideas!

So keep everything secret. The exhibition will be a smash hit.

Get back to me soon.

Warm wishes,

Inge

Sonya read those lines three times but couldn't make head or tail of them. She wasn't supposed to tell Diane anything? After all, wasn't Diane Inge's cousin? She'd already been told everything before Sonya got there. Was Inge afraid Diane would tell her distant relatives in Germany? But why? This hush-hush stuff was an absolute mystery to Sonya. It was all too late anyway.

She half heard an announcement over the loudspeaker. All the passengers immediately hurried to one side of the ship. Excited chatter filled the room. The man who'd been sitting behind her was suddenly standing beside her seat.

"This is something to see. Come on."

She was so surprised that she stuffed the papers into her backpack and followed him up on deck. He stretched out his hand the way he'd done back when he tried to grab the windblown paper. At first she saw some slight movement in the water, then a fin—no, a dozen fins. Shining gray backs dove up and down in the water with them. A harmonious, elegant, frolicsome round dance.

"Porpoises," the man said.

A girl beside them shouted into her cell phone, "Mom, I see whales!"

Sonya exchanged knowing glances with the stranger. *Like Inge*, she thought, *making a whale out of a little porpoise.*

"That island over there," the man said, "is Savary Island. Are you up on your history of this place?"

"No," Sonya replied.

"Come, and I'll tell you about it over a cup of coffee."

Sonya nodded. *How easygoing these Canadians are.* Although . . .his accent didn't sound Canadian, or British either. A coffee—she could chance that. The ferry landed in twenty minutes, and then she'd be free again.

"Where are you from?" she asked on the way to the cafeteria.

"I originally grew up in South Africa, but I've been in Canada for fourteen years. And you?"

"I'm from Switzerland."

She noticed he wore expensive-looking hiking shoes, high-tech ones.

He bought her a coffee, and they sat down at a bistro table.

"Are you on vacation?" He didn't mention that he'd seen her before.

"No, I'm here on business." Before he could ask another question, she said, "I remember now that I've read something about that island. There were Indian fights there, right?"

"Yes, the Haida from the northwest conquered Savary Island hundreds of years ago; they beheaded the men and carried the women off to be slaves."

Sonya sipped her coffee.

"The Haida were a warlike tribe; they terrorized the entire west coast—nobody was safe from them. But their art, their carvings, and their ornaments are simply divine."

Was he an art dealer? Or maybe a historian?

He studied her.

"You definitely must go to Haida Gwaii, the islands of the Haida. They're also called the Queen Charlotte Islands."

"How do you get there?" she asked, more out of politeness.

"Take the ferry from Prince Rupert."

She laughed.

"What's so funny?" he asked.

"This is the third ferry I've been on now. I'm taking the Prince Rupert ferry in two days—that makes four. I haven't been on this many ferries in my whole life!"

She suddenly stopped talking. *"Don't pass on any details about your trip."* She stirred her coffee and looked at his hands, which lay relaxed on the table, his cup between them. Not a paper-pusher's hands. Too muscular. No ring.

"The passage to Haida Gwaii can be very rough. The strait, Hecate Strait, is notorious for its storms. They're very dangerous. The most dangerous waters on the west coast, they say. But the Haida paddled across it in their dugout canoes."

She might have found his remarks didactic, but his quiet intonation was pleasing. Not blasé, not officious.

"Then I certainly won't be going there. I'm scared of storms, especially on the water."

He didn't take his eyes off her.

"Be motivated by something bigger than your fear."

"What would you suggest?"

"Curiosity, ambition . . . the urge to do research, maybe a love of animals . . ."

His lips were trembling slightly, as if he were suppressing a word that was on the tip of his tongue.

"There are lots of wild animals there: birds, whales, seals, bears. You should go by all means."

"Are you a tour guide?" she couldn't resist asking.

He grinned, and wrinkles appeared on his cheeks.

"No. Why do you ask? I'm a mining engineer. But I'm interested in Canadian aboriginal history. I hope I haven't bored you with it."

She was within a hairbreadth of telling him about Nicky—who loved aboriginal history—when the loudspeaker requested passengers to go to their vehicles.

They got up, and he held out his hand.

"I'm Robert Stanford. I'm pleased to meet you."

"The pleasure's all mine," Sonya said, walking away.

While waiting in her pickup for the ferry to land, she thought about her conversation with the stranger. Nicky would have wanted to know everything about the First Nations. At least early on, at the time she came into his life. Later, Nicky was close-mouthed toward her, which she took as normal. A new woman in his divorced father's life—not an ecstatic idea for a thirteen-year-old. And a historian on top of it. History was anything but cool. She could see his lack of interest just by looking at him. She was the complete opposite of Nicky's mother; Tonio's ex was a bundle of energy, whizzing around like a ball in a pinball machine. Sonya, on the other hand, was factual, reflective, unathletic, a cerebral person. Nicky's mother was loud and upbeat.

But Nicky was very interested in First Nations. He even went to Zurich's North America Native Museum with her. There, they came across a native wood-carver from Vancouver, who was in Switzerland on a visit and carving a totem pole for the museum. By the time Nicky turned fourteen, his First Nations phase was over.

She told him once, "You are history, too, Aragorn." (She named him after the prince in *Lord of the Rings*, because he didn't like the name Nicky. He called her Galadriel after the Elf that was—of course—played by Cate Blanchett in the film.) "Do you realize that?"

A deprecating look.

"You've already got fourteen years of life behind you."

An uncomprehending blink.

"You're making history, for yourself, for others. Your life, that's history. *Your* history. It's exciting! You'll see one day how exciting it is."

For his birthday, Sonya gave Nicky a chronicle of his young life: a binder with photographs and newspaper clippings and collages and documents. There was a section about a trip to Munich with his basketball club, where his team missed the same train that derailed and killed eight people. She digitized a picture with Nicky in between his heroes, Eminem and Ronaldo. There was a transcript of his interview on the local radio station after he won a snowboard race, and his designs for the ski club's pennant. Everything was there. Documented.

He didn't say much, just: "Really pretty weird."

But he showed the binder to his friends, Tonio let on later. When she began looking for clues shortly after the tragedy, she found the binder in Nicky's room. Nicky had added slots for photographs. There were many pictures missing, although he'd numbered slots for them. She found a blank page at the very back with his name on it and a cross signifying *deceased*. In Nicky's handwriting.

Nicky had composed his own obituary.

CHAPTER 11

A prize-winning garden extended in front of the dining room of the B and B in Comox. The proud owner mentioned the award as she handed Sonya some fresh-squeezed orange juice. But Sonya was so nervous that she hardly gave the garden a glance. She didn't touch the freshly baked muffins. When the B and B owner remarked how brave it was of her to travel alone, Sonya's stomach started to flutter. Why had she got herself mixed up in this business? Maybe she wouldn't be able to bear whatever it was that was awaiting her in Prince Rupert.

She went up to her room to pack her bag when her cell phone buzzed.

"Hello, Sonya, it's Diane."

Sonya sat on the edge of the bed with a sigh of relief. She wasn't alone in this strange country.

"Where are you?"

"In . . . Powell River."

Shit. She was lying already. All because of Inge; and she didn't even know why.

"Listen, Sonya, I have to go on a rather long business trip. But you can usually reach me on my cell."

"OK, Diane, I've got your number."

"When are you taking the Prince Rupert ferry?"

Sonya hesitated.

"On Monday."

"Monday? I thought it was Friday. Isn't that what you said?"

"Maybe . . . I'll have to check and make sure."

Her stomach was in a knot. She'd brought this on herself. This was absurd.

"There's something I wanted to ask you, Diane. Your friend Holly told me about a Swiss lady who was at one of your parties who'd wanted to live out in the bush for a while. Can you tell me more about her?"

There was a pause.

"Hello? Diane?"

"I was just thinking about it. I don't know who you mean. I'll ask Holly, OK? So long. Take care."

After driving a few miles, Sonya had the feeling she was on the wrong road. The key intersection the people at the B and B had told her about simply never appeared. She drove on without any idea where she was. It wasn't until fifteen minutes later that she saw the sign: "Campbell River." Now it dawned on her. Of course. People here were used to completely different distances! *Sonya, this is Canada, the second biggest country in the world!* She'd read that British Columbia alone was twenty times bigger than Switzerland. *Think big, baby.*

The road meandered through farm country where black-and-white cows were grazing. A church appeared now and then on the roadside, much more modest than churches in her homeland. She was tempted for a minute to go and learn about the history of one of these wooden buildings, but she wanted to move on.

She'd felt impatient since talking to Diane. If the unknown Swiss lady at the party was indeed Odette—and the timing was actually right—then . . . then she might have the first concrete clue to her whereabouts. The dream she'd had back then had held her in its grasp, and it reminded her every day why she was here. Odette was stumbling through a thick forest with blood on her temples, calling for help. Sonya had woken up with a tight throat and couldn't move at first. But she absolutely had to turn on the light because she was so terrified; she had left it on until sunrise. Ever since that nightmare, Sonya felt with every fiber of her being that Odette must be in Canada.

She certainly didn't mention her dream when she was finally able to talk to Odette's mother. Eight weeks had passed since the crash, which is how long it took Sonya to pick up the phone. Initially, she didn't want to speak to Odette; she simply couldn't. She was in shock. First, the news of the death of the two of them, then the letters. Her best friend had betrayed her with her own husband. Sonya simply went underground, hiding in her home. She didn't want to see anybody, talk to anybody, and Odette didn't even try to contact her.

When Sonya had recovered enough to look for answers to her questions, Odette had vanished. Nobody seemed to know where she was. Not her friends, her employers, or her neighbors. Odette was surely hiding from her, so Sonya finally asked Odette's parents. But she didn't really expect to get anything out of them. Odette had broken off from her parents when she was twenty-four. She had wanted to live her own life, without the constant pressure of her parents' expectations. Sonya knew this pressure all too well; like Odette, she was an only child, and this was one of those invisible bonds that tied them together.

Sonya was surprised when Odette's mother answered, "Yes, we know where she is, but Odette doesn't want anyone to know. She wants to be left in peace. By you, too, Sonya."

She stuck to her guns.

"I must speak to her. It's extremely urgent."

"I'm sorry, Sonya, but that is expressly what our daughter wished. We can't make any exceptions."

Sonya lost it.

"You can't simply run Odette's life!" she shouted into the phone. "I have a right to speak to her. She owes it to me."

"I'm so sorry," Odette's mother whispered, almost in tears. "Believe me, Sonya, I'm so sorry. It is all so awful. But I can't help you. You know how hardheaded Odette is; you know better than anyone."

For the first time, Odette was in league with her parents—and against Sonya herself! After that, Sonya had screamed and raged for hours in her empty home until she fell into bed, exhausted. Sleep gave her a temporary respite from her inner turmoil.

Nonetheless, Sonya didn't tell a soul about the letters—not Odette's mother, not even her own mother. Didn't her parents always believe it had been a mistake to marry Tonio? She wouldn't have been able to admit that. There were things that were better kept under lock and key.

My dearest Tonio, I'm not giving you up. You are so much more than I dared to hope for from life. Not one experience, not one pleasure can equal the power of my love for you.

Now the Pacific loomed up on the right side of the road. People were walking along the beach, throwing sticks into the sea, their dogs jumping frantically into the waves to go after them.

Sonya stopped and dialed Inge's cell phone, but she saw there was no reception. Frustrated, she packed her device away and drove on. The road got lonelier. Trees had been cleared away on both sides with only stumps left: defenseless, abandoned, like hacked-off limbs. Tree roots stuck up over a raw, churned-up forest floor. Now a few trucks came toward her with tires as big as pool tables. As they roared past, she caught a glimpse of their loads, which were as big as houses. The trucks pulled precariously lashed-down tree trunks, many of them as long as three telephone poles.

Two hours later, the road climbed. The woods to the right and left blocked her view. Dark clouds were gathering on the horizon where mountain peaks displaced the sky. Her pickup was now the only vehicle on the road, which made Sonya uneasy. Was she on the right road? The gas needle was getting perilously low, and it occurred to her that she hadn't a reserve gas can. There was no trace of a gas station here. The next town could be hours away.

The faster she got there, the better. She pressed the gas, and out of the corner of her eye, she saw a large shadow running across the road. A deer! Her brakes squealed, and with a crash the pickup broke through bushes on the shoulder.

Sonya sat there, her heart hammering, her hand still clutching the wheel. Then she began to shake.

Somebody knocked on the window, a woman with thick glasses, looking at her with alarm. A man in a woolen hat stood behind the woman.

"Are you hurt? Can we help?"

Sonya could only shake her head.

Hours later, in her comfortable room in Port Hardy, she was just able to recall a few details: the hot tea the couple offered her, the calming words, the relief that her truck wasn't damaged except for a few scratches and could be hauled out of the bushes with a cable, and the fact that she could drive safely behind her rescuers' SUV to Port Hardy.

CHAPTER 12

"You sound a bit stressed," Inge said. "Is anything wrong?"

Her voice sounded as close as if it were around the corner.

Sonya was on her hostess's phone; Inge was paying for the call.

"Inge, can you explain why I can't tell Diane anything? She surely knows about the exhibition already."

"I sent you an e-mail—didn't you get it?"

"No, but explain it to me now."

"Read my message, it's all in there. I—"

"No, Inge, tell me now."

"OK. An immigration official phoned Diane about you."

"Why?"

"Diane says it's purely routine, a random check. They just want to know if you were telling Customs the truth. You know, after 9/11 there's a bit more surveillance in North America."

"I still don't get it. Why should they go after me of all people? I don't look suspicious."

"Look, now you're getting worked up. That's why I didn't want to tell you about it."

"And what's Diane got to do with it?"

"Nothing. That is, the less she knows, the less she can tell the police about you."

"The police? So it was the police, then?"

"Sonya, calm down. They were immigration people. If she doesn't know anything, then she doesn't have to lie to them."

"Lie to them? What for? I'm not doing anything illegal!"

"Sonya, listen to me. Legal or illegal isn't the point. It's only a routine check, believe me. We simply don't want to jeopardize our project. You don't want that either, my dear. Better safe than sorry, right?"

"Inge, all this secrecy is making me anxious. I've already had to lie to Diane."

"That's not so bad, nobody is getting hurt. Why create problems when there's a way around it? By the way, we're getting twenty thousand euros for the exhibition. Isn't that terrific?"

Sonya was about to ask who was donating it, but Inge went right on talking.

"And Else Seel, are you moving full speed ahead? Have you read the material I gave you?"

"I . . . um . . . I'm a good way along."

"Well, that's wonderful. This call is sure to be expensive. Send me an e-mail; we've got to keep costs down. So long!"

Sonya was furious after their conversation. She went to her room, put some things in her backpack, and started off for downtown Port Hardy. The brisk sea air couldn't cool off her fuming brain. How much simpler it would have been just to go to the Vancouver police and ask: How exactly did my husband die? But the very thought of it sent cold shivers down her spine. *Police in a foreign country, far away from family and friends. Far from protection and safety.*

Let sleeping dogs lie.

She discovered in the Internet café that Inge hadn't sent any e-mail at all—at least, there wasn't one in her inbox—and she got even more upset. She was on the point of writing her a stiffly worded note when she discovered an e-mail from her mother.

From: H_H_filli71@yahoo.com
Sent: September 8, 16:58
To: Sonya Werner
Re: Theft

My Dear Sonya,

I'm pleased that everything has gone well on your trip to Canada so far. What good luck that your wallet turned up!

Nevertheless, this incident makes me worry. I don't wish to alarm you, but I read so much about identity theft these days. There are criminals who steal personal data (like bank accounts, insurance numbers, birthdays, and marital status) and they pretend to be that person. They loot their accounts or they commit crimes in the robbed person's name. I hope nothing like that has happened to you. Any criminal would have had enough time to copy your bank card and credit cards. Maybe he took your wallet to the police so you would think you are safe. Perhaps it would be a good thing to regularly check your credit card statements and your bank accounts.

I think of you often and wish you good adventures.

Your Mama

Sonya took a deep breath. They were all like that. *I don't wish to alarm you.* And then they showered you with jeremiads and dark warnings. How was she supposed to stay calm? Maybe Tonio was right, throwing all those pieces of advice to the wind. *"They're prophets of doom and gloom,"* he'd said.

Her mother was a capable woman with a good head for business. But Sonya was her only child. She protected her as if she were herself—especially because Sonya's father was usually away. She had the unfortunate habit of dramatizing everything and always thinking of the worst-case scenario. You had to steel yourself. Sonya understood only too well why Else Seel had kept her mother in the dark about immigrating to Canada until the last minute. One day, Else had her hair cut short and wrapped it in paper; she put it on the table and rather harshly opened it for her mother to see. *"Mother, no complaints. Help me pack quickly, because I have to leave for Quebec in a week on the* Empress of Australia *out of Hamburg."*

Sonya suddenly didn't feel like writing Inge anymore. Let other people wallow in fearful theories; she was busy enough with the logistics of her trip. She left the Internet café and walked to a bench on the beach promenade. The gray ocean languidly rolled in before her. Fog patches obscured the islands along the coast. She began to leaf around in her documents, and a sentence she'd marked in color caught her eye: *"Apart from her work at the bank, Else Lübcke took history and philosophy at the Humboldt University."*

Anyone interested in history had to be a kindred spirit. But when Sonya turned to Else's poetry, she felt, as always, rather confused. She thought most of the lines pompous, often awkward, sometimes even embarrassing. But she wasn't a scholar of German, after all. Maybe she should look in the poems for clues about the woman, the historical Else Seel.

Sonya got hung up on one passage.

I long for those who are my equal
And common folk mean naught to me.
I yearn
For those like me, who know, and feel,
And breathe beauty and know what art is.
Yes, I pine for kindred spirits
But have I none but for the shades.

Sonya raised her head. Screaming gulls circled a point in the water, dove, and rose high again, shrieking.

Then why did Else marry a trapper in the bush, a partner she couldn't discuss art and beauty with, who didn't read books? Someone who really didn't know who she was, or what moved her deep down? For whom she had, however, written her most moving poem after he died in 1950: a confession of love from a woman consumed by mourning.

That year, George Seel had come back from a strenuous trip surveying with some engineers in the mountains. For weeks he'd spent his nights in a tent in bitter cold and had wasted away to a skeleton. He didn't feel well, and went to bed. Else was in the kitchen, cooking and chatting with him through the open door, and suddenly he stopped talking. George Seel was dead at just sixty years old.

I had my arms about you still;
Then what I sensed was death.
The conclusion of all things,
And I wished to go along with you.

At that moment, in the worst way, Sonya wished she could have written a poem like that for Tonio. But his death was not the end of all things for her. For her, there was no end to anything.

Else and George shared a history that was unique and intense: the cabin in the woods, many hard years, a few good ones, and the two children.

My history was taken from me, Sonya thought to herself. *It was replaced by another one, and I don't even know what it is.*

Not yet.

When she returned to the B and B, a woman from the common room hurried toward her, greeting Sonya like an old friend.

"Hello! I've just discovered that you come from Germany, too."

The woman in the RV. The same woman that had stared at Sonya so inquisitively and annoyed her.

"I'm Gerti, and this is Helmut."

She pointed to a man in a green armchair.

"Hello," Sonya said and turned to leave.

"Do come and have a cup of tea with us," Gerti said.

The man stood up and pointed to a chair. "Please, come and sit here." He was of retirement age like his wife. They were people with lots of time.

Sonya was grasping for an excuse, when the manager of the B and B appeared with a cup of tea in her hand.

"Oh, how nice that you were able to meet your friends from Germany," she exclaimed.

Your friends from Germany. Sonya sat down. Questions rained down on her at once. Where was she from? Oh, from Switzerland! Kreuzlingen!

"Well, by golly! Helmut, I can't believe it!" They were from the same neck of the woods, from Ravensburg. "Who'd have thought it possible!"

"I know Ravensburg quite well." It slipped out involuntarily. "I go shopping there now and then."

Gerti looked as if she wanted to hug her on the spot.

"We go over the border often, don't we, Helmut? It makes for a nice outing. Everything in Switzerland is just so neat and tidy. And you've kept your Swiss francs, which is the right thing to do—we've got a fine kettle of fish with the euro. Everything's so expensive now, it's a catastrophe. Almost as expensive as in Switzerland, right, Helmut?"

Gerti didn't take her eyes off Sonya as she was burbling away. She said they had friends in Kreuzlingen and they always paid a visit to that cute museum with a gorgeous garden and those unbelievably beautiful roses climbing up the wall, and they simply had to have a coffee in the nice café next door and some strawberry cake, it was so marvelous.

"What's that café, Helmut?"

"Die Rosenlaube," her husband replied.

"Die Rosenveranda," Sonya corrected him.

"Yes, that's right, so you know it, too!"

"I work at the Dreiländer Museum."

The woman stared at her openmouthed.

"You . . . work there . . . Well, I'll be jiggered! Helmut, did you hear that? Well, it *is* a small world—we just saw it. You work at our museum! Your last show, about the history of vermin, that haunted me for weeks afterward, didn't it, Helmut? Though we don't have any pests in our house, of course. We're very neat. But it was quite interesting. And the show before that . . ."

Sonya listened absentmindedly. She'd brought this on herself. Now she was no longer anonymous; now she represented the museum—no, she *was* the museum. Gerti and Helmut would tell dozens of friends and relatives about their meeting. *Guess who we met in Canada!*

Admittedly, the thought of the Rosenveranda's strawberry cake was a pleasant one, and Sonya sensed something like melancholy rising inside her. Gerti was still going on about food.

"We're going to the Chinese restaurant near the harbor today. Would you like to join us for dinner?"

"Thanks, but I've already eaten at a Japanese place. I can recommend the restaurant. The sushi is delicious."

She got up. Gerti extended her hand.

"Then we'll go there, won't we, Helmut? We haven't had Japanese food for a long time. It's so expensive at home."

"Yes," Helmut affirmed.

"We'll see each other on the ferry," Gerti said as Sonya was leaving. Sonya only heard the key word *ferry*. Back in her room, she grabbed her cell phone to call BC Ferries. After five minutes of the music of the spheres, a voice came on.

"I'd like to confirm my reservation for tomorrow," Sonya said.

"Glad to. What's your booking number?"

The booking number. Shit, she hadn't thought of that. The note with the number was somewhere, but where? She didn't have a clue.

"Can we do this without the number?" she asked hopefully.

"Can you give me your name and credit card number?"

More music, and Sonya studied the tacky landscape picture on the wall.

"Yes, you're booked," the voice burst in. "Nice you're traveling with us again."

"What do you mean 'again'? It's my first time in Canada."

"Oh, excuse me. I see on the screen that a Sonya Werner booked the same passage three years ago."

"How can that be?"

"I see now that this Sonya Werner used another credit card number. So, yes, maybe it's only a coincidence."

"Yes, of course, many thanks," Sonya replied.

She sat there for a while and thought about it. Was it possible . . . ?

Then she dismissed the thought. *Sonya, don't be paranoid.* There were other Sonya Werners in this world for sure. The Inside Passage, the west-coast cruise—hundreds of foreigners booked it every year. It was a coincidence and nothing more.

CHAPTER 13

Although it was four thirty in the morning, the woman working for BC Ferries looked like a dew-bedecked rose. Sonya, on the other hand, felt like an absolute wreck. It was one of those nights that would have been better spent with a book or music: no thoughts of sleep, and her mind kept spinning like a merry-go-round.

The woman passed her ticket through the open bars.

"Lane twelve, please. Have a nice trip."

Sonya got in line, and her stomach felt queasy again. She hadn't had breakfast, but that wasn't the reason. She'd be in Prince Rupert that evening. Suddenly the small city was so close, almost within reach.

As the line of cars rolled into the belly of the ferry, she suddenly realized she hadn't taken her seasick pills. She couldn't remember where she'd put them. *It will be all right*, she thought to comfort herself. She locked the truck and took the elevator up.

Once she was on deck, her nose picked up the smell of coffee, scrambled eggs, toast, and bacon. Unable to resist, she renounced her dietary rules yet again. She loaded up a tray before the cafeteria filled up with hordes of travelers. She grabbed an unoccupied window table and poured hot water over the tea bag. More and more people spilled into the room. She noticed once again that most of them were couples. Not one woman was having breakfast by herself. Better to be happy by yourself than unhappy as a couple, Inge always said. Inge was a happy person. She'd been single for twenty years until she met Wilfried on a blind date. "Wilfried's the icing on my cake," she said, "nothing more, nothing less." Inge was one to talk. She never had whipped cream, always sticking to her diet.

"May I join you?"

A voice dealt her an electric shock. It was the mining engineer. Robert something.

"You remember me, or so I'd like to think?"

Just like her, he had a loaded tray in his hands and looked as if he hadn't slept a wink. That put her in a conciliatory frame of mind.

"Of course," she answered nonchalantly, something she'd picked up from Canadians.

He sat down and heaved a sigh.

"I don't know why I got on this ferry; I normally fly to Prince Rupert. But you've got to see the Inside Passage once in your life, like Niagara Falls or the Rockies."

"Do you go to Prince Rupert much?"

"Lately, yes. On business, like you."

He gave her a knowing look. He probably hoped she'd tell him more about her reason for traveling. Instead she asked, "Do you travel a lot?"

He appeared to be delighted with her interest.

"Yes, actually I do. It comes with the job. May I ask what your business is?"

"I'm a historian. I'm studying the history of immigrants from Europe."

She'd crafted that answer carefully, a most innocuous option. *Just be consistent. Consistency is above suspicion.*

He cut the yoke of his fried egg, and it ran out.

"Are there many Swiss in Prince Rupert?"

"It's not just the Swiss, there are Germans and Austrians," Sonya replied; she felt it was about time to change the subject.

But the engineer wouldn't let it go.

"But you are Swiss, or am I mistaken?"

"Yes, that's right, but I work for a German employer."

That wasn't really a lie. After all, Inge was German.

"Do you have any relatives here?"

"No."

"If I can be of any assistance in your work . . ."

"Thanks, that's nice of you, but I've a number of contacts already."

She was fascinated by the way his strong hands spread peanut butter on his thin piece of toast—very focused, almost lovingly.

"I have Austrian ancestors. I think they come from Linz." He pronounced it *Lins*.

Then something popped into her head.

"What's a corporate security service?"

He dropped his knife in surprise.

"A corporate security service? In what context? Where's that coming from?"

"I read something about it on the Internet. Apparently they work for industry, oil companies, diamond mines, and gold mines. Things like that. But what exactly do they do?"

Two hairline creases formed around Robert's mouth, which was otherwise so relaxed. He took his time answering.

"Why do you think that I of all people would know that?"

"You're a mining engineer, after all. I thought you might have heard of it."

"Well, I suppose they are people who guard gold shipments, for example. That's the first thing that comes to mind."

"So it has nothing to do with espionage?"

He placed his toast on his plate forcefully and wiped his hands on his paper napkin.

"Is this part of your research?" he asked, attempting to smile without total success.

Sonya was alarmed. She'd gone too far—she realized it now. She had to get out of these dangerous waters as fast as possible.

"I read a lot of crime novels," she replied, standing up and reaching for the teapot. "I'll go get some hot water."

He pointed to the front.

"Over there, by the cutlery. Then you won't have to line up."

At the counter, Sonya smelled pancakes. It was too tempting. *So get in line.* When she returned, there was no maple syrup, so the engineer got up.

"Let me . . ."

"No, no, I'm already up." Sonya fended him off.

After the first pancake, she knew that something unpleasant was up. Her stomach was full, and the ship was rocking. The ferry dove deep into the troughs of the waves and swerved upward. Her tablemate seemed unperturbed.

"Have you any pills for seasickness on you?" Sonya inquired.

"No, sorry," he said. "I took my last pill this morning. You don't feel well?"

"I have an odd feeling in my head. It's all so . . . so peculiar."

Suddenly, he was staring at her. Was he afraid she'd dump the contents of her stomach right onto the table instantly?

"Do you need to lie down? Have you booked a cabin?"

Sonya shook her head, which made her even dizzier.

"Do you want to lie down in my cabin? I'm happy to let you use it. And I'll find some pills for you."

He was already standing.

"No, no, thank you very much. I . . ."

At that moment her ears picked up another voice.

"Sonya, there you are! I said to Helmut, I hope she didn't miss the ferry. Didn't I, Helmut?"

It was Gerti and Helmut from Ravensburg. Sonya saw them as a blur and felt hot.

"I think I'm going to be sick," she stammered helplessly.

She tried to stay standing but lost her balance. The engineer reached out his arms to catch her. No success. She fell against something soft, voluminous. Gerti's bosom. Strong hands grabbed her by the hips and shoulders.

"Good grief! Sonya . . . Helmut, I told you that Sonya would have it too for certain, the same as you. It's from the raw fish at the restaurant. Hold her up, she must be taken care of at once . . . Get her backpack, Helmut!"

Sonya heard the engineer's voice as if in a fog, but she couldn't understand what he was saying. A confusion of voices. Gerti was loudly protesting, and she heard Helmut in the background. Somebody took her arm. There were people right and left. Lights, corridors, doors. She lay down. And then there was water on her lips. Warm. Rocking. Noises in the far distance. Submerging. Deep. Blackness.

CHAPTER 14

"I can't remember a thing."

Exhausted, Sonya looked at the woman in the white doctor's lab coat. "My . . . friend thinks it's food poisoning. I had sushi the day before."

"Your symptoms don't indicate food poisoning," the doctor explained. She spoke with a barely audible Asian accent. "Food poisoning doesn't put you into a deep sleep and cause memory loss."

Sonya looked past her to a poster on the wall of a grizzly bear climbing out of the water. In big letters above it: "Khutzeymateen Grizzly Sanctuary."

The doctor's voice brought her back.

"Have you taken any drugs?"

"You mean medications?"

"No, drugs, narcotics."

Sonya blushed as if she'd been caught in the act. That was the last thing she needed. It was good that Inge wasn't there.

"No, no. Never. No." She shook her head. "Why do you ask?"

The doctor looked straight at Sonya with her almond-shaped eyes.

"We found traces in your body. There are drugs that work exactly like that. Your condition's a good match."

Several seconds went by before Sonya had processed this information. *What does that mean? What really happened on the ferry?*

The doctor put her notes on the table beside her.

"That's all I can tell you for the moment. If you want to know more, we'll have to send your blood to a lab—mind you, at your expense. I have to leave the decision to you. Are you traveling with your friends?"

Sonya sensed the skeptical look in her eye.

"No, I happened to meet them by chance, in Port Hardy."

"They were with you on the ferry?"

"Yes, they put me up in their cabin, she and her husband."

The doctor leaned forward.

"Keep a close watch on yourself. And drop in if you don't feel well." The doctor got up. Sonya saw how small-boned she was, more fragile than she herself.

Sonya went out onto the street, and Gerti was waiting for her. She wore a bilious green blouse and Bermuda shorts.

"Well, that was quick," she said. "If that isn't a good omen. Come on, there's a coffee shop right over there."

She put her arm in Sonya's and pulled her to the other side of the street.

"Helmut's still in the First Nations museum. He's interested in aboriginal history."

Sonya hadn't said a word. She was too knocked out.

Gerti plopped onto a comfortable sofa at the front of the café.

"Can I get you something?" Sonya asked, to reciprocate.

"Coffee with whipped cream, dearie."

Sonya ordered a medium latte for herself: decaf, organic, with low-fat milk.

"So what did the doctor say?" Gerti asked, scooping the cream off her coffee with her spoon. Her fingernails were neatly manicured.

"The doctor said it wasn't food poisoning."

Sonya dropped the information like bait.

"Indeed? Did she say that?" Gerti seemed disappointed. "Well, what was it, then?"

"She doesn't exactly know. They have to test my blood in a lab."

"Don't get yourself involved with that; they just make money off tourists. I've heard that so many times. You have to pay cash up front, you see. Canadians get everything paid by the state. Helmut had the same thing happen to him when—"

"Gerti, please tell me again precisely what happened."

"You still don't remember?"

Sonya raised her hands helplessly.

"No. I still don't."

"Well, Helmut and I had more trouble with our reservations . . . But that's not important. I first saw you in the cafeteria. Helmut wanted a linden-blossom tea because his stomach was upset; he'd felt awful the whole night. He didn't sleep a wink, as you can imagine, and I couldn't either . . . But it's not your fault, Sonya, I don't mean to say that it's because you recommended that Japanese place—no, I don't."

She licked the whipped cream off her thin lips and put a reassuring hand on Sonya's arm.

"But Helmut definitely picked something up there. He had a sushi appetizer—"

"But I had that, too," Sonya added.

"See, see?" Gerti exclaimed triumphantly. "So Helmut wanted a tea and . . . But isn't that . . ."

Sonya looked where Gerti was looking. A man was studying the café menu and then walked away.

Gerti was thunderstruck.

"That . . . that's the man who was sitting with you in the cafeteria."

Sonya looked at her keenly.

"He was sitting at my table?"

"Yes, of course. And when you stood up and almost fell over . . . he didn't want us to help you, not one bit. Helmut had to take your backpack away from him. He didn't want to let go of it!"

Gerti was trembling with indignation.

"Who didn't want to let go? Helmut?"

"No, that man. But I knew right away that he wasn't with you. He didn't even speak German. We didn't let him have it. We must stick together when we're abroad, mustn't we?"

Sonya's head was buzzing.

"What happened next?"

Gerti made a broad, expansive motion, as if she were about to wrap the whole world under her wings.

"We took you back to our cabin, put you to bed, and you went to sleep. Helmut and I let you sleep. My mother always said: sleep heals everything. And then we thought it best to take you to our hotel."

"Helmut drove my truck?" They must have found the keys in her backpack, of course.

Gerti folded her hands. She seemed pleased with herself.

"We could never have allowed you to drive—in your condition. Just imagine."

That was the first thing Sonya could remember, waking up in the hotel.

"You're an angel, Gerti," she said. "What would I have done without you?"

Gerti beamed.

"We won't ever forget it. No one at home will believe us. Isn't it crazy?"

When Gerti disappeared into the restroom, Sonya investigated her backpack. Her video camera was there, the little camera, her wallet. She unzipped a hidden pocket in the back, where she kept her itinerary and her information on Tonio's Canadian trip. Her secret pocket. It was empty. She rifled through the backpack. Nothing.

Her heart started to race. Had someone gone through her backpack and filched her notes while she was dead to the world? Or had she mislaid the papers? Quickly, she tried to remember what information they contained: Tonio and Nicky's hotels, the stores where Tonio shopped, their excursions, everything she'd taken off Tonio's credit card statements. But who'd find the information of any use?

Helmut came through the doorway and headed right to their table. He was wearing a fisherman's hat.

"We did it," he announced. "We're off on a grizzly tour in three days."

He beamed at Sonya, evidently in a good mood. His stomach problems seemed to have vanished into thin air.

"There's still room for you if you'd like to go. You wouldn't want to miss this," he said to Sonya.

Sonya knew at once that he meant the Khutzeymateen Grizzly Sanctuary. She'd read about it. It was the only protected area for grizzlies in Canada. Tonio had been there on a guided tour. That was the only way you could get in. It had cost him a fortune, but when she saw his credit card statement, she wasn't very surprised. She'd known by then that he'd sold his favorite plane in Switzerland without telling her.

"That would be nice, but it's too expensive, unfortunately," she replied, looking at two disappointed faces. "I actually have to look for another accommodation. Hotels aren't part of my budget." She gave an apologetic laugh.

Helmut and Gerti exchanged glances. The silent understanding of a long-married couple.

"We didn't want to cause you any hardship," Gerti explained. "It simply seemed to us to be the best solution."

Sonya's stomach seized. She had just managed to snub her rescuers.

"You're both wonderful," she said to placate them. "I'm so grateful to you for everything . . . Can I buy you a piece of that marvelous chocolate cake I saw on the counter?"

"Good idea. I love these massive Canadian cakes. Helmut, you will have to pass on this; I'm sure your stomach can't take it now."

Sonya walked to the counter, and she instinctively glanced through the window to see if the mining engineer might still be there.

CHAPTER 15

Sonya left the youth hostel, which had a pink facade straight out of a Western. She'd had a rather busy night. Some young people had come in from the ferry after midnight and noisily moved into their rooms. At least one of them had washed his clothes in the bathroom during the night. When she slipped into the bathroom that morning, clothes were still dripping from every possible spot, even from the shower curtain rod. She settled for a quick wash, turning the tap on full in revenge.

A little later, she was on the street with an umbrella under her arm. It was time to view Prince Rupert. Standing on a hill, she saw passing tankers and ships on the Pacific. Islands dotted the coastline, as if someone had grown them out of the ocean by the dozen. The fresh smell of the ocean and damp wood lay over the city. Many houses on the main street had boomtown facades higher than their flat roofs and looked straight out of pioneering times. It wasn't even raining.

Prince Rupert might well have been an important port, but otherwise the city didn't have much to offer. Did Tonio come here on account of the grizzlies? Or did he know somebody in the area? The question went around in her head, though she only wanted to focus on Else Seel today. Else went to Prince Rupert by herself now and then, when she wanted a whiff of city air. There was, after all, a five-story hotel, big stores, cafés, and an asphalted main street. Else would eat in the hotel restaurant, go to the movies, and meet people. In the deep woods, she must have gotten tired of the roof hitting her on the head. Once, Else wrote, she met a retired pastor from a German congregation in Los Angeles who spoke authentic Bavarian. He immediately began to dream up a film based on Else's life: *From the Hurly-Burly of Berlin to a Log Cabin in the Wild* is what she wrote later. Sonya could empathize with him.

That must have also fascinated Ezra Pound, who was held in an American psychiatric institution in Washington, DC, after World War II. He was interned for anti-American propaganda speeches he'd made in Italy and for sympathizing with the Italian fascists. Pound was accused of high treason, but he was declared mentally ill. Else entered into a correspondence with him in 1947 after she'd read a newspaper report of his institutionalization. Pound importuned her again and again to write him in detail about her life in the wild.

Sonya looked back out toward the ocean. Before her, the green island forest gleamed like wet seaweed in the pale sunlight. Sun in Prince Rupert!

She wanted to spend that day researching an incident from Else's diary. When Else was once in Prince Rupert, a person she knew from her home district looked her up. He'd discovered Else's name in the local paper under the heading "New Hotel Guests." If Sonya could dig up that edition of the paper, Inge's eyes would pop.

At the library desk a young lady with an open, friendly face turned to her. Sonya made her request.

"Which paper do you mean: the *Prince Rupert Daily News* or the *Evening Empire*? We have both on microfilm."

"Back to when?"

"Around 1912."

Sonya felt like throwing her arms around the librarian's neck.

"That's wonderful! What paper from that time do you think would have a list of hotel guests?"

The clerk thought for a moment.

"I'd say the *Daily News*. Do you have the exact date the German lady arrived?"

Sonya fished out her notebook.

"It must have been 1931."

Which was when Else was pregnant with her daughter Gloria.

"Come with me, I'll show you how the search function works."

Less than fifteen minutes later, Sonya found the page with the announcement and printed out a copy.

Then she had an idea. She went back to the main desk.

"I'd like to look up something more recent. I'm interested in September three years ago."

"But of course," the young woman responded. "I'll look it up on the computer."

Sonya's hands were moist as she looked through that month. September 11. The bodies were found the day before. That is what the police in her hometown of St. Gallen told her. But nothing. Not a word through September 22. And again nothing. She went through page after page. How could that be! A seaplane with two people on board; the pilot and passenger dead. There must be a report in the *Prince Rupert Daily News*. She started again from the beginning. There it was—the headline. "Two European Tourists Dead. Tragic Ending to a Holiday." A brief article. Sonya double-checked the date. September 29. Nineteen days after the crash!

Impatient, she began to read.

The rescuers found the bodies of the pilot and his son near Captain's Cove, about five miles from Kitkatla. The plane, a DHC-2 Beaver, must have hit at full speed. The pilot was apparently unaware he was heading straight for the water. It was raining hard at the time, and visibility was poor. Those aboard were Tonio Vonlanden, a Swiss man, and his seventeen-year-old son, Nicky. The Beaver was leased; the police did not release the owner's name.

That was it. A few lousy lines. Sonya kept looking and chanced upon a brief item from the beginning of October that year. It said that the bodies had been transferred to Switzerland. The police had no further information about the crash of the two European tourists.

It was all so peculiar . . . So the plane was rented; therefore, Tonio had not bought it. Perhaps he couldn't because he was a tourist . . . Sonya's search had exhausted her. She thanked the woman, who called after her: "Do go to the museum in the harbor. It shows the history of our area. I have a friend who works there."

But Sonya already knew where she was going. She turned around.

"How do you get to Captain's Cove?"

CHAPTER 16

The road zigged and zagged like a hunted rabbit. Sonya thought she was lost already. Then a broad bay came into view, and so did a flat, factory-like building and a bright blue gabled house next door. Sonya saw the words "Greenblue Air" on the gable, and her pulse beat faster. As she slammed the truck door shut, she saw a seaplane rattling up to the sky some distance away. The air was cool; a gentle breeze came off the ocean and blew her hair into her eyes. It smelled of fish.

She entered the company's building, which was divided into an office on the left and a waiting room on the right. Some people were sitting on orange plastic chairs, and the faces turning toward her were almost all from the First Nations. Flights, times, and destinations were listed on a board on the wall. One name struck Sonya: Kitkatla.

"May I help you?" A woman rose from her seat.

Sonya spun around, as if she'd been caught doing something illegal.

"Is that the only flight to Kitkatla?" She pointed to the board.

"It's the last one today, but there are two tomorrow: one at eight and the other at three p.m."

"Are there same-day return flights?" Sonya asked.

"Five p.m. is the last return. Would you like to make a reservation?"

Sonya hesitated.

"How much does it cost?"

"A round-trip flight is a hundred and eighty dollars."

The charge mustn't show up on the expense report for the museum. She whipped out her credit card.

"The morning flight, please."

She signed the receipt, but there was an uneasy feeling in the pit of her stomach. She strolled down to the landing dock, where two seaplanes were moored. A tall, slim figure was busy with one of them. She only saw his back. *Tonio!* She was rooted to the spot. She saw him come around the plane. She saw him throw his sports bag onto the jetty, check the stowage space, jump nimbly onto the jetty planks.

Tonio, she wanted to call out, but her throat was choked up. The figure picked up his bag, straightened his baseball cap, and took off his sunglasses. She stared at the man as if he were a ghost.

"Hello," he called, a little puzzled. "Looking for something?"

At first she couldn't utter a sound.

"No, I . . . I was going to Kitkatla, but not until tomorrow, I . . ."

She fell silent.

The man laughed.

"Well, you've come to the right place. I'm flying to Kitkatla tomorrow. Are you the new nurse?"

"No . . . I'm on vacation and just wanted to see the area in a plane."

"Tell them in the office that you want to fly with Sam." He put his bag down and took off his baseball cap. He looked up at the sky.

"Let's hope the weather tomorrow is as good as it is today."

Another look at her face, and he laughed.

"Don't worry. We only fly if the weather's safe enough. Believe me. Now, I need a cigarette and coffee."

He walked up the ramp, but Sonya didn't budge an inch. She was incapable of thinking straight. Her breathing was shallow. An eagle soared over the water. It flew calmly and effortlessly, riding the wind. Sonya had read that for the natives, the eagle was the messenger of the gods. But what was the message the gods were sending her right now? She listened for a long time but only heard the ocean swishing, the gulls screaming, the boats chugging. She filled her lungs with the salty sea air and made her way to the parking lot.

Her nose smelled cigarette smoke. At the back of the building, the pilot, Sam, was sitting on a beat-up kitchen chair. Out of the wind, naturally.

"Care for a coffee?" he shouted.

Sonya politely declined.

"Where are you from anyway?" Sam carried on blithely. "Your accent. Are you from Holland?"

"No." She stopped. "I'm only passing through . . . Have you been with Greenblue Air for long?"

He blew smoke into the air.

"Seven years. But I've been flying for twenty-six years."

Now that she could take a closer look, she saw he wasn't at all like Tonio. His face was harder, more deeply lined; his eyes burned like those of a person who'd lived through a lot. Not from commercial, phony adventures, Sonya thought. He wasn't a world-weary sportsman getting his kicks; it must be from the dangers of living in the Canadian northland. And smoking, of course—that leaves its mark, too.

Sam dragged on his cigarette.

"I used to fly in the Arctic, and over the tundra. There's just rocks and muskeg there. And snow and ice in the winter. I took supplies to small lumber camps."

Sonya came closer.

"So you're a bush pilot?"

He nodded.

"Those were the days, up in the Arctic. Once I blew a cylinder in my Otter. A DHC-3 Otter, and I had to make an emergency landing. I was stranded for four days in the Barren Lands until help arrived. But a guy like me sometimes gets lucky. An Air Canada pilot flying the polar route to London caught my SOS signal. He passed it on."

"You must be a very experienced pilot," Sonya said.

Sam laughed dryly.

"We're all prima donnas here. Greenblue wouldn't hire a pilot who didn't have at least six, seven thousand hours. On a seaplane, I mean. Would you like to sit down?"

He got up and offered her his chair, but Sonya declined.

"I must be going." She added, hesitating, "I've heard that seaplanes crash frequently."

Sam looked mystified.

"Greenblue planes?"

"No, but in this area."

He took another drag on his cigarette, and then he threw the butt on the ground and stepped on it.

"I could show you five places on the map in the office where friends of mine have gone down. The weather's bad here. Wind, squalls, fog, rain. It can change very fast. First you get the sun, and you barely turn around and you've got rain and fog. Are you worried about tomorrow morning?"

He looked at her with those burning eyes.

Sonya lowered her eyes.

"A little. What about you, you're not afraid?"

"I'm good, I know that. I'm always five steps ahead of my plane. You have to be even stronger than it is."

He lit another cigarette, turning toward the bay.

"It's probably one of the trickiest areas in North America, I mean as far as the weather goes. There's no radar, no control tower, nobody to talk to. You're all by yourself up there."

The fact that Sonya was listening so attentively seemed to spur him on.

"Are you staying here long?" he asked.

"I don't know yet."

She made as if to leave but changed her mind. She had to seize the opportunity when it came.

"If this region is so dangerous, are foreign pilots permitted to fly here?"

"In principle, yes, if they present their flying license to our transport authorities and have it confirmed. Whether they *can* do it, that's a different matter. Some guys come up here from the south and think they know better. No way. We're strict about VFR."

"What's VFR?"

"Visual Flight Rules. You'll see for yourself. There's nothing else. Even if we've got GPS and maps on the monitor. Sit beside me tomorrow. I'll show you."

Had she gone too far? Had she aroused too much curiosity? It was time to go.

"Thanks a lot, Sam. That was very interesting."

Sam's eyes stayed on her a few seconds too long.

"It was my pleasure," he replied.

Backing out of her parking place, in the rearview mirror she saw a black SUV gliding past. Sonya glanced quickly at the driver. The mining engineer!

She felt hot. What was he doing here? She instinctively gunned it, looking in the mirror after a few hundred yards. The black SUV was following her. She quickly turned into a side street. At the next intersection, she went left and then took an immediate right. She didn't have the foggiest idea where she was, but she zoomed through a residential district. All of a sudden, she was on a straight road leading to the main highway.

A few minutes later, bathed in sweat, she parked in front of the youth hostel. Never again, she swore to herself, would she tell herself that she was being too suspicious.

CHAPTER 17

It was just seven a.m. Sonya was already sitting in one of the orange plastic chairs in the Greenblue Air waiting room, as if she were checking in for an international flight. It didn't matter to her; she hadn't really slept a wink that night anyway. She wore a long-sleeved, tight-fitting T-shirt with a deep décolletage that revealed more than she actually intended. That was a lie: it was intentional. Why shouldn't she look seductive?

Somebody quickly opened the door. A tall dark-haired woman rolled in a suitcase that was bursting at the seams.

When she saw Sonya, a smile spread over her face.

"*Ach, hallo,*" she said, as if they'd known each other for years.

"*Guten Morgen,*" Sonya responded in surprise. "Are you German?"

"Canadian, but originally from Germany, from Mainz. And you?"

"From Switzerland."

"I thought so. I heard you on the telephone, in the hostel."

Sonya couldn't get her head around it. She thought she could waltz around here in complete anonymity, and now a strange woman was telling her she'd heard her talking to Inge on the phone. She'd had Inge call her on the house phone because the reception on her cell was so bad. Inge was audibly amused that Sonya was staying in a youth hostel.

"So you immigrated to Canada?"

The young woman kicked her suitcase aside and sat down beside her.

"Yes, I've been living here for thirteen years. Not here, but in Vancouver. I only come here to work."

"What's your line of work?"

"I'm an outpost nurse—a flying nurse." She laughed easily. "I fill in for nurses on vacation in outlying areas about six times a year. Otherwise I work in a Vancouver hospital in the emergency room."

Her glossy black hair kept falling over her eyes, and she'd push it back behind her ears.

"And where are you flying to?" the nurse asked.

"I'm taking a sightseeing flight with a short stopover in Kitkatla."

"I'm working in Kitkatla! That is, I start tomorrow. Come to the nursing station, and I'll give you a guided tour if you like. By the way, I'm Kathrin."

Sonya marveled at how simple everything was here, how friendly people were with one another. It was a completely relaxed mode of existence. "I'm Sonya." She felt a warm, soft feeling spreading inside.

Kathrin disappeared into the washroom. There were only two other people waiting for the flight.

Suddenly, Sam stood in front of her, his face more furrowed than the day before.

"We can get going," he announced. "Is this Kathrin's suitcase?"

Everyone here knew everyone else.

"She'll be right back," Sonya replied.

Sam stood with his arms akimbo, relaxed.

"You've picked a magnificent day. Visibility couldn't be better."

Kathrin came back, and he took her suitcase. Then he said hello to an old native man who was lugging a cardboard box on his back.

"Hey, Joe, going home?"

"About time, Sam," the man replied. "This town is getting more and more frantic."

"You're right, Joe, and it's going to get worse with the new container port—you heard about that. Leave that box there. We can carry it down for you. Let's go!"

On the way to the landing dock, Kathrin explained, "Sam's an experienced pilot. He'll get us there safely."

"Do I look that worried?"

Sonya once again cursed her face, which couldn't conceal anything.

"A little." Kathrin laughed her bell-like laugh.

The plane only had seven seats. Sam helped her into the seat beside him. "You'll see best there," he said. Kathrin sat down next to the old man and began chatting with him right away. Sonya followed Sam's directions, putting on the headphones so she could hear his voice over the wire.

"We must always be on the lookout for eagles. An eagle has no natural enemies so it doesn't avoid planes. An eagle can do a whole lot of damage."

"What type of plane is this?" she asked.

"A DHC-2 Beaver."

Tonio's fatal plane. Sonya swallowed.

Sam started his engine, and they glided over the water out into the bay. The early morning shimmered in fresh, delicate colors. The sky dissolved into a diaphanous watercolor.

The chug of the motor gave way to a roar, and the Beaver took off.

"We're going up to a thousand feet. Here, have a look."

Sam pointed to a miniscreen, where yellow shapes stood out against a blue background.

"That's a GPS map. We can see our position on it."

Sonya looked down through the window. The coastal islands were so close that she could clearly make out trees, swamps, and isolated houses. Prince Rupert was already behind them.

Sam looked at her sideways.

"Here's where there are powerful wind gusts. Three planes have hit the trees during takeoff."

Sonya focused on a canary-yellow seaplane in a cove on a small island. It sparkled in the green like a sunflower.

Little sunflower. Tonio's term of endearment for her.

She had only gone up once with Tonio in his plane, on a jaunt to Milan. Much to her surprise, she liked flying. But when her goddaughter had given her a present of a hot-air balloon flight, she gave the voucher to Odette; wild horses couldn't have dragged her to it. But Tonio's light plane was something else. That was fun. Something they could share. But then Tonio had suddenly stopped flying. There were no more high-altitude flights together. No floating above the clouds. "It costs too much right now," he explained. Then he sold the plane and took the money to go off to Canada. It simply made no sense.

But she could very well comprehend his inability to resist flying a seaplane in Canada. After all, he'd got his pilot's seaplane license during a long stay in Alaska. And that was precisely what proved fatal for him and Nicky.

"Do you see that island on the horizon?"

Her eyes followed the direction of Sam's arm.

"That's Bonilla Island. There's a weather station there. That's where we get our weather reports. If the wind on the island gets up to forty-five knots, it's about fifteen knots less in the bays."

Sonya looked back. Kathrin's eyes were closed. She hadn't put the headphones on and appeared to be asleep.

The Beaver made for an island. A few wooden huts with tin roofs lined the shore.

"That's Oona River. I bring them the mail three times a week. It's an old Scandinavian settlement."

Sam eased up on the throttle.

"The water's not deep in that bay. You have to stay precisely in the channel and hope a whale isn't swimming out."

Sonya saw a man running on the landing dock, while Sam laughed and waved at him. "Come and catch me!" he joked. He turned to Sonya, telling her, "I don't have any brakes." She looked at him in alarm. Then he laughed some more.

The Beaver touched down on the water in an amazingly soft landing, which Sonya acknowledged with a thumbs-up.

Sam's dark eyes twinkled. He was pleased with himself.

The Beaver glided straight for the dock, and the man arrived just in time to pick up the mailbag.

Kathrin poked her head from behind.

"Everything OK?"

Sonya nodded.

Then they left the bay and were on their way to Kitkatla. Before, it had just been a name. Now, suddenly images would accrue to it. Sam said something she couldn't understand, motioning with his head to the left.

"That's where it came down, the Beaver."

Sonya instantly froze when she heard him say, "Three, four years ago. All the passengers were dead."

Sonya stared at the surface of the water. So it was here that it happened. Here's where they lay in the ice-cold water, where their bodies were smashed up, where they left this world. Did Nicky die first? Or did he watch his father die? Were they both killed at once, as the Swiss authorities assured her? She couldn't get these questions past her lips. Sam wouldn't have known the answers anyway. Instead she asked, "Where was it exactly? Where?"

"We're flying right over it now. It's a difficult spot in bad weather. Winds collide from everywhere, from all directions." He made a face. "You can really get hammered here."

The water was in motion, like a wet, crumpled gray cloth. There was no place you could fix your gaze upon, only this infinite, broad ocean roughed by the wind. The waves had a silvery gleam, like fish scales. What power emanated from this ocean! An eternity dissolved in water. The longer she watched the incredible expanse far below, the smaller she felt. A tiny bit of life, of fate; and lives and fates were like the arching waves of this mighty, incomprehensible ocean. So many tragedies and disasters, so many cruelties occurred. Who had any right to claim being exempt? Life wasn't fair—how foolish to insist it was! Perhaps an eagle was about to deliver a message from the gods: you can only survive life humbly, by staying small before the powers, the forces, the dispensations that are so much greater than your own life.

Sam's voice brought her back from far away.

"The pilot underestimated the conditions. That happens frequently."

Sonya was silent for a long time. She'd expected anything and everything: that she'd break out in tears, or faint; that she'd feel mounting rage; that the scene of the accident would release some sort of unknown, overpowering emotion. Maybe her demons would break out of their cage, and she'd finally be rid of them.

Then she would be able to flush the little pink pills—that wrapped everything in indifference—down the toilet. That's something she could not have done, but now she felt . . . almost nothing. It wasn't that she didn't give a damn; her soul hadn't turned cold. She felt something like . . . objectivity. The urge to accomplish her mission. A feeling of obligation toward Tonio and Nicky: to discover the truth about their deaths.

Her voice was calm as she asked Sam: "These accidents, are they so frequent that they're not worth reporting in the newspapers?"

He looked her straight in the eye.

"The newspapers. We don't give a damn about what the papers say. We don't need to read them. We know when something happens. We know everything, sooner or later."

Sonya thought it wise not to ask any more questions.

The Beaver's nose tilted forward. Sam was starting his approach.

"Kitkatla," he announced.

CHAPTER 18

Sonya's knees wobbled as she walked along the jetty. It felt strange to feel terra firma again.

Kathrin shrugged.

"There's no taxi. We'll have to walk. But it's not very far."

"There are cars here?" Sonya asked, immediately regretting her naïveté. She'd never been on a small island with a First Nation village on it, but her question didn't bother Kathrin.

"Cars come in on the Prince Rupert ferry. But you can get along quite easily without a car, at least most of the time."

Sonya grabbed a handle of Kathrin's heavy suitcase, and they walked up the unpaved main street. The village houses looked relatively new, or at least seemed in good condition. At any rate, they weren't run down like houses on many First Nation reservations that Sonya had read about in the papers. She was struck by so many trampolines in front of the houses. Suddenly, there were loud, excited shouts. Children came running from everywhere, and the two of them were soon surrounded by a babbling crowd. Sonya smiled shyly at the dark-skinned faces.

"We knew you were coming today," a girl in a colorful parka and sneakers shouted.

"So who told you?" Kathrin stroked her hair.

"Molly!"

A boy pointed at Sonya. "And who's that?"

"This is a visitor from Europe who'd like to see our nursing station."

As they worked their way through the crowd of children, Kathrin explained that Molly was the nursing-station receptionist, and she spent most evenings with her. There really wasn't much to do here in Kitkatla, no entertainment other than TV. Sometimes they played bingo when the parish organized a bingo night.

Kathrin said hello to some men repairing their fishing nets by the roadside, and Sonya followed her lead. Salmon filets were drying out on wooden stands. The nursing station was behind a Catholic church. A large sign announced that Kitkatla was an alcohol-free reservation and listed the regulations. People who drank faced a possible six-month sentence.

Sonya was surprised how bright and modern the nursing station was, but she bit her tongue so she wouldn't seem like an ignorant European. Kathrin introduced her to the staff: the nurses, the psychologist, the caretaker, the nursing-station head, the community nurse, and of course Molly, the receptionist.

Sonya had come to Canada to mourn the death of two loved ones. And here she was in a circle of welcoming strangers who treated her like a long-lost daughter, sharing their grilled salmon, potatoes, and steamed carrots with her.

That afternoon Kathrin took her on a short hike up a hill behind the village. Kathrin had packed pepper spray, not because of bears but "because dogs roam in packs here." Sometimes there are more dogs than people in Kitkatla, she added. That's when they shoot dogs that are off a leash.

Sonya walked faster. She'd have liked some pepper spray as well. She'd had enough bad experiences with dogs. But standing at the edge of the coastal forest on the hilltop with Kathrin, she forgot about them. The view was breathtaking. A labyrinth of tree-covered islands spread out before them, and high mountains rose up into the smoky blue sky. Sonya expected to see seagoing ships of early explorers pop up among the islands and Indians hurrying to the beaches, unsuspecting of the looming threat to their existence. The two women sat for a long time, gazing out at the ocean and the village at their feet.

With Odette, times for relaxation had been rare. She always seemed to be under pressure, always getting ready to climb a peak in Alaska or for a trekking tour in Yemen, or a river cruise in France. To Sonya, she seemed driven by an insatiable craving for achievement and success and a desire to be better than everyone else.

Wouldn't Odette rather have sat on a rock like this and left all her cares behind? Or watched bald eagles circling overhead? She would certainly have been interested in what Kathrin was saying: that people in Kitkatla belonged to the Tsimshian tribe and had been in the Prince Rupert area for about five thousand years. Sonya thought about it: five thousand years ago, the Pharaoh Djoser built the famous step pyramid at Saqqâra, the first monumental building made of stone in world history.

"There's a rock not far from Prince Rupert," Kathrin said, "that has the impression of a body: the head, torso, legs, and arms. A Tsimshian legend tells of a man who fell from the sky. He was once expelled from the village community of Metlakatla. He left, but returned one day to say he had been in the sky and fallen back to Earth. The villagers said: 'We don't believe you; prove it!' So he took them to that rock, and the villagers looked at the imprint of his body and were astounded. Here was proof that he'd fallen from the sky. The community forgave the man and took him back in."

The man who fell from the sky. There are no imprints on the ocean, Sonya reflected. No traces. No proof. Nobody is resurrected from the dead. Otherwise she might be able to forgive, just as the Tsimshian did.

On the way to the jetty, Kathrin urged her to see the Queen Charlotte Islands. "Or you'll be sorry."

"I'll give it some serious thought," Sonya assured her.

"You could also go see Jack Gordon there. He used to live here, but he's in Queen Charlotte City now."

"Who's Jack Gordon?"

"He's the pilot who found the bodies in the plane that crashed."

Sonya was startled. So Kathrin hadn't been sleeping at all. She had heard her whole conversation!

"Why did Jack move away from Kitkatla?"

"Not from Kitkatla. From Prince Rupert . . . I think he'd recovered too many dead bodies over the years . . . After that disaster three years ago, he just quit and moved out. Something must have happened that made him leave. Jack wasn't the kind of guy to just simply stop."

Sonya made a snap decision. The Queen Charlottes. Jack Gordon. She must get there.

Sam's Beaver appeared minutes later.

"I had to drop somebody off at Rainy River Lodge, a fisherman from Austria," he apologized. Sonya was sitting beside him in the otherwise empty plane. She was only half listening. She waved good-bye to Kathrin until she couldn't see her anymore. She wanted to come back someday and find time to hear stories of the people who'd been on these islands for thousands of years.

When she looked at Sam, she knew immediately that something was up.

"We've no time to lose," he said.

Sonya noticed a gray veil over the water.

"The weather's changed, hasn't it?"

"Yes, and this is only the beginning. But we can still make it."

The Beaver gained altitude. It behaved quite normally at first, but then it unexpectedly began to vibrate and shudder violently.

"Everything OK?" Sam's voice could be heard in the headphones. Before she could answer, somebody else was on the air. Loud static and crackling garbled the conversation. She heard another man's voice, while staring through the windshield into gray nothingness.

"Did you get that?" That was Sam. "There's fog up in Alaska. Thick as clam chowder. Very dangerous. And a lot of fog between Dundas Island and Wales Island and Tree Point."

She found it hard to concentrate. She felt her throat tighten. What was this about Alaska—they were much farther south! Alaska—what did she care about Alaska!

"If the glacial water from Portland Inlet hits warmer air from the Pacific, there's fog. Then it's better to fly over land than over water."

She realized he was rattling on to take her mind off the danger.

"But there's no land here," she shot back.

"Don't worry, we—"

A downdraft suddenly pushed the Beaver downward. Sonya's stomach shot up like a rubber ball.

"Dammit!" Sam muttered.

The plane was bouncing up and down like a yo-yo.

Sam's distorted voice came through to her.

"It's not far now. But if it gets worse, we'll descend."

"What?" Sonya shouted.

"We'll get down. Emergency landing. Understand?"

"Down where? On the water?"

She yelled so her voice wouldn't sound so frightened.

"Of course. It's a seaplane, right?"

Sonya looked at Sam for a split second. He was grinning! She couldn't believe it.

"Heads up, I'm going to make a slow descent."

Sonya closed her eyes, but that didn't make it any better. She felt she was in the middle of a nightmare. Her worst fears were about to be realized. An emergency landing on the ocean, in the midst of a raging storm. *Is that it? Do I have to die this way now?*

The Beaver seemed to be hurtling straight at the water. Out of the corner of her eye, she saw Sam's hands working the levers and controls.

"Prepare for landing!"

His words weren't a question but a warning. Sonya had no idea how to prepare for anything. There was nothing she could do except not scream in panic.

The plane veered sharply, looping back, and Sonya saw some green. Land! Then she saw a landing stage, a house, and a yellow seaplane. She took it all in for a fraction of a second. Then they splashed down hard. Spray washed over the windshield. Sonya bounced between Sam and the door. The Beaver tipped dangerously on its side and came upright again, wobbling.

"C'mon, now," Sam urged. "C'mon, c'mon."

Gusts of wind pushed the plane over on its side again and again. But Sam skillfully righted it every time. This phantom dance seemed to last forever. They were so close to shore, their salvation. But the wind held them captive.

"I can't bring 'er in, I just can't bring 'er in!" Sonya heard Sam exclaim. She didn't respond. There was nothing she could do. Or was there?

"We've almost made it. You're doing great, Sam, we'll make it."

Her voice sounded firm as the Beaver headed for a point of land. A blast of air pushed its nose to the left. And then—then the plane sailed into the cove all by itself. Sam finally killed the engine. They looked at each other in relief.

"Are you a good broad jumper?"

Sonya grasped what he meant. She dismounted hand over hand onto the pontoon, while the wind and rain whipped her face. She gripped a strut firmly with her right hand, and her feet helped keep her balance on the pontoon. Then she jumped, landing on the bank, slipping, but grabbing hold of a tussock and pulling herself up.

He threw her a line that she lashed tightly around a bollard.

Not until she'd finished did she feel her heart pounding and her legs shaking. Her jacket was soaked, a heavy weight on her body.

Sam looked up at the house.

"Let's see if George is in. Funny that his dogs didn't come down."

Sonya followed right on his heels in case the dogs suddenly ran up. The house seemed oddly substantial, almost stately for its wild surroundings. The builder had placed great store by having large windows, though now they were dark. At the back door, Sam turned the knob. It was unlocked.

"George? Hello?" he shouted into the house.

Nobody answered. Sam brought Sonya inside.

"He's not here. He's probably riding out the storm somewhere."

They went up some stairs to the main floor, and Sonya took off her wet hiking shoes. She followed him tentatively through the living room into the kitchen. The rooms were filled with warmth.

"Can we just barge in like this?"

"Of course. His door's always open. Particularly in an emergency. Coffee?"

He took two cups from the draining board and put them on the table.

"He's made a fire. He probably hasn't been gone long."

Sonya hung her jacket on a chair. Even her T-shirt was damp. She resisted the temptation to take it off and let it dry out, though the thought was tantalizing. She took a look around. There was a wood stove in the corner, with two wing chairs in front of it; huge stuffed animal heads hung everywhere: moose, bear, mountain lion, wolverine.

The coffee machine gurgled.

"I'll be right back," Sam told her. "Gotta use George's RT."

Sonya saw him in the hall pulling a lever and talking into the mouthpiece. He was evidently calling Greenblue Air.

Sonya poured some coffee and found an open can of condensed milk in the refrigerator. She heard an electric generator humming somewhere.

She sat down. The hot coffee thawed her out. So what if it was decaf or organic. She had a sudden feeling of lightness, almost weightlessness. She had escaped from a great danger; she was safe. Nothing else mattered.

Sam walked across the living room.

"We aren't the only ones stranded. The storm took everybody by surprise."

He piled sugar into his coffee.

"That's how it is up here, eh? Always full of surprises." He grinned.

Sonya looked out the window and saw the two planes rocking.

"Where can George be? His plane's here."

"He probably took his boat to go fishing and is waiting in a cove for the weather to clear."

"Does he live alone?"

"For some years now, since his wife died. He's a real loner, a lone wolf. A lot of men up here live like he does. Solitude can be attractive."

Sonya brushed her damp hair off her forehead. A drop of water fell on her nose. *All alone out here.* Suppose George had an accident with an ax or a chain saw? Or fell off a ladder? Who'd get him to a hospital? Would he even be found in time?

Sonya recalled a passage in Else Seel's book. In March 1936 during a bad winter with temperatures of thirty below zero, George Seel was away again, setting his traps. Else and her two children kept to the main room, eating and sleeping in front of the large iron stove and its constantly crackling fire. Suddenly her ears began to hurt and her glands swelled up; she ran a high fever and didn't have the strength to chop a water hole in the ice-covered lake. She was desperate. Then Else heard a knock at the door. A neighbor she'd known for a long time had dropped by. An inner voice had urged him to look in on Else and her little children. Else wept in gratitude. That same winter an elderly man froze to death in his log cabin. The neighbors found him weeks after he'd died, frozen stiff, still clutching the stovepipe.

"Tell me about Switzerland," Sam asked, interrupting her thoughts. "I've never been there."

Sonya was surprised. Had she told him where she was from?

"Switzerland is heavily settled, not like here. People and houses everywhere. A lot of the mountains have cable cars with an inn at the top. You've got to go a long way to live in seclusion."

"That's probably why so many tourists like it here, because there's so much room. A little too much room for my liking."

"Too much room? There can never be too much, Sam."

"Well . . . it's easy for people to hide up here, people who don't belong at all, eh? They can carry on their dirty business, and nobody can lay a finger on them."

He poured another cup.

"Our coastline is so long. Who can really patrol it? Not the coast guard or the police. It's impossible. There's too much land and too few guards."

"You mean smugglers?" She was thinking about her chat with the fisherman in Powell River.

"Yeah, them too. Crooks once tried to smuggle some Chinese into Prince Rupert. They were stuck here for weeks. Then the government deported them. People are hard to overlook. You can hide other things more easily. But I—"

He stopped. A noise. Sonya heard it, too. Was George back?

"George never leaves without his dogs."

He listened intently.

"Could be a wild animal. I'll go look."

He tramped down the stairs and slammed the door. All she heard for several minutes was the howling of the wind, maybe the rush of the ocean, and the humming generator.

Again, that quick, sharp noise. It came from inside the house—she was positive. She went softly on her stocking feet into the living room and discovered a door to the right that must lead to another room. She took a few steps toward it and was about to put a hand on the doorknob. She still held her coffee mug. Was it better to wait for Sam? She felt like a burglar.

Then she heard a scratching sound. Quite clearly. Quite near. She jerked backward, slipped, and lost her grip. The mug slipped out of her hand and shattered on the floor.

Before she could recover from the shock, she heard a mewing. A cat!

Sonya turned the knob. Something black shot by her, and a draft shut the door immediately. Sam was back; she hadn't heard him come in.

"It's a cat," she shouted. "It was shut up behind this door."

"A cat? I didn't know George liked cats. Maybe there are rats in this place—that really is some black beast."

The cat rubbed against her legs. Sonya found a bag of cat food, filled a bowl, and gave it some water. The cat gobbled it down at once.

"I heard something break when I was outside," Sam said.

"Yes, that was me. I dropped my mug." She gathered up the larger pieces and cleaned up the puddle beside the cushioned chair. Sam handed her a broom and dustpan, and Sonya swept up the remaining pieces, mopping her brow.

"What are we going to tell him?"

As if she was ever going to see George at all!

"Not to worry. It's just a cup."

Sonya noticed how clean the whole wooden floor was, as if someone had just gone over it with a damp mop. She had an eye for things like that. She studied the larger broken pieces of the cup and made out parts of colorful cows and a few written letters. Maybe it was a souvenir from Cowpuccino's Coffee House in Prince Rupert, where there were close to a hundred images of cows hanging from the beams and wooden pillars. Maybe she could buy the same cup there. She dropped the pieces into a pocket of her green down jacket.

Sam was back on the RT. Apparently he wanted to be sure that he could risk going ahead with the flight. Sonya looked out the window. The two planes were moving only slightly now. The wind was hardly stirring in the branches of the firs. Black ducks were wiggling through the water in near-military formation. Black ducks. A black cat. If that wasn't a bad sign!

"We can chance it."

Sam was standing behind her, and when she turned around, she almost fell against him. They stood for a second in this physical proximity. Then a soft mewing sound broke the spell.

"Are you ready?"

"Yes, I don't want to stay here alone!"

She pulled on her jacket, though it was still wet.

The cat was licking itself in front of the fire.

"Will she be OK? She has to be able to go out."

Sam laughed.

"There's a little window open in the basement. Good that you're worrying about the cat and not the flight."

An almost eerie calm lay over the ocean. The storm had dissipated as quickly as it had come. The Beaver took them up effortlessly, and Sonya saw the yellow seaplane shrink below them to a tiny point until it was invisible.

Not a word was exchanged between Sam and Sonya, as island after island flashed by below.

Out of the blue, he commented, "Robert certainly won't be able to fly out today."

"Who?" Sonya asked.

"You know Robert, don't you? Robert Stanford?"

She tried to be nonchalant, inquiring, "What's with this Robert Stanford?"

"He's an old pal of mine."

"You've known him a long time?"

"Yes, I've often flown him in and out up there in the Arctic."

"What was he doing there?"

"He's a mining engineer. He sees if it's worthwhile to exploit mineral deposits. I mean, financially."

"Is that why he's in Prince Rupert?"

"Dunno. He didn't want to talk about it. These things are hush-hush sometimes. Because of the stock market and whatnot. And because of the competition. That figures all right."

"Is he a . . . I mean, do you know him well?"

Sam's answer was not forthcoming; he was concentrating on landing. The Beaver made a turn for the water. Sam maneuvered the plane into the bay with impressive accuracy.

Sonya landed on the wooden dock with shaky legs. Her ears were buzzing. She turned to Sam as he was mooring the Beaver.

"Sam, I want to thank you . . . for that rescue."

He stood up, surprised.

"Rescue?"

"I mean . . . We could have, I could have . . . It could have gone badly."

"Not with Sam, Miss Switzerland. Not with this Beaver. I arranged it so you'd have something to tell them back home."

She couldn't tell by his look if he was kidding. He wasn't the kind of man to reveal much about his feelings.

"You were fantastic," she affirmed, hoisting on her backpack.

"Don't mention it. By the way, he wanted to talk to you, but you took off on him."

"Who?"

"Robert Stanford. He's staying at the Best Western. In case you're interested."

"Thanks," she replied, raising a hand in farewell. "See you."

"Yep." Sam tapped his baseball cap and turned away.

CHAPTER 19

When she came down for breakfast the next morning, she was well rested. She saw him immediately, and he sprang from his chair.

"Can we go talk somewhere?"

She looked around. The table in front of the kitchen was already taken. It must have struck him as strange to find her in a place like this. So what.

Cowpuccino's Coffee House popped into her mind.

"Let's go down to the old port."

He nodded, opening the door for her.

How did he know where she was staying? Did Sam tell her? People here seemed to know everything about everybody so quickly, though many of them lived in some sort of isolation. She stole a glance at Robert Stanford. Good-looking, for sure. Good-looking without being ostentatious. A strong, open face turned toward hers.

"I was relieved to hear you got back safe and sound."

"What do you mean?"

"Things could have easily gone wrong with that sudden change in the weather. But Sam's very reliable."

Sonya didn't get it. Why should Robert Stanford care whether or not she came back safe and sound? Why was he here? But she reined in her impatience.

"I've heard you can't fly out right now," she said.

"Right. Actually, I just got back today."

"So where were you?"

"Unfortunately, I can't say. For professional reasons."

They didn't speak until they got to the café, where only a few tables were occupied. They sat in a bay window with a view of the colorfully restored harbor buildings.

"What can I get you?" he asked.

"A chai tea."

Suddenly the incident on the ferry crossed her mind. *Maybe somebody slipped something into my tea.*

She stood up.

"Oh, let me get it," she said. "I haven't had breakfast—I'll see what muffins they've got."

He gave her an indefinable look but didn't argue. When Sonya returned, he fixed his eyes on her.

"I was worried about you. After you got sick on the ferry. It all happened so fast."

Sonya spooned off the foam from her Indian spiced tea.

"That German couple—you know them?" Robert asked.

"Yes, I do." She had no desire to elaborate on her relationship with Gerti and Helmut.

"I'd gladly have helped, but those two abducted you—they really did, you know that?"

"Mr. Stanford . . ."

"Please, call me Robert."

"I won't beat around the bush. According to the doctor who saw me in Prince Rupert, somebody slipped something into my tea in the cafeteria. A drug."

His face froze. He seemed to be thinking with his eyes, which were brown and speckled with green.

"What did you say?" he finally asked. "What kind of drug?"

"The doctor didn't know exactly, but it put me into a deep sleep and made me lose my memory."

"Did they find any traces in your blood?"

"No, but I had all the symptoms to indicate it was a drug."

He looked puzzled.

"Did you ever leave your cup unattended?"

"Yes . . . On the table you and I were sitting at."

Her words had the desired effect.

"So you think . . . You think that I . . ."

"It's possible. I must take that into consideration."

Now it was out. Raising his cup, he looked out the window and took a slow sip, as if playing for time. The cup rattled when he put it down, and he leaned toward her.

"When you went to get water for your tea, did you ever take your eyes off the teapot?"

Sonya searched her memory but drew a blank. She didn't want to let it show; she felt too vulnerable.

"It's . . . possible. I may have gone looking for sugar or milk."

"Who was standing near you?" His voice was a bit penetrating.

"No idea. I was tired, and there were lots of people in the cafeteria."

"Think hard. Maybe something will come back to you."

She did some polite, hard thinking.

"No, sorry," she said. "I can't remember anyone in particular."

He wouldn't let it go.

"Were there people around you?"

"Yes, I think so. Surely there were people around me; the cafeteria was pretty full."

"You did go and get tea, didn't you?"

She avoided his penetrating gaze by staring up at some cow postcards on the wooden beams.

"Yes, I can always do with a pot."

He rubbed his chin with his palm. She couldn't stand the tension.

"Where are you going with this, Robert? How do you explain all this?"

He rocked his cup back and forth, always catching it at the point of falling over.

"I know this upsets you, and rightly so—it's not a simple situation. But . . ." He hesitated.

"But?"

"If it was a drug . . . maybe there was a misunderstanding."

"A misunderstanding?"

He looked her straight in the eye.

"What I'm trying to say is that maybe someone thought the pot was for both of us. An outsider could have taken us for a couple, get it?"

"I don't get anything about—"

"Maybe it wasn't an attempt on you, but on me."

Late that night Sonya tossed and turned in bed; she was kept awake by slamming doors, loud music, and foot stomping.

"*An attempt,*" he'd said. Her thoughts were a confused whirl. She had to find out more about this Robert Stanford. She hadn't managed to weasel any more information out of him in the café. He wanted to talk about her instead: about the emergency landing, about Kitkatla, the nursing station, George's house, the black cat. Even about Else Seel.

She had talked and talked to keep him on the hook. To soften him up for *her* questions. But when she tried to get him to tell her who was after him and why, all he replied was, "That's what I'd like to know, believe me." She got nothing out of him, nothing whatsoever.

"When are you going to the Queen Charlottes?" was the last thing he asked her.

How in heaven's name did he know that, too? Did Sam tell him? She kept it vague.

"Probably sometime soon."

He had dropped a remark as they were saying good-bye.

"Distances seem huge here. But to tell the truth, it's a small world. Word gets around fast."

She couldn't read the serious look in his eyes, and now she just wanted to be left in peace. That's why she stood up and said dryly, "That's how it is everywhere these days, don't you think?"

He seemed to want to respond, but all he'd said was, "Next time, don't forget your seasick pills."

The noise in the corridor died down. How late was it? Probably past midnight.

Suddenly somebody hammered at the door. She didn't want to open it at first, but the pounding didn't stop. *No more youth hostels*, she thought, staggering toward it.

The young lady from the office was there and handed her a cordless phone.

"Phone call for you."

Sonya reached out in a daze.

"Sonya?"

She recognized the voice at once. Robert.

"Listen. Don't take the ferry tomorrow. You understand what I'm saying? Don't take it tomorrow."

"What? Why? What are you saying?"

"Don't take the ferry tomorrow. Go another day."

"Why? I wanted—"

"I can't explain it now. I'll do that later . . . Believe me, it's for the best. I'm sorry. I didn't want to upset you. I just don't want any more problems."

"What makes you think that—"

"Later. Everything later. Just go to bed and sleep tight."

Then his voice was gone. She handed the girl the phone as if it had burned her hand.

CHAPTER 20

Sonya felt the warm sun on her face as she walked through downtown Prince Rupert, but she was boiling inside. What was that guy Stanford thinking? Calling her up in the middle of the night, tossing out a warning, leaving her dangling without a word of explanation! What infuriated her even more was her own cowardice. She could take the ferry anyway. It damn well wasn't right for a perfect stranger to be sticking his nose in her business!

She yanked open the door to Ziggy's Internet Café, zeroed in on a computer, and entered Robert Stanford's name into the search engine. There were many hits. The first was a magazine article, without much text, and several photographs. She began to read feverishly.

The Canadian geologist Charles Fipke, son of an Alberta farmer, was obsessed with the idea that there must be diamonds in the Canadian Arctic. Not just a few small chips here and there but giant deposits that could be exploited commercially. His idea was reinforced by the fact that De Beers, the powerful South African diamond concern, secretly took soil samples from the banks of the Mackenzie River in the early 1980s. De Beers had a worldwide monopoly in the diamond business at the time. But what the people at De Beers did not know was a well-known fact among Canadian geologists: that when the glaciers advanced hundreds of miles into the interior of the country, they moved coarse gravel with them. All that diamond prospectors really had to do was follow a glacier's path to discover the source of the diamonds. But it is difficult to reconstruct a glacier's progress. After years of futile searching in the interior, Fipke started to collect soil samples in the tundra, about 300 miles from Yellowknife. But he told people in Yellowknife, the capital of the Northwest Territories, that he was looking for gold.

In that region Fipke found quantities of indicator minerals for diamonds. He discovered a diamond-rich vein of kimberlite under a lake, Lac de Gras. Fipke teamed up with the Australian mining company BHP Billiton, and they amazed the world in 1991 with news that they had discovered huge diamond deposits. Their Ekati Diamond Mine was the first of its kind not only in Canada but all of North America. By contrast De Beers found nothing. "The persistence and success of small exploration companies helped break De Beers's global monopoly," says Robert Stanford, a Vancouver mining engineer.

Sonya printed out the story, then clicked to the website of a company called Shining Mountain Explorations. Robert Stanford was listed as an outside consultant.

His name also appeared in a report from the BC Ministry of Energy and Mines. Downloading the document took ages.

Sonya went over to the counter.

"Do you have organic coffee?"

"No," the girl at the counter said, "but our mocha with whipped cream is very good."

Sonya looked at her, dithering. Caffeine. Chocolate. Whipped cream. She did the numbers. She'd made three hits on the Internet. Three sins. It was a wash.

"OK, a mocha," she conceded.

She went back to her computer, and was shocked to find that the ministry's report she'd downloaded was fifty-six pages long; it was about security issues in the mining industry. Sonya scrolled through the text until she came across the section on diamond mines. There, she read that Canadian diamonds would compete with the best in the world, and their origin could be proven conclusively. This was of major importance, the report stated, because Canadian diamonds were clean, politically speaking, unlike diamonds from certain African countries that financed brutal civil wars. Unfortunately, criminal elements tried to forge documentation for "blood diamonds" and pass them off as Canadian diamonds—machinations that must be eliminated by all means. Sonya's eyes wandered farther down and spotted a passage.

We are greatly concerned in particular by the infiltration of Canadian mining by organized crime. The police are increasingly combating this development through undercover investigations.

Undercover investigations. Sonya had read enough mystery novels to know what that meant. Undercover agents. Spies.

She found Robert's name in a footnote, where he was quoted as an information source. Sonya would dearly have liked to know what information he had given to the government.

While she was at it, she decided to look up the other stranger, the man in the Granville Island Market who had found her wallet. She entered the search word *Camelian*, landing on a company's home page that she'd already seen in Vancouver. She reread everything very carefully. Then she pulled up the list of places who'd used this company and their websites. She clicked on a few of them at random—and stiffened. A very familiar face was staring out at her: short black hair, big dark eyes, a beaming smile. Diane Kesowsky!

She rooted around frantically, opening page after page, forgetting the time and where she was.

"Sonya! Hello!"

She nearly fell off her seat.

"What a coincidence! We've been looking all over for you! We were afraid you'd gone away, right, Helmut?"

Gerti stood before her in a salmon-pink blouse and red pants, her face beaming. Helmut stood behind her, slightly embarrassed as always. Then Gerti discovered the pile of printouts.

"Surely you're not working on your vacation, or am I wrong?" She looked genuinely appalled. "Helmut, we must lure our Sonya out to eat something. How about lobster—you can't refuse that!"

Lobster. She suddenly realized how hungry she was.

"I . . . don't eat lobster—matter of principle," she replied, ignoring the disappointed look on Gerti's face. "Those poor lobsters are thrown into boiling water alive."

She knew she sounded like a missionary, but she didn't care.

"Oh, I see . . ." Gerti was actually speechless for a moment. "Salmon or halibut would work, too, wouldn't it, Helmut? There's a good restaurant next to Cowpuccino's Coffee House, you know the place already."

Sonya was startled. How did Gerti know she'd been there? But Gerti babbled on.

"We've something to celebrate." She winked at Sonya know-ingly. "You survived that awful storm—that's a good reason to treat yourself to something nice."

This time Sonya followed up on it: "How do you know that, too?"

"Helmut was down there, at Greenblue Air. We wanted to go on a sightseeing flight. They told him about it."

Helmut interrupted her with unusual force.

"Gerti, stop yacking. Sonya can't even pack up her things in peace."

In the restaurant, Sonya chose the bass, although she didn't know if her selection was politically correct. Gerti talked during the meal about her three daughters and her grandchildren and the new teaching methods in schools and how everything was much more complicated for the children. Sonya showed inter-est at regular intervals, though her thoughts were elsewhere. She could hardly wrap her mind around what she'd just found out on the Internet.

Diane—owner of an exploration company specializing in dia-monds. All that crap about a jewelry designer! Inge was obviously way off base. Diane was a trained geologist, apparently a well-known expert in a male-dominated industry. A woman with a serious career. She'd found indications of diamond deposits in the Canadian territory of Nunavut, but lost approval for exploiting them because an Australian company had already acquired the mining rights. Evidently things weren't all above board, because Diane's company sued the Australians, who settled out of court for a considerable sum. Sonya read on the Internet that Diane used the money to finance a new expedition, this time at a secret location so nobody could beat her to it.

"You should try this wonderful wine, Sonya. It's from British Columbia."

Gerti gave her a glass for a toast. Sonya thought she had another reason to celebrate—a valuable strike in the web archives.

"Your health!" she called out to the group.

"Now you must tell us about your adventure; we're all on pins and needles!"

Her adventure. Nobody ever wanted to know about her adventures. This was something new. Tonio's adventures, yes, and Odette's adventures. Her past experiences had always seemed so uneventful beside other people's. Sonya looked out onto the ocean and saw a seaplane disappear in the distance. And then it poured out of her: Kitkatla, the nursing station, Kathrin, the storm, the emergency landing, the black cat behind the door, the motley crew of guests in the youth hostel—she delivered it all in the same extremely meaningful tone she'd used when reading her history papers in class.

The effect wasn't lost on Gerti and Helmut. They constantly exchanged astonished or concerned looks according to the events she narrated, garnishing her report with brief comments.

When she'd finished—they were already having coffee and dessert—Gerti exclaimed, "Good heavens, you lead a dangerous life! What else are you planning to do?"

"Oh, I'm going to surprise myself," Sonya said, a little tipsy. She didn't give out her next destination, even though Gerti kept asking for it. That adventure was to be hers—and hers alone.

It wasn't until she was in her bleak youth hostel room that something crossed her mind. Funny. Gerti and Helmut hadn't said a single word about their trip to the Khutzeymateen Grizzly Sanctuary. It was as if they'd never been there.

CHAPTER 21

The ferry lurched ponderously through the high waves, and Sonya lurched along with it. The rain whipped the passenger-area windows, and the ocean seemed like a huge hungry monster. Sonya was so sick despite her seasick pills that she wanted to lie down in her cabin. Now she fully believed what she'd heard: that Hecate Strait was among the fiercest waters in the world.

Lie still, lie totally still. The first hour of the crossing was over, so that left five. It was a mystery how the Haida were able to cross these raging seas in sixty-foot-long canoes. Did they get seasick, too?

She heard a sudden voice, as if through a fog. She could only make out the words *arrival* and *vehicle* and *twenty minutes.* She rubbed her eyes. Had she been sleeping? She dragged herself over to her sink and wet her pale face with water.

The heavy swell had let up. She caught a glimpse of phantom shapes through the window—dark hilly shadows: Haida Gwaii, the "Islands of the People." Sonya hurried downstairs and wandered from deck to deck until she finally found her truck. That had been some kind of trip!

She discovered in no time that the name Queen Charlotte City was a charming exaggeration. She'd barely driven into the village with its little harbor when she was outside it again. She picked out a cheap boardinghouse with ducks grazing in the surrounding meadows. Her room had a telephone and a coffee machine, which she switched on at once.

Then she struck out on a tour of the "city." It was drizzling, and a low fog hung over the bay. Not too far from her boardinghouse, a building housed the Northern Cold Air office next to a landing facility for seaplanes. But she felt too tired after the long crossing to find out about Jack Gordon. She went to Rainbow's Gallery instead, a store with a motley collection of flotsam and jetsam plastered on its facade. Inside, she found Haida artworks, jewelry, and souvenirs, but not a particular book she wanted. She was directed to the only bookstore in town, hidden away at the end of the main street in a standard residential house. She snaked past tables and corners. The owner was at a computer in the last of the book-stuffed rooms. Two eyes behind gold-rimmed glasses swiveled up in her direction.

"You've come to the right place." The man welcomed her.

"What makes you think that?" Sonya responded in amazement.

"I know because an obsessed person's face lights up like that. What's your field?"

"History."

"Interesting, interesting."

The book dealer stood up. His hair was cut short like a monk's, and his glasses glinted.

"So what are you looking for?"

"A book on Haida history."

"Nice accent. Where are you from?"

Once again that irritating accent betrayed her. And she had to go through the whole spiel again. Why she came. Why she was interested in the Haida. How she knew about the Queen Charlottes. She also told him about Else Seel and the exhibition, that Else came to this place and had written a poem about the Haida.

"Else Seel? Name doesn't ring a bell—and she lived here?" he asked, surprised.

"No, she only visited here, on a steamer, I think, in the thirties or forties."

"Interesting, interesting," he repeated.

He took a book off a shelf.

"Read this, then you'll be up on Haida culture."

He also handed her a colorful brochure, which she leafed through. An outfitter offered kayak trips, boat trips, and expeditions to Ninstints, one of the legendary deserted Haida villages, protected since 1981 by UNESCO as a World Heritage Site. Unfortunately that was a little too late, Sonya read, because nineteenth- and twentieth-century anthropologists and explorers had looted the cultural treasures from those now-dead villages.

The book dealer, inspired by her obvious interest, delivered a little lecture.

"The Haida lived on these islands for thousands of years, from seven to ten thousand. They were the kings of the seas. They traveled in their canoes from Alaska to Vancouver Island."

"And to Savary Island."

"Yes, yes, yes—so you're up on that. Rather brutal warriors, the Haida. They took men and women from other tribes to be slaves."

He went back to his computer to print out the receipt.

"Have you seen Haida art? It's phenomenal. Their pieces are even exhibited in Europe. Since you're here, you've got to go to the deserted Haida villages in Gwaii Haanas, a national park. That's why I gave you that brochure. You'll never forget it. Oh, by the way, my card."

Sonya read the name: Ian Fleming!

"I'm only here a few days, unfortunately," she parried.

Ian was undaunted.

"You know, I'm going to Tow Hill on Sunday. Have you got hiking boots? We could hike out to Rose Spit. That's the cradle of the Haida. Their Bethlehem, so to speak. As a historian, you've *got* to go there."

She thanked him for the offer, saying she'd think it over. As she was just leaving, he ran after her.

"If you want to know anything about women who lived out in the bush, you should talk to Kara. She's a person I know. She lived out there for years."

Now he had Sonya hooked at last. She told him where she was staying, so this Kara could get in touch. Then she walked back to the boardinghouse with her book under her arm. She didn't read a word; she'd hardly lain down before dropping off to sleep.

Sonya went down to the reception desk at nine the next morning and asked the lodge's owner about a garage to have her tires checked.

"Somebody's waiting for you over there," the man told her.

Sonya saw a woman approaching her.

"Are you Sonya?"

"Yes?"

"I'm Kara. Ian told me about you."

"Yes, of course. Word gets around pretty fast here!"

"Well, we don't miss a trick. When do I ever get a chance to chat with a historian from Switzerland! I haven't had breakfast," she said. "Can we go somewhere?"

Sonya could have guessed that the day's specials would be irresistible. She ordered the Fisherman's Breakfast: steamed salmon, eggs, potatoes, and toast. Fishermen on Haida Gwaii had to live on something, after all. The salmon was buried under a thick yellow sauce. *So what,* she said to herself; she had to get her strength back after yesterday's woes. Kara ordered eggs on toast with mushrooms and bacon.

Right off the bat, Sonya said, "So, the suspense is killing me. Tell me about your life in the bush."

Kara took a sip of dark black coffee.

"I lived in Victoria as a child. I was a real city girl, but I wanted something different. I got married at eighteen; my husband and I moved up north and bought some land in the Kispiox Valley. Very remote, I tell you. We had horses, chickens, cows, a large vegetable garden. But that wasn't all. We also had a lumber mill. I had to help continually with cutting down trees. That was tough."

She drew a hand across her face as if wiping away her worry lines.

"It was backbreaking work—eleven hours a day. There was no entertainment, no variety. Just work and more work. We couldn't afford any machines; we did everything with old primitive tools. But worst of all was the isolation. I didn't have any neighbors. Nobody came to visit. And I like to be with people."

Kara poured herself another cup of coffee. Sonya listened with bated breath.

"So much for the dream of a life of solitude. No marriage can withstand it. At least mine went all to hell. Now I've bought some land in this town. I wanted neighbors; I'd had enough of the bush." She laughed. "Maybe for you this city is a hick town out in the sticks, but for me it's a bustling city. I've taken up painting again. That was impossible before now."

Sonya looked at her, spellbound. Kara seemed to understand why.

"Many European women dream of a life in the wild, eh?"

"Yes, of course. But I'm not sure they can even conceive of what it's really like."

Else Seel definitely could not, Sonya thought. She certainly suffered culture shock. But whatever drove her away from Berlin must have been worse than all the hardship, all those disappointments in her life in the wild. She did have neighbors, though not very near. There had been occasional dances at the Wistaria Community Center, and Else was able to get away now and then. To Haida Gwaii, for instance. Nevertheless . . . Else loved the bush above all else. It became her homeland.

"Else certainly didn't have it easy," Sonya told Kara, who was listening attentively. "But she and George had a common goal, and that was survival." She recalled a passage in Else's diary: *"Teamwork, yoked together, the children in the cart that must be pulled, it must go on. There's no way around it, no arguing about it."*

But then there were times when Else bumped up against her limits: for instance, when George came back from a weeklong patrol and announced he'd found gold. He'd been traveling for two months, continually panning river deposits. Then he'd found a black rock containing gold granules and thought he had discovered a vein—there was a broad border of gold dust in his pan. But it was only pyrite. Fool's gold. His hopes were dashed.

Before that, Else had had to put things on credit in the store because they were out of money. She couldn't even bake a cake for her birthday. The couple had to give their only cow to the neighbors because they couldn't afford hay, and there was only a can of condensed milk for the children. Else made coffee once a week, which had to last for seven days. They fried dry bread in the frying pan. Else ultimately took money out of her German savings account to buy flour, lard, and fuel. But George had taken almost all of those precious things with him on his search for gold. He came home shortly before Christmas, empty-handed. Is he the fool or am I? Else asked herself. Sometimes she wept in desperation.

Kara nodded her head vigorously.

"Believe me, I've had those intense feelings myself—not only about physical survival but about self-esteem."

She stopped for a moment.

"It's risky for an artist to be isolated."

Sonya agreed.

"Else's poetry declined in that demanding environment," she said. "She had no social interaction, no German culture nearby. She probably had no inkling of this beforehand, and perhaps she never did recognize this downturn."

Sonya said the last sentence more to herself than Kara.

But Kara chimed right in: "You don't know until you've tried it yourself, believe me."

As they got up, something crossed Sonya's mind.

"Do you know a Jack Gordon?"

Kara looked somewhat taken aback.

"Please, I only want to know about plane rides here," Sonya said.

"He doesn't go up anymore . . . He's a complicated person." She put some money on the table. "But he might talk to you. Just don't mention his daughter—or fatal accidents."

"Why?"

Kara gave her an inscrutable look.

"The less you know about it, the better."

CHAPTER 22

Sonya could hardly believe it: she was on a ferry again.

The people in the Northern Cold Air office told her Jack Gordon lived on a neighboring island, in the village of Sandspit. Fortunately the crossing only took twenty minutes; the sea was calm and the sun was out.

The trees had all been cut down in Sandspit. Sonya found her gas station right away; it was on the main street paralleling the ocean. The cashier pointed out Gordon's house. A large sheepdog sat in front of the entrance. Sonya wheeled around.

"Is that dog dangerous?" she asked the cashier.

"If the dog's there, Jack's home, too, eh?"

"I'm afraid of big dogs."

"He's never done anything to anybody."

Sonya just stood there, as if the dog were the cashier's problem.

"I can go get Jack, if you'd like."

Sonya thanked him, relieved, and then she heard shouting and barking. Three minutes later, the cashier returned with a brawny man.

"There she is."

Jack Gordon looked rather displeased.

"I was just leaving."

"It won't take long. I just have a question for you."

They went outside, and Sonya noticed that Gordon smelled of cigarette smoke.

"I heard you're the pilot who found that crashed Beaver three years ago near Kitkatla."

"I don't talk about that." He turned to go, but Sonya stayed right on his heels.

"It's very important to me. I've come all the way from Switzerland for this."

His dark eyes narrowed.

"Who are you, and who told you about me?"

Sonya ignored his second question. She didn't want to put the nurse, Kathrin, in an awkward position.

"I lost my husband and stepson in that crash."

It was out on the table. She'd played her highest trump. Her instincts told her it was her sole chance to get this guy to listen.

Gordon eyed her in silence.

"I want to know what happened to them, how they died. It's the one thing I can take back home."

The big sheepdog sniffed her pants. But her fear of Gordon's answer was greater than her fear of the dog.

Jack finally opened his mouth.

"No chance you'd know this, lady, but people get killed regularly on the ocean. Life's like that up here."

He put his hands on his hips, scuffing the ground with the heels of his leather boots.

"Were they both dead when you found them?"

He didn't answer right away.

"I carried the dead bodies in my plane. That's all I can tell you. You'll have to ask the police if you want to know more. Bunker, come!"

He started to move away, and the dog followed.

"If it was your son, wouldn't you want to know exactly what happened?"

Gordon whipped around so fast that the dog started barking. Sonya couldn't be stopped.

"He wasn't even eighteen years old. He didn't deserve to die like that."

Tears welled up in her eyes.

"I've got to go, I've told you already. Where are you staying?"

"The Ocean View Lodge."

"Yeah, I know the place. Look, I'll call you when I'm back."

He got into his truck, and the dog hopped in after him. The door slammed shut, the motor roared, and Gordon stuck his head out the window.

"What's your name?"

"Sonya Werner."

"Sonya, sometimes it's better not to know the truth, eh? Believe you me."

"Who organized the search party? Who told you where they'd gone down?"

"I heard it on the emergency radio. Your husband . . . he wasn't very cautious. And with a kid . . . It was far too dangerous. It was irresponsible." He raised his hand. "Hey, Sonya, all the best."

His car rolled onto the road, and her eyes followed him. Jack Gordon would never call her, that much was clear. Her red truck was parked next to the pump, like a loyal ally. She gassed it up with tears in her eyes.

The cashier looked embarrassed when she came to pay.

"He's not a bad sort," he explained. "But he's had some bad times."

Sonya silently watched him process her credit card.

"His daughter had an accident. She was an only child."

She kept silent. Waiting.

"She was driving down a road in the woods, and a moose ran right in front of her. A giant bull. Came through the windshield. Killed her instantly. The moose, too."

"How long ago was that?"

"About two years, eh?"

"Thank you," she said. "Thanks for everything."

CHAPTER 23

Sonya felt as if she were in a stupor. She hadn't gotten enough sleep. And to top it all, the loud music of Bonnie Raitt came from two speakers at the rear of Ian's green Ford Explorer. On Skidegate Inlet she caught a glimpse of ancient Haida totem poles that were a must-see—but not now. She closed her eyes. *Just don't make me talk.*

Ian sang along with the songs, occasionally drinking coffee from his thermos and praising the beautiful weather. Sonya cursed her lust for adventure. What had she gotten herself into? She didn't have to prove anything to anybody, but now there was no going back.

An hour later the asphalt gave way to packed dirt, and Sonya was bounced back and forth on her seat. She couldn't even think of dozing. The Ford Explorer blew dust all over the bumpy forest road. Lichen hung from the fir trees like tinsel. A blackish-green bog shimmered through the underbrush. The car hopped from pothole to pothole.

"We'll be there soon," Ian shouted.

And a vista did in fact open up in the forest. A river flowed under the roadway, fanning out into the ocean, and Ian drove beside the water toward the sandy beach.

"North Beach," he announced, like a tour guide.

He drove over the sand strip as if it were a runway, close to the water's edge. Not a soul could be seen. The milky sun cast a mysterious light on the white sand. Silvery bleached tree trunks lay about like bizarre sculptures. The rain forest stretched out behind the beach, dark and spooky.

Ian parked a few kilometers farther along in a gap in the forest, right behind the dunes. He surveyed the surroundings.

"We have to remember this spot so we can find it again."

Sonya pointed to a tree trunk that had washed ashore; its twisted branches made it look like a dragon.

Ian nodded. "We'll recognize that."

He looked at his watch.

"It's twelve now. We've enough time."

Sonya found walking easier than she'd thought. The fresh, salty air did her good, and she felt more relaxed.

For the first half mile Ian regaled her with Haida creation myths, such as how the pointed beak of the raven—a mythological bird for the Haida—opened the seashell enclosing the first humans. The people were afraid to crawl out, choosing to stay in the warm, safe shell. Then the raven pictured for them how gorgeous the world was, with its long white beaches, mountains, and the ocean. The people became curious and saw that the raven was right. And so they began to settle the world.

Sonya thought the legend was much more beautiful, more heartening, than the story of Adam and Eve and their expulsion from paradise. She picked up a pretty shell now and then, or a fist-sized abalone shell, and stowed it in her backpack. The sun was warmer. Ian monopolized most of the conversation, which was her heart's desire.

Early in the afternoon they found a path through the bushes that ended an hour later in a long dune-grass meadow.

"This is a real bird paradise," Ian said, pointing to the nests and the birds that were fluttering up. They emitted excited calls. Sonya had become somewhat tired, but their biggest challenge still lay ahead. They had to clamber over a field of debris-like stones, logs, brambles, and clumps of grass that bordered the ocean instead of walking along a sandy beach. The ground had a thousand trapdoors, Sonya soon realized. A cold wind blew off the ocean. The sun had gone behind some clouds. When they reached the tip of Rose Spit, Sonya collapsed on the ground, exhausted. They had arrived at the place where, according to the Haida myth, humans first came into the world. *Naikoon* was the Haida name for this spot—"long nose"—and Sonya thought that was most appropriate. She was shivering.

"On a clear day," Ian started to say—and she finished the sentence with him—"you can see all the way to Alaska."

They laughed and took pictures of each other before starting back. Sonya kept stumbling and hurt her hand on a pointed broken branch. Twice she dropped into deep holes beneath the underbrush, her concentration flagging; her feet began to hurt.

"At least it's not raining," she said more or less to herself when they reached the dune meadow with the bird-nesting area. Ian mumbled in agreement, picking up the pace. Sonya could hardly keep up, but she was used to this from her forced marches with Tonio. The allée-like path through the woods seemed endless. Had they really walked so far? Finally the white beach appeared; a veil of mist was gradually settling over the coast. Now Sonya realized what was motivating Ian. At first, only fine, almost transparent patches of fog glided toward them. Then a wall formed suddenly, as thick as billowing smoke from a factory smokestack.

"Yucky, pea soup," she heard herself say. She still wasn't frightened. They couldn't get lost. The path simply led along the beach.

But walking became increasingly difficult. She kept sinking into the sand, much more than on the way in. Ian was also moving more slowly.

Everything looked all of a piece. The white sand, the white fog, with the invisible ocean sounding behind it. They could hardly see three feet in front of them. Suddenly it hit her: they wouldn't be able to find the car! The forest was completely out of sight, as well as the driftwood. Everything was all white. The dragon—their signpost! They would unwittingly walk right by it.

"The car," she gasped.

Ian kept going ahead, answering her.

"We're not there by a long shot, and maybe the fog will be gone by then. That often happens around here."

She was so tired, she wanted to sit down and not get up again.

"Can we take a break?"

"Sure," Ian said, turning around. His voice had a resigned edge to it.

Sonya ate her last apple. There was barely a pint of water left.

"How far to the car?"

He looked at his watch.

"Probably two hours."

Two hours! Her spirits sank. But she didn't want to appear weak.

They started moving again. Sonya counted her steps. That had helped her on her excursions with Tonio. Up to a hundred, then back to the beginning. It gave time structure and concentrated her energy. She mustn't let Ian out of her sight. Then she'd be alone—lost on a never-ending beach. When did it get dark here?

"We'll make it all right," Ian said, as if reading her thoughts. Then with forced cheerfulness: "You'll enjoy telling your family about this adventure."

The remark seemed familiar. Hadn't Sam come out with something like that? But . . . what family? Her family had all passed away.

Ian worked to keep the conversation going.

"The Haida used to scatter swan's down on the ocean near Rose Spit to placate the storm spirits and sea monsters. Children couldn't laugh," he said. "That would provoke the monsters. Nobody dared spit in the ocean there."

Sonya thought she was hearing Tonio's voice telling her about Nepalese Sherpas who would offer gifts during the puja ceremony to curry favor with the mountain gods. Tonio was impressed by such respect for the mighty mountain. But Sonya thought that was what many mountain climbers lacked. They constantly left garbage behind on their climbs: oxygen bottles, aluminum cans, synthetic containers, clothes. Mount Everest was covered with it. The mountain was just an object to these climbers, a vehicle for their urge to conquer. Everything else was subordinate to them. But Tonio never wanted to talk about it. He said repeatedly that she'd never get it; outsiders just couldn't get it.

That's how he saw her. As an outsider. A person who didn't really belong and who therefore had no say.

When Viktor, who was on the rope with Tonio, fell to his death in the French Alps before his very eyes, it was Sonya who Tonio sent to console Viktor's wife. Tonio could look danger right in the eye but not the mother of Viktor's three children. Tonio refused to hear what Viktor's wife had to say amid her tears; but Sonya would never forget her words.

"They're all just egotists, pure egotists. Men like my husband should never bring children into this world. Mountains were always more important to him than our family. Don't let Tonio get you pregnant, Sonya; your kids don't deserve it. And Tonio's a coward, that I have to tell you. He didn't even have the guts to come here. But you watch: Tonio won't be put off by what happened to Viktor—he'll go right up the next mountain."

And that's how it turned out. The subject of Viktor's death on the mountain was taboo; Tonio never mentioned it—as if his friend had never existed.

How odd I'm thinking about this now, Sonya thought. *Here, on a sand beach in the Queen Charlotte Islands.*

At that moment huge shadows appeared in the fog, then they dispersed. Dark shapes loomed up against the white background. A monster seemed to lie on the sand. Sonya was rooted to the spot, and Ian approached it.

"A dead seal," he shouted. "Best to give it a wide berth."

Too late. A rotting-animal stench hit her nose. Two eagles settled down on a weathered tree stump some distance ahead. Sonya kept close behind Ian. She looked back. The eagles were now perched on the animal's corpse.

Sonya grabbed Ian's arm in her excitement.

"I see them!"

"What?" Ian looked at her, mystified.

"The eagles! I can see them! The fog's lifting!"

He threw his arms up into the air in triumph.

"Didn't I say so? Let's go, it's the last lap. It's not much farther."

In spite of her exhaustion, she felt she'd sprouted wings. The fog retreated more and more. She could clearly see the forest edge.

After more than an hour, they finally reached the dragon-shaped tree trunk. Sonya could have cried in relief. It took every last ounce of strength to drag herself over the barricade of driftwood to the forest's edge.

Ian fished around in his backpack, and then he searched his jacket and pants pockets. Sonya watched his frantic movements.

"What's up?"

"I can't find my car keys!"

Did she hear right? That couldn't be true.

Ian started his search again from the beginning. His backpack, his pockets, pants, and jacket pockets.

"Where did you put them?"

"I thought in this side pocket. But they're not there."

He emptied his backpack out on the forest floor. No keys.

"Is the car locked?" She didn't recognize her own voice.

"There's a central locking system."

She sank down on a mossy spot.

"I don't understand."

Even Ian looked desperate.

"What a fuckup."

Sonya looked at her watch. It was six thirty and probably a three-hour walk to the fork in the road where a sign pointed to a campsite. If anybody was staying there, of course. And they'd used up their water.

"I've got to go meditate," Ian said. "The Haida gods will help us."

He walked toward the beach.

Sonya looked at him nonplussed, and then she shouted, "You've got to do *what*?"

He turned around.

"I'll meditate—the solution is sure to come to me."

He's crazy. He's gone nuts. Sonya could have screamed. Her mind raced. What would Tonio have done in this situation? She knew one thing for certain: he wouldn't have shown a bit of nervousness or fear. He would have coolly sized up the situation and decided the necessary steps. If Sonya was upset about something or worried, he'd always say: imagine the worst thing that could happen. That always snapped Sonya back to reality. If she tried to depict the worst-case scenario, the situation often stopped being terrifying.

Sonya remembered the rock pools in the woods. They definitely wouldn't die of thirst. Maybe they'd have to spend the night out in the open, in the middle of a forest filled with bears. The black bears were bigger on Haida Gwaii than anywhere in Canada. The mere thought of them made her shudder.

Then she saw Ian assume the lotus position, his palms turned outward, his face toward the ocean. She took the opportunity to crouch behind a tree. While she was relieving herself, she heard Ian's voice from the beach. He was calling upon the gods—unbelievable!—instead of looking for his keys in the sand.

Time passed. She sat down on a log near him and waited for his meditation to end. A fierce urge seized her to throw a handful of sand at his head. And another. And one after the other. She felt twinges of a rage more powerful than all the sea monsters in the Pacific's deep.

Her hand clutched some sand. Then she heard something. A noise. A soft hum. She looked along the length of the beach. Was something moving? No, it was a hallucination. Desperate, wishful thinking.

But the hum didn't go away. Now Ian was moving, too.

"What's that?" he asked, looking around. Then he shouted, jumping to his feet.

"A car! A car! I see it! It's coming closer."

Now she saw it, but she was petrified. Would the driver see their two tiny figures on the beach? Or just turn and go back?

As if on a given signal, they both ran toward the vehicle. Ian kept throwing his arms up like a victorious racer at the finish line. The car came nearer and nearer, straight at them, then stopped. Somebody got out.

"Heaven sent you!" Ian shouted at the driver. "We need somebody to take us back."

"I can see that," Robert Stanford replied. He wasn't looking at Ian, but at Sonya. She could read the relief in his eyes.

"Get in."

On the way back, Ian sat beside Robert and described their experiences; to Sonya's surprise, he left out his appeal to the Haida gods. She stretched out on the backseat; her limbs were heavy as lead. Robert tossed in a "Got it" or "No kidding" every now and then. Sometimes she sensed his gaze in the rearview mirror, but she avoided it. She didn't want to look at him or think about why he'd shown up at North Beach, and she gradually drifted off.

Robert woke her up gently when they reached her boardinghouse in Queen Charlotte City. He helped her out of the car. She offered no resistance to his strong hands. Wearily, she made a good-bye gesture to Ian, back in the car. Robert helped her up the stairs to the front door, and the owner opened it.

"There you are!" he exclaimed. "I'm so glad everything turned out OK."

Sonya gave him a wan smile. Looking at Robert, she felt dizzy.

"I don't know how to thank you. I . . ."

He quickly put his hand on her shoulder.

"Get some rest. We'll see each other tomorrow."

She lurched up the stairs, dragging her backpack behind. Her fingers shook as she unlocked her door. Something white lay on the carpet. A folded piece of paper. She opened it clumsily.

Words in block letters. They swam before her eyes.

THERE WERE MORE THAN TWO PEOPLE ON THE PLANE.

CHAPTER 24

First, Sonya's video showed an establishing shot of the whole totem pole, then the details of its carving, with the eagle at the top, then the frog, the killer whale, and the raven. Then the field of view slowly widened to get the context: the imposing appearance of the Old Masset Haida chief's house, the tall bulrushes with more bushes behind them, and the sandy beach. Then the strait on the horizon and the forest on the opposite bank. The fluffy clouds in the blue sky above. Then a panning shot to the other side and the colorful painted houses of the Old Masset First Nation.

Sonya put her video camera down and sat gingerly on a washed-up log. Every leg muscle hurt. She wouldn't let herself in for a hike like that ever again. She noted the time and place in her video log. Else Seel didn't see this pole on her trip to Old Masset; it was more recent, as Sonya could tell at first glance. Besides, it was painted red and black. Else had written about unpainted totem poles. This one was a fine showpiece nevertheless.

Sonya read Else's poem on the Haida with renewed interest.

I am your woman
gathering cedar branches early in the morning
to weave your whip.

They were wet with sweet drops
and still thinking of the night.

Sonya lowered the book. What*ever* was that supposed to mean? She sighed. Poetry wasn't her strong suit, which left the historical facts.

Else's steamer had moored in New Masset. She had danced until two in the morning with the ship's doctor, a blond Dutchman, *"my first and last dancer."* Else must have enjoyed those trips: she loved sociable people, loved to hear the stories of their lives, and, yes, she liked to spend an evening dancing with another man. Especially if he was good-looking.

That night on the steamer Else slept badly. She dreamed that her dog had died, that the chickens had starved to death, and the cat vanished. She wanted to rush back to the cabin in Wistaria. And yes—when she returned she found the coyotes had preyed on her rooster and four hens. Her dog had been poisoned by an unknown hand. Upon her return, Else went to bed running a high fever. George postponed his departure for the mountains by a day, massaging her while she sweat. Then he left her to her own devices.

Sonya's gaze wandered from her book to the strait. She imagined Else's steamer pitching its way out of the inlet.

So I'm not the only one to have bad dreams, she thought. *Odette, covered in blood, in Canada.* Else would have taken that dream seriously. She would have understood Sonya's misgivings.

There were more than two people on the plane.

Was Odette on that plane? Did she and Tonio and Nicky go down together? Did she survive and go into hiding? What were Odette's parents keeping from her? Or the police? Odette's father was a man of great influence, the president of the Swiss

Parliament. He could pull plenty of strings if necessary. She was now more determined than ever to hunt down the truth.

Sonya raced back to Queen Charlotte City as fast as Else had rushed back to Wistaria after her nightmare.

The owner of the boardinghouse was just coming out of his office.

"Your friend was here," he said. "The same guy as yesterday. I told him you hadn't left yet. He'll drop by later."

"Did he leave an address or phone number?"

"No, he didn't. Do you know where he lives?"

Sonya dodged the question.

"Did you tell him where I was going yesterday? To Rose Spit?"

"Yes, he seemed very worried. I said you were with Ian, but that didn't put his mind to rest—he *is* a friend of yours, eh?"

"Yes, yes," she said quickly. "Thanks for your help."

She stopped on the stairway.

"I'm taking the Prince Rupert ferry back tomorrow."

In her room, the answering machine was blinking, a message from Ian Fleming asking how she felt. Kara wanted to talk to her, too. Sonya dialed her number, but there was no answer. She'd talk to Ian later. She opened the bureau drawer and took out the note. She studied it for a long time, as if it could speak to her.

She was convinced that this mysterious bit of information came from Jack Gordon. Given recent events, she figured that Jack had revealed something he really shouldn't have. But who told him not to, and why? The police? Why didn't the newspapers report that somebody else was in the plane besides Tonio and Nicky?

She felt a hollow sensation in the pit of her stomach and decided it was time to have a long talk with Robert Stanford. She had a brainstorm about where to find him: a mining engineer would be moving around on these islands by air for sure.

She hurried down to the Northern Cold Air office.

"Do you know when Robert Stanford's coming back?" she asked an agent. "I'm picking him up."

The woman didn't seem the least bit surprised.

"Bob? I think in about an hour. But let me check that."

She thumbed through her papers.

"He'll be here around three thirty."

Bull's-eye. Sonya was pleased with her powers of deduction. She sauntered over to Rainbow's Gallery and bought an elaborately woven cedar-bark basket for her mother and an argillite carving of a whale for Inge. She was still puzzled about what to get for her father; it was so hard to find presents for men. She once bought Tonio a wrist pedometer that read his pulse and gave the height above sea level. It was among his personal effects sent from Canada to Switzerland that arrived along with the bodies.

Shortly before four, Sonya was on Northern Cold Air's landing stage. She heard the roar of the plane before she could see it, and then she watched Robert disembark. He saw her immediately and didn't seem fazed. He looked like an explorer returning from an expedition: pleased, but a bit rumpled. Why did he fly all over the place anyway?

He made for her straightaway.

"You look as fresh as a summer's day. Are you well rested?"

She folded her arms over her chest.

"Yes, but you don't seem to ever get any rest."

He looked at her, smiling.

"And to hear that from *your* mouth, you flighty creature."

He walked up the wooden stairs to the street with her.

"Let me get a quick shower, then we can go have some fish, if you'd like."

"Where's your hotel?"

"I'm at the White Raven. There's a good restaurant nearby. Can I pick you up in maybe half an hour?"

It was, in fact, only a few hundred yards' walk, but her aching muscles reminded her of her heroics the day before—and of Robert's wondrous appearance on the beach.

The restaurant near the White Raven was almost full. Sonya ordered clam chowder, and Robert, whose damp combed-back hair gleamed, ordered halibut. Then he looked at her expectantly. She could smell the fresh scent of his shaving lotion. He wore a soft cotton sweater and jeans.

"Why are you here?" he asked.

Damn. *She* had wanted to ask that first. Instead his hand was already on the tiller. She felt resentment rising up inside. She felt she constantly had to account for her trip, as if so many people found her presence unwelcome. But then she thought of Jack Gordon and the note. Of Kathrin the nurse, and Sam the pilot. Of Diane, and the man who found her wallet, that mysterious security man. And Gerti and Helmut. All friendly, helpful people. Or was she kidding herself?

Robert's eyes were glued to her. Now his gaze wandered down her long slim neck. She felt the golden pendant burning on her bare skin where her leaf-green collared shirt was open.

She lifted her chin. She wasn't going to make it easy for this self-confident man.

"To answer your question . . ." And then she talked about Else Seel: her life in Berlin, the ad in the paper, her immigrating to Vancouver, and meeting George, the trapper. She described their life together in the cabin and Else's correspondence with Ezra Pound.

Robert was all ears, and when she'd finished, he said, "I can well imagine why you found this woman fascinating, Sonya."

She fished a piece of clam out of her bowl.

"Really? Why?"

"The parallels are unmistakable."

She dropped the clam beside her plate. What was he saying, parallels? What did this man really know about her?

He watched her in amusement.

"C'mon Sonya, you must have picked up on it, too. You come to Canada by yourself; you're a cultured, intellectual city girl; you love adventure and nature, so it seems, and . . ."

He didn't go on, because the waitress arrived to fill their wine glasses.

Sonya took the opportunity to change the subject.

"Do you have a family?"

"I've been divorced for three years . . . I think I left my ex-wife alone too much. I was often away for long periods. It comes with the job."

"Was your job more important to you than your relationship?"

"All I've got is this job. It's very specialized. You just can't hop over into another profession. But it's true: I love this work. Especially because it's enormously exciting. Right now, there's so much exploration for new deposits of raw materials, and new mines are being constructed. I'm well paid."

Sonya put down her spoon.

"Men can afford the luxury of focusing on their job. But— what happens to their partners and their children?"

"You love your job, too, Sonya. I hear it clearly in how you describe things. Would you be willing to give it all up?"

"I don't have a family—well, I don't have a family anymore. My husband and my son were killed a few years ago."

She looked past him, at the ships in port.

"Here, in Canada."

He didn't say anything, waiting to see if she'd say something more. But she wasn't in the mood, she was sad from her confession. Then he leaned back.

"I'd like us to take a little walk down on the beach. Would you like that?"

She nodded.

Robert paid and helped her on with her jacket.

They drove to Skidegate in silence, past the totem poles and the main lodge of the Skidegate First Nation. The beach was deserted, and the sky stretched out over the neighboring islands. A wind came off the ocean and cooled Sonya's burning face. She pulled up the zipper on her jacket, ambling beside Robert, who was also bundled up. She could picture him scrambling around in mine shafts in freezing temperatures, looking in the ground for traces indicating riches beyond measure—or maybe leading to fraud and deception. Who knew what a mine would actually yield, except experts like Robert? Their opinion had to be trusted—and their critical eye feared. Above all, they had to be prevented from leaking secrets, until all security measures were in place. Their knowledge meant either a lot of money or ruin. Sonya had read up on this in her printouts.

Robert was the first to break the silence.

"So the dead Swiss pilot was your husband."

She couldn't really tell from his tone of voice whether he was asking a question or making a statement. He obviously knew of the crash, perhaps from Sam, and had put two and two together. She decided to lay her cards on the table.

"Yes."

"And the boy was your stepson."

She gave him a sideways glance.

"But you already knew that, didn't you?"

He didn't reply, keeping his eyes to the ground. The approaching evening made his face darker.

She picked up a stone and threw it into the water.

"Now tell me, Robert. What exactly happened? What's being hushed up? Was a crime committed? What do you know? And why are you following me?"

She looked him straight in the eye. He picked up a shell and tossed it from one hand to the other, looking out to sea. As if playing for time. Heavy waves crashed on the beach.

"Look at the ocean and this marvelous beach, the huge sky above, and the mountains behind them. These incredibly dense forests. This country is so magnificent, so splendid, it always takes my breath away. But a lot of people don't see the trees and the mountains and the ocean. They only think about what's under them. Gold, silver, copper, diamonds, oil, gas, uranium, zinc, any natural resources whatsoever. And there are immense energy deposits on the ocean floor around the islands here, around Haida Gwaii. I'm talking about natural gas. That's all some people think about when they hear 'Haida Gwaii.'"

"People like you," Sonya interjected dryly.

"I used to be like that, you're right, but . . . I've changed. I firmly believe that you've got to manage these resources responsibly, so that they spell out a future for people and are sustainable. I'm convinced that in many places in the world nature is more important for human survival than the exploitation of natural resources."

They walked side by side along the gravel beach. The declining light of the sky was reflected in little puddles.

"I'm here to advise the Haida on how to protect their rights to their own natural resources. I do the technical side; lawyers handle the legal end. The Haida want to know how mining companies operate and how decisions are made. They're smart and don't want to be ripped off."

Sonya saw a white dot on the horizon. The Prince Rupert ferry.

Robert stopped.

"When money and economic interests are on the line, you can count on strong opposition. Powerful governments want a piece of the pie, and influential corporations, but also . . . criminal elements."

"I've heard that organized crime has infiltrated the diamond industry here."

He whirled around.

"Where did you hear that?"

"Saw it on the Internet."

"You're interested in diamonds?"

Sonya hesitated. She hadn't intended to hold anything back, but she wasn't quite so sure now.

"I looked up your name."

"My name? Why?"

"Research is my job; doing that comes naturally."

Robert frowned.

"So, what did you find?"

"Nothing about you, but . . ."

He waited.

"But the name of a woman I know."

He looked at her inquiringly. Since she'd gone so far, she might as well spit it out.

"Diane Kesowsky."

He said nothing, but it was clear her name was familiar. He tossed a shell away in a high arc; it fell onto a split rock and shattered to pieces. The rock was dug into the sand like an eagle's talon.

Sonya's gaze was fixed on him.

"What's the story with my husband, Robert?"

He dug his hands into his jacket pockets.

"Your husband got mixed up in some stupid business. He was flying his plane in an area he didn't know a thing about. He was reckless. A gambler, if you ask me. Especially because he put other people's lives at risk."

"I've heard that more than two people were on board," she blurted out.

He stared at her for a long time, and she'd have given a million pennies for his thoughts. If he was wondering how she knew, he didn't let on. Maybe he realized now that she could catch him in a lie. But he had a surprise up his sleeve.

"There were four people in all."

Sonya gave a start.

"Four! Who were the other two?"

"The police aren't making that public knowledge. The investigation's ongoing—that's why the cops are keeping some facts to themselves."

"What? They're still investigating? Nobody told *me*!"

She kicked the sand in anger.

"Your husband had nothing to do with the other two people. It was pure coincidence that they were flying with him. At least, that's how I see it."

She looked at him dumbfounded, not knowing what to think. He returned her stare, looking concerned.

"How come you know all this, Robert? What have you got to do with it?"

He pursed his lips.

"I worked for a certain firm a while back that was exploring for diamonds. A person working for that firm . . . this person was suspected of cooperating with crooks."

"And that person was on the plane?"

"Yes. But that's all I can tell you."

"And the fourth person? Was it a woman?"

"No. But I really can't tell you anything more. Believe me, if I could, I would. But I'm sworn to secrecy for professional reasons. I sign contracts barring me from talking about my work. Those secrets could be worth billions. If somebody finds diamonds somewhere . . . then my goose is cooked."

He looked very serious. His eyes were riveted on her. She had a sudden impulse to lay a hand on his cheek, but she turned away, confused.

Her legs began to move. When she was far enough away from him, she sat down on a rock. The infinite ocean seemed to mock her. How insignificant she was. How presumptuous of her to try to fathom her fate. Life happened, and the wise person submitted to it without offering resistance. How much simpler to explore the fate of others. One's own life was too near, too immediate, too inescapable.

Maybe if she knew the whole truth, she'd be unhappier than before. Robert was right: certain secrets must be kept. *Demanded* to be kept. *It could cost me my life.*

Robert was standing exactly where she'd left him, an erect, lean figure. As vertical as a totem pole, facing the sea.

She walked back slowly. He turned and saw her coming. *A man who can wait patiently*, she thought. His face softened when she was beside him.

"Shouldn't we head back?" he asked. "It'll be dark soon."

She ignored the question.

"Why did you warn me . . . that night, why did you say I shouldn't go to Haida Gwaii?"

"Because you were being followed, and people wanted to find out by whom and why."

"Who's following me? And why?" she continued as calmly as possible.

"That couple from Switzerland."

She couldn't believe her ears.

"Gerti and Helmut? You're not serious! They're here on holiday!" She really felt like laughing. "They were away for five days in Khutzeymateen, for the grizzlies."

"No, they were not."

He took her by the arm, and they started walking.

"No, they were there. And Gerti and Helmut are from Germany, not Switzerland, they—"

"Sonya, those two were not in Khutzeymateen, believe me."

Her instincts told her he was right.

"Then where were they, for God's sake?"

"Hard on your heels. At Greenblue, they asked where you were going."

Sonya had to sit down. The wet sand dampened her pants, but she didn't care. Robert squatted down beside her.

"Don't worry. They're not on the Queen Charlottes. They were misdirected. They thought you were already on the highway to Vancouver."

"Who misled them?"

"People who saw to it that you could get on with your research without interruption."

"Who? And why should anybody want to keep me from my research?"

"It was simply a precaution; there's no real danger."

"Is this another one of your secrets?"

"Yes, it is," he replied. He helped her to her feet. His hands were surprisingly warm. *Watch out! He's one of those guys looking for danger. Here's another one with secrets.*

"You've got secrets, too, don't you, Sonya?" Robert said calmly. She couldn't see his eyes anymore because it had grown too dark. What was he driving at?

"I don't expect you'll let me in on them. Everything in its own time. Come on, I'll take you back—you're shivering with the cold."

In the car he suddenly blurted out, "There's one secret I *can* tell you. Ian Fleming wasn't calling to the gods while he was meditating on the beach."

"Come again? How do you know that Ian—"

"He was calling me on his cell phone. I was in Old Masset at the time."

"I don't get it. Have you known him for long? Why did you need to know that Ian and I—"

He touched her arm lightly, smiling.

"Now that really is top secret."

CHAPTER 25

A storm was raging the next morning. Rain splattered on the windowpanes. Sonya couldn't find the ducks that were usually on the meadow at this hour. The ferry wouldn't be running in this weather, the proprietor had announced, so she extended her stay by a night.

Something else unforeseen had happened. She could no longer hear with her right ear. The ear canal was completely blocked. The only thing for it was to go to the health clinic through driving rain. The modest building cowered against a steep slope as if it were trying to be invisible. Sonya waited only a few minutes until the community nurse called her name. She talked nonstop, washing out Sonya's ear until the pressure was gone. It soon became clear that she knew Kathrin.

"She was a vacation replacement a year ago. She's in Kitkatla now, eh. I must give her a call sometime, so we can get together. Are you staying here long?"

"No," Sonya answered. "I actually wanted to go back today, but the ferry—"

"I know, I know—this dreadful storm. Always messes things up. But better to wait a bit and get to Prince Rupert safely, eh?"

Sonya paid her bill and offered her hand. The nurse squeezed it but didn't stop talking.

"There was an accident a couple of years ago with a Swiss lady, somewhere around here, I can't remember where, but she was badly hurt. At any rate, she had to be taken by helicopter to Vancouver—that much I remember."

"Did she survive?" Sonya asked, excited.

"No idea. I just heard about it vaguely. Maybe Kathrin knows more. I was up in the Yukon when it happened. There aren't many serious accidents on the island. You get a bit out of practice. Now Kathrin, she's got a lot of experience because she works in emergency, but I—"

Someone called the nurse's name.

"Yes, I'm coming. Excuse me, I'm needed . . . It was nice chatting with you."

As Sonya walked downhill to the main street, her pulse pounded stronger than the rain on the roofs. Maybe she had her first clue about Odette! An accident. Robert said there was no woman on the plane that crashed. So what accident was this? Had Odette been lying paralyzed in a hospital? Was that what her parents kept quiet about?

Robert knew more than he was letting on. Sonya turned at the harbor and headed toward the White Raven. The receptionist didn't search on the computer for long.

"Bob checked out today," she said.

"But the ferry—isn't running today," Sonya stammered.

"I don't know if he's on the island or not. Sorry."

"Did he leave a message or say why he left so quickly?"

"Bob only reserved until today. I made the reservation myself."

The woman was friendly, but Sonya was annoyed just the same. How dare she be so familiar as to call him Bob! As if he were a good friend.

He'd simply flown the coop.

Sonya stormed out of the hotel and fought her way through the wind and rain. At the boardinghouse Robert hadn't left a message on her answering machine or at the desk. But a package had arrived for her. She unpacked it in her room and stared at a brightly painted native dancing mask on the cover of an illustrated book. She had browsed through that big book in the bookstore for a while, but hadn't bought it because it was so heavy.

On the spur of the moment, she put on rubber boots and raingear and went outside.

"Ah, here comes our intrepid historian," Ian exclaimed in delight as she planted herself in front of his desk. "Have you recovered from all that strain?"

"Thanks for asking. Tell me, how do you know Robert Stanford?"

Ian's eyes grew big as he looked at her. He certainly hadn't expected her to be so forward. But Sonya was too incensed to be polite.

"Bob? He's in here often. He's interested in Haida Gwaii."

"How did he know about our hike to Rose Spit?"

Ian looked down at the floor.

"I didn't keep it from him."

"Who's talking about keeping anything from anybody? Why did you tell him?" She couldn't conceal her exasperation.

"I wanted to avoid problems."

"Problems? What kind of problems?"

He hemmed and hawed.

"Well . . . that I was going there with you."

"Why should that cause problems? I don't understand."

Drops from her wet rain jacket rolled off onto his desk. Ian fidgeted with a pile of papers.

"I didn't want any misunderstanding. I simply told him I was showing you Rose Spit. He was OK with that."

Sonya was wide-eyed.

"He was what? He doesn't have to agree to anything! You don't have to get his consent. I'm—"

"I know, I know." Ian turned around. "It hadn't escaped my notice, of course, that he had a particular interest in you, if you catch my drift. I didn't want to get in his way. Who comes into the shop first gets served first. That's how it is, eh?"

Sonya was speechless. What was this guy saying?

"So you think . . . you think that Robert and I . . . that we . . . Did he suggest anything like that?"

Ian brushed his hand over the stubbled hair on his head.

"Well, if you really want to know—but not a word of this to Robert. He said, 'Keep your hands off her. I'm interested in her.'"

He saw Sonya's flabbergasted face and raised his hands apologetically.

"I thought somebody had told Bob that the two of us were going to Rose Spit together. And that he came to me to stake out his turf. That's logical, isn't it?"

Sonya took a deep breath. She couldn't believe what she'd heard. But Ian was already off again.

"I wanted to go out there with you anyway. In any case, I thought it was great fun. And Robert thought everything was fine . . . Or isn't it?"

He gave her a cautious look.

"Yes, of course," Sonya quickly agreed. She was starting to figure some things out. Robert had seen her go into Ian's shop—he was surely hot on her trail—and he had quizzed Ian about their plans. He let Ian think she'd hooked up with him, or at the very least that he was interested in her. So he made Ian her guardian. How clever.

Robert was playing a double game. That was clear. He was following her, spying on her, maybe protecting her, too, but for inscrutable reasons. Gerti and Helmut were tailing her! How could she be taken in by such crap!

And now Robert had vanished into thin air. How could she have trusted him? After all she'd been through with Tonio, she should at least have learned something! You can never be too vigilant.

Ian still stood before her. She almost felt sorry for him.

"I had an awful lot of fun, too," she assured him. "I'll never forget that experience."

"If things don't turn out with Robert, come back here . . . But he's one cool guy, eh? I can't say a word against him."

"Definitely." She wiped what remained of the rain from her face. "I'll definitely come back here someday."

And for a moment she believed it, too.

"I unpacked the book today and—"

"Just a minute," Ian said. His attention was diverted by a customer who'd just come in.

"There's a card in it," he said to her hurriedly, and then he gave Sonya a friendly good-bye hug.

Back at the boardinghouse, Sonya learned that the ferry would be leaving that night. She began to pack at once, putting the heavy tome at the bottom of her suitcase. She had long forgotten about the card.

CHAPTER 26

"What's that noise?" Inge asked.

"Fishermen boozing it up because they caught a big fish," Sonya explained.

"Where have you wound up, for heaven's sake?"

"I got a room at a fisherman's lodge because it looks like a proper log cabin. I must spend at least one night in a Canadian log cabin."

She was speaking from the phone booth in the lodge hallway because her cell phone had no reception yet again. Her voice fought against the caterwauling of the men drinking whiskey and vodka around the fireplace in the common room.

"Tell me, what's the time there?" Inge asked.

"One in the morning."

The racket from the guests had kept Sonya awake so she decided after midnight to phone Inge. It was already ten a.m. in Switzerland. A burning question was on her lips.

"Inge, did you know that Diane's exploring for diamonds?"

Silence on the line.

"Inge, are you still there?"

"Yes, sure. But those drinking buddies make it really hard to understand you. Where did you hear that anyway?"

"I read it somewhere."

"Oh, those old tales about diamonds. They're not true, but Diane can tell you about it. I don't have precise information . . . Are things moving along with Else Seel?"

Sonya suspected Inge wasn't telling her the whole story. But she knew her boss well enough to sense this wasn't the time to push her.

She didn't tell Inge that when she discovered that Kathrin was no longer in Kitkatla, she'd planned to return to Vancouver as soon as possible. Unfortunately, nobody in the nursing station wanted to give her Kathrin's phone number or address in Vancouver. Sonya could only leave her phone number. Then she'd tried to reach Sam, but he was off somewhere. A little bird in her head told her that in Vancouver she'd sort out the puzzle of Odette's disappearance. Odette must be the key to Tonio's death.

The next morning over breakfast, Walt, the lodge proprietor, told her that the old hospital in Hazelton was no longer standing, but Sonya preferred to check it out for herself. She tried to explain to Walt why she absolutely must find it. No event in Else's journey had captivated her so much as Else's exciting trip to the Hazelton hospital and then back to her cabin in Wistaria.

"She and her baby almost died," she recounted to Walt, fishing the ice cubes out of her orange juice. She hated ice cubes.

Else, who hadn't been quite two years away from Berlin, wanted to have her first child delivered by a doctor at all costs. George came with her and then left her to go trap marten in the mountains. The birth went well, and Else started back to Wistaria in January 1929, with her newborn child.

"It was twenty below zero, and she took the train to Burns Lake alone with her newborn," Sonya continued.

Walt went into the kitchen, and she heard him cracking eggs.

"Yes, we often get temperatures like that around here."

He probably didn't understand why she was so fascinated. But nothing would stop her; she knew the description of the trip by heart.

Else and her baby had gotten off the train at Burns Lake at two in the morning. Else felt her way carefully across the icy platform to the hotel where she'd booked a room. The bedroom was ice-cold because the wood stove in the corridor heated the floor but not the rooms. The windows were iced over, and Else shivered in bed. In the morning Else's infant was turning blue, so she took him into the only heated room: the waitresses' bedroom.

A car brought Else to her next lodging, a B and B on François Lake. George finally showed up a few days later to see Rupert, his newborn son. He was beside himself with pride and joy. But he went across the lake the very next day, supposedly to have a beer. And he didn't come back. He'd found a farmer from Wistaria with a sled and seized the opportunity to get hunting in the mountains more quickly.

Sonya almost choked on her orange juice. She called into the kitchen where Walt was frying bacon.

"Imagine that: he up and left Else and the baby behind."

His answer was the hiss of grease. She kept on talking all the same.

"Else had to wait until the lake froze over so she could get across by car. The wife of the B and B's proprietor wanted to visit her daughter in Prince Rupert and was closing her house to guests, so Else had no choice but to head out once again even though the ice on the lake wasn't yet stable enough to cross."

Sonya shuddered as she narrated.

"A game warden intended to drive his old Ford over the ice. He'd tied long poles to his car to prevent it from sinking if the ice broke. At first he refused to take Else and her child along, but she persuaded him. They drove past open cracks in the ice, and Else was terrified that they'd break through and drown in the ice-cold water. But, as if by a miracle, they reached the other bank safe and sound, where a number of men anxiously awaited their arrival.

"The warden felt encouraged to go back across the frozen lake alone. But this time his old car crashed through the ice, and he just managed to jump out and save his life.

"It might have been the death of Else and her baby. How she must have felt when she heard about it!" Sonya added. *"A death in the ice-cold water, and the child could have died,"* Else wrote afterward. She and Little Rupert spent the night on the opposite shore with some people they knew, and they left the following morning by horse-drawn sled, driven through the deep snow. The trip took the whole day, and Else kept checking to see if her boy continued to show signs of life. Her fear was well founded. A woman from those parts had tightly wrapped up her own baby for a journey home—too tightly, as it turned out. When she took the child out of its covering, it was dead. Suffocated.

"They arrived at Ootsa Lake that evening. Else's body was so stiff from the cold that she couldn't get down from the sled on her own. But Rupert was alive.

"You see," Walt said after he left the kitchen and sat down beside her. "That shows how hard it is for parents to know when to protect their kids and when to risk it. Both can cost a kid his life."

Sonya stared at him. He'd understood exactly what she had tried to say. She felt unmasked somehow and only added, "And George didn't come back from hunting until a month later."

Sonya traveled to Hazelton around noon. The clinic was on the other side of the valley, in the First Nation reservation, so she had to cross a hanging bridge over a deep gorge.

Walt was right: the original building was gone and had been replaced by a flat, factory-like building. The faces she saw in the waiting room were almost all native ones. In one of the hallways, she came across a photograph of the old hospital on the wall. It looked rather like a summer residence.

Sonya filmed the clinic from the outside, the massive mountains around it, and the native houses on the hills. Then she drove along the brown, tumbling Skeena River toward Burns Lake, surrounded by the magnificent colors of the deciduous trees that sparkled deep yellow, orange, and glowing red in the sunshine. She felt a sudden wave of happiness. Until she caught herself wondering, did Robert Stanford maybe have children somewhere?

CHAPTER 27

So here was François Lake, where Else Seel had endured the fear of death during that bitterly cold winter. Maybe it was because of the warm autumn sun that Sonya found the body of water almost idyllic. She stood at the rail of the little ferry—not another ferry!—that was floating her truck safely to the other shore. The outlines of low hills snuggled against the silvery-blue sky like long, outstretched sleeping cats. It was tranquility Sonya saw, not the bush. She felt the pleasurable excitement that comes when names you only know from books become reality.

She parked her truck on the shore in front of a little weather-beaten wooden house with a sign over the door: "School." This couldn't be the schoolhouse Else's children attended. Sonya went up to the modest building next door that housed the administration of the local Cheslatta tribe. A young woman was just coming out of the door.

"Is this the school of Wistaria?" Sonya inquired.

"No, their school used to be on Ootsa Lake. Wistaria no longer exists. Their houses were flooded because they built a dam upstream."

That was old news to Sonya, but she hoped to find a few houses that had survived the rising level of Ootsa Lake. The young native woman pointed to a shed behind the school.

"Why don't you ask my grandfather if you want to know more. He's going on seventy; he was alive when it all happened. He's in there carving a canoe."

Sonya thanked her and got her notebook and video camera out of the truck. The shed door creaked loudly when she pushed it. At first she saw just a partly dug out canoe, but it took up the whole length of the room. A man was scraping the inside of it with a tool. He looked up when she came in, and she introduced herself, saying she heard in the band office that he was carving a canoe. The old native wore jeans, a purple shirt, and a baseball cap; his face resembled the ridged bark of a hemlock. She couldn't read the enigmatic expression in his eyes.

He looked at her, asking no questions, then simply started to talk.

"My grandfather carved the last canoe in this area. From a cottonwood tree like this one here." He stroked his finger over the wood. "That was in 1946."

He went to the workbench and came back with a black-and-white photograph.

"That's my grandfather. He belonged to the killer whale clan."

Sonya calculated—1946 was five or six years before a Canadian company built the dam that raised the water level of Ootsa Lake and gradually flooded out the houses of both natives and white settlers. She asked the old man about that, and he turned his face away.

"They flooded my village. Now everything's gone. They also flooded the place where our ancestors were buried."

He worked silently on the canoe for a few minutes and then picked up where he'd left off.

"I was seventeen at the time. We lived in log cabins by the lake, or back in the bush. We had only two weeks to clear out our houses. We had to leave a lot of things behind."

He went to his workbench and switched to a different tool. His movements were economical, measured.

"We call the land here the Hungry Plains since we had too little pasture for our cows."

She watched how he peeled off shavings from the dugout canoe, using ancient knowledge that might well die out with him. She asked if she could film him as he worked, and he nodded his assent. When she walked out into the sunshine a little later, she felt she was resurfacing from a long forgotten age.

She continued on her way, past cow pastures interspersed with small wood lots, past small farms by the road. The landscape reminded her a bit of Switzerland. She turned off at the place the old native man had described; she went along a broad gravel road that had apparently been built for the giant oncoming trucks that appeared sporadically carrying tree trunks. At times she couldn't see the road for the dust; she heard gravel popping against her truck and soon discovered a hairline crack in her windshield.

She geared down, luckily, because shortly afterward a herd of goats drifted over the road seeking shelter in a dilapidated farmhouse. Exhausted, Sonya stopped the truck and looked around. A little white church was on the right, surrounded by a bare wood picket fence, as if the church were an animal threatening to escape. Sonya's heart jumped for joy. That must be the church that Else and George Seel attended for years, even in the depths of winter. That's where their children, Rupert and Gloria, were baptized! A cross over the door was all that indicated the plain house was a church, and a chimney stuck out of the roof instead of the old belfry. The snow-white facade was newly painted; but otherwise time seemed to have stood still. Sonya got her video camera and shook the door. It was locked. She looked over at the derelict farmhouse, which appeared to be unoccupied; a car with no license plates was rusting away in the tall grass in front of it. She heaved a sigh. There was no view of the interior, but what great light for outdoor shots!

A few miles farther down the road, she found the community hall the settlers in Wistaria had built. It was right by the road-side—so inconspicuous that Sonya would have passed right by if she hadn't been looking for the sign, "Wistaria Community Hall." The hall resembled a functional farm building, with no windows facing the road.

Sonya looked up Else's description in her book. So here's where the onetime daughter of a German estate owner had danced for so many nights, to the music of a guitar, violin, and accordion band. *"The big, strong men lifted the ladies high in the air, whooping with delight,"* Else wrote. After the dance the sleds pulled up,

the young people were on horseback, and dogs yapped excitedly among the sleds and horses. The crowd dashed down the steep slope until they came to the road leading to the side roads, where the sleds disappeared to reach the farms.

Sonya looked up at the hall. She couldn't fathom Else at all at that moment. This could *not* have been what the lady from Berlin had dreamed of! Dances in this unadorned building and sandwiches at midnight? Surely she hadn't given up her life in Berlin—the passionate all-night discussions with her fellow students and the history and philosophy lectures at Humboldt University—for this. In Germany, Else had just had her first successes as a writer:

a short story in 1921 and other contributions to newspapers and magazines. She must have dreamed of a future career as a celebrated author.

And then she chose to live this completely dull life in Wistaria among uneducated people who had no idea of culture! A few paltry dances were the highlight of her social life. But why? Sonya looked around. From the crest of the hill, she saw the vibrant blue water of Ootsa Lake down in the valley. The thick forests that covered the hillsides in Else's day had been cleared, stripped, robbed of their wildness. The place looked—to Sonya's eyes at least—much tamer and less threatening than in Else's account. But what a contrast to the Berlin of the twenties!

Of course there'd been that unhappy love story. A married man. And a famous author, to boot. The Danish writer, Martin Andersen Nexø, who lived in Germany from 1923 to 1930. He was twenty-five years older than she was, her mentor, and she fell in love with him. And then the usual happened: Nexø decided to drop her. Else was bitterly disappointed and felt as if the literary scene—the people in it, the entire Old World—had suddenly rejected her. She wanted to turn her back on them, to forget, to start a new life.

Sonya could empathize with Else's feelings of abandonment, born out of pain. Reinventing yourself. It happens time and again. But did Else realize what was awaiting her in Canada? Did she want to lose her former life in order to gain one here: one in which you were in danger of freezing to death in winter—chopping ice from the lake for drinking water, baking bread year round, salting down meat, and tending the garden?

Sonya had had long discussions with Inge about this, and now she had to admit Inge was right. Something must have happened in Germany, something that drove Else away. Her dark secret. A secret that only a radical break would help Else to overcome.

Else, what are you hiding from me?

CHAPTER 28

An hour later, Sonya was sitting across from a thickset man with deep hanging eyebrows, who'd sooner talk about George Seel than Else.

Alan Blackwell was his name; he'd gone to school with Else's children. The museum director in Burns Lake had given Sonya Blackwell's address. She found his house at the end of a bumpy country dirt road. She was in luck: Blackwell and his wife happened to be cleaning out their house, since they wanted to move closer to Burns Lake. Nonetheless, they dropped everything and invited Sonya in for tea and cookies. Now she was sitting with them in a kitchen filled with boxes.

Sonya guessed that Alan Blackwell was in his midseventies. She was quite excited about interviewing a witness from Else's early days on Ootsa Lake, but his first words were about George Seel.

"He was a really likable guy—caring, but rough and hardy. You must know that trappers had a tough life back then. They'd leave on snowshoes at the beginning of November and be gone until Christmas."

He looked at Marion, his wife, a white-haired wiry woman, who listened quietly.

"They would be back at Christmastime for a few days and then be off again until March. They caught marten, and lynx, and otter and beaver in the spring. They used leg traps."

Sonya imagined the animals trapped, suffering, panicking, completely at the trapper's mercy. She shuddered, and her reaction didn't go unnoticed.

"It was hard on animals and people. Trappers had no contact with the outside world. Suppose George froze to death in his hut up there—nobody would have known. Those were tough times, but it was the only way to earn a little money around here."

Sonya took notes. Alan Blackwell needed no encouragement to keep talking.

"George was good-looking, a dashing fellow. But he could be dirty." The old man laughed. "Some trappers told tales about him: that he'd come back from the bush in his cold, filthy clothes and would climb into bed with Else first thing."

"Were they both happy?" Sonya inquired.

Blackwell looked at his wife again.

"When George and Else were together, they seemed happy. She never complained about him, and he always described her as a good wife."

"Wasn't he a hopeless dreamer? I mean, his futile search for silver and gold."

"He was a dreamer, right enough. He found silver and thought he'd be rich. But those prospectors, they're all dreamers, you know."

He paused and had some tea.

"At times she did seem unhappy."

Sonya waited.

"She was frequently alone. I know she was a poet. As for me—I think it's odd she chose to live that kind of a life . . . if you think about where she was from." He coughed. Sonya had heard he was a soldier in Europe during the Second World War.

"My mom came to Canada from England. She'd been engaged to my father's brother, but he was killed in the First World War. Then my dad asked her to marry him after that."

He rubbed a heavy hand slowly over his arm, as if it hurt him there.

"Mom told me later that she cried every night before going to sleep their first three years here. She hadn't the foggiest notion about the life she'd gotten into in Canada. But she got used to it and didn't want to leave."

Sonya listened, fascinated. Else ultimately didn't want to leave as well. Mainly because they were better off financially in the 1940s when those crushing money worries had gone. That's when they expanded their home, adding a stable and a large barn. George bought some sturdy cows that had calves, and the Seels tried their hand at cattle farming, buying over two hundred acres for hay, with a creek and a river. After the war, Else would ship CARE packages of food to relatives and friends in Germany. George bought a chain saw, and two horses for Rupert. Life seemed to be easier.

And then disaster struck. The Ootsa Lake settlements were doomed. A Canadian company near the town of Kitimat built a dam for hydroelectric power that reversed the flow of the Nechako River. The water level of Ootsa Lake rose higher and higher.

Sonya asked Blackwell about the flooding. He took her to the edge of his garden, to an unobstructed view of the lake in the valley and the forested slopes of the mountains on the horizon.

"The lake used to be a hundred and fifty feet shallower," Blackwell remarked. "The men from the company said the lake level was going up and gave us very little time to pack up our things. The settlers got a rotten deal for their land."

Sonya caught the bitter resignation in his voice. The Seels had to give up everything—their house, stable, barn, gardens, berry bushes, flowerbeds, fir trees, meadows, their glacial stones, and their hay field. The imminent flooding wasn't the only hard blow Else had to suffer. In 1950, George died at the age of sixty.

Everything can be taken away from you from one day to the next, Sonya thought, looking over the lake. *And it hasn't happened just to me.*

When they were saying good-bye, Marion Blackwell pressed a note into her hand.

"Give this lady a call; she's the daughter of Else's neighbors. I've told her you'll be coming by."

Sonya saw the old couple in her rearview mirror, standing before the house they'd soon be leaving behind; their honey-colored Labrador was by their side and their black cat was at the door. They waved good-bye for a long time.

Sonya rolled down the window. The sun was burning hot: much too hot for September, she reckoned. She was driving over a stony back road to a boat launch on Ootsa Lake. At the lake, there was a broad clearing and a meadow covered with colorful foliage. The water glittered as if covered with stainless steel. Sonya sat down in the grass and unpacked some bread, cheese, tomatoes, and pears. A gentle breeze made the leaves dance in the air, and the autumn light glowed. Sonya had the sensation of breathing gold dust. Trees were all there was to see on the far shore.

Sonya walked down to the beach and washed her hands. Then she sat on the shore and read the *Vancouver Sun* she'd bought in the supermarket that morning. The first thing she saw was the picture on the front page. A man in his midforties held out his hands to the reader. Instead of fingers, there were just stumps. She read that this mountain climber and two of his companions had climbed Canada's highest mountain, Mount Logan, and then run into a snowstorm. They were pinned down on a ridge for three days; they had been lashed by sixty-five-mile-an-hour winds that blew away their tent. The men expected to die, but a helicopter got them out. Their rescuers had risked their lives. Sonya browsed through the interview with this mountaineer, who was the father of three children.

Mountain climbing is egotistical, I'll grant you that. But it's an addiction, and like any addiction, you hurt the people you love best . . . Dying's easy. Any idiot can do that. It's the people you leave behind who have to deal with it . . . But I can't quit. Every day's an adventure. The euphoria on a mountain—I can't explain it. It's uncomfortable, dirty, cold, it's all damn hard. But it makes you happy . . . I'll get prostheses, and then I hope to climb again . . . I wish I could say I'll never do it again. I know that would make the kids happy. But I can't say I can promise them that . . . I don't believe I've learned anything from all this. Because I don't think I'd have done anything differently . . .

Sonya crushed up the paper and got into the car, fuming.

She had done everything wrong. Wrong to marry a man like Tonio. Wrong to trust him. Wrong to put her life on ice. Wrong to waste time and energy on the circumstances of his death. It's stupid to say they're just egotists and don't know what they're doing. No kidding! They know exactly what they do to other people. And they go do it anyway.

She didn't stop shaking until she drove onto the ferry an hour later. She looked at her watch. Too late to find the address on the note, and she was too tired anyway. She went back to the same boardinghouse.

She made tea in the guest area, picked up her Haida art book, and flopped onto the sofa. She got lost for a while among those witnesses to an almost vanished world. But her mind kept coming back to the conversation with Alan Blackwell. He must have admired George Seel. Boys need male role models to imitate; Nicky admired his father the same way. He was so looking forward to a Canadian adventure with Tonio. Just Nicky and his father in that magnificent country; an adventure he could regale his friends with. She'd observed to Tonio, "Good you're seizing this opportunity. Nicky will soon be gadding about with a girlfriend." Not that he had one at the time. Two years before, he'd dropped one like a hot potato. But Tonio found condoms in Nicky's jeans when he was doing the laundry. Who was he sleeping with? he'd asked her. Sonya was not all that surprised; after all, Nicky was almost seventeen. It's good he uses condoms, she assured Tonio, who just frowned.

She had to admit to herself that this incident had opened her eyes as well. She quickly realized how muscular Nicky was, displaying his powerful thighs when he went around in shorts. The boy looked damn good, and Tonio must have noticed that, too. But Nicky was still a dreamer who'd withdraw into his fantasy world. What did he dream or fantasize about? Nicky hardly told her a thing. She wrote it off as a phase, speculating that maybe she shouldn't keep mothering him like a little boy. Hadn't he thrown these words at Tonio and her just before the trip: Don't tell me what to do. What do you know about life anyway?

Her eyelids got heavy; the book slowly slipped from her hands. Something white fell out. An envelope. She tore it open and pulled out a card.

Dear Sonya,

This book is to remind you of the beauty and the magic of Haida Gwaii. Maybe you will return under happier circumstances. You are a fearless, marvellous lady, and I feel honoured to have met you.

I'd like to keep in touch.

Do call me. My cell phone number is below.

All the best,

Robert

It was Robert who had given her the book, and not Ian! She reread the words and visualized Robert's face: the knowing eyes, the faint smile in the corners of his mouth. She went to her room and dialed the number on the card. She heard an automated voice: "The customer is unavailable. Please try again later."

She threw the phone onto the bed.

Then she took a long shower, letting the water run over her body until she was finally able to relax.

CHAPTER 29

Alice Harrison took Sonya into the living room, where a TV blared full volume. Her husband sat in an armchair. She leaned over the walker beside him.

"This is Sonya, from Berlin. She's here because of Else and George," she shouted into his ear. The old man regarded Sonya through watery eyes.

"Alford is ninety-five," Alice announced proudly. "I'm eighty-seven."

She sat down on the sofa, full of energy.

"We ran the Wistaria post office; my father was the postmaster, you see. Please sit down . . . I often went to visit Mrs. Seel on horseback. Her house was cozy. She had many cross-stitched quilts. But she was lonely, of course."

It was difficult to follow the old lady's flood of words, which Sonya could barely hear over the blast of the TV. Sonya peeked at the screen. A football game.

"Alford was a trapper like George. But he was never away as long as George was. Else called him *Georg*, in German. Did I pronounce it right? George was a good provider, proud of his family. But he didn't take care of himself. He smoked."

She closed her eyes and stopped talking. Then she shot up from the sofa.

"He raised beavers. How many beavers did George have?" she shouted at her husband. "How many beavers?"

"Two. A pair." Sonya had trouble hearing his weak voice over the sports announcer's commentary.

"Else had to take care of the beavers," Alice continued. "She was one smart person. Very different from George. She was very emotional."

"How did she show that?"

"When the government built a road to their bay, the workmen knocked down several fir trees. Mrs. Seel was beside herself. She screamed at the men. 'You can't cut down my trees!' But they sure could, take my word for it."

"Were Else and George happy together?"

Alice reflected. Sonya could plainly see that question made her uncomfortable.

"They made the best of it. George was a good neighbor. He looked good, he worked hard. She really didn't complain. Except . . . if he didn't come home the day he promised to. I believe he was proud of her, but he had a peculiar way of showing it. Come with me. I've a lot of photographs."

She jumped up, amazingly nimbly, and returned soon with her hands full of albums. Sonya got itchy fingers. Pictures for the exhibition! She would have to persuade the old lady to lend her some.

Alice asked her to sit beside her. The pictures were small: black and white, with white, frilly edges. Sonya's practiced eye saw everything.

Else at a picnic with Wistaria schoolchildren, sitting in the grass, wearing a broad-brimmed hat.

Else with her daughter Gloria, looking sturdy; her facial features were harder and broader than in the portrait Rupert had of her as a girl.

Else with her infant in the snow, the infant warmly wrapped. Her hair was cut short and lying close to her head.

George Seel with Rupert in his arms, posing in a chair in their house. A big, strong man and a tiny baby.

Sonya went excitedly through the pictures, imagining them enlarged in the museum. Alice Harrison chatted on continuously, so Sonya could just forget her questions.

"George had several accidents. He once burned his neck with a lamp, which left him with deep scars. He was faithful to her though—I have no doubt about that. But why Mrs. Seel chose that kind of life, I don't know. We didn't ask many questions at the time. She received a lot of books and newspapers in the mail. They were essential for her."

Her monologue petered out. Sonya waited. She couldn't believe how well she could summon her own patience.

"We were at the Seels' the night before George died. George was lying down, and he looked exhausted."

Alice grew silent. Alford got up from his armchair, bracing himself on his walker, and she jumped up, hurrying over to him. Eighty-seven, Sonya marveled, and looking after a ninety-five-year-old husband.

"I have to take care of Alford now," Alice said apologetically.

"I wanted to ask if you would lend some of these pictures for me to copy." Sonya was on her feet as well.

"Come back around two, when Alford's asleep, and I'll have some time."

Alice left her husband standing for a few seconds, giving her visitor a spontaneous hug.

"Your questions brought back old times. That's lovely."

Later that afternoon, Sonya was singing as she hurtled down the highway. An envelope of pictures was in her bag. She could hardly believe what a haul that was. Though she still hadn't cracked Else's secret, she felt she was closer than ever. She'd be in Vancouver soon, perhaps in two days. She was convinced some vital discovery awaited her there. All roads seemed to lead to Vancouver.

A huge truck blocked her view of the road. She was getting ready to pass when her cell phone beeped. A text message. *That Swiss woman nearly died. Info at the VGH.*

Sonya stared at her phone as if it would cough up the meaning of the mysterious message. What did VGH mean? Who sent this unsigned tip? The nurse in Queen Charlotte City, who had mentioned the injured Swiss woman? But she didn't have Sonya's phone number!

That reminded her that she'd sent Diane a message telling her when she'd be coming back to Vancouver. The message hadn't been answered.

On an impulse, she called up Robert.

"Yes?" His voice sounded far away.

"It's me, Sonya."

"Sonya! Where are you?"

"On the way to Vancouver. And you?"

"In a meeting. Wait, I'll pop out."

She heard a door close.

"Sonya, listen. Jack Gordon is dead."

"Who?" She could hardly understand him.

"Jack Gordon. You met him on the Queen Charlottes."

Sonya was too bewildered to ask how he knew that.

"Don't talk to anybody about this. Get to Vancouver as quickly as possible. I'll be there soon. Sonya?"

Her thoughts were racing. Should she be afraid?

He interpreted her silence correctly.

"I didn't mean to scare you. We just have to be cautious. Are you OK?"

"Yes, but it's all so confusing, so—"

"We'll see each other soon. Please be a little patient. I'll explain everything. Please."

"OK." What else could she say?

"I've got to go. See you soon, eh?"

"Bye for now. And thanks, thanks for the book."

Sonya got back on the main road and stepped on the gas.

Just stop thinking. Stop feeling. Keep moving forward. As fast as you can. Get away, from everything. Away. From Robert and his mysterious ways. From Tonio and the past. From the pain and this whole nightmare and the memories. Don't wake up in the morning with everything the same, as if there's no escape.

Would she lead a normal life again? Would she ever be happy?

She had to slow down: two RVs were moseying along in front of her. She'd already passed several of these rolling elephants, but more of them kept looming in front of her. Too many of them.

She reflected on her years with Tonio. Was she happy back then? She'd been restless, *that* she remembered. Constantly searching. Searching for . . . something extraordinary. She hadn't wanted what was "normal." She wanted to break free. And if she couldn't do it alone, then she wanted to do it with somebody else. But she never succeeded with Tonio. The adventure, risk, danger—those were his domain. Compared to Tonio, she only felt more anxious, more cowardly, keen on safety. Not that he ever criticized her for it. He'd never implied in the least that she wasn't up to him as far as taking risks went. No, it was her inner voice that scolded and denounced herself, over and over.

But now, at this moment, it was *her* adventure, her voyage into the unknown; she was in the thick of it, all alone. She felt anger, confusion, rebellion, impatience. But not fear.

She swerved into the passing lane and gave the truck some gas.

No, her life would never be the same again. Sure, people had experienced serious change: Her mother's life changed after she learned that her father's sudden death wasn't from a heart attack, as she'd been told repeatedly as a child, but a suicide. Inge's partner had learned he had prostate cancer. Tonio's ex had lost her only child.

And Odette? Her life had changed. Assuming she was still alive. Odette's life could never be the same again.

"I can no longer imagine a life without you. Without my beloved Tonio. My life is now finally whole. From now on and forevermore."

No, Odette, from now on and nevermore. *For you and for me.*

CHAPTER 30

Everything looked so idyllic: the Provincial Park sign, the road through the woods, the picnic tables on the meadow by the little lake. Sonya was looking forward to the food she'd bought from the supermarket deli on the way. She parked her truck and was happy to see an elderly couple eating at a stone table. They gave her a friendly wave. It was a good thing not to be alone.

The sun's rays cast a narrow, shining stripe on the lake, like a diamond-studded bracelet. Sonya thought of Diane. She'd be in her apartment in a few days, with a hundred questions. She'd have to be vigilant, weighing her words carefully.

She locked the truck, and a sign pointed to the washroom. The facility was surprisingly clean. She washed some fruit and tomatoes and strolled along the path back to the parking lot. Suddenly, she sensed a threat. An odd, intense smell pierced her nostrils. Out of the corner of her eye, she caught sight of a shadow. A shock went through her like a bolt of lightning.

A bear was about fifteen feet away, a giant animal. He appeared to be taken by surprise as much as she was. They both stood rooted to the spot for some seconds. The truck was too far away, and the bear was directly in her path. Good God!

The bear's head moved. She could see its little eyes, its pointed snout. Then she heard it. A deep, threatening, nerve-shattering roar. Emitting an *"ugh ugh ugh,"* it stood upright.

Don't run. Just don't run. Never run away from a bear.

But she turned around and ran for her life.

To the washroom. Back to the washroom.

She got to the building, literally jumping into the nearest stall, the one for the disabled. She locked the wooden door fast and realized at once that it offered no protection. It was completely open above and below. A heavy bear could easily smash the partition, shatter the wood with one blow of its paw.

Sonya tried to listen, but her heart was beating too loudly, her breath was too fast. Her blood was rushing.

Oh, God, I don't want to die!

Where was the bear? What was it up to?

The couple at the picnic table. Did they see the bear? Did it see them? What were they doing?

I hope they come and help me. I hope somebody comes and helps me!

She didn't dare move. Standing stock still in the cubicle big enough for a wheelchair, she spied a metal grip on the wall.

There! Wasn't that a cracking sound? Then nothing. For a long time, it was quiet. An occasional puff of wind blew through the room with a soft rustling sound. Other people must be coming to the park. More cars. They would definitely shoo the bear away. Bears didn't like crowds of people.

But ten wild horses wouldn't get her out of that stall. A bear was running around out there!

Shivering, Sonya felt abandoned, defenseless. Then she screwed up her courage and got up on the rim of the toilet bowl. She saw nothing but a trail and heavy underbrush. It would soon be dark. Should she call for help? Why had she left her cell phone in the car?

She knew bears very rarely attacked people. They ran away most of the time. But maybe this bear was used to people, and a lot of tourists were dumb enough to feed bears. It certainly would have found the scraps that thoughtless visitors hadn't disposed of properly.

If only she had a walking stick or an umbrella. She had a Swiss army knife in her rain jacket, but what use was that? Then she had an idea. She opened the screwdriver in the knife and unscrewed the metal bar on the wall, turning and turning until all the screws were out. The bar was in her hand in a few minutes. It wasn't a weapon, it wouldn't protect her, but she somehow felt less vulnerable. Now she just had to muster up the courage to open the door and sneak out before it got dark. But she stayed sitting on the rim of the toilet bowl.

Then she heard footsteps. Very clearly. They were coming nearer.

Somebody came into the washroom, slammed a toilet door, locked it. Human sounds. Sonya listened as if in a dream.

After there was a flush, she shot out of her prison.

"Help me, please! There's a bear outside!" Sonya gasped.

The young woman wore a colorful headband. She looked surprised.

"Did you see it?"

"Yes, it was very close. I ran into the washroom, and I didn't dare go out!"

Sonya didn't give a damn what the woman thought of her. She could have flung her arms around her neck in relief.

"Did you find that in there?" The woman stared at the bar in Sonya's hand.

"I had to have something to defend myself with, don't you see?"

The woman smiled as she washed her hands.

"Where are you from?"

"Switzerland."

"Well, well. Where I live there are lots of bears. I always carry something with me."

She pulled a rather long can out of her enormous jacket.

"It's pepper spray," she laughed. "I've never tried it. But you must get very close to the bear and shoot it in his eyes. Too close, for my liking."

She put the can back.

"I don't think the bear's still there," she assured Sonya. "My friend is waiting in the parking lot with our dog, Tucker. He would have barked long ago; he can smell a bear in a second. Would you like to have this spray?"

Sonya hesitated, then nodded.

They walked back to the parking lot together, and Sonya could see her red truck in the twilight. She'd never felt so much love for her truck. A mud-spattered jeep kept it company, and a long-haired man waited next to it, smoking. His sheepdog was sniffing around her truck.

Then another RV drove into the lot, two people got out, and Sonya couldn't believe her eyes.

She'd escaped from a bear. But not from Gerti and Helmut!

CHAPTER 31

A steaming plate of spaghetti was put in front of her. She didn't give a hoot about anything else. All she felt was a fierce, raw hunger.

"Dig in, my dear Sonya. It will give you strength."

Gerti refilled her wine glass. Sonya had made sure that her hosts were drinking out of the same wine bottle. Just in case.

"You must be hungry as a bear."

Helmut laughed at his silly joke. It was the first time Sonya heard him laugh so heartily.

Gerti finally pulled up a chair.

"Who'd have thought we'd see you again, right, Helmut? But it's a small world, I always say."

She heaped grated cheese on her spaghetti.

"And we've had to save your skin once again. Isn't that a scream!"

That triggered more guffaws from Helmut.

"Funny shooting iron, that, a weapon from the john, a 'bear killer,' right out of those old Karl May novels."

Sonya didn't recognize the author. But Helmut had done the wine justice, an excellent gewürztraminer.

How could Robert ever imagine that this couple—yes, a bit possessive, but warm-hearted—were up to no good! The reason the two of them showed up here of all places was simple: Prince George was on the way to Vancouver. Everyone had to come by there. But then she thought, weren't the two of them supposed to have returned to Vancouver long ago? She learned half an hour later what had held them up. They spelled out in detail all the stops on their tour: Nass Valley and the lava beds from early volcanic eruptions, the historic Indian village of 'Ksan, a visit at the Alaskan border, the Salmon Glacier near Hyder, colossal Babine Lake, and a flight over the mountains near Smithers.

Sonya listened, thinking to herself: *Nothing's going to scare me anymore. I'm alive. I've survived.* She didn't protest when Gerti and Helmut insisted she sleep in the bunk over their cab. She was too tipsy, too exhausted, too relieved. Just get to sleep and don't think about anything. A barking dog was the last thing she heard before falling asleep.

When she opened her eyes, she was lying on soft moss. Sunlight filtered through the firs standing around her bed like mighty pillars. She looked around, confused. Squirrels on the branches uttered sharp calls. Where was she? Nothing but thickets and tall trees surrounded her. She leaped to her feet. Woods, just deep woods. She made her way through the undergrowth. Fir branches hit her in the face. Spider webs stuck to her eyes. She climbed up embankments, waded through swamps, crossed streams, balanced along rotten tree trunks lying on the ground. She was encased by swarms of gnats. Her inner compass drove her on westward, faster and faster, farther and farther.

What was that? A dog barking! But her hunger and thirst were stronger. A house. People. She walked into a clearing, into a meadow in front of a log cabin. A woman was hanging up the washing. She would save her, most certainly. But the woman ran screaming into the house at the sight of her. She stopped, shaken. What was the matter? A man came through the door. He was holding a gun in his hand. She looked down at herself. Saw her brown, shaggy coat. Paws. Long pointed claws.

No, no, she tried to shout, I'm not a bear, I'm—But the bullet hit her, exploding in her body.

Sonya awoke with a start and hit her head on the ceiling. Two figures were standing like guilty poodles in the camper kitchen.

"Now we've gone and woken you," Gerti apologized. "I'm sorry—it's because the john door slammed shut."

Helmut said nothing. They were both dressed and all cleaned up.

Before Sonya could say a word, Gerti motioned with her hands.

"You don't have to get up this instant; we'll go for our morning walk, and you can shower in peace and quiet." She pointed to a milky pane of glass behind her. "When we're back—how long will we be, Helmut, an hour? Then we'll have a very hearty breakfast with all the trimmings."

She waved and scooted off outside with Helmut in tow.

Sonya sank back into the mattress. So here she was, with Gerti and Helmut in their RV. Of all things. A curious bear had turned up, and she had thrown all caution to the winds, looking for protection like a chick under a mother hen's feathers.

She looked out the slit window above the pillows. Her truck was nowhere in sight. It was on the other side; she'd locked it up securely as always. She reached under her pillow and looked in her shirt's breast pocket for her passport and car keys. All there. No cause for alarm. She slid off the bunk and slipped into the shower. When she opened the RV door, she felt a cool, damp breeze. She could climb into her truck and drive away. Gerti and Helmut wouldn't be able to catch up, not with this monster of an RV. If there was anything to Robert's warning, then she had to seize the opportunity and shake them off.

Then she saw the orange tarp. Somebody had placed a plastic tarp over the front of her truck and weighed it down with stones. Someone wanting to keep fir needles and leaves off her truck, although the leaves bedecked the tarp. She knew she owed it to Gerti and Helmut's thoughtfulness. It was a tarp just like the one on the RV's windshield.

An SUV turned into the parking lot. Two men in uniform got out, and one came up to her.

"Hi, I'm the game warden. Are you the lady who saw a bear yesterday?"

"Yes, yesterday evening. It was over there." She pointed to the trees.

"A little too close," the man exclaimed, screwing up his face. "Anything happen?"

Sonya shook her head.

"We'll catch it and release it in the wild."

He pointed to an oversize barrel in the back of the SUV.

"Two people are taking a walk in the woods. Tourists," Sonya offered.

"When are they coming back?"

"About twenty minutes."

"We'll be here till then. Let us know if there are any problems."

They started to unload the barrel.

Gerti and Helmut were right on schedule, and Helmut whipped out his camera when he saw the bear trap. The two good-natured game wardens posed for him.

"Oh, the bear. We'd completely forgotten about it!" Gerti exclaimed. "But you can't always think the worst."

For breakfast Gerti toasted some crusty Swiss bread in the little RV oven; she'd bought it in a Swiss bakery in Smithers. Sonya just couldn't be angry with Gerti, not even when Gerti constantly interrogated her.

"When are you going back to Switzerland?" she asked.

"My flight's on September the twentieth." Sonya didn't say that she was toying with the idea of staying longer.

"And what are your plans until then?"

"I'm going to the archives at the University of Victoria. And maybe I'll take in a whale-watching trip. I've always wanted to see whales."

She wanted to change the subject, but there was no sidetracking Gerti.

"That's a good idea. We know a fabulous B and B in Victoria. When will you be there?"

"I've already got a room, right on campus. It's really just practical."

Gerti and Helmut's exchange of glances didn't escape her.

"You academics, you've got your international contacts, don't you? When do you get to Victoria?"

A loud chirping made them all jump: Sonya's cell phone.

"Hi, it's Diane."

"Diane! I—"

"Sonya, I'm calling from a long way away. I'm up north. I won't be back for a week. But you can still stay at my place. The super has my key. Give him a call before you get there. Have you something to write with?"

Sonya looked around. Helmut was in between her and her backpack, but Gerti immediately guessed what she needed and pushed over the blackboard and chalk they used for playing cards.

Sonya wrote down the phone number and a name.

"Diane, will we still see each other?" Sonya knew that her voice almost sounded desperate.

"For sure. I'll be back in time. Has everything gone well?"

"Yes, everything's fine. Thank you. I'm very glad—"

"Don't mention it. Hey, I gotta go. See ya."

Sonya put her cell phone away and saw that Gerti was looking at her expectantly.

"A friend in Vancouver," she explained. "I'm meeting her tomorrow. So I must get going right away." She smiled an excuse. "It was nice seeing you again."

"Yes, it's been a fantastic coincidence," Gerti exclaimed. "When I tell them back home, not a soul will believe us, right, Helmut?"

"For sure," her husband affirmed.

Sonya left shortly afterward and felt a bit wistful. There were two sandwiches in her backpack that Gerti had made.

By the afternoon, the lumberjack city of Prince George lay far behind her. Then the realization hit her that she hadn't erased the telephone number on the blackboard.

CHAPTER 32

It was evening by the time she got to Diane's apartment. She could hardly believe that she'd gone off on that trip and was back. It felt a bit like a homecoming. Her heart beat faster as she rang the super's bell; she had let him know she was coming. The super welcomed her like an old friend. Sonya almost had tears in her eyes from gratitude.

It smelled of flowers in Diane's apartment; a large bouquet on the dining room table bade her welcome. A few lines on some stationery lay beside it:

The fridge is full, so help yourself to anything including wine and vodka. I don't exactly know when I'll be back, but I'll call.

PS The name of the man who took the Swiss lady to my party is Vince. Give him a call.

And there was a phone number. So Diane hadn't forgotten Sonya's question. A wave of warmth came over her. She'd met so many friendly people on this trip! Including Diane, who let her have her apartment in complete confidence, bought her flowers, and stuffed the fridge. As a thank-you for all this, she was expected to mislead Diane to keep the immigration authorities in the dark. What crap! Not even Inge knew Sonya's real intentions.

Sonya fetched her bag from the car, heated up a can of soup, and took a hot bubble bath. But she couldn't simply "wash off" those recent events as if they were sweat on her skin. Robert's words popped into her head.

Jack Gordon is dead. Like a bolt of lightning. *Jack Gordon is dead.*

It was her last thought before she dropped off to sleep and her first when she woke up in the morning.

After her first cup of coffee, she called Vince's number. A sleepy voice came to the phone, and it dawned on her that it was Sunday. She stammered an apology.

"No problem," he responded. "I'll make some coffee, OK?"

Sonya laid out for him what she wanted to know. How well did he know the Swiss lady he escorted to Diane's party? Vince had no trouble remembering her.

"I met Yvonne in the Opus Hotel bar in Yaletown. Pretty as a picture, that Yvonne. Are all Swiss women that pretty?"

"Naturally," Sonya parried. "Did she have short hair?"

"No. She had long blonde curls."

There was no way that could have been Odette, unless . . . unless she was wearing a wig.

"Was she by herself?"

"She came to Vancouver alone, but then we hooked up."

"How long did she stay?"

"About a week, maybe ten days. Then she got to know another Swiss woman. They wanted to do the Inside Passage together, so I had to say so long, beautiful Yvonne! She left me brokenhearted."

The Inside Passage. He had no idea how valuable this information was. He chatted on through the drinking noises.

"I always wanted to see her in Switzerland but was too busy. We don't have as much vacation as you Swiss people. Yvonne had six weeks' holiday fully paid. What decadence! You can count yourselves lucky that—"

"Do you have her address? Her phone number, e-mail?"

"Yes, I think so, let me take a look . . . one second . . . Here she is, Yvonne Berger."

Sonya wrote down the number.

"And you? Are you here on vacation?

"I'm here on business. But many thanks for your help."

"Well, then, good luck—and give that Swiss lady my best."

Sonya didn't waste any time and immediately called up Yvonne Berger.

A woman's voice answered.

"Hello?"

"My name's Sonya Werner. I—"

"What's your name?"

"Sonya Werner."

"Sonya Werner? I can't believe it!"

"I beg your pardon?"

"How'd you find me?"

The voice was noticeably amazed.

Sonya hesitated. Should she give Vince away? The woman spoke again.

"You got my number from Odette, right? Odette told you?"

It took Sonya's breath away. The woman knew Odette!

"I knew all the time that she thought it was completely wrong."

"Excuse me, but I don't follow. What did Odette think was wrong?"

"That business about your name. I'm sorry, it just popped into my mind. I didn't mean to cause any trouble."

Sonya tried to hide her excitement.

"How did it happen?" she asked guardedly.

"It was off the top of my head. Odette had a book with a lot of photos and things, and your name was in the front. That's how I came across it. It was all because of Vince."

A book with Sonya's name in it! Sonya needed to sit down.

"Why because of Vince?"

"I met him in Vancouver. He followed me everywhere and didn't leave me alone. When I told him I was leaving, he wanted to come along so bad. He was like a leech. He was a sweet guy, but he stuck like glue. That's why I booked the ferry in your name, so he couldn't find out what ferry I was on. I knew this would catch up with me someday."

"The ferry from Port Hardy to Prince Rupert?"

"Yes, exactly. And then—"

"How did you meet Odette?"

"Odette? On the plane. We sat next to each other, and she was terribly scared."

"Scared? What for?"

"She was scared of flying, of course. Her face was all green— really, I'm not exaggerating. And she'd taken pills beforehand."

Odette afraid of flying! She'd never uttered a peep about it— but they'd never flown together.

"She was so sick," Yvonne went on. "She asked to hold my hand and clung to it like a lifesaver. I kept up a stream of mindless chatter to distract her. We prevented everybody around us from sleeping. Jesus, was that a crazy flight!"

"But why did you both take the Port Hardy ferry?"

"Odette put the idea into my head. She'd invited me out for a meal in Vancouver, you see." She interrupted herself. "Are you a relative?"

"No, I'm a friend."

"I thought so. That's why Odette dragged that album around with your name in it."

The mention of the album gave Sonya a jolt.

"So you had lunch in Vancouver," she said impatiently.

"Yes, at her invitation, in gratitude, so to speak, for being a lifesaver. That's when she told me about the Inside Passage, how beautiful the ferry ride was to . . . What's that city again?"

"Prince Rupert."

"Yeah, right, and I said right off the bat, 'Hey, that's for me, too.'"

"Did she say anything about her plans in Canada?"

"Her plans? How do you mean? You'd best ask Odette yourself. We didn't get along very well after that. She probably told you I was a fraud. But it was just my dumb idea. Nothing more. It was a stupid thing to do."

"I won't hold it against you," Sonya added hastily. "All I want to know is what happened, exactly."

"I really shouldn't have told you all this, but that's me. Don't give any of this a thought."

"So Odette found out you used my name because you told her?"

"Yes, but that's when we met for a second time. We went shopping in the Granville Island Market. She called herself Antoinette the whole time, but I knew her name was Odette. I saw it on the card, you know, the customs card you have to fill out on the plane. So I saw her name was Odette and not Antoinette."

"How did she react when you questioned her?"

"She was evasive. She claimed that Odette was short for Antoinette, but of course I didn't buy that. I told her it's not a crime to use a different name, and then I admitted I took the ferry under your name because of Vince. Wowee! Did she ever hit the roof!"

"She got mad?"

"And how! She made all sorts of accusations. After that, things were pretty tense. But I remember the whole affair even today. I hope you won't hold it against me."

Sonya heard a voice in the background.

"I've gotta run," Yvonne said, "but one thing I'd like to know. Why didn't Odette tell you about the name business? It's been years since then, at least three."

"We've lost sight of each other for a long time."

"I hope you've got no hard feelings. I'm really sorry for her."

"It's OK," Sonya replied. "I appreciate your frankness. That book—that album—it had an orange binding, didn't it? The book with my name in it?"

"Yes, that's very likely. She always carried it around with her, on the plane, at meals, everywhere."

"Thank you, thank you so much," Sonya said, and then she said good-bye.

CHAPTER 33

Sonya went through the apartment and out to the patio as if in a trance. A dull roar flowed toward her from the nearby bridge. Gull screams ripped through the fresh, salty morning air. Sonya was on fire inside.

The one thing on her mind was that orange book. Odette had carried it with her. Yvonne Berger's words still echoed in her ears. She always carried it around with her.

Sonya had an orange-colored book as well, with Odette's name in the front. It was gathering dust somewhere in the attic; she hadn't looked at it for years. But Odette took hers on her fateful trip to Canada. Why?

The book was their friendship pact. When they had been blood sisters at fifteen years old. For a whole year they'd filled the album with mementos of their youthful euphoria. Sonya pasted inspirational pictures and wrote thoughts on them. She entered quotations, sketched a dream dress for Odette to wear in an imaginary film, made a list ranking her favorite songs, and utilized her newly acquired knowledge of French to compose a poetic motto for Odette borrowed from the French singer Juliette Gréco: *belle se rebelle.*

And time and again a note: *Dear Odette . . .*

After a year, they exchanged albums. Odette had sketched a lot. Writing wasn't her forte, but she could draw: a lot of comics and mood pictures and portraits as well. She'd glued in little mementos: pressed flowers and leaves, newspaper clippings, horoscopes, movie tickets, train and bus tickets, even a mosaic of colored bits of yarn.

In later years Sonya recalled that enthusiastic phase with amusement and some embarrassment. And then came a time when she totally forgot the orange book.

But Odette didn't. She had it with her in Vancouver.

Why did she meet up with Yvonne anyway? Were those the hours that Tonio was spending with Nicky? Was Odette hiding from Nicky? Where was Nicky when they were fooling around? Why did Odette call herself Antoinette? An allusion to Tonio? Or to cover her tracks? Sonya couldn't make head or tail of it.

At least she knew now that it was Yvonne Berger who booked that ferry as Sonya Werner. And now she knew for certain that Odette was in Vancouver three years ago. Same time as Tonio and Nicky.

But there were loads of unanswered questions.

It was time to track down Kathrin, who worked in the emergency room of a Vancouver hospital—Sonya's sole clue. Kathrin had mentioned the name of the hospital where she worked only once. To Sonya's ears, it sounded like *Zurich*. The first letter surely wasn't *Z*, but maybe an *S*. In the phonebook, she went down the hospital listings and came across Surrey Memorial Hospital. Her heart leaped.

She dialed the number and asked for Kathrin in Emergency.

"Kathrin Ritter?" a voice asked.

"Yes," Sonya confirmed, hoping it was the right person.

"Is it urgent? We don't put through personal calls during working hours."

Sonya replied quick as a flash.

"When's her shift over? I'm a friend and would like to pick her up."

"Just a second . . . She gets off at one p.m. Can I leave her a message?"

"Yes, please. Tell her that Sonya from Switzerland called."

After hanging up, her decision was a foregone conclusion. She spread out a map of Vancouver and found the suburb of Surrey in the southeast. She noted how to get there and was off. She was at the Surrey Memorial Hospital an hour and a half later. The reception desk informed her that Kathrin Ritter would be out right away.

"How did you know where I was?" Kathrin asked.

It happened that they were both hungry, so they went for a quick meal nearby.

"I should have given you my number in Kitkatla." She handed Sonya her card. "What have you been up to all this time?"

Sonya was happy that she had an immediate excuse to talk about the Queen Charlottes and her visit to the community nurse.

"That would have been Brenda," Kathrin acknowledged. She described a woman exactly matching the person who'd mentioned the injured Swiss woman. Brenda had told Sonya that Kathrin knew more about it.

"She said that? That's a surprise." Kathrin scrunched up the empty sugar packet between her fingers. "You know, I'm not supposed to talk about patients."

"I don't need medical details. But I might know the woman. She might be an old friend I've lost contact with."

Kathrin hesitated. "I . . . It was like this . . . The police told me at the time that I wasn't to breathe a word. Let's say there was something about this case . . . an exceptional situation. I don't want to put my job on the line, you understand."

"Yes, I do. But there must be people who know about it."

Sonya told her about the text message on her cell phone. *That Swiss woman nearly died. Info at the VGH.*

Kathrin raised an eyebrow.

"I can't imagine who that could be, but I can confirm this much for you—don't tell who you got it from—that the patient was transferred to the VGH."

"What's the VGH?"

"The Vancouver General Hospital. I doubt whether they'll give you any information there. A patient's privacy is protected by law here."

Sonya sighed. She always seemed so close to her goal and then banged up against a wall. But she wasn't giving up yet.

"Did the case cause a sensation? I mean, was it in the papers?"

Kathrin shrugged. "I don't know. It was at the end of my stay in Kitkatla. I usually go for two, three weeks. I'd be surprised if the police released the woman's identity. After all, it was hush-hush."

Sonya stirred her tea. It was cold, and she was lost in thought. She'd just nibbled away at half her tuna fish sandwich. Maybe she could dig something up anyway. If the accident was that bad, the news must have spread like wildfire. Or had everyone been muzzled?

Not everybody. Not the person who sent the text message.

Kathrin snapped her out of her meditation.

"This woman . . . she's very important to you, eh?"

"Ye-e-e-s," Sonya said slowly, her stomach suddenly cramping painfully. "Yes. She's the key to a tragedy in my life."

Kathrin looked at her with empathy, in silence.

"But I'm not blaming you at all," Sonya assured her. "I understand."

"I'm sorry not to be able to help, I—"

She stood up quickly. Sonya sensed she was about to say something. She rose to her feet, and Kathrin gave her a hug.

"I wish you all the best, and . . . sometimes a door opens up all of a sudden, believe me."

She said it so empathically that Sonya drove back to Vancouver with newly awakened hopes.

At the entrance of Diane's apartment building, a figure emerged from a row of parked cars. She gave a start.

"My God, you gave me a fright!"

"Don't I do that all the time?" Robert Stanford said with a wink.

CHAPTER 34

"I don't know what to make of you," Sonya said, though she had to admit that her assessment came very late in the game. Robert had taken her to an Indian restaurant. *You're a troublemaker, an indecipherable, web-weaving spider. I'm not going to get entangled in your web.* Sonya kept these thoughts to herself, scrutinizing him with knitted eyebrows.

"How can you get to know me if you keep avoiding me?"

His voice was gentle, his eyes steadily fastened on her. She turned away from his attractive face, which she almost touched spontaneously in a moment of tenderness on a Haida Gwaii beach.

"Sometimes you have to take a chance even if there might be a catastrophe, don't you think?"

Catastrophe? What was he talking about?

He rolled his linen napkin from one hand to the other. Sonya followed his movements as if hypnotized.

"You're so close. Don't throw in the towel. Be persistent."

"*You're* telling me that? I've had the impression all along that you wanted to keep me from getting to the bottom of it."

The waiter came to take their order. Robert helped Sonya choose from the many unfamiliar dishes. Then they fell silent.

Robert spoke up first; it was clear that he'd been waiting for this moment.

"I think I ought to tell you about myself, then you might understand me better. I was born in South Africa, in Cape Town, but I wasn't there long. My father was a mining engineer, like me. He worked all over the world: in Africa, Northern Europe, Asia, America, Canada. He was always on the move. It wasn't easy for us children or for my mother. She had three girls and two boys; I was the second youngest. I think we moved about fourteen times during my childhood and teens."

She saw this was a struggle for him. Apparently, he didn't find it easy to get intimate confessions out.

"We couldn't settle down anywhere, and I didn't want to when I grew older so that unavoidable farewells wouldn't be difficult. My parents' marriage ultimately fell apart, but interestingly enough, not because my father was away so much. It was because he retired. I believe my mother couldn't stand being with him all the time. She didn't want somebody butting in when she was planning her day."

"And you became a mining engineer as well," Sonya remarked.

He laughed.

"Right. It was something I knew and was familiar with. I was already down in the mines with my father when I was allowed to as a kid. I loved being with him."

Robert had a faraway look in his eye.

Sonya straightened out her napkin on her knees and picked up the thread of the conversation.

"My family moved just once," she said. "I think I was a year old. We always lived in the same town. But I longed to go abroad very early. An uncle left us his diary and photos of his months-long trek across Australia. That fired my imagination. It was a revelation for me to know a world existed beyond the high Swiss mountains. A place that was vast and boundless."

The waiter covered their table with plates and steaming bowls. Sonya took in the exotic aromas. At this moment she made peace with her decision to accept Robert's invitation.

"Have you traveled a lot?" he inquired, passing her a bowl. "That's spinach in coconut sauce."

"A little, but not as often as I'd have liked."

She'd never gone with Tonio on his expeditions to North America, Asia, and Africa. Why hadn't she insisted just once on traveling together without climbing a high mountain in record time, taming white-water rapids, or making a forced march— without the eternal pressure to achieve that Tonio always gave in to.

Sonya was always afraid it would bore him to, say, go up to an alpine meadow for a glass of fresh goat's milk in an alpine hut. Or simply to listen to the birds in the morning. He was always on the go out of fear that life was too short. His biological clock was ticking against him.

Robert broke into her thoughts.

"But now the travel bug's got you; it's unmistakable. You've acquired a taste for adventure."

"Someone with a taste for adventure? Is that how you really see me?"

"Sonya, how could I not see you that way! You've got a certain curiosity, a glint in your eye. You've acquired a taste for it. It's a disease that's difficult to heal, I can assure you."

She saw the roguishness in the deep corners of his mouth.

"Another bull's-eye, Mr. Soothsayer. I must confess I'd like to take a trip to a place unknown, just for the sheer pleasure of it. Just to see what happens when you don't make any plans."

"In my experience, the unexpected happens whether you make plans or not. We rarely have events under control, don't you think?"

She gave him a questioning glance. Where was he going with this? She stabbed a bite of tandoori chicken with her fork, taking her time responding.

"Perhaps . . . That might well be. Things elude you more often than you expect."

"Isn't that the attraction?"

"It's not always attractive. I mean . . . always chasing something. Of course, you, a mining engineer, want to find gold, or whatever. But is the search an end in itself? Is the hunt the only point?"

He smiled.

"You're doing a pretty good job of figuring me out. But you know, I'm only indirectly involved in a hunt. I just analyze whether a mine's worth exploiting, what machinery's needed, mostly what the whole thing costs."

"Have you ever actually discovered any mineral deposits?"

"No, that's for prospectors and geologists. They're the hunters, not me. Maybe some people are driven; that's my impression, at any rate. Or else they wouldn't put up with all those years of hardship—the crap, the cold, the disappointment. People like Chuck Fipke simply can't stop exploring. He could have retired after he found those diamonds. He's so rich he doesn't have to turn over a single rock ever again. But I've heard he's at it again, somewhere in Africa." Robert put some rice on his plate. "Your take on my job may be too romantic. I don't get into the game until the treasure's been found."

"Who's in on these secrets?"

"You mean after something's been found?"

Sonya nodded.

"The geologists send rock samples to the lab. The results come back and you must keep them under lock and key. Nothing must leak out until the business partners and the stock market are informed. That's always enormously nerve-racking. More rice?"

They ate in silence for a while, Robert as deep in thought as Sonya.

"And when will I become privy to the secret?" she asked unexpectedly.

He looked surprised, but then he understood.

"In about a week."

"Can you tell if I'm in any danger until then?"

"Not if you stay in Vancouver."

She nearly dropped her fork.

"What do you mean?"

Robert took her hand and gave it a quick squeeze.

"Please trust me, Sonya."

"Tell me, what happened to Jack Gordon?"

"He wasn't careful."

"What's that supposed to mean? Not careful how?"

"That's what the police are investigating."

"How was he . . . What happened to him?"

She didn't dare utter the word *murdered*.

"He was found in his boat, choked to death." Robert turned monosyllabic all of a sudden.

"What—choked to death?" Sonya wouldn't be put off so easily.

"With a rope."

She couldn't visualize it.

"Was he lying in the boat?"

"No, he was half in the water."

Sonya struck a bullying attitude, as if that would make him more talkative.

"When did it happen?"

"Probably late in the evening. It might have also been an accident; the police are investigating. Maybe he was drunk and got tangled up in the rope and strangled himself."

"One more weird accident in this neck of the woods, don't you think?"

The waiter brought chai tea, and Robert looked grateful for the interruption.

"Hot and sweet, just the way I like it." He poked his nose into the steam rising from the cup. "The tea will do us good after this feast."

"It can burn you sometimes," Sonya said. "What about that?"

He studied her with an inscrutable look, as if trying to look into her soul.

"You're one stubborn lady, Sonya. You know, as I do, that there are things you have to do, no matter what the consequences. You have to do them so life goes on. Sometimes you simply have to go for it and see that you don't get destroyed doing it." He took a careful sip of the tea and closed his eyes for a second. "Not really hot enough, but nice and sweet." He grinned, but turned serious right away. "You almost never get destroyed, believe me. You usually win."

"I'm afraid." It just slipped out.

This time he grabbed her wrist so that it almost hurt.

"Good," he declared. "Good. Keep that fear like a talisman. It'll protect you."

She took back her hand. "I'm afraid because I don't know anything, understand? Because nobody tells me anything."

"You already know a lot, Sonya, believe me. It's all a matter of time. But that's critical at this moment. We just need more time."

She was about to tell him that her stay in Canada was slowly winding down, but he didn't stop talking.

"Sonya, you must absolutely take a trip in a kayak while you're in Canada. We could paddle together to Twin Islands. It'll be sunny tomorrow. You won't regret it—it's fantastic. When can I pick you up?"

There was an imploring note to his words. Sonya wavered. The Else Seel archive wasn't open until Monday, and she was leaving on Sunday. That gave her an extra two days in Vancouver.

She wavered again. He knew all too well that her resistance was for naught. All those experiences she'd denied herself for so long, and here was this man telling her: You can do it, Sonya. Let's do it together. But who was he, really? A redeeming thought popped into her head: no matter what happened, she'd be back in Switzerland in ten days. At home. Safe. But now she was here, in another country, living more intensely than she had for God knows how long. It was . . . what was it? Surely she wasn't on adrenaline. Was it the celebrated thrill, the blood rush that was the feeling of freedom?

"Is ten early enough?" she offered.

He stuck his thumb in the air, as if they'd just made a deal.

Sonya was in her bedroom when she noticed that the notebook where she recorded everything on her trip was missing. She looked in her backpack, in her half-unpacked suitcase, in the kitchen, on the living room table, in the bathroom. Nothing. She returned to the bedroom. Maybe she'd stuck it in the night-table drawer from force of habit, though she had no recollection of it.

She opened the drawer. Something was indeed in there, but not a notebook. A piece of paper, folded twice.

Was it the e-mail she'd printed out in the Internet café that afternoon from an anonymous sender linking her to the home page of an animal rights group? It was evidently part of a campaign against shooting grizzlies. Walt immediately came to mind, the proprietor of Fisherman's Lodge. Maybe he thought she'd be interested because she'd quizzed him so much about bears during her stay. It was the only explanation that seemed to fit. She'd hit "Reply" and asked the sender to keep her e-mail address confidential. She didn't like it when data was passed around without her permission.

Lost in thought, she unfolded the sheet, which wasn't a copy of Walt's e-mail. The headline that hit her wasn't about grizzlies at all. It was a newspaper article, or rather a copy of one that included a photo. An all too familiar face. Only much younger. Surely it wasn't a coincidence that it was in this drawer.

Her hands trembled. How in the world did this article get here?

CHAPTER 35

Sonya's nerves were stretched to the breaking point. Fortunately, Robert couldn't see that because he was stowing their backpacks in a hollow space in their kayak. He couldn't see all that much of her anyway: her upper body was encased in some armor popularly called a "life jacket," and a heavy oval rubber skirt was around her hips. She wore the inevitable baseball cap and waterproof shoes. Sonya felt like a duck—absurd. But Robert was in high spirits and held out his hand.

"C'mon. I'll help you get in."

She teetered into the water, and he showed her how to bend the paddle between the kayak and the sea bottom for support. She slipped awkwardly into the hatch, and it seemed to take forever to fasten the rubber skirt over the opening. Robert held the kayak patiently all the while. Then he got into the hatch behind her. They floated leisurely out of the bay. They were in Deep Cove, a coastal town near Vancouver. Their paddles poked into the water.

With each stroke the kayak shot as lightly as a fish through the water. A soft gurgling and hissing came from around the kayak's yellow synthetic hull. Sonya's nervousness melted away in the warm autumn sun. Much to her surprise, she felt weightless, at one with the kayak. The water was so clear that she could see pink starfish swimming up. A sudden feeling of happiness filled her. Robert waited a while before breaking the silence that enveloped them both.

"How's it feel?"

"Magnificent," she shouted ahead into the strait that was surrounded by mountains.

They glided along the coast, past houses only accessible by boat. Bald eagles circled high in the sky, as light as a feather. Sonya paused now and then to relax and take in the surroundings. A zigzagging round dot immediately captured her attention.

"Robert, over there!" she shouted.

A seal ogled them, curious. After a while, it coiled up like a spring and dove. Sonya hoped it would come back, but a motorboat was approaching and making waves. She felt vulnerable in the kayak, though Robert had assured her it was difficult for a two-seater kayak to capsize. She was about to ask if he thought they would collide, when the motorboat suddenly turned away. As it zoomed past, she saw the man at the wheel. He looked familiar somehow, but she couldn't place him.

She tried to look at Robert, but it wasn't easy in her position.

"Still liking it?" he shouted forward.

"Yes, very much," she replied.

Twin Islands came up much faster than she'd anticipated; the islands were covered with bushes and trees. Robert expertly steered the kayak through the rocks, guiding them to a sandy spot on shore. They got out and climbed up a rocky hill, choosing a sunny stone slab to rest on. Robert piled up plastic containers and little packages beside her: smoked salmon sandwiches, sushi, potato salad, fruit, and muffins. Sonya was astounded.

"Where did you ever dig up these delicacies?"

"Dig up? You're asking a mining engineer that question? Out of the ground, naturally." He gave her a wink. "It's Canada, after all. I just had to poke around a little."

She laughed. "Since when does sushi grow in the ground?"

"They're like truffles in France, didn't you know?"

She savored her smoked salmon.

"Do you need a pig to sniff them out as well?"

"What are you thinking! I can smell deposits half a mile away."

He stuck his nose in the air defiantly.

"And now I can smell a special treasure. It looks like a pearl, shining bright and perfectly formed. You need kid gloves to handle it."

She made a face.

"I think you're smelling a boiled egg."

Robert chastised her with a look.

"Eggs don't smell like exotic wildflowers."

"Ah!" Sonya took off her baseball cap, running her hand through her hair. "You're smelling my new body lotion. You're not a very good treasure hunter."

"You're wrong, Sonya, big time." He pulled a bottle of wine out of his backpack.

"Pinot Grigio from a Canadian winery."

"Wine! What a wonderful idea! But isn't drinking alcohol on a public beach prohibited in Canada?"

Robert passed her a paper cup.

"This wine is well camouflaged. And anyway, it is also prohibited for cultured European ladies to refuse Canadian wine."

She took the cup in her hand, undecided. Robert saw her hesitation; then he gave her a mischievous look.

"Shall I go first? Would that reassure you?"

She was caught. But she had no intention of apologizing. He should know better than anyone that she had every reason to be wary. Robert filled his cup.

"I raise a glass to this wonderful day and to the wonderful lady I am allowed to share it with."

He took a swig, licking his lips.

"I'm more a fan of South African wine, but Canadians are catching up, I must say."

Sonya sipped her wine and smacked her lips.

"Mmmm."

Robert grinned. "Thank you for your judicious and balanced opinion, and from a historian."

He dipped a piece of sushi in soy sauce. Sonya stared dreamily at the waves rocking the seaweed. That's exactly how languid she felt. She laid her head on her rolled-up Windbreaker and stretched her limbs. Only the lapping of the water and the distant hum of a generator reached her ears. Robert lay down, too. His body's proximity distracted her. It was indescribably exciting. So much so that she had to break the silence.

"Robert, do you actually know Diane Kesowsky?"

"Why do you ask?"

It was the wrong answer. She sat up.

"You know I'm trying to piece a puzzle together."

"Ah." He kept his eyes closed.

"I looked her up on the Internet. I saw she was looking for diamonds and that an Australian company beat her to it. She took them to court, and now she's exploring for diamonds again. I didn't know all that."

Robert sat up.

"Is she a friend of yours?"

"She's a distant cousin of somebody I work with. But Diane never told me about . . . about her discovery."

Robert's eyes were directed steadily at the water.

"Diane Kesowsky is a well-known figure in our business, first, because she's an excellent geologist, and second . . . there aren't many women in the industry; mining has always been male dominated."

He filched a piece of carrot from a container.

"The diamond industry is a small group of people. Everybody knows everybody. Or at least you think you know them. But that's all changing."

"Why?"

"It's not enough just to find a diamond. That's only the beginning. You've got to construct a mine and the whole infrastructure along with it; you need to pay experts. That costs lots and lots of money. Extraction is very expensive, particularly in the Canadian North. It's terribly cold up there. It gets down to forty below, the ground freezes, and long columns of trucks have to travel over a road made of ice."

"An ice road?"

"It's an ice road that forms in winter. In summer it's all lakes and muskeg and impassable."

"And where does all the money come from?"

"Mainly from big companies. They've got the requisite finances. Small exploration companies can't get enough capital together. Unless . . ." He hesitated. "Unless you look for money from murky sources, from backers who'd rather stay invisible but are keen to make money."

She looked askance at him.

"Has this something to do with Diane?"

Robert stood up.

"There's always a lot of rumors in my line of business, but I've never been a part of it. You should ask your friend directly."

He sounded almost gruff. The two of them packed their things in silence. A shadow had fallen on their delightful day. They walked back to the kayak, and Robert waded into the water, offering his hand as she climbed in. Sonya was about to take it, but she stumbled and lost her balance. Before she knew it, she'd plopped rather clumsily into the water.

Robert quickly got his strong arms under hers and lifted her up. Gasping for breath, she leaned on him with her full weight. He drew her toward him and held her for a second. Her face rested on his shoulder. She felt him briefly press his head to hers. Before she could begin to think straight, she heard the soft buzz of a cell phone in his breast pocket. She disengaged herself.

"Did you hurt yourself?" he asked. His eyes, his lips, were very close. She shook her head in a daze. He was holding her gently by her hips.

"Sit down for a second. I'll be right back."

He went off, and Sonya heard him talking. She waited with shivering limbs. Her pants were soaked; her feet were swimming in her waterproof shoes; her baseball cap was in the water. When she got up to fish it out, her shoes squeaked, and the sound made her laugh. She put the skirt on, climbing into the kayak using the paddle.

Robert came on the run.

"Are you running away from me? Did I scare you so much?"

Sonya looked up at him, managing a smile.

He fastened her rubber skirt, touching her a number of times as he did so. She sat very still and let it happen. Then he slowly maneuvered the kayak around the islands and out into the inlet, where they encountered a fresh, oncoming breeze. Sonya paddled strongly to keep warm, her damp hands rubbing a little on the shaft with every move.

They found their rhythm, and the kayak raced over the water.

"Everything OK?" Robert bellowed from the rear.

Sonya was about to say she was getting blisters on her palms when she saw a large motorboat coming straight at them.

"He'll see us, won't he?" Sonya shouted.

Robert didn't answer. He stopped paddling.

Then he shouted, "Sonya, undo your rubber skirt!"

"What?" She didn't understand him.

"Undo the skirt from the kayak, fast!"

His voice wouldn't stand for any delay. Sonya did as she was told, desperately holding on to the paddle with one hand. The boat was heading straight at them.

"What's that damn idiot doing!" Robert shouted, paddling frantically.

The boat still was heading straight for their kayak. Sonya looked around. To her horror she saw a boat heading toward them from the opposite side. Then she heard a loud, piercing ship's horn blaring over the water like a siren. The kayak rocked dangerously in the high wake from the boats. Robert was making for shore, where some boats were moored in front of a house. Sonya's hands hurt, and her arms and shoulders, but she kept paddling, staring at the approaching house.

A woman ran along the dock.

"I saw everything from my living room," she shouted, gasping for breath. "Those idiots and their expensive boats run around at top speed endangering people's lives. It's a scandal!"

"May we stay here a little?" Robert said.

"Of course. Wait, I'll help you."

"Sonya, get out first; I can hold the boat steady."

She was so stiff she thought she'd never make it over the railing. But the woman, a strong fifty-year-old, grabbed her arms and pulled her up onto the planks. Then she bent down and held the kayak so Robert could swing himself up.

"Thanks a lot," he said. "You're an angel."

He put a hand on Sonya's shoulder. "You're completely soaked," he declared. "Is it possible for her to dry her clothes?"

"She'd better or she'll catch her death," the woman replied.

Robert squeezed Sonya's shoulder.

"You were magnificent. You did everything right. I'm very impressed."

"Come," the woman said before Sonya could answer. "You need a nice hot cup of tea after that shock."

Robert nodded for her to go.

"Go ahead, I'll be right along."

The woman took her up some wooden steps and into the house. In the living room she wrapped Sonya in a wool blanket and quickly brewed some herbal tea. Never had a drink tasted so wonderful! Sonya thanked her warmly.

"Your hospitality is a minor miracle."

Her hostess beamed in satisfaction.

"I'll fetch a few dry clothes, and then we'll pop your wet things in the dryer."

On the way out she ranted about the "rowdies" who made the waters around Deep Cove unsafe with their racing around. "They're just spoiled brats, with rich parents."

Sonya only half listened. Through the high front windows she could see Robert on his cell phone, pacing up and down the dock like a tiger in a cage. Then she saw a small motorboat approach the dock. Robert walked toward the boat, the driver hopped over the railing, and Robert welcomed him with a slap on the shoulder.

Sonya stood up to see better. The two men had their backs to her, but then the driver turned and looked up at the house.

Sonya gave a start. It was the person who'd whizzed past their kayak that morning, the man at the wheel she thought she'd seen before. And now she remembered where: the Granville Island Market, at the table with Diane! The man who turned in her wallet, and who might have made copies of her credit cards and her ID!

At that moment, her hostess came in with a bundle of clothes. She also noticed the two men on the dock.

"Is that someone you know?" she asked.

"Yes, an acquaintance," Sonya replied.

Soon after, Robert came into the room.

"Nothing beats a wool blanket; all that's missing is the camp-fire," he joked.

"I'll show you a room where you can change," her hostess said. "Hot tea's coming right up."

When a warm and dry Sonya left the house a half hour later, Robert looked at her, relieved.

"We're going back by motorboat," he declared.

Someone else, a stranger, was standing at the railing. She turned around, perplexed.

"Where's the other guy?" she asked. "I know him, he's a security guard."

Before Robert could respond, the boatman held out his hand.

"Hi, I'm Rick. Welcome aboard."

She looked at the men, puzzled. Had she made a mistake? Did she confuse this boatman with the stranger in the market?

"We can trust Rick," Robert said with a reassuring nod. "He's the most experienced sailor I know."

In the boat, Robert put a life jacket on her.

"Not that we'll need it again," he said.

She sat down in the lee at the stern. The house that so kindly took them in receded, and the yellow kayak with it, still on the dock. Then a man came out of the house. The security official! She suddenly realized he'd go to the kayak and fish out her waterproof bag from the stowage area, the bag she'd forgotten. He'd find the newspaper article in the bag: "Tragic Death of a Daring Mountain Climber in Canada," with the picture beneath the headline. A beaming bride was walking with Tonio through a gauntlet of skiers. But the bride was not Sonya.

CHAPTER 36

"Please put these on when you handle the pictures," the archivist requested quietly, handing Sonya a white pair of nylon gloves.

Sonya promised, peering past him at the dolly with cardboard boxes and file folders. It must be in there: Else Seel's secret. Eager with anticipation, she signed the admission form, looking at the archivist expectantly.

"What would you like to see?" he inquired.

"Photographs, poems, diaries, stories, letters, family documents." Sonya rattled off her list like a railway-station conductor announcing the timetable. The archivist—wearing cotton shorts as if it were the middle of summer—put one carton after another on the table.

"May I ask how you got interested in Else Seel? It's rare for anybody to come here for these, especially from abroad."

"As I said, she'll be part of an exhibition about women who emigrated alone." It took some effort to curb her impatience.

"But why her, of all people?"

Sonya weighed an answer that would best satisfy his curiosity. To her own surprise, she heard herself say, "Because she's like me somehow."

"Aha," the archivist acknowledged.

He didn't venture to ask any more questions, and she smiled at him in gratitude, sitting down at the heavily laden table. The room was gloomy; small windows let in some dim light. The archive was on the ground floor of a multistoried building at the University of Victoria, but Sonya wasn't interested in her surroundings. She immediately plunged into the volumes in front of her. The odor from the cardboard boxes was familiar: the smell of old paper and stale air. As she leafed through the documents with respectful fingers, everything dissipated from her—her exhaustion, her sadness, the faint pain around her heart. She could forget Robert and the security guy and her tense experience in Deep Cove. Her thoughts stopped racing back and forth like startled birds. Calm settled in, and intense concentration.

She put on her gloves and began with the photographs. Look at this! Else Lübcke, shortly before departing for Canada: a young woman in a dirndl on an alpine pasture; mountains were in the background, and her long hair was pinned up, combed away from her face. She sifted through the pile slowly. One much larger photo captivated her instantly. Else was standing barefoot on a rock jutting out of a mountain lake. Her white pants were hitched up high, a man's shirt was stuck in her waistband, and her hair was looped in a loose knot. Her face was partly turned away from the photographer, a hand braced casually on a hip; her eyes were on the water where the mountain peak was reflected.

In that luminous moment—Sonya could sense it—Else was at one with her environment, at one with nature. A moment of happiness and freedom for the young poet from Berlin. Water, mountains, stone, herself. Sonya saw a quiet ecstasy in that relaxed face, a feeling Else might have experienced only on her hikes.

Then there was a picture of Else and her husband at the bottom of the pile, dated 1942. Else was already forty-eight and now rather plump; George looked like a young, thin tree trunk next to her. No wonder she found him appealing, that guy George; Sonya could well understand why. Next she held a postcard that Else had written George shortly before she arrived in Vancouver, during her train trip across the continent. She wrote that she was having palpitations. And he shouldn't be shocked because she had her hair in a bob. She said nothing about her feelings. What must have gone through her head during those days before she met him? An unknown man, an unknown country, all bridges burned!

Sonya couldn't wait any longer. She reached for the little black notebook in front of her. Else's private, unpublished diary. The beginning. She opened it clumsily.

"You don't need gloves for that," the archivist said, passing her table. But she kept them on; her hands were moist. The first thing that struck her was the delicate, somewhat casual handwriting on the closely written pages. It crossed her mind that Else must have written whenever and wherever she could—and not always sitting comfortably at a table. She kept a diary for twenty-three years, and now Sonya read the first entries, written in Canada.

> . . . *the Great Unknown One, the day after tomorrow I shall see him—Georg. I took thoughts of him with me through the night—I could not sleep. The tension of my anxiety and hopes was unbearable. I burned as with a fever, my body was burning—who was it I was going to meet?*

Sonya dropped the notebook. She couldn't sit calmly any longer. She rushed through the archive door into the glaring light of a large room, where students sat at their computers. Some of them began whispering. She ran to the washroom and cooled her hot cheeks with water. To her astonishment her face in the mirror looked fresh; her slightly reddened skin glowed. She winked at herself in the mirror, with a soupçon of self-irony.

When she returned to her table, the archivist gave her a searching look. She read through the diary for that fateful day, the day they first met. September 5, 1927.

I arrived, and saw Georg and was at ease. Thank God. I am very happy and have hope, and if all goes well, then a few printed characters in a newspaper have brought me happiness. Yes, dare, bet, and win. G. is a good and whole man, and that is the best thing there can be.

The shrill ring of a telephone sounded in the background. A man's voice started a conversation. Sonya read on.

There is a knock; Georg enters, shy, embarrassed, tall, broad-shouldered, with hardened hands. The two of us cannot speak, stammer; finally, I manage to laugh. He sits down and I take his hat off his head, still laughing. Then things went better.

Someone was standing beside her, and Sonya raised her head reluctantly.

"We're closing now," the archivist announced.

She nodded but absolutely had to read on.

Otherwise I am firmly convinced that Georg and I will have a very happy marriage; not only does he meet all my expectations, he surpasses them by far.

So it was all that simple for Else, Sonya reflected. Those words sounded so confident. That must have been how it was.

"*You think too much,*" Tonio often said. "*Trust your feelings and just go with them.*"

Else trusted her feelings. "*I arrived, saw Georg, and was at ease.*" She didn't torment herself with doubts—*how will it work for us, I'm a Berlin intellectual, he's an uneducated trapper who can only write a letter with some effort.* Sonya, on the other hand, always agonized during her brief marriage. She never really trusted in her happiness. Had they really found happiness together? They were so different, she thought. How could it stay that good forever? When she found Odette's letters, she felt validated. Tonio lacked something; all that time, there had been something missing.

"I'm sorry."

The archivist snapped Sonya out of her unhappy memories, and she packed up quickly.

"I'll be back tomorrow."

The computer room was noticeably emptier. Sonya sat down in front of a screen and checked her e-mail. Inge's e-mail came up. "How's the archive going? What have you turned up? Don't keep torturing me! I'm losing sleep over this!"

Sonya went through the rest of her e-mails. She stopped at one of them. Someone had sent her a link to the website of the Raincoast Conservation Foundation, which protected bears. But the page wasn't sent by Walt from Fisherman's Lodge. It was another anonymous sender; there was a single sentence at the top: "Go through the links very carefully!" What in the world did that mean? Was somebody trying to stick her with a computer virus? That didn't seem plausible, so she clicked through the links: the grizzly's range, the grizzly's way of life, recent research results, sightseeing tours for ecotourists, statistics on incidents with grizzlies.

Sonya was indignant. What was all this? She quickly scrolled through until she came to the incident statistics. Suddenly she was riveted by one thing. An incident involving a grizzly. Three years ago, in September, near Prince Rupert. Sonya didn't hesitate. She called up the foundation only to get the answering machine. She left her phone number and backed it up with an e-mail. Whoever sent her this knew more than anybody. That person wanted to share what he or she knew by circuitous routes. She was willing to play his little game.

CHAPTER 37

Sonya was in a great mood the next morning. The conservation organization still hadn't replied, but the head of the German department, who was responsible for the Else Seel archive, had just given her the green light. She could have several original documents for the museum show. Sonya could have climbed every tree on campus for joy! She instantly sent Inge an e-mail with more exclamation marks than words. *Today's my lucky day*, she thought to herself, storming like a marathon winner through the archive door.

The boxes of documents were ready and waiting. She immersed herself at once in Else's world, shutting out everything around her. *"Georg and I will have a very happy marriage."* This certainty was inspirational for Else in the first days after she arrived. Sonya wanted to find out more. Every line, every page of the diary opened up a new reality for her. *"And I suddenly realized: solitude. If you scream, nobody will hear you. That pierced my heart like a knife."*

Else Seel, a brand-new wife, learned fast and painfully what her new life would be. It would be filled with loneliness. Sonya imagined her sitting in her primitive, remote log cabin on Ootsa Lake. Winter had already burst upon her, one of those long, hard northern British Columbia winters. George didn't show up for many weeks, walking his lines where foxes, wolves, weasels, and martens met their end. There was only silence and Else. *"Yes, I'm doing well—but I don't have a husband—so it seems. But Georg stays home after Christmas, thank God."* Those stays were brief. Else wrote time and again: *"Georg is away, Georg is away."* She sat by the window, yearning—and keeping watch for his canoe to appear on the lake. *"Small ice floes floating on the lake like the tears I do not shed. No, I do not weep so easily anymore."*

Sonya was stunned. This was *not* the woman she'd read about until now. Such outspoken confessions just hadn't been there. In Else's German publications, she portrayed herself as a fearless, energetic, tough pioneer's wife who overcame every obstacle and stoically faced any hardships. But in her personal, uncensored, handwritten diary, a vulnerable, sometimes anxious, frequently self-doubting woman laid her heart bare.

> *Married, marriage—strange, powerful words, like distant mountains which lie—for me still—somewhere in the distance. But they will come nearer, or rather, I will come nearer to them, quite near, and then there are two possibilities: they crush you, or you climb over them, high up into light and clarity.*

The more Sonya read, the more it looked as if Else was crushed, rather than lifted up. When George was lying with her, she was unable to show him her love.

"There is always a barrier between two persons, always a barrier like the gate in front of a train flying past."

Sonya couldn't deceive herself: George stayed a stranger to Else. They were strangers to each other. He was jealous when she stroked the cat lovingly; she was jealous when he couldn't keep his hands off their infant Rupert. Else complained that she had to bake bread instead of writing a novella. She began to long for a like-minded spirit, a soul partner.

Sonya dug out the letters she wrote to Ezra Pound. She read and read, surprised by Else's intimate, almost erotic tone. A one-sided exchange—yes, verily! Pound seldom wrote her, only a few paltry lines now and then. Else, on the other hand, wrote several pages at a time, telling her correspondent much that was personal. Else didn't realize until almost ten years later how much Pound exploited her candor and her commitment. Sonya couldn't comprehend why it took a disappointed and embittered Else so long to ultimately break off contact with him.

And her disappointment with George? Sonya stumbled upon an explosive entry in 1932 when the family's financial situation was catastrophic. *"But it is so damn hard for me and I cry often, as I did today. Good that no one is looking after me, so no one can see it."*

Else toyed with the thought of leaving George and Wistaria and settling somewhere else.

"I must stay and hold on, or I would already have been over the hills and far away, making a living once again."

She wrote seven years later: *"Georg did not say good-bye when he departed ten days ago—even this bond has been torn asunder."*

Sonya set the diary aside, overwhelmed by a flood of contradictory thoughts and feelings. How naive she'd been to take Else's published story at face value! As a historian she ought to have known better. Words can deceive, disguise, mislead. How quickly you can arrive at the wrong conclusion.

She should have taken that into consideration. *Context, Sonya, context.* She was displeased with herself. There were more important factors she ought to consider. Else was no superwoman. She suffered and complained, felt fear and desperation. George Seel could not see her for who she was: an artist thirsting for intellectual debate, with deep emotions and complicated thoughts. He wanted a woman who baked bread, salted moose meat, raised his children, and played hostess to his neighbors and pals. When George was away, Else smothered half the bed with books. But the two of them stayed together all those years until his sudden death. When George died, Else felt as if her life had been robbed of its meaning. She had indeed loved him, in some way or another.

Sonya picked up the diary again, and a passage caught her eye.

Over the last four months, I've seen him for precisely four days! It is passing strange: he makes an appearance now and then like a stranger, brings with him a few stormy days and nights, then rushes off. And am I not happy, deep down in my heart? By nature I am not one for continuity, I, so shifting, undisciplined . . .

The last sentence cut Sonya to the quick. She read it over and over. Did Else not want to be tied down? Could she not stand having a husband in the house all the time? Did George's long absences give her the freedom she so desperately needed? That would mean Else's loneliness was also her freedom!

Sonya couldn't help thinking about her own marriage. Tonio hadn't wanted a wife who did the same things he did, who was like him, who thought like him. He said that often enough. She felt he was telling her the truth at the time, but she had doubts later.

Her cell phone buzzed. She'd forgotten to turn it off. The archivist's head shot up at the sound, and she quickly left the room.

"Were you the person who called concerning the bear incident in Prince Rupert?"

It was a male voice. The animal rights group.

"Yes, thank you for returning my call."

"Are you from a newspaper?"

"No, I'm . . . I'm a researcher."

"May I ask what you are researching?"

"Human misconduct concerning wild animals." Sonya surprised herself with her rapid, spontaneous answer.

"Ah. You didn't call last week?"

"Last week? No, certainly not."

"I thought . . . we had a call last week about the same incident in Prince Rupert."

She pricked up her ears.

"Who called?"

"I don't know. Normally my colleague processes inquiries. She mentioned something, but I don't really know."

"Can I speak to her, please?" Sonya asked instantly.

"She's just gone on holiday. Maybe you can call back next week?"

Sonya could have cursed, but that wouldn't have helped. She politely ended the call.

It was already late in the afternoon when she made a startling discovery . . . She'd been searching for such a long time, and suddenly it was in her hands. No doubt about it. Here it was, staring her in the face.

Else's secret.

From: yh6t9abeil@yahoo.com
Sent: September 20, 17:02
To: Inge Stollrath
Re: Found it!!!!!

Hello Inge,

You were right as (almost) always! There *was* something in Else Lübcke Seel's life that drove her to Canada. And I've found it: the motive, the mystery, the decisive moment! You will give me a gold medal. Or a raise. I shall accept both.

I got on the trail by reading Else's unpublished story "The Old Lion." I'll spare you the details, but it's a thinly disguised depiction of her liaison with the much older Danish author Martin Andersen Nexø. As you know, he was married and wouldn't legalize his relationship with Else. She was about thirty-two at the time. Else drew inspiration for more or less all her works from her life experience—a poet cannot help but be autobiographical, in my unliterary view.

In any case, I jump into the story, whose heroine was named Elise. I'm reading it pretty attentively, page by page— and then it hits me like a thunderbolt: *And so I leave, with those words in my heart and a child below it.*

I keep reading like a woman obsessed and come to another passage:

She writes to Mark [i.e., her lover] and tells him everything. He replies in beautiful, powerful words that flow so easily from his practiced pen, which has the whole of life at its command. Elise knows that her condition, too, is at his command, and she thinks: he shall be master over life and death—if he grants life and warmth, then he shall receive life and warmth; but if he is cold as death, then life must be extinguished.

At this point—you can just imagine—my temperature shot up, but farther along Else is crystal clear and leaves no doubt.

The next day Elise writhed in pain. Her legs were stretched out like arms, imploring, pleading in vain for mercy. She whimpered as her body was torn open. She heard blood dripping and glimpsed for a moment the doctor's stained hand. A stream of agony went through her body as if an ice sheet were cracking apart.

The young doctor lifted her up gently. Else was weak and lay still in his arms. He saw her pale, tear-stained face. Her eyes were shining at him, bravely and truthfully, and as she stood up leaning on him like a brother, she asked in all seriousness, "Did I do wrong?" He leaned over, and his face expressed complete understanding as the words came out like an inspired idea: "No, because you're still a child yourself."

At this point, I had to go to the bathroom for a drink of cold water. The world was spinning before my eyes.

Of course, I wanted to check my discovery in the secondary literature and did, just before closing time. Angelika Arend, a German-Canadian academic, wrote in an article on Else's love poems:

Else was deeply hurt by the pain and humiliation brought by a man twenty-five years older than she—whom she loved and admired, who sexually abused her for a pleasurable diversion. Aborting her child cast her into deepest despair. We may assume that this radical break [Arend means her emigration to Canada] was a desperate attempt to put a firm end to it, and would enable her to make a fresh start and go on living.

Dear Inge, I wish Else's secret weren't so gloomy, because the abortion must have been traumatic, apart from the fact that it happened in the twenties under difficult medical circumstances.

Now I'm pooped. I'm going to find myself a pizza and get to bed.

Your exhausted Sonya

From: soneswunder@swifel.com
Sent: September 21, 07:10
To: Sonya Werner
Re: Soooooo impressed!

Dear Sonya,

Just read your news. Am utterly bowled over by your research! Will have to give it more thought in peace and quiet. Can't now because Wilfried is in the hospital with a slipped disk. From gardening!

Get back to you soon. Everything you're doing is really, really terrific!

In haste,

Inge

CHAPTER 38

Sonya had a feeling of déjà vu. She was watching for a ferry yet again, this time to take her truck to Tsawwassen, a ferry terminal near Vancouver. She leaned against the pickup and held her face to the morning sun. Just for a few minutes, she promised herself, a little bit wouldn't hurt. The light and air were hugely refreshing after all those hours in the dark archives.

Plumbing the depths of another person's life had liberated her from her own unresolved issues for a few days. Now she was creeping around silently on tiptoe. The newspaper article on Tonio's death she found in the drawer—how did it get into Diane's apartment? Did Diane know more about Sonya's secret mission than she was letting on?

How was Robert connected to the security agent? He hadn't explained it after the Deep Cove episode. He hadn't even tried—as if he had no inkling that she found it all suspicious, that she didn't believe in coincidences any longer. Doubtless he was worried about her, but if he was sorry to have endangered her life, he hadn't uttered a word about it. Her resentment distanced her from him. Her anger ended up being most opportune—because of it she needn't worry about other much more threatening feelings.

She hadn't quizzed Robert about the security guy. Perhaps that was a mistake, but the events in Deep Cove were so overwhelming, all she wanted was to be alone, to take one little red pill and go to bed.

Her cell phone buzzed. Where the hell had she put it? She reached into her truck through the open window.

"Hello?" she answered.

"Sonya! Good I caught you!" A woman's voice spoke.

Finally.

"Where are you, Diane?"

"In Yellowknife."

"Where?"

"In Yellowknife. In the Northwest Territories. Way up north."

"When will you be back?"

"I don't know yet, but certainly not before you go. I'm really sorry."

Sonya's mood sank to rock bottom. Was Diane avoiding her intentionally? She thought lightning fast. She absolutely must talk to her—she was determined to. Sonya wouldn't leave for Switzerland before talking with Diane.

"I could go to Yellowknife." She hastened to add, "I've always wanted to see the North. And I desperately have to talk to you, hear me?"

"Sonya, where I am now, you need a snowmobile and fur underwear!"

Diane wasn't taking her at all seriously. What the hell. She'd find out soon enough.

"If that's all, it's no problem," she replied.

"I *would* like to see you again, Sonya. It's too bad it just won't work. You'll certainly come back some other time, right?"

"I'll be back for sure."

Diane misunderstood her again.

"You can give the key to the super or drop it in the mailbox."

"I've things to do here, so I postponed my flight."

"OK, you should confirm your seat," Diane continued. "Have a good trip, and let's hear from you."

"I'll do that, I prom—"

The connection was lost.

Sonya took down Diane's number; it was on her phone's display.

She booked a flight to Yellowknife immediately upon arriving back in Vancouver that afternoon. She was unbelievably lucky: the flight left the next day. She booked a room in Yellowknife using the number she'd just noted: the Redwood Garden Motel. She'd had enough of Diane's stonewalling. Sonya would teach her a thing or two about stubbornness. You can't shake a historian off so easily.

Then she wrote an e-mail to Inge: "Coming home two weeks later."

She packed her carry-on bag. She took the green winter jacket she'd worn in Prince Rupert to the cleaners for express service. She had cleverly packed thermal underwear and a warm hat and gloves for Canada.

That night she slept deeply and soundly—she'd done what she could. But her restfulness dissipated that morning. Almost everything went wrong. First the taxi got stuck in traffic; then she lost more time at the cleaners while the clerk fussed around for a black plastic bag containing the items found in Sonya's jacket pocket. Luckily, the taxi driver waited patiently, so she just made her flight to Edmonton and caught the connecting flight to Yellowknife.

On arriving, she was welcomed by the huge stuffed polar bear that kept watch over the airport concourse. On her way to the exit, she saw a group of ruddy-faced men wearing hats, jackets, and backpacks—all camouflaged. Moose antlers held down with brown duct tape sat like a figurehead on their baggage cart. Trophy hunters. *Welcome to Yellowknife*, Sonya said to herself. A banner in front of the airport proudly announced: "Diamond Capital of North America."

She glanced at the steppe-like vegetation. The cold was unmistakable; they were just two hundred and fifty miles from the Arctic Circle. The thought was exciting and scary at the same time. What business did she have here, for God's sake?

She took a taxi to the hotel and asked for Diane at the registration desk. "My friend's expecting me," she lied without blushing.

"Diane's left already," the pale young receptionist said.

A cold shiver ran down Sonya's spine.

"But she was here yesterday. She made a special point of telling me when she called."

"Sorry, but she checked out this morning."

"This morning!" Sonya wanted to scream those words. The whole trip all for naught. Maybe Diane was in Vancouver right now—to see Sonya off. Why didn't she tell Diane her plans? Too late now.

"She's coming back in about a week," the girl ventured timidly.

"So she didn't go to Vancouver?"

"No, I don't believe so. She's probably out there."

"Out there?" Sonya understood less and less.

The receptionist simply stared at her. Then the penny dropped.

"She's at work out there, right?" Sonya said.

The receptionist nodded.

"How can I reach her? Or leave a message that I'm here?"

"I don't know. You'll have to ask around. Somebody in the Explorer Bar might know. That's where everybody goes."

"Excuse me—who's everybody?"

"Prospectors and workers from the mines and diamond companies. The bar's not far."

She tore a map off a block and showed her where the bar was. Sonya took the map and her keys and started upstairs.

"Oh, yes," the girl called after her, "do go see Scott Dixon. Maybe he can help you."

"Who's he?"

"He's got a store where everybody working in the field goes shopping. He sells equipment and things."

"And fur underwear," Sonya muttered as she went upstairs. Scott Dixon. She filed away his name.

In her room, she checked the time: five thirty. A good time to hit the Explorer Bar. The notion made her stomach tighten. She didn't like going to a bar alone, especially if it was sure to be full of probably drunk roughnecks, and she'd have to talk to some of them. But what did she have to lose? she asked herself to soothe her feelings. Nobody here knew her.

She walked along an almost deserted Franklin Street to downtown Yellowknife. The bar was in a commercial building resembling an East German concrete prefab. She crept her way inside behind a group of young people. The bar was jammed. A thick cluster of customers blocked her view of the bar. She figured immediately that there were about as many women as men, so she wasn't conspicuous. No searching eye sized her up; no head turned toward her.

Everyone had a glass in hand. She stood behind a broad back in a bright blue fleece vest. It was hot; the concentrated body heat in the room felt greater than the heat of the sun on a Caribbean beach. Sweat formed on her forehead, and beads of moisture dripped down the back of her neck.

The blue vest moved ahead, leaving an opening. The bartender gave her an inquiring look.

"A glass of beer," was her startled reply. She never drank beer in Switzerland.

"What kind?" he asked, rattling off a list of names.

"That one," she answered, pointing to a glass of beer on the bar.

The bartender asked her something else, but she simply nodded.

A minute later she was standing in the totally packed, dimly lit bar, holding a glass as big as a tulip vase. The place was loud, and the air stifling. She moved in a slow circle, not knowing what to do.

Then she saw him. He was sitting at a little round table, yacking noisily with some men: the fisherman from Powell River. What was he doing here? She vaguely recalled that he once worked in Yellowknife, but she couldn't remember what he did. She fought her way over to him, frantically scouring her brain for his name.

He happened to look in her direction, and she simply said, "Hi!"

He hesitated, and then his face broadened in surprise.

"What the hell . . . You're here! Our historian from Switzerland! Hey, guys, this is . . ." He had trouble with names, too.

"Sonya. And what's yours again?"

"Dave."

He stood up. Now it clicked: Dave Gallagher had once been a gold prospector somewhere around Yellowknife.

"C'mon, siddown! I'll be a monkey's uncle! What brings you up here?"

"I'm looking for a friend, Diane Kesowsky. We were supposed to meet in the motel but missed each other. "

She sat down beside a red-haired hulk with his shirt collar open. An amulet on his chest looked like a bear claw.

"Sonya's from Switzerland," Dave explained to the men. "She's doing an exhibition of women who left the country. She's looking for Diane Kesowsky."

"Diane!"

The men looked at one another. The hulk spoke.

"We'd all like to know where she is."

Everyone laughed. They had weather-beaten faces and calloused hands. It was friendly laughter. Out of sheer nervousness, Sonya took a big swig of her cold beer.

One of the men spoke up.

"Nobody up here says where they're going. Get that? It's a big secret."

"We just know she's rooting around in the dirt somewhere near the Arctic Circle," a bearded man chimed in. "I have no idea what she's gonna find there."

"I made a special trip here," Sonya said. "Maybe somebody can contact her?"

"They'll have a satellite phone, but only insiders know the number. Maybe—"

"The helicopter guys at Arctic Blue Air," his buddy interrupted. "Sonya can leave a message there. Diane hired Arctic Blue for sure."

"I thought she always used Joe Thirkell's pilots." That was the red-haired giant.

"No way. They work for Tetra Earth Mines. Arctic Blue made a lot of flights yesterday, I hear."

"Well, don't you know a whole damn lot, Ted!"

The men laughed again.

"Ted's our little spy!"

"The spy who came in from the cold."

Now they all roared with delight, and Sonya laughed along with them—it couldn't hurt.

"But it's a long way from Sweden to Yellowknife," Ted declared.

"Switzerland, not Sweden. Believe me, I never thought I'd wind up here." She drank another quick gulp of beer.

"Yeah, the North's a really big draw. Watch out, because if you're up here once, it'll never let you go."

"Like our good old buddy Dave. Comes to Yellowknife every year to freeze his ass off." The hulk emitted a hoarse chuckle. "The ocean at Powell River is warm as bathwater by comparison."

"Sonya, we've got five seasons in Yellowknife—early winter, midwinter, winter, late winter, and the coming winter."

Sonya joined the thunderous laughter. The beer made it easier. She looked over at Fisherman Dave. It struck her that he hadn't said anything, leaving the conversation to his drinking buddies.

"I've got to go soon, I'm tired," she said.

"You need somebody to take you to your motel?" Dave asked instantly. She quickly accepted his offer.

"Are you coming back, or do we gotta go see you in Switzerland?" one of the men shouted.

The gang was having a grand old time.

Outside, Sonya took a deep breath. It didn't matter at all that the air was frosty. Dave walked her over to a beaten-up truck.

"Did you drive to Yellowknife in that?" she asked.

"No, it belongs to a buddy of mine. I still know a lot of people here from the old days."

He started the engine.

"Did Diane actually say she would see you up here?"

"Why do you want to know?"

Dave waited for a moment.

"There are lots of rumors in this town, and rumors about Diane. Nobody knows what she's up to. But . . ."

"But what?"

"She goes in and out of the police station a bit much."

"What's that supposed to mean?"

"There was this murder up in the tundra."

"What's Diane got to do with that?"

"It happened in her camp. When she was looking for diamonds."

"What kind of murder? What happened?"

"It was one of her prospectors," Dave replied. "He was found with his throat slit, but the murder was never solved."

"So what's going on now?"

"People are saying that the cops are onto something."

"Onto Diane? Is that what you're saying?"

"They're only rumors, eh? What's she doing at the station all the time?"

Sonya had the impression that Dave was uneasy. Was he worried for Diane? Or about something different?

"Dave, you did tell me in Powell River that there's organized crime around here. Mafiosi you've got to watch out for. You think Diane has something to do with that?"

"I said something about the Mafia?" he said, leaning on his horn in surprise. "It was probably the beer talking. No, Diane has nothing to do with that. But in Vancouver, that's where some people probably wish they'd been a bit more careful."

"More careful?"

"Some guys robbed them blind, promised them the moon—but it was all made up."

"What?"

"The drill tests, the surveys, the paperwork. It was all hot air. But one mining engineer—they couldn't buy him. He spilled the beans."

It was Sonya's turn to be surprised.

"Do you happen to know his name, that engineer?"

"Gotta think . . ."

"Was it Robert Stanford?" Her pulse was throbbing.

"Yeah, maybe, Bob Stanford, very likely. He was the key witness in the trial of those crooks. Honestly, I wouldn't like to be in his shoes."

"Why?"

"I'll bet those gangsters will try anything to get rid of him. If you take my meaning. But he's probably got bodyguards or something. I would if I were him."

Sonya was dizzy, and she knew it wasn't from that one beer.

"Yeah, it's a rough business, you can trust me. Wherever there's money, they crawl out of their holes like rats. And a few decent people—or people who were thought to be decent, suddenly ditch their morals overboard."

He gave a humorless laugh.

"You can't blame them—who wouldn't want a million or two in the bank? I would, at any rate. Wouldn't you?" He gave her a sidelong glance.

"Why not?" she shrugged. "But you can't take it with you. And you can't eat diamonds or gold either."

He made no response, but he spoke up again when she was getting out of his truck.

"You know, there's really nothing better than sitting in my boat having a fish dinner with a beautiful woman. But then—then I feel the pull. I have to come up here again. I'd like nothing better than to head out on the tundra and find the richest vein of gold the world has ever seen."

He shifted into reverse.

"It's just human nature. And anyway, you're searching for something, too. Or am I wrong?"

"Believe me, Dave, it's not gold I'm looking for. Thanks a lot for the ride."

Before the door slammed shut, she heard him say, "Don't kill yourself, Swiss lady."

CHAPTER 39

Sonya was standing at Arctic Blue Air's check-in building at eight the next morning. Fog floated on Great Slave Lake like a concentrated blob given off by dry ice. The lake looked like the ocean: no horizon and holding out the promise of an unknown world. A notice was posted at the entrance of the airline's office: no flights today because of fog. The door was locked. Sonya walked down to the landing dock, where several planes were waiting for better weather. Not a helicopter to be seen, and no landing field.

Perhaps she was in the wrong place. She took a look around: there was nobody to ask. She was drawn to the sign on the old cabin across the way: "Wildcat Cafe." The little house and its weathered wooden boards could have been on a Swiss alp. Its door was shut, too. She spied a poster proclaiming it was built in 1937 but not announcing when she could expect to get a coffee. Then she heard a key turning. A pudgy young man with a scarf around his neck opened the door.

"Sorry for the wait. Come right in."

Sonya sat down at a rough-hewn wooden table and ordered a hearty breakfast of bacon and eggs. The man with the scarf took her order and doubled as the cook. She killed time by scrutinizing reproductions of old photographs on the wall: gold diggers with their primitive tools, shacks like sheds with tiny windows to keep out the brutal winter cold.

"We have a pretty good pea soup out here," the cook said, setting a giant steaming cup in front of her. "I can tell you, it's better than the mosquitoes in summer. How long have you been here?"

"I came yesterday."

"Well, you're lucky. This summer was a disaster. The mosquitoes invaded the town in masses. They crawled in everywhere: in your eyes, ears, and nose. It wasn't safe to open your mouth. You could only go out with a net over your head. Dogs and cats—even birds—were driven half-crazy. Forget mosquito spray. Not worth a damn. That's how it was; right, Sven? Never been so bad?" he said. He addressed a man who just came in.

"Holy shit," the customer exclaimed, taking off his battered cowboy hat, "that damn plague! Don't even mention it. Just bring me a cup of boiling hot coffee and something to bite into."

The man sat down at a table diagonally across from her. He wore a red-checkered flannel shirt and a cheap leather jacket.

"Here on a visit?"

"I guess I obviously look like a tourist," Sonya smiled back.

"You're dressed too pretty for Yellowknife. Nobody goes around looking like that. Or are you looking for work?"

"No, I was going to go on Arctic Blue, but the office is closed."

"Too dangerous, can't see damn anything today. You wouldn't see much of the area."

The cook brought him coffee and a muffin.

"I've heard they've got helicopters, too."

"Yeah, they do, but not for tourists, just for companies and prospectors. Too expensive for normal people. Nobody can pay what they're asking these days."

"Are you talking about houses?" asked the cook, who'd only heard his last words. Sonya's breakfast had arrived.

"Naw, helicopter flights."

"Nobody can buy a house either," the cook said without emotion. "After diamonds took off, all hell broke loose. More and more people came in, and they can't build houses fast enough. You know where I sleep? I share an apartment with four people. Haven't even got my own room and I pay a fortune. It's insane."

"Before that," said Sven, "you could pick up a house for a song. Then the gold mines were finished, and nobody had a job. Until that Chuck Fipke guy showed up."

"Yes, I've heard of him," Sonya said.

"People here knew that Fipke was up to something. But the sly old fox told everybody he was looking for gold. Who'd ever think of diamonds? Not me. Nobody would've. But that's how it was. People made jokes about it. They said the best Fipke would find in the tundra would be brown caribou turds."

"Did diamond fever take off after that?" Sonya inquired.

Sven chomped on his muffin.

"No, it took a while. Not like a gold rush. Nobody runs around town with a bag full of diamonds. You need machines to get at the real rocks. Have you ever seen a rough diamond, eh? Not specially pretty, no it ain't."

Sonya owned a single diamond, in a ring. Tonio's wedding present. She came across an advertising slogan some time later: "A gift as lasting as love." She didn't wear that ring anymore.

"Do you know what a test drilling costs? Fifty thousand dollars. That's not for small-time prospectors like me. That's only for big companies."

"But Fipke wasn't wealthy by a long shot. How did he get financed?"

"He scraped the money together, but the mine—he didn't build it. BHP Billiton did, Australians—a giant company. Fipke's a billionaire today for sure, I can't imagine him not."

"Do you know Diane Kesowsky?"

The cook was about to give her a refill but stopped. He glanced from Sonya to Sven, who took his time answering.

"Who doesn't?" the cook admitted.

Sven cleared his throat.

"She could be a billionaire, too. But . . ." He paused for far too long a time. "People say she let go of a claim too fast. Somebody else got the land. And that somebody found diamonds afterward like plums in a Christmas pudding. All you can say is tough shit."

"Tough shit?" the cook interjected. "I thought it was fraud."

"Rumors—you know the rumor mill in Yellowknife. As many rumors as ravens. And you know, we've got more of those birds than any place in the world."

Sonya decided to put her cards on the table.

"Diane is an acquaintance of mine. I'd like to get in touch with her since I'm here. Her camp's out in the tundra. And she's said to have a contract with Arctic Blue for helicopters. Do you know how I can get hold of her?"

The men stared at each other in silence.

"Do you know anybody who flies to her camp?" she added.

The cook turned to Sven, who scratched his head.

"Are you with the cops?"

"Who? Me? What makes you think that?"

The cook giggled nervously. "Listen, Sven, you're overdoing it, eh?"

Sven muttered something incomprehensible.

"Hey, send her to Scott Dixon," the cook suggested. "If anybody's flying out to her, he's sure to know."

"The man who runs the equipment store?" Sonya asked.

"Yes, the man with the store, who's seething with the most unbelievable anger in his belly."

Sonya had an uneasy feeling as she went to look up Scott Dixon. Now they thought she was a cop! What fear was driving the people around here that they were so afraid of spies? Or was it an archaic attitude of pioneers, who loved their freedom and independence most—and so avoided the guardians of the law like dogs avoided the whip?

Yellowknife's harbor district, where she was walking, took her back to the time of the gold rush in the thirties and forties. The old shacks of the early gold hunters huddled against a rocky hill. She thought they looked less comfortable than the houseboats in the bay, with their shiny colors seeping through wispy billows of fog. Farther away from the shore, along Franklin Avenue, Yellowknife looked more like a city, with its multistoried commercial buildings and a modern parliament building on the outskirts.

Scott Dixon's store was in a side street and resembled an ancient warehouse. She would have loved to pack the interior decor into a shipping container just as it was and send it off to her Swiss museum—so strong was her feeling of being transported back to the past despite the modern snowmobiles and machines. Faded ads for long-obsolete products dozed on the walls, keeping huge aluminum propellers and orange life jackets company. Sonya was sorry her video camera was back at the motel. She discovered several snowmobile-racing trophies on an old-fashioned metal rack, together with well-worn ring binders and a filing cabinet straight out of a prewar film. A dusty pane of glass behind the counter separated a tiny packed office from the sales area. Around the window frame were out-of-date calendars featuring businesses that had probably died. The cash register, she guessed, would have to be as old as Yellowknife itself. From 1937.

The office door opened, and a squat, thin man stuck his head out, shouting, "Be right there!" Sonya heard him arguing excitedly on the telephone about prices and quantities and delivery dates. She couldn't resist sitting on a snowmobile. Her hands held the ends of the handlebars. She fantasized that she was whizzing over a vast snowy plain high up in the Arctic, with nothing to see but ice and an endless horizon. She would cross the whole white continent alone, a packed sled in tow, and at night in her tent fill her diary with entries that would later become historical quotations in books.

"That just came in, the latest model," an unexpected voice announced behind her.

She felt blood rush to her face.

"I actually don't need a snowmobile," she confessed.

"Oh, everybody can use a snowmobile. How do you expect to get around in winter?"

Scott Dixon threw his hands in the air, but she could see that his sales pitch was staged. He must have recognized at once that she was a clueless tourist.

"You can certainly sell a lot of them now that people are rolling in dough from the diamonds," she said, dismounting.

Dixon rubbed both hands over his narrow, nearly bald skull.

"Diamonds? The companies have them all—Rio Tinto, De Beers, BHP Billiton. And they don't buy anything here, eh? They got their own supply sources."

He leaned on the counter. Sonya could hardly believe her eyes, but there was in fact a pencil behind his ear. She'd loved to have packed him into a container, too.

"But after all," she said, "it was the small exploration companies that did the searching. The big companies came in later and bought them out."

"Ah, the lady is informed. Where are you from anyway?"

"From Switzerland."

"Switzerland, how interesting. Chuck Fipke's ancestors were Swiss, I believe."

"No, they were German, German settlers who'd first immigrated to the Ukraine."

"You seem to know everything to a T." He scratched his temple with the pencil.

"I took history," she said, as if that validated her interest in diamonds.

Dixon didn't seem to care. Instead, he said, "I well remember the day when Fipke came into my store. He bought sixteen thousand dollars' worth of supplies. I didn't have the slightest idea what he was digging for out there." He shook his head. "Fipke offered me shares in his company to pay for the goods, you understand. For an all-purpose vehicle, a generator, lamps, a portable stove. Things like that. Two cents a share. But I turned it down. Better sixteen thousand in my till than a bunch of worthless papers."

He took a green page from the table, crumpling it up.

"I'd had my fill of those treasure hunters who promise you paradise and want everything for free. Not from me."

He paused, as if he still couldn't rightly comprehend what happened back then.

"He came back in the fall, bought four snowmobiles and several sleds, and rented an ATV. Fourteen thousand dollars for the lot. He offered me shares again, this time for fifty cents apiece. I refused him again."

He bent down behind the counter for a second, laying a note-book before him.

"Do you know how much those shares were worth later?" He whipped out his pencil and scribbled some numbers on the paper. He looked at Sonya meaningfully.

"I'd have gotten eight hundred thousand shares. A year later, a share was worth forty-four dollars. That makes thirty-five mil-lion dollars." He shook his head. "When I hear the name Chuck Fipke, I think to this day—even today I think: Will I ever see another opportunity like that in my lifetime?"

Sonya could have held his disappointment in her hands. He stuck the pencil back behind his ear.

"I'll let you in on something. Today's the first time I've crunched the numbers. I couldn't bear it until now. I couldn't have survived the shock of my stupidity."

He looked around his store.

"I could have shut this place down long ago. Finished. *Finito.*"

"But you still have customers," Sonya added cautiously. "I've heard that Diane Kesowsky buys things here."

He raised his eyebrows.

"So you know that, too."

"Diane's a friend of mine." She told him the story about miss-ing her in the hotel. "Can you tell me how I can get ahold of her? Can you put me in touch?"

The answer came quick as a flash.

"I can let Don know—he flies to her camp."

Sonya could have jumped for joy.

"When's Don going?"

"Not today. Maybe tomorrow. I'll let Diane know you're here. Drop by tomorrow morning around eight thirty."

"You're in contact with Diane?"

"She calls me on the satellite phone."

Two men came through the door, and Dixon said hello. Then he went back to Sonya.

"What's your name?"

"Sonya Werner."

He repeated her name.

"No problem. I know."

What does he know? she asked herself when she got to Franklin Avenue. Would he really be able to remember her name? But she had to trust him; her hands were tied.

She made a beeline for her next goal: the local museum. She simply had to see the relics of Franklin's disastrous polar expedition on exhibit talked up in her travel guide. The odyssey of Sir John Franklin had always fascinated her, partly because of Franklin himself but also because of his ambitious wife, Jane, who goaded her husband into making reckless expeditions. Sonya was struck by the fact that Franklin's corpulent build didn't make him look like a born leader of an expedition. But Lady Franklin was determined to help him gain fame by sending him to the coldest, most inhospitable part of the world. In another era she would probably have thrown herself into such ventures, but Victorian society would have stifled her urge to conquer in person.

In the museum, Sonya immediately asked the way to the Franklin room. She was magically drawn to two models of Franklin's ships—the *Erebus* and the *Terror*—that were caught in the ice. In a plexiglass box she found objects from a lifeboat that Franklin's crew left behind on King William Island: comb fragments, a violet-tinted lens from some snow goggles, a brass button from an officer's uniform, the meager remains of a boot heel, a few nails.

Sonya studied the pitiful legacy, fascinated and saddened at the same time. Here were scraps from an expedition hoping in vain to find the famous Northwest Passage. Franklin was almost sixty at the outset. About one hundred officers and men died under cruel circumstances, in part because preparations for the voyage had been inconceivably inadequate. When no news came of the expedition, Lady Franklin organized search parties from England. But for twelve years search after search came back empty-handed. There were published oral reports from Eskimos saying that some members of the expedition had eaten their dead comrades. Lady Jane rejected them.

This longing for . . . greatness? For a place in history? Franklin had achieved it with time. Lady Franklin angrily convinced leading experts in England to praise her missing husband as the discoverer of the Northwest Passage.

Sonya was put off by her behavior. She'd never have pushed Tonio to risk his life so he could go down in the annals of history. Even when he told a friend in her presence that he wanted to cross the Arctic on skis someday, all by himself, and was sorry he hadn't done it, even then she simply let it be. She never brought it up, though she knew what was making him restless: he wanted to do something special in his lifetime, to achieve something big that would raise him above the masses. He wanted a legacy to outlast his brief human life. She knew all about that type of desire from biographies and history books—and she knew its consequences, for individuals and all mankind.

Had Tonio hoped she could understand this ambition of his? Franklin had the assistance of his wife and her stubborn campaign. He'd paid for it with his life and been blamed for the deaths of people entrusted to him. Tonio had died without making his dream a reality. Without having tried at all.

Dearest Tonio,

We share something that only we understand, that joins us like earth to water. We've known each other from time immemorial; it was always there, and now it's come true. Inviolable.

Sonya sat down on a bench in front of the glass box, and the tears came. Her pink pills were in her backpack, but this time she didn't want her tears to stop. She cried uncontrollably to herself in the quiet of the museum's gloom. She wept for Tonio, for herself, but mostly for Nicky. Nicky was as young as many of Franklin's hired men, still in their teens, who suffered unimaginable torments. They starved and froze to death before their lives had really begun.

She barely noticed when an elderly visitor passed by, asking if everything was all right. She just nodded. Yes, everything's OK. She'd opened the floodgates, and her feelings had not pushed her off a cliff. The man went away and brought her a glass of water.

"Take your time," he said, disappearing as silently as he'd come.

She'd no idea how long she'd been sitting there before she summoned up enough strength to step outside into the world. The receptionist at the motel gave her a funny look. Sonya hadn't taken the trouble to clear her swollen red eyes. She eventually saw that the young woman was handing her a note.

"For you."

The message was brief. *Be ready in front of the motel at seven.* No name. No information.

"Who's this from?"

The receptionist had already gone back to her computer.

"I have no idea. I wasn't here when it came."

Sonya was too exhausted to find out anything more.

In her room, she dumped out her "Arctic" clothes on the bed and everything she'd need for a flight to Diane's camp. She wanted to be prepared. Out of her backpack, a black plastic bag emerged. What had they found at the cleaners anyway? She looked inside: there were broken fragments, pieces with written characters. A *Ü*, a *K*, a scratched *H*. Typical! She always collected all sorts of junk in her pockets. She tossed the bag into the wastebasket.

She thrashed around before falling asleep. Had she thought of everything? How would Diane be when they met? What if she simply stonewalled her? Then she'd be faced with a heap of broken pieces, and everything would hinge on Robert.

Pieces. A hasty grab for the lamp: the light, the wastepaper basket. The bag. The fragments. Those letters. How could she have missed it? At that moment she knew she wouldn't be falling back asleep.

CHAPTER 40

Feeble lamplight illuminated the motel entrance. The night was pitch-black on all sides. No fog, no rain—just a slight, cold wind. A metallic sound came from somewhere, like a glockenspiel gone awry.

Whenever a car drove by, Sonya stiffened up. Her stomach was in an uproar. Suppose the note was a trap? She should have gone and asked Scott Dixon who was behind it. She could be kidnapped. Her body would never be found. Nobody would ever find out what happened. Robert wouldn't have a clue where she was.

How stupid to think of him just now. She *did* want to avoid him, after all—him and the surveillance of his retinue. Whoever they were. Whatever mischief they were up to. A man had been killed out there in the tundra, his throat slit.

Big headlights blinded her, and a small white bus turned into the motel's parking lot. The door opened.

"Sonya?"

"Who are you?"

"I'm Cameron from Arctic Blue Air. Are you Sonya?"

The man wore a cap with earflaps.

"Yes," she replied, but she didn't budge.

"Can you identify yourself?"

Surprised, Sonya fished her passport out of her backpack. It wasn't until the man had the document in his hands that she realized how rash she'd been.

"I must ask you a few security questions," the man said. "What did you find on the table in Diane's apartment when you got back from your trip?"

The man had a friendly voice.

"Flowers," she responded. Should she have refused to answer?

"What color were the sheets in your room in Vancouver?"

But this was absurd. Still, she answered obediently. "Purple."

"And what's the name of the partner of your favorite friend in Germany?"

"Inge's partner? Wilfried?"

He gave back her passport and smiled.

"You passed the test. Hop in."

He reached out to take her backpack, but she didn't give it to him.

"It's OK."

They drove through the dark in silence. When some lights appeared in the distance, she recognized the area around the airport. The bus stopped before a hangar, and they entered an adjacent building.

"This is Sonya," the driver announced to a young woman in uniform, who came up to her directly.

"I must examine your baggage and your pockets before we can take off," she said.

"But of course," Sonya said, feeling more relaxed now. She handed over her backpack but didn't let it out of her sight.

"I'm taking you to the chopper. Duck under the rotors and don't get on until I tell you."

The woman took her arm and led her to the tarmac, where the droning helicopter was waiting. When the young lady signaled to her, she crouched down and walked under the circling rotors. She sat next to the pilot, who motioned for her to put on her seat belt. His facial features were unmistakably native.

She put on her headphones.

"Hi, Sonya, I'm Don. First time up in a chopper?"

"Yes, but I hope it isn't yours."

"It *is* today." He grinned. "I've been flying for nine years. There's been a heck of a lot going on since they found diamonds."

"Do you go back and forth all the time?"

"Yeah, I carry people and supplies, though most of the supplies go on small planes. They're cheaper than choppers."

Sonya looked down but couldn't see much in the dark. The pilot kept talking, going on about "claims" and "stakers." After asking several questions, she finally understood what this was all about. Don flew prospectors up to the tundra to stake claims on land where they wanted to look for diamonds. He explained that mineral rights belonged to the Crown, so the Canadian government had to give people permits. If you wanted to extract minerals, you had to pound marked wooden stakes into the ground at prescribed intervals and register the marked area with the local Mining Recorder's Office.

Sonya could understand that much in spite of the roaring engine.

"When diamonds got hot," Don continued, "it was already winter. God, that was a race! Everybody wanted to go up there and grab another claim. Chuck Fipke and BHP Billiton got the best locations. And then De Beers got into the act. Millions of acres were claimed, all of it by chopper. That was big money, I tell you."

Sonya wondered where Diane got the money to fly to and from camp. She hadn't seen any signs that she was rich. Explorations must cost millions. Who was backing her?

She listened in silence, which stimulated Don's talkativeness.

"We had whiteouts, like, every winter, everything white, only white—we saw nothing, not a thing. And then our GPS would fail; the screen would suddenly go dark. The staker had to get out his topographical map and peek out the windshield to see if the ground was visible. It was nuts, absolutely nuts."

"Did you land every time to plant the stakes?"

"Yes, that was the agreement. Chopper down, staker out, stake in, then the staker jumps back in, the chopper takes off, and so on. Absolutely nuts."

Dawn came. Sonya could see little rises in the landscape, and then something below shimmered, like a mirror.

"Is that a lake down there?"

"What? A lake? Probably is. There are thousands of lakes in the Territories." He laughed. "Pretty much all water down there. You'll see. Of course it all freezes in winter, and just you try and hammer a post into the ground! That's a job for an idiot. But there are tricks."

"What tricks?"

"Simply tossing the stakes out of the chopper onto the ground, which isn't quite right, of course. But if anybody said that it wasn't properly staked out, we'd just say a bear pulled the stakes out."

He laughed, and Sonya joined in.

"Are there bears in the tundra?"

"Bears for sure. Grizzlies. And wolves and moose and caribou and foxes. They're the worst."

"Foxes? But there are a lot of foxes in Switzerland, too."

"Ninety-five percent of the ones here are rabid. You'd better not get bitten."

Sonya shuddered. The wilderness was so unsafe.

The sun came up, and the spectacle nearly took her breath away. The tundra was bursting into fabulous colors—red, purple, wine red, rusty red, all glowing in a way Sonya hadn't seen before, with cheerful yellow tufts here and there.

"It's gorgeous!" she uttered spontaneously.

"That's our ancestors' hunting grounds. It's still our territory."

Sonya could hear the pleasure and pride in Don's voice.

"What's your tribe?"

"I'm Déné. Our village is Rae, not far from Yellowknife."

"Is mining permitted on that land?"

"They probably would have taken the land from us, but we defended ourselves. They had to negotiate with us, all of them: Rio Tinto and BHP and De Beers. A lot of Déné work in the diamond mines now."

He pointed to a dot in the distance.

"The camp."

Sonya strained, scouring the plain. Not until the helicopter turned sideways did she spot white shapes among colorful bushes and bare slabs of rock. They evoked the houses in Monopoly. Now she saw a lake bordered by a bright strip that was probably sand. A few miserable windblown firs huddled together in small groups.

The helicopter dropped down and landed, and Don shouted something she didn't understand. The door opened, and Sonya ran under the rotors until she was out of their range. Two men hastily unloaded crates from the helicopter. The pilot waved and took off. One of the men, a redhead, came toward her, carrying a crate on his shoulder.

"You must be Diane's friend," he said. "You just missed her, but come with me."

Sonya picked up her backpack and followed him.

"What do you mean, Diane's not here?" she asked.

"She has to finish a job in the field, but she'll be back," the man replied. He was young and strong, and Sonya noticed that he carried a gun.

The tents were surprisingly far away, so they looked quite small. The cold cut into her face. Sonya stumbled over half-mushy, half-frozen tundra dotted with islands of low bushes. She waved her hand frantically, trying to beat off the mosquitoes swarming around her head.

"Did you spray yourself?" her companion asked, looking back.

Sonya shook her head. Her spray was in her backpack.

"Then don't stop or you'll be eaten alive. Keep moving, keep moving all the time."

He's making fun of me, Sonya thought. As they came closer, she counted nine tents, and they weren't the conventional ones. White tarps were stretched over a wooden framework. Proper doors led inside, and chimneys poked out of the gabled roofs.

The man went to a tent door and pushed it open.

"The kitchen," he said. "Where we like it most."

Warm air hit them.

"Gwen, we've got a guest. Her name's Sonya!" he called out over the tables and chairs. There was movement behind an antiquated stove, and a muscular woman with bare, tattooed arms appeared from among the makeshift racks.

"Hi," she called back. "But I can't put a guest in the frying pan. Did you bring any food?"

"Whaddya think this is?" He pointed to the crate beside him.

"I can't see it, but I can smell it. It stinks suspiciously like bear shit." The cook guffawed. "I'm Gwen." She motioned to Sonya to come in. "How about a strong cup of coffee? You look like you've been bit by a vampire."

She brought her a thermos and a cup.

"Sugar and milk's over there." She pushed the crate to the back of the tent, which made the floorboards shake. Then she sat beside Sonya at the table nearest the warm stove.

"It's potatoes and smoked trout today. Some of our boys caught them in the lake, and I smoked them in the shed next door over a green Arctic willow fire. Where you gonna find that in a Vancouver restaurant?"

"It must be delicious," Sonya said, and her stomach made its presence felt again. She took off her jacket. The stove glowed. Gwen's face gleamed.

"So you're Diane's friend from Switzerland."

Sonya smiled. "Apparently word's got around."

"Sure, we've got to know who's coming into camp."

She got up to fetch a plastic box of cookies.

"Eat or you'll drop dead on me."

Sonya helped herself.

"I didn't get a lot of sleep last night," she explained.

"We didn't either—a bear came sniffing around, probably smelling the fish. Our guys took their guns to bed with them so they weren't completely alone." She laughed again, a deep belly laugh. "The racket was too much for the grizzly; he took off pretty soon. Betcha nobody went to the can last night, eh?"

"Where's Diane?" Sonya inquired for the second time that day.

"Out there. She'll be back in two, three hours. When they come in, they'll be hungry as wolves."

Gwen got up on her feet.

"Why don't you help me cook? You must know how to peel potatoes, or don't you do that in Switzerland?"

"We don't eat potatoes in Switzerland, didn't you know? We only eat cheese and chocolate."

Gwen whinnied.

"Yeah, sure. And spaghetti grows on trees, oh yeah, sure!"

She disappeared and came back dragging a sack of potatoes.

"I almost forgot. Diane told me to show you the camp." She waved at her to come along. Sonya grabbed her jacket while Gwen put on a fleece. The cold wasn't as biting because the sun was stronger. The white tents sparkled like snowflakes against the red-brown-gold of the vegetation. Gwen pointed to a large plastic cubicle.

"The john."

She took Sonya to a shed that a man had just gone into. Inside, she pointed to grayish-black, tubelike chunks on a rough-hewn table.

"Here's where we store the liverwurst," she joked, making a face.

The man—gaunt, bearded—laid a hand on the stony material.

"These are core samples from over six hundred feet down."

He stroked the long, thin tubes. They were broken apart at many points.

"They're sent to a lab in Vancouver," he continued. "They look for indicators in them."

"OK, smart-ass, tell her what indicators are."

Gwen walked around the shed as impatient as a wild animal waiting for food. The man fumbled around with his quilted cap, but he didn't seem offended.

"Indicators are minerals that occur along with diamonds. If you find a lot of them, then diamonds are usually near. You can often only see them under a microscope, like garnet—it's red. Chromium has a black shine, dioxide green, and ilmenites—"

"OK, Mr. Hot Shit Geologist, we don't need more details."

"No, no," Sonya contradicted her. "This is very interesting. I read that diamond-rich stones are often found in depressions beneath lakes in the tundra."

The geologist's face brightened.

"That's correct. Volcanic eruptions force diamonds to the surface. You find them in enormous kimberlitic pipes shaped like carrots. When magma breaks through the earth's surface through the pipes, it brings diamonds up with it. Glaciers form depressions later that get filled with water."

Sonya was amazed that he spoke so openly. Now she was certain that Diane was exploring for diamonds in the area. Perhaps not every significant location had been staked out and gobbled up by a global company. Had she thought she could find a major overlooked deposit? Gwen snapped her out of her thoughts. She was obviously fascinated by diamonds, too.

"These damn things are three billion years old—can our stupid human brains even take it all in?"

The geologist pulled at his beard.

"People don't care how old diamonds are. They're only interested in how much money they can make."

Gwen kept quiet. Sonya saw them exchange glances.

"OK, I've got to get going," the geologist announced. "I've got to get all this packed up before the chopper comes back." He checked his watch.

Gwen waved her hands, agitated.

"Holy cow, we'd better get cooking! At least people can eat *my* gems." She grabbed Sonya's arm and dashed outside.

"Nobody in these camps is normal. Everybody's a little cuckoo up here. That's why no alcohol, not one drop. Or else there'd be trouble."

Sonya's antennae quivered.

"What kind of trouble?"

"Squabbles, brawls. Anybody could go berserk at any time."

"Stabbings?"

Gwen stopped on the spot.

"Who told you about that shit?"

"A guy in the Explorer Bar."

Gwen opened the kitchen door. As they were going in, she muttered something like, "If I ever catch those bastards . . ." But Sonya wasn't sure she'd heard right.

Gwen pointed at the mountain of unpeeled potatoes.

"Just pretend they're diamonds, then it's easier."

She grinned. Sonya stared at the large knife Gwen gave her.

"Here." Gwen also handed her a pail. "Just toss—"

She was drowned out by the sudden roar of an engine. "What the fuck—"

Gwen stormed out, and Sonya came right after her.

CHAPTER 41

Sonya just caught a glimpse of a small plane diving at the camp before Gwen yanked her to the ground. Then they heard a shot. And another. Sonya screamed. Somebody else screamed. Gwen.

The engine noise receded quickly, and the hand clutching her arm relaxed. Sonya saw the terror on Gwen's face; then she saw blood running down Gwen's arm.

"C'mon," she urged, pulling her into the kitchen.

Sonya had practiced the drill hundreds of times in First-Aid. She knew the questions to ask by heart, the preparations, how to check the wound, the patient's condition.

"Those goddamn bastards," Gwen howled.

"Relax. Is there a camp doctor?"

"No. I'm bleeding. I'm gonna bleed to death!"

"Relax, Gwen. Let's take a look at your wound."

She felt the spot to see if there was a bullet beneath the skin. She bent Gwen's arm slightly to see better. The bullet must have passed through.

"Are there any clean dish towels?"

"In the box on the shelf."

Sonya snatched some towels, pressing one on the bleeding wound. Gwen whimpered.

The geologist threw open the door.

"They fired at us!" he bellowed, unable to contain himself.

"Get me the first aid box," Sonya ordered.

"What the hell—"

"The first aid box, quick! Over there, behind the fridge, on the rack!"

That was Gwen.

Patient is coherent and logical, Sonya noted to herself.

She found the iodine in the box and disinfected the wound. Then she applied a tourniquet.

"You've got to get to a hospital as fast as possible."

"The chopper should be here any minute," the geologist said. "Where's John? And the cops—we've got to let them know. And Diane."

There was a racket. The geologist was at the door in a single bound. A man with a gun burst in: John, the young man who'd met Sonya at the helicopter.

"Gwen, Jesus Christ!" he exclaimed. "I heard shots, but—"

"She's got to get to a doctor, that's got top priority," Sonya interrupted him. She secured the tourniquet.

John was already out the door, followed by the geologist.

"Blow them away, the sons of bitches," Gwen called.

"Shh," Sonya cautioned. "You must keep very still."

Sonya got painkillers out of the emergency box, and Gwen washed them down with a single gulp of coffee. Sonya bedded down her patient on a table.

"They've been after us forever," Gwen muttered. Maybe it was good to let her talk, Sonya reflected; it would keep her mind off the wound.

"Who?" she asked.

"They're after our claim, they want it by hook or crook."

"Who?"

"Goddamn bastards."

"You know who fired the shots?"

"I can well imagine. Rudy's to blame for everything. He should never have gotten mixed up with those guys."

"Who's Rudy?"

"Diane's ex-boyfriend." Then she shut up, as if she'd said too much.

"He probably didn't know what he was getting into," Sonya said, almost in passing. She had to feel her way carefully.

"He knew exactly what was up, that backstabber. Too bad he drowned before he was caught."

"He drowned?"

"They fished him out of the ocean, dead . . ." She bit her lip. "You got another pill? It hurts like hell."

"Sure," Sonya replied.

They heard another engine, but farther off this time. The geologist threw open the door. "The chopper's here. Gwen, you can get between John and me, so we can hold you on both sides. That'll be quickest."

"I'm coming, too," Sonya spoke up.

"No, somebody has to stay here. We'll take her to the chopper, and I'll take her to the hospital. John's coming right back."

She looked at him, aghast.

"I do *not* want to be in this camp all by myself!" she exclaimed as emphatically as she could.

"It's just a few minutes. John'll be right back."

Sonya shook her head.

Gwen stepped in.

"Can't Sonya come with me?"

"She's staying here," the geologist repeated. "I've got to go get backup." He said "backup," not "help" or "the police."

Before leaving, the geologist took a parka off a hook on the wall and laid it carefully around Gwen's shoulders. Sonya pulled up the zipper.

Gwen looked at her and grinned crookedly.

"Good that the Red Cross was invented in Sweden."

"Switzerland," Sonya said automatically.

Gwen laughed.

"Gotcha!"

"*Schlaumeier*," Sonya retorted.

"What?" Gwen shouted from the doorway.

"That's 'smart-ass' in Swedish." She waved good-bye.

"Watch the stairs!" She heard John warn them. Then the helicopter door was shut.

Just a few minutes—but Sonya was alone. Suppose the plane came back? *Just don't panic*, she told herself. She had to distract herself. The potatoes. She began peeling. And peeling and peeling. Thirty more minutes passed without a sound. No trace of John. Water. Where do they get water here? From the lake, of course. There must be a pump around someplace.

She picked up the plastic pail beside the fridge and anxiously felt her way outside around the tent. Dead-on, there was a pump. She put the pail under the spout and pumped the handle several times. Nothing but squeaks. Maybe it was driven by electricity, a generator. She pounded the handle in exasperation, and suddenly a strong jet of water poured into the pail.

At that second, she heard it: a hum, growing louder. The plane was coming back!

CHAPTER 42

Sonya left the pail behind and scooted around the corner of the kitchen tent. She could see the plane: red and white, like the Canadian flag. It was flying very low and made a quick turn toward the lake. She ducked along the tent. Another turn, now lower—the plane was making its approach.

She started to run, and her bootlaces came untied from their metal hooks. She fell but immediately picked herself up. Not the kitchen. That's the first place they'd look. Panicked, she ran to the shed where the core samples were. She stumbled over the door-step, shutting the door behind her. It was pitch-black. She opened the door a crack to let in some light. She saw the plane on the lake but no people. Her eyes feverishly searched inside the shed and stopped at a pile of boxes. She could hide behind them. She closed the door and crawled behind the barricade. Her heart was beating so wildly that she had trouble listening. What were the attackers doing anyway? Were they watching the tents for signs of resistance? Where was John? Was he ambushing them somewhere with a gun? The geologist wanted to go for backup. What kind of backup? Didn't they have a satellite phone to let the police know?

There—something was there! Voices. Shouts. A chaos of voices. Still, there were no shots. Maybe John had gone off on the helicopter. Maybe she'd simply been left behind.

She heard hurried heavy footsteps that came closer and closer. Sonya didn't dare breathe for fear that someone could hear her through the thin fabric walls. The door burst open. More footsteps. Then a soft scraping: the sound of soles turning on their axis. Then a loud snort. The intruder left the shed.

"Will! Will!"

It was a woman.

"Will, the door's unlocked. But everything seems OK."

Was she hallucinating? She knew that voice! Now— again—louder.

"I said everything seems to be OK."

Sonya stood up, feeling her way along the boxes. She peeked around the corner and saw a woman with short black hair standing at the open door.

"Diane!"

The person whipped around as if struck by lightning. Sonya reeled ahead, blinded by the light. Her hand tried to hold on to the pile of wooden crates.

"Look out!" Diane shouted. Too late. Sonya's arm was strong enough to send the wooden boards crashing to the floor, along with the irreplaceable core samples that shattered into a thousand little pieces.

The two women stood there horrified for several seconds. Then Sonya's entire body began to shake.

"I'm . . . so sorry," she stammered. "I . . ."

But Diane wasn't listening. She was focused on a point on the floor.

"Shh," she whispered, as if hypnotized. She bent over and picked up what looked like a lump of coal. In the ray of light coming through the open door, Sonya saw a flash on the round surface.

"Good God," Diane murmured. Her face was in rapture, like a kid staring at her first Christmas tree. Then she suddenly looked tense. She slowly laid the broken piece of stone back in the wooden box.

"Don't tell a soul what's happened, you hear me? You don't want to get blamed for wrecking a core sample, right? You could never pay for it."

Then she took Sonya's hand and led her outside.

"I'll take you to the kitchen," she said, closing the door behind her, but after a few steps, she came to an abrupt stop.

"Sonya," she said, giving her a hug. "Neither of us is going to give up, right?"

Sonya was too dazed to answer. She still felt terror in her limbs. She let Diane drag her along like a puppet.

All of a sudden, everything came back.

"Gwen's been hurt, a plane . . . they shot at us—"

"Yes, I know," Diane interrupted. "We'll talk about that, but I've an important thing to take care of first." She squeezed Sonya's hand. "It must have been a tremendous shock for you."

She spoke to Sonya as if she were a kid that had fallen off a bicycle. In the kitchen John, the redhead, came up to her.

"Where the hell were you?" he shouted at the sight of Sonya. "I couldn't find you anywhere!"

"Where's Will?" Diane fired back at him. Sonya's eyes scanned the tables, where men and women sat before empty plates. They'd apparently come with Diane. *Mealtime*, Sonya thought.

"On the john," somebody bellowed.

Some people laughed, but their nervousness was apparent.

"Take care of Sonya until I'm back," Diane said. She smiled at her in encouragement, then disappeared.

Sonya was instantly surrounded. People took her to the table, conjuring up a hot bowl of soup out of nowhere. She saw two men busy at the stove and was bombarded with questions.

While she was answering, it seemed as if everything had been just a bad dream.

Finally it was her turn to ask a question.

"Who were those guys in the plane, and why did they shoot at us?"

A sudden silence.

Then a young woman spoke up.

"Don't worry your head about it. They won't be back. Would you like some fish?"

All eyes were on the stove.

"Still ten minutes," came an answer. Steam rose from the huge pot she'd filled with potatoes earlier.

"Sonya should certainly know about it," John interjected. "After all, she was in the thick of it, eh? It's no secret. She maybe saved Gwen's life."

He didn't wait for an answer but began at once.

"This here claim"—he pointed around vaguely—"was registered by Diane four years ago. In other words, she bought it from a prospector from Yellowknife who didn't want it anymore. He hadn't found anything and was out of dough, but Diane was convinced he hadn't looked in the right places. Some of us were already working for her then, including me. We were all hoping, big time. We dreamed night and day about a fantastic diamond mine. Didn't we, Peggy?"

"And how!" the woman next to Sonya agreed.

"Diane had a small exploration company, a handful of people, and a little money—just enough for a few test drillings. It was in September, like now, so it got dark early, and the ground was beginning to freeze. We were down to our last five thousand dollars for one last test drill—the very last one. Rudy said we should forget it."

At the mention of Rudy, Sonya felt the tension in the room.

"Diane wanted to, too," Peggy added.

"We all wanted to," John continued. "But it was our last chance. Rudy took a last sample to the core shed, where the core samples were chalked up before being shipped to the lab. Whatever happened there, there was no one else in the shed. But Rudy must have secretly switched the samples."

"Switched?" Sonya looked inquisitively at John.

The rattle of cooking and the hiss of hot water filled the silence.

"Rudy sent plain old crap to the lab instead of the original core sample." John's voice exuded anger.

"He replaced the sample with ordinary blue clay that had no indicators," Peggy filled her in.

"Why did he do that?"

"Because he was a crook," she said.

"Because he guessed—or knew," John said, "that the sample was a surefire winner. That we'd struck a rich diamond deposit."

"C'mon, everybody, soup's on!" The voice from the kitchen came like a bugle call. They all stormed to the counter near the stove. Only Sonya stayed in her chair, in a daze. Her thoughts were whirling around like mad, but before she knew it, a heaping plate was in front of her. She'd forgotten how hungry she was.

A ravenous quiet reigned for a while. Then John picked up where he'd left off.

"You know, we suspected early on—not immediately, but when the lab report came back that there were no indicators—that just couldn't be."

Sonya thought about the flash of light in the shed but was careful not to mention it.

"We talked to Diane, but she didn't want to listen at first. She simply didn't believe it. Rudy was"—John ran his fingers through his bushy red hair—"she was engaged to Rudy."

"But she listened to Robert," Peggy chimed in.

Sonya dropped her fork.

"Bob Stanford's a mining engineer," John explained. "He's incorruptible. He's the one who finally scraped up the money."

Sonya stopped eating.

"Money? For what?"

"For a second drill hole, right beside the first one. Diane did it on the sly."

"You should tell her why it came to that," Peggy urged him.

"Robert learned that Rudy was secretly hunting around for financing. He needed the dough to buy the claim. He told several people with money that Diane's company would soon abandon her claim and then he'd register it under his name, and it would be a safe bet."

"A safe bet?"

At that moment the door opened. Sonya felt a cold draft on her shoulder. Then a hand.

"Eat up," Diane ordered. "We're flying to Yellowknife in an hour."

CHAPTER 43

Dear Inge,

I'm wondering about you. And even more about myself.
It's amazing that it took so long for me to catch on, and just
as amazing that you thought I'd never find out. No, of course
you never thought that. You only hoped I wouldn't notice
anything until people discovered everything about me.

But it still isn't entirely clear to me how much you knew.
It's not really that important. The main thing is, I know now.
At some point my powers of deduction did kick in. Maybe
my intuition as well. But you fooled yourself. You thought
you knew everything. You thought you could risk it, but you
can't toy with people.

We only know a part of the truth. Haven't we often talked
about that? But now it's too late. Fate has run its course. I'm
not suffering the consequences all by myself. You imagined it
would be different, right? I can assure you: Your shock right
now is only the beginning. The worst is yet to come.

Sonya

The lake was blueberry blue, like saturated ink. Its water
turned into sparkling silver stars wherever the sun's rays hit. Egg

yolk–yellow bushes lined the shore, backed by the flaming-red creeping vegetation. Sonya drafted her e-mail to Inge in her notebook, stuck it in her backpack, and stretched her legs out in the sand. She could just make out the backlit white tents, like blurry dots. A herd of caribou grazed on the other bank.

Swarms of insects circled around her face. She applied more of the stinking mosquito repellent that made her skin smart. The anger bubbling inside her repressed any fear of bears or wild gunfire.

Suddenly she heard a person panting and the tread of heavy boots. A hooded figure approached.

Sonya froze.

"What the hell are you doing here? I've been looking all over for you!" Diane stood in front of her, out of breath.

"I'm waiting."

"You're waiting? But not here! The chopper lands on the other side of the lake. You know that."

Sonya didn't budge, didn't look up.

"I'm waiting until we can finally have that face-to-face."

"But I told you—in Yellowknife. Now's not the time, you can see that. C'mon, get up, we've got to go."

"No, Diane, first we talk."

"Are you nuts? The chopper's coming any minute now."

"It can wait." Sonya was more decisive than she'd been in her whole life.

"No, Sonya, it can't. It costs me a thousand bucks an hour."

Sonya cocked her head.

"Cut it out, Diane. That thing you want to take to Yellowknife is worth a fortune by itself."

She didn't miss seeing Diane go bug-eyed. Diane was dumbstruck for a minute. Sonya got up and shook the sand off her pants.

"You think I'm stupid? You think I don't know why you're in such a rush to leave camp? I've seen too much, haven't I?"

Diane remained silent.

"I'm not getting into that helicopter until we've had a talk."

Diane slipped her hand into her jacket pocket. The next thing Sonya saw was the muzzle of a revolver.

"You've no choice, Sonya," Diane said in a voice like broken glass. "This is my once-in-a-lifetime chance, and I'm not gonna blow it."

Sonya felt no fear. Not even consternation. Only emptiness. A gaping hole.

"Is this how you treat people you find inconvenient? You simply knock them off just like the man who was knifed?"

The hand holding the revolver began to tremble. Diane's face turned pale. Suddenly Sonya grasped who she had standing before her: This woman had spent years traveling an area as big as some European countries looking for any indication of diamonds. She'd spent cold nights in thin tents, collecting thousands of rock samples without results, getting financing together time and again. And only to be cheated by her fiancé. Everything had gone down the toilet. And now she was just a hairbreadth away from her goal.

Smarter to get out of her way and follow orders.

"Get your backpack."

Sonya picked it up.

"Along the lake and then left."

She stumbled ahead, blinded by the low sun. The ground was a gleaming red carpet. She couldn't see the helicopter in the glaring light, but she could hear it.

Diane grasped her arm.

"We've got to hurry. We're flying to Vancouver tonight."

"We?" Sonya found it hard to keep up with her.

"I've got to take you along. You're absolutely right—you know too much."

"So who has a problem with that?"

The noise got louder, and now a shiny metal insect appeared in the sky.

"People with money. Get it? Now we need buckets of cash." She shouted her words over the tundra. The force of the rotor blades flattened the bushes.

Sonya did get it. As if dreaming, she could see a tarmac in front of her with planes landing, planes being unloaded. She saw earthmovers, excavators, hoisting cranes, and a crater in the ground as if a meteor had hit. She heard a constant rattling and banging and pounding all over that wasteland.

"So that's it, it's the money?" she bellowed back.

Diane shook her head. She raised a fist up to the sky and spread her middle and index fingers. A victory sign. The helicopter landed, and two men jumped out and greeted Diane, who shouted something at them. She'd put away her pistol. After Sonya got into the helicopter, she noticed somebody else behind the pilot, in the second row of seats. The stranger flew with them to Yellowknife. They made a quick stop at Sonya's motel, where the stranger watched Sonya pack her things. Then he took them to the airport, where Diane took out her pistol.

"It doesn't shoot bullets, just blanks—it's to scare off bears. Actually, it doesn't make a bang anymore, it gave up the ghost long ago." She gave a sheepish grin. "Extraordinary times call for extraordinary measures."

She gave the warning pistol to the unknown companion, who tossed it into a garbage can without a word.

Sonya was hardly able to think straight. It was as if a bizarre film were passing before her eyes. No matter how hard she tried to make the plot add up, it simply wouldn't. Diane handed her a piece of paper.

"Your plane ticket."

"I've got one, but it's for the day after tomorrow," Sonya said.

"You don't need it anymore. Mission accomplished."

"So in Vancouver I'm free to go?"

Diane took her by the shoulder.

"That would not be convenient. Let me explain some more in the waiting room."

They sat out of earshot of the other passengers. Even their guard—Sonya assumed he was a hired security guard—stood several feet away, although he didn't take his eyes off them.

Sonya raised her shoulders and shivered.

"God, there's a draft in this place."

She opened her travel bag, rooted around in it briefly, and pulled out a scarf. Surreptitiously, she turned on the microphone of her video camera. The conversation could begin.

"So how did Rudy die?"

"Who told you about Rudy?"

"Some people in the camp. So how did he die?"

"In a plane crash."

"Where?"

"Near Prince Rupert."

"In a seaplane?"

"Yes. And your husband was the pilot."

There was a pause.

"You've known this the whole time?"

"Yes, but I couldn't tell you."

"Why not?"

"I wanted to wait until you asked me. I know these events are painful for you. Maybe you didn't want to find out too much. What you know can hurt you."

"Is Tonio . . . Did my husband do anything criminal?"

"Nothing points to that. But Rudy had a way of dragging well-meaning folks into his dirty business."

"What kind of dirty business?"

"I thought someone already told you."

"I want to hear it from you."

"OK. It was four years ago. We'd taken over a big claim that was almost twenty square miles: the place we were just at. The camp was built right on the spot. I was convinced we'd find diamonds there. The only question was, where? We were damn lucky to get that claim. It was karma for me, something had to come of it."

"Karma? What are you talking about?"

"More or less all the key areas up there were claimed ten years ago. When the diamond rush got underway, anybody who could fly there made claims where it looked promising. Later on, a prospector in Yellowknife wanted to dump his claim. He probably needed money fast. Or he thought it wouldn't bring anything in. We found out about it in time and pounced."

"Tell me more about Rudy."

"Don't be so impatient. The story's rather complicated . . . So we found it out by chance and bought the prospecting rights. It was a miracle, a genuine miracle."

"But you drilled and found nothing until the last drill hole."

"Rudy was the one to collect the core samples. He must have suspected we hit a bull's-eye. In the shed where the core samples—"

"What's the matter?"

"Let's sit a little farther away from these people. We don't want any eavesdroppers."

[Rustling]

"All of us trusted Rudy. As a geologist, he was often in the shed all by himself. And that's where he switched the core sample with a fake one."

"The one he sent to the lab."

"He'd probably been planning it for some time. That's what I believe today. He must have been harboring his scheme for a long time."

"Even when you first met him?"

[Pause]

"I don't know, Sonya. I loved him. I didn't notice anything. How well do you really know a person?"

[Pause. Throat-clearing sound.]

"Did you know what your husband was up to in Prince Rupert?"

"No, I still don't to this day. Do you?"

"I know he flew a plane to Rainy River Lodge."

"What's that?"

"It's a floating hotel for fishermen, about half an hour from Prince Rupert."

"But Tonio didn't fish. He was never interested in fishing!"

"He booked a room for two people for three nights."

"For him and Nicky."

"Maybe his son wanted to go fishing."

"But—"

Your attention, please. The flight to Edmonton has been delayed by approximately ten minutes.

"Damn. We might miss our connection to Vancouver."

"It's just ten minutes late."

"If you only knew how . . ."

[Silence]

"Did Tonio . . . Where did he and Rudy meet?"

"There are witnesses who say they met at the lodge. Rudy went there to meet potential backers for the diamond mine."

"But he didn't have a mine."

"No mine, but he had my claim."

"You handed over the claim to him?"

"Rudy knew I wanted to give up the prospecting rights to the claim. It would have cost me big bucks to hold on to it. I was broke again by that time. I'd gone through all my cash."

"That's when he latched on to your claim."

"Yes. He used straw men. But I found out too late."

"Too late? You mean after his death?"

"No, before then. Robert Stanford told me he'd heard through the grapevine that Rudy was seeking investors for a diamond mine. He told them he knew of a deposit that couldn't miss—he'd had a survey done. One of the investors got in touch with Robert to learn more about Rudy."

"Why Robert?"

"He has an excellent reputation in the business. And he knows what's what in the tundra."

"Then what happened?"

"Robert informed me. It was . . . I had to believe him. I fought it, but . . . I had to do something. We decided to take the investor into our confidence, and he played along. He persuaded Rudy that he was very interested, so Rudy showed him more documents. Things couldn't move fast enough for him. No money, no mine—simple as that."

She paused.

"Did Tonio and Rudy work together? Is that what it boiled down to?"

"The police couldn't find any evidence. Tonio's role in the whole affair is very mysterious. Probably Rudy simply wanted to go to Vancouver that day, and there wasn't a flight early enough for him. So maybe he asked Tonio to fly him to Prince Rupert. The lodge manager gave testimony that your husband actually wanted to postpone the flight, but Rudy could always get people to do things for him against their better judgment."

"So the fourth passenger was the investor?"

"Who on earth told you about a fourth passenger?"

"A pilot on the Queen Charlottes—the pilot who was first on the scene of the crash."

"Good Lord, Sonya, do you have his name?"

"I'd have to look in my notebook. But Robert told me that he died recently. What does that mean? What's with him?"

"That's what I'd like to know, too. That's—"

Calling all passengers for Flight 345 to Edmonton. Your plane is now ready for boarding.

"Wait," Sonya said. "Tell me who the people were who shot at us."

"Some crazies looking for revenge. Let's go."

"But—"

"Later, Sonya."

CHAPTER 44

Sonya made up her mind never to tell Diane that she'd recorded their conversation. In the plane, the more she thought about the news she'd just heard, the more confusing it seemed. There were too many inconsistencies; Sonya didn't see any logic to it, particularly how Tonio was involved. And then that mysterious investor who suddenly got into the act. But you can't interrogate the dead. So some things had to remain unknown. Was that really all Diane knew?

Sonya knew better than to ask Diane more questions in a full airplane. Tiredness overcame her suddenly, and Diane had to wake her up before they landed in Edmonton. With the security guard, they were the last to board the Vancouver flight, and Sonya dozed off once again.

In Vancouver, she was still only half-awake during the taxi ride, and when she walked into Diane's apartment, she could have kissed the marble floor. She dragged herself, robotlike, to her room, dumping her backpack onto the floor.

"You can go right to bed, but the door has to stay open," Diane ordered. The guard was standing behind her.

"Why?" Sonya squinted in the glaring light.

"We have to keep an eye on you. Nobody can utter a peep until we've informed our backers and the stock market."

"Who's 'we'?"

"A few people are coming over to discuss crucial business matters. I'll get you some earplugs so you can sleep."

Sonya saw her alarm clock indicated twelve thirty a.m.

"Can I at least go to the bathroom?"

"Yes, but no cell phone!"

Sonya rubbed her face. Tired as she was, she couldn't even have entered a number.

She heard voices later in the distance, then nothing at all.

The silence must have woken me up, Sonya figured out the next morning. She rolled over under the soft covers. Then she remembered the earplugs. It was still very quiet, even after she'd removed them. Only the monotonous murmur of traffic came through the windowpanes. Then she noticed the door was closed. Where was her guard? Where was Diane?

She slipped into a bathrobe and crept upstairs to the living room. Champagne bottles were on the table amid a dozen empty glasses. She wanted to turn on the coffeemaker, but grinding the beans would rouse the whole house. So tea it was.

Then she saw a white piece of paper on the table. A press release from the Thunderrock company and its president, Diane Kesowsky. It was short, nothing fancy: "Thunderrock Inc. in Vancouver has discovered a diamond deposit so promising that the world's largest mining company will be financing the project."

There were two hastily scribbled sentences at the bottom in Diane's handwriting: *Am at the office. Why don't you have breakfast with my other guest?*

A second guest, who was sure to be one of the nocturnal champagne drinkers. Sonya decided that under the circumstances she needed a double espresso. To hell with any late risers. The grinder rattled like a steam locomotive. But nobody stirred. Maybe the guest had already left.

Sonya showered and got dressed. Then she went to the Granville Island Market and bought some hard-crusted European bread. She went by the table where she and Diane had sat, where she had "left" her wallet. How long ago was it? At least three weeks, but it seemed like an eternity.

When she got back, she heard someone in the shower. Then she noticed a second cup of espresso in the kitchen. The guest had served himself. She didn't feel like having breakfast with some stranger; there was no time for idle chitchat. She had to get ready, book a flight back to Prince Rupert. She hurried into her room.

Now she could use her phone again undisturbed.

Somebody had texted her: "*Why don't you call back? Don't you want to have a new experience? Robert.*"

The noise from the shower stopped. She quickly called Robert's number and heard a soft ring somewhere. That must be Diane's telephone. Robert didn't pick up. Then a door opened on the floor above, and she could hear the ring distinctly.

That ring! Sonya realized.

She went up the stairs in slow motion, crossed the living room, and stopped in the hallway.

Robert was holding his cell phone. A bath towel was casually wrapped around his hips, and pearls of water rolled down his naked upper body. His wet hair was brushed back, making his facial features stand out more.

"Did my surprise work?" His eyes twinkled.

"Who let you in?" she retorted, though of course she already knew the answer.

"Diane didn't want to, but I blackmailed her."

She stole a glance at his damp, shining skin, his broad shoulders, his strong arms.

"Diane wouldn't let herself be blackmailed, I don't buy that."

"Oh, yes, she would. I told her I'd tell everybody she threatened you with a starter's pistol."

Sonya nearly dropped her phone.

"How the hell did you know that?"

"She told me yesterday, no, tonight—after two or three glasses of champagne. I believe she wanted to clear her conscience. But let me throw on some clothes, then I'd like to whip up my famous omelet for you."

Sonya couldn't suppress a smile.

"Don't forget to put on your apron," she called, circling around the living room. She picked up the empty bottles and glasses, tossed the crumpled paper napkins in the garbage, and wiped the table clean.

Robert was back amazingly fast, wearing a loose, freshly ironed shirt with the top two buttons undone. She smelled a scent that must be thousands of years old—still absolutely effective. Robert looked at her in silence. Sonya suddenly realized how dangerously close he was. She fought like a drowning person against the waves looming over her. She thrashed about with her words.

"Did Diane delegate you to guard me? Her bodyguard was standing by my bedroom yesterday."

Amused, Robert shook his head.

"I think Diane's nerves were shot. She was just that far from her goal; she wanted to get to Vancouver as quickly as possible to get the contract with that company. They were thinking about a merger with another exploration company. And the news had to get out pronto before anybody got wind of it. The stock market calls the shots so often these days. Everything hung by a thread."

She nodded toward the empty champagne bottles on the kitchen counter.

"Did you take part in this revelry?"

He slowly rolled up his sleeves, revealing two tanned arms.

"Yes. I haven't had champagne in a long time. I had something important to celebrate, too."

She raised her eyebrows. "Apparently there's nothing that puts people in a better mood than the prospect of lots of money."

She'd barely gotten the words out when she was embarrassed. She didn't have the right to make fun of Diane and her team—including Robert, who was obviously admired by them all.

He said nothing at first. He opened the fridge and took out a carton of eggs, cracking them open into a bowl. He washed his hands and flipped a towel over his shoulder.

"Aprons aren't my thing, as you can see," he said. "Would you like pepperoni, onions, and fresh mushrooms?"

Sonya nodded. "Can I help?"

"Sure. Could you chop the pepperoni?"

They orbited each other in the tight kitchen like mutually attracting planets that still kept their distance. Sometimes Robert slightly brushed against her, leaving behind a glowing spot on Sonya's skin. He beat the eggs for a while, then stopped.

"*My* champagne celebration was because you came back to Vancouver in one piece," he confessed. He went back to work, not looking at her.

Her hand kept turning the kitchen knife around.

"Yes, others weren't so lucky," she said.

He stopped stirring.

"Oh, I nearly forgot—Gwen's doing well considering the circumstances. She lost surprisingly little blood; the doctors were very impressed that the tourniquet was applied so efficiently. Where'd you learn that?"

She felt a rising wave of relief. Gwen was safe.

"How wonderful! I'm so happy that—Ow!"

She felt pain for a second, and then blood dripped from her finger. Robert went to grab the dish towel on his shoulder, but she called, "I'll be right back!" and rushed to the bathroom. She stuck her finger in her mouth, utterly improper. What was crucial at that moment was to stop her tears from coming, tears of joy and exhaustion. She didn't want Robert to see them; they made her look vulnerable and weak. She stuck a bandage on the cut and freshened up.

"Everything OK?" she heard Robert ask.

Going back in, she managed a smile.

"I've taken first aid courses—two dozen, easily. At least all that effort wasn't wasted."

She stuck her bandaged finger in the air like a trophy.

He laughed.

"I think we should first have our omelets and put off the explosive topics till afterward, before more calamities happen."

He offered her a glass.

"And perhaps we should start off with a toast."

She accepted the glass.

"To the great diamond strike," she said.

"To Sonya, who never loses her poise or her faith in people," he countered.

Her hand was so shaky that she spilled some champagne.

"You don't mean me, surely?"

Instead of replying, he pointed to the plates.

"The omelets are getting cold."

Her appetite surprised her, winning out over her nervousness. She praised Robert's cooking, which he received with evident pleasure.

They ate in silence for some time.

"I'm waiting," he said at last.

"What for?"

"For your questions. I know they're on the tip of your tongue."

"Don't court disaster."

"Who's talking about disaster? I'm happy to be peacefully sitting here having breakfast with you."

She snapped up the bait.

"Who were those people in the plane? Why did they shoot at the camp?"

He spread some peanut butter on his toast.

"A while back, a suicide happened in Diane and Rudy's camp. One of the dirt baggers killed himself."

"What's a *dirt bagger*?" Sonya asked.

"They're the ones who collect earth samples for the lab to test for indicators. It's done before deep drilling can begin. This guy was a student, one tough hombre. That's what he appeared to be, at any rate. What Diane didn't know was his medical history. He'd been suffering from deep depression for several years. Everybody felt awful about his death. It was very sad."

"Did he kill himself with a knife?"

"Is that the rumor in Yellowknife?"

"No, there's talk of an unsolved murder."

Robert chewed slowly, taking his time to answer.

"That's the family's version. His parents and siblings don't want to face up to the truth. I think it was frustration that drove him to it. Diane and her team didn't find anything after all that test drilling and had to throw in the towel. After all that hard work and all their hopes. The dream of finding diamonds is a powerful motivator—but the fall afterward is all the harder. Nobody knew what Rudy had up his sleeve back then."

He crumpled up his napkin.

"The student's family felt cheated. They'd not only lost a loved one but the dream of getting rich quick."

"But that's no reason to go out and shoot people. They were probably drunk. It's like the Wild West! Gwen could have been killed!"

"You too, Sonya."

"Gwen shielded me with her body."

"I owe her my most profound gratitude—it was actually all my fault."

"Your fault? I don't get that."

"I asked Diane to let you go to the camp. I wanted you to see a camp, to experience that atmosphere up there, to stand in the tundra, in that unbelievable vastness . . . And, OK, yes—to see a test drill. I wanted you to enter the world where I so often work."

He picked up one of the bottles.

"There's a bit left over. Shall we kill it?"

Sonya nodded, though she realized it would make her even more light-headed after Robert's confession.

"Diane couldn't refuse my wish, and I knew it."

Sonya sipped her drink.

"I was struck by how cold she was when she returned to camp after the shooting. So detached. As if it were no concern of hers and nothing had happened. She didn't even tell the police."

Robert stared out the window.

"Nothing else counts at a time like that but diamonds. There's no place for any other emotions. Prospectors, treasure hunters, geologists, soldiers of fortune—they're all driven by this obsession. It's stronger than hunger or sleep, stronger than love. If you're not made that way, you won't last in this business."

He stopped talking, still staring out the window. How much she loved that intelligent, open face, the quiet seriousness there. But she couldn't let it distract her, certainly not now. She didn't have much time left.

"Does that mean they do things just this side of what's illegal? For them, does the end justify the means? Is that why the police weren't called in—because they'd discover things that were secret?"

Robert shifted his gaze back to her. Did she read dismay in it, or was she simply imagining things?

"Companies like Diane's have their own security services. She's hired specialists. The police can't be everywhere, especially not all over the Northwest Territories."

He ran a hand through his drying hair.

"The greatest danger is temptation. People who give in to it sooner or later fall into the clutches of organized crime."

"But that has nothing to do with the plane and the shooting, right?"

"No. But it might have something to do with your husband's death, and your stepson's."

Her eyes were glued on him. She was waiting.

"It's become clear that Rudy had a rendezvous with people who wanted to launder money from drug dealing. Put the dirty money into a diamond mine—lo and behold! Now it's legal. At some point, the whole business spooked him; he didn't want to give up control of the project. But the gangsters probably couldn't be gotten rid of so easily. They wanted a foot in Canada. That's why Rudy was so desperate to find new financing."

Sonya looked more closely at Robert's hands. What would he do if she gently stroked them? The back of his hand, the sinews and veins, the soft places between his long, strong fingers.

He took her silence the wrong way.

"I don't want to cause you further pain."

"No, no, go on. I've got to find out at some point."

"The police aren't ruling out that the crash wasn't an accident."

"But?"

"Perhaps it was murder, but that's only a suspicion. There's no evidence, no leads, no concrete clues."

"So I will likely never find out."

"No, we will likely never find out."

How familiar that felt! How often had it occurred in the history of mankind: no clues, no witnesses, no evidence, no certainty. Events were irrevocably lost to science—to the memory of following generations. Strange, she didn't feel any sadness. No despair, no angry protests. Just resignation. Was now the time to bow to the inevitable?

She fiddled with her necklace. She'd found out some things despite it all. For instance, that the man at their table in the market was a security agent for Diane's company. Diane wanted to check Sonya out to make sure she was the person she claimed to be. The security agent had an hour to verify her ID, her personal information, and her banking arrangements. That same man steered the boat that drove Robert's attackers off before they could crush their kayak.

"I've heard about the trial in Vancouver and your part in it," she said.

Robert folded his hands on the table.

"In retrospect, I should never have exposed you to that danger," he mused. "But you never know how far some people will go. The audacity of those rats surprised even me. But they didn't get away."

"They were caught?"

"Yes. But they weren't the masterminds, of course. Just small fry. Still, you should never call it quits."

"Was that the news you wanted to tell me? Your text message came too late. That guard wouldn't let me check my cell phone."

Robert leaned forward.

"Your German friends showed up here. They asked the super about you."

"What? Gerti and Helmut?"

He nodded and asked, "Are they really as innocuous as you think?"

Sonya took a deep breath, stalling for time before answering. She'd left the super's phone number on the blackboard. But even then—how did they find out where she was staying? What's more: Why did they want to find out?

"Did the super tell them what they wanted?"

"Diane's guard found out they told him you'd left something behind in their RV. He took it without another word. The super is obviously very security conscious."

"What did they give him?"

Robert pushed an envelope toward her. She tore it open, and little red pills dropped out.

"For my allergies." She blushed. She'd never even missed the damn things. Robert didn't say anything, he just watched her.

The ring of Sonya's cell phone delivered them from their embarrassment. She heard a voice.

"Lions Gate Hotel."

Tonio's hotel. Her pulse raced.

"Yes?"

"We found an envelope, with photographs belonging to a Mr. Vonlanden."

CHAPTER 45

Robert dropped Sonya off at the Lions Gate Hotel. She'd suspected instantly they had Nicky's photographs. Tonio never printed out photos on his trips. He hated piles of printouts.

Sonya held Robert's car door open and looked at him.

"I'm so lucky to know you," she said. "You've become very important to me."

Then she went off, not waiting for his response. The words had cost her nearly all her courage; she needed what was left for what awaited her. The lobby looked gloomier than the last time and was surprisingly empty. This time a man stood behind the computer at the reception desk. His badge read "General Manager." When she told him why she came, the man already knew. He'd called her himself.

"My staff told me your husband was in a fatal accident," he sympathized, handing her an envelope. "I hope these pictures bring you a little consolation."

"It's such a surprise," Sonya replied, "but I'm very happy."

"I found the bag in a drawer. It had an envelope that was supposed to have been picked up at the time, but . . . it didn't happen. As you can see, we don't throw things out."

Sonya managed a smile.

"That speaks for the quality of the hotel."

The manager thanked her for the compliment.

Out on the sidewalk, Sonya let the sea breeze caress her forehead. She clutched the bag, as if it could be ripped from her through some unfortunate circumstance. She took a window seat in the *crêperie* next to the hotel, forgetting to place her order until a young man behind the bar called over to her.

"I'm waiting for somebody," Sonya replied, opening the bag. She found a normal, colorfully printed envelope from a camera store. A bright green label had words printed on it: "*For Odette.*"

She took out the pictures and went through them feverishly. All the pictures were of Vancouver: a silhouette of the glass-covered inner city, the cruise ships at Canada Place, the North Shore Mountains, the Capilano Suspension Bridge, street scenes, the steam-driven clock in old Gastown, a seaplane in the harbor. There were no revelations, no clues pointing to imminent events, no people that she knew: only strangers in the city crowds.

Wait, there, in the last picture—Tonio's silhouette, half-covered by a passerby. These were typical tourist shots, and not particularly good ones at that. They distinctly bore Nicky's finger-prints: shot too fast, with no feeling for structure or perspective. Nicky didn't have any artistic standards—unlike Tonio, whose photos were a source of income. Nicky had a cheap camera, his fourth, because he always kept losing them. She'd given him this one as a present.

A haggard young woman staggered past outside; her deep-set eyes indicated drug use. There were no pictures of things like that; Nicky had always had a certain shyness toward people. When they invited guests over, he'd quickly disappear up to his room or go to the movies. Odette would shrug when she told her about it, saying that was normal for teenagers. Nicky was just a bit introverted, she said. Fortunately, Odette had a good rapport with him. When she came to visit, he'd show his face. She knew how to draw him out.

Sonya went through the stack once again, slowly. Why had Tonio left Nicky's nondescript pictures for Odette? Why had Nicky given them to him in the first place? Wouldn't he have wanted to keep them himself?

She looked in the envelope again. No negatives. Just an advertisement for the camera store, which wasn't far from there. Then something caught her eye. A promotion: two for one. That was it! A customer got two copies of the pictures for the same price. Nicky gave his second set to his father, who for some reason left them for Odette. But why? So Odette could see where Tonio and Nicky had spent their time together? This explanation didn't seem very convincing. Odette could have found that out from Tonio directly.

The waiter arrived at her table.

"Would you like something to drink while you're waiting for your friend?"

"Unfortunately I'm out of time," Sonya replied, putting away the pictures. She hurriedly left the *crêperie* and walked to Davie Street, where she'd seen a travel agency.

Once again it all went amazingly fast. By one o'clock, she had in her hands an e-ticket for a flight to Prince Rupert. She had exactly three hours to get to the airport.

CHAPTER 46

From: soneswunder@swifel.com
Sent: September 24, 22:36
To: Sonya Werner
Re: The worst is yet to come?

Dear Sonya,

You're right: it was only a question of time. I knew from the outset that the truth would come out someday. At some point you would hit upon the crucial evidence and connect the dots. It was inevitable.

I'm guessing it was the newspaper article that put you on my trail, right? It was missing after my Vancouver trip. I showed it to Diane at the time. You probably found it somewhere in the guest room, where I stayed during my visit.

That you of all people found the article—I call it karma. You'd probably call it just a coincidence. But we were never on the same page there. I've long known that a Swiss man by the name of Tonio Vonlanden flew the plane carrying Diane's former fiancé, but I didn't have a clue until recently that Tonio Vonlanden was your husband. You go by the name of Werner, of course, and you weren't in the newspaper photograph.

Believe me, I didn't have the slightest idea—until a museum visitor told me you were Tonio Vonlanden's second wife. She said how hard it must be for you to have lost a husband and stepson. The visitor assumed that our exhibition of funeral practices since the Middle Ages was maybe a catharsis for you. That was on your day off, and I was glad you didn't have to listen to her speculations.

I'd always assumed your husband died in an accident in the Swiss Alps. You never talked about it, but I could see nevertheless that you were suffering.

That same day I hurried home to talk to Wilfried. Rudy is Wilfried's brother. See, we're all connected: Diane, Rudy, Wilfried, me, you, Tonio, Nicky. Rudy was the black sheep of the family, but I didn't know that initially. I got to know Wilfried through Rudy when I was first in Canada. Wilfried was in Vancouver at the same time that I was. I've hardly told a soul about it for Wilfried's sake. He didn't want to be linked to Rudy. But now it's out, and he told me that evening that you ought to know.

Wilfried and I were completely in a state that evening. You should know that it wasn't clear to us what part Tonio played in the tragedy. Nobody knew exactly what went on in Prince Rupert. And you of all people had to become my colleague! Naturally I wondered later if our connection was really just a coincidence. You know what I mean. But then Wilfried and I came to the conclusion that you couldn't have known about Diane and Rudy.

The police in Canada declared the circumstances of the disaster classified information. Wilfried was questioned several times about Rudy—interrogated, I should say, which helped him figure out a lot of things. Then it was suddenly announced that the police investigation was closed, and evidently that wasn't true.

After talking to the museum visitor, I thought you ought to know the truth. Just looking at you, I could see what was the matter. There's no one in the world who could live with that pain in their eyes. There has to be healing, or else it's like a cancer. I didn't want you to find out about it from the police someday—when it would be too late anyway. I thought that you ought to find it out for yourself, little by little, the way you discovered things as a historian. I thought that was the easier way to go about it. And if your heart hurts too much, you still have your head to deal with it.

I arranged everything: the exhibition (I'd wanted to do that for a long time, I must admit. Else Seel was handed to me on a silver platter), the trip, your stay with Diane. I took a risk—that, I admit. But I don't toy with people. You decided on this trip because you wanted to go, Sonya. You were ready for it. I'm prepared to live with the consequences. Am I shocked? Yes. But better a shocking ending than a shock without end.

Sonya, I hope you won't forget, in spite of everything, how dear you truly are to me.

Yours,

Inge

CHAPTER 47

A knocking, softly at first—then it became louder and louder until it banged like a drum.

Sonya was jolted out of her sleep. She screwed up her eyes. The drumming noise that woke her was rain, a real downpour that attacked the skylight over her bed.

She plumped up a pillow behind her, leaning back on the headboard of the canopy bed. She was surrounded on all sides by frills—butter-yellow and pink flower patterns, embroidered vines—and shiny brass.

It wasn't to her taste, but her B and B in Prince Rupert felt like a luxury hotel compared with the youth hostel.

She pushed the curtains aside. The dreary view was not promising. She groped for her cell phone on the night table with a sigh. She'd already stored the number.

"Greenblue Air. Good Morning. How can we help you?"

"When are you flying to Rainy River Lodge?"

"Not until tomorrow, at two p.m., we return at four."

"Is Sam the pilot on that flight?"

"No, Sam's not flying till Friday. He goes to Rainy River Lodge at noon. The weather's supposed to be better on Friday. How long are you here for?"

Friday. Two days of waiting. Two long days. But she needed Sam. She needed him for her plan.

"OK, I'll go Friday."

"That's probably better. We don't know if we're flying at all today. The weather's terrible. What name is the booking under?"

"Sonya Werner."

The breakfast the B and B owner set before her lifted her spirits. She wolfed down the homemade pancakes with blueberry jam and whipped cream and the subsequent fried eggs, sausages, and home fries. The rain had to be counteracted with something. Her full stomach made her so tired that she went right back to bed. She just wanted to sleep all day to make time pass more quickly . . .

A ring jerked her out of her slumber. A guy named Fred was on the phone. How had he gotten her number?

"Fred, from Raincoast Conservation."

She was wide-awake in a flash.

"Yes, this is the right number. Did you find out anything?"

"I can give you a little information. It certainly wasn't simple. The police officers we talked to were very tight-lipped. Because of the privacy laws, you know."

"I can imagine."

"Well, there is something to report. The victim you were inquiring about was a rather young lady, a tourist from Europe."

"From Switzerland?"

"We weren't told. This tourist rented a camper—apparently by herself—so she could go to a lake near Prince Rupert."

"Do you know when that was?"

"I only know the date of the incident. It was three years ago, on September 14."

Sonya's heart stopped for a second. The plane had crashed on September 10. Fred had more to say.

"The woman parked by Kitsumkalum Lake. She was attacked there early that evening by a female bear that had buried the remains of a deer nearby. You see, the bear was protecting her kill."

"Naturally," Sonya replied.

"The lake is rather remote, but fortunately there were some fishermen in the vicinity. They heard the victim's screams and came to her aid."

"How did . . . the incident play out?"

"We could only ascertain that the wounds were severe. Evidently, the lady was able to drag herself to her camper, probably since the bear was distracted by the fishermen's SUV. In any case the bear was no longer in sight when the fishermen got to the camper."

"How did they know?"

"Apparently they saw the blood right away, blood everywhere. From the wounds . . . The lady was still conscious; she'd probably been conscious the whole time in spite of the serious wounds to her head and face."

"Did she survive?"

"Yes, that's certain. But the bear didn't. The game wardens tracked her down and shot her."

Sonya actually didn't want to hear that. What she'd just heard was appalling enough.

"You don't happen to know where that woman is now?"

"She was flown to Europe when she was stable enough."

"Can you give me her name?"

"We don't have it—the police have cloaked the details in secrecy. I've probably already told you more than I should have."

"I'm genuinely thankful. It's—"

"There's one important thing I want to tell you. Bears aren't aggressive by nature. She was only defending her food. People often forget that when they're out in the wild, they're intruding on animals' habitats. People don't pay any attention. And this lady was traveling by herself—that's not smart. She was colossally lucky that there were fishermen nearby. Otherwise she'd have—"

"Yes, I see what you mean."

"There's always a reason why these things happen."

"Yes, there's always a reason, I agree with you. The bear couldn't help it, and the woman either. Thank you very much for your efforts."

She went to the bathroom and splashed cold water on her face. A tourist from Europe. That could be anybody. Thousands of tourists traveled through this province. Odette would never have gone off in a camper, and after all that had happened. Why should she? Odette at a remote lake—the very idea!

But then why did that anonymous e-mail tip her off to Raincoast Conservation? Who was behind it? She took a terry-cloth towel and started to dry her face, when she suddenly stopped. Of course! She remembered talking about the Swiss patient with Kathrin, the nurse. *Sometimes a door opens up all of a sudden, believe me.* Kathrin's words of farewell. She had opened a door for Sonya without revealing a medical secret.

Sonya couldn't stand her flowered room anymore. Within minutes she was wrapped up in raingear and marching through torrential showers to the center of Prince Rupert. Before she reached the library, the wind was bending the ribs of her umbrella. She stood at the front desk, dripping wet, until the young librarian, who had been so helpful her first time there, appeared. She recognized Sonya immediately.

"Oh, here you are again!" she exclaimed. "Is your investigation moving along?"

"Thank you, yes." Little rivulets trickled off Sonya's jacket onto the floor. Then the scales fell from her eyes. Of course, that must be it! That's where the text message came from when she was coming back to Vancouver.

"VGH stands for Vancouver General Hospital, correct?" she whispered, so nobody else could hear.

The young woman blushed.

"The woman admitted there, was she Swiss?"

"Very possibly. But you didn't get it from me. Promise?"

"My lips are sealed."

So it might well have been Odette. But what business did she have going to a secluded lake? Is it possible she was ignorant of the crash? Had it been kept from her?

Sonya left her wet jacket by the desk and cast a glance at the newspapers that were there as she went past.

A large picture on the front page caught her attention: it looked like a dark lunar landscape with a glossy iceberg in it. She spread out the paper and read the caption: *Core sample with a two-carat diamond.* Then she read the report.

Sensational Find in the Arctic

Yellowknife, NWT. The chief geologist and president of Thunderrock Inc., Diane Kesowsky, couldn't believe her eyes when she took a closer look at a core sample in her camp. On its broken surface lay a sparkling diamond! Finding a visible diamond in a core sample is as rare as finding a black polar bear. And a two-carat diamond at that—it borders on the miraculous. "We changed all the locks on the shed and on the tent with the computers," Kesowsky said. "Then we cut the phone lines."

The delighted geologist brought the core sample in person to Vancouver the same day, well stowed in a backpack. She now has a contract in her pocket for the construction of a mine in the tundra two hundred miles from Yellowknife. The world's largest mining company will build it. Kesowsky is on her way to becoming a multimillionaire. But she will invest her future income in more diamond exploration in Canada. "I'm convinced that giant deposits are still out there," the radiant CEO stated.

Sonya put down the paper. She'd helped Diane make a sensational discovery! The core sample she'd inadvertently pushed off the rack had fractured at the precise location of the diamond. Diane must have realized in a second what she held in her hands. She had to be certain that no one in the camp, including Sonya, would ever breathe a word about it. Where did all that certainty come from? *"The two of us will never give up,"* she'd said to her in the camp. Perhaps that was the deal Diane was secretly offering: she wouldn't get in the way of Sonya's Canadian investigation and—even more critically—Diane wouldn't tell the police about it. She knew Sonya wouldn't jeopardize their unspoken pact. What a brilliant woman she was!

Sonya found a computer and searched under Rainy River Lodge. She pulled out her notebook and began to take notes.

A floating hotel on the mainland coast south of Prince Rupert. Rustic-log-cabin style. A fisherman's paradise. Pictures of guests carrying giant fish in their arms like babies, fish being weighed. Salmon, halibut, red snapper. The place is wildly expensive. Transportation and one-night lodging: 1,000 dollars. A week's fishing with guide and boat, all inclusive: 6,500 dollars.

Where did Tonio ever find the money to indulge himself like that? The trip to Canada alone must have cost him a pretty penny. He admitted it really broke the bank, then said, "but this may be my last trip with Nicky, just the two of us."

My last trip with Nicky.

Surely he didn't know . . . Definitely not. She shook off the idea. That was impossible.

She got to her feet, put on her wet jacket, and said good-bye to her helpful informer at the main desk.

At the supermarket, she bought some Crazy Glue. Back in her room, she carefully glued together the broken pieces of the mug with the odd characters. *Finally*, she thought, when she'd finished. *Finally the time has come.*

CHAPTER 48

At the crack of dawn, Sonya's cell phone shook her out of her sleep.

Her voice was a mere croak.

"Hello?"

"Sonya? It's Sam here. You want to go to Rainy River Lodge?"

"What? Sam? How . . . I . . ."

"I can take you there today. You've got to be at Seal Cove at nine."

Sonya finally found the light switch, but it took a few seconds for her to decipher the time on her alarm clock. Almost six!

"Today? I thought . . . They said . . . the weather . . ."

"The weather looks good today. I've got the time to take you there. So nine o'clock it is."

"Wait, wait! I've got a flight for Friday—"

"You're flying with me personally. Be happy. The flight's paid for. See you soon."

"Sam—"

The phone went dead.

When Sonya was in the air with Sam, she heard the rest of the story. First, he told her in detail how he knew that the weather that day—which was actually his day off—would be better than everybody predicted. Then he explained that Greenblue Air had told him that a certain Sonya Werner had asked for him.

"We pilots always want to know who our fans are." He chuckled, visibly pleased with himself.

"Sam, that's not the point. I want to know who's paying for this flight."

Sam turned serious.

"Sonya, don't make things difficult for me. It really had nothing to do with me."

"Sam, did you call Robert?"

"OK, yes, I did."

"Who do you think you are!"

He hemmed and hawed. "I thought it might be of interest to him."

"What would be of interest to him?"

"He was always so concerned about your safety, eh?"

"Sam, that's a joke. I don't need a chaperone."

"Don't get upset. Bob and I are old buddies. He'd do the same for me."

"What's that?"

"Well, like . . . sharing news."

"Sharing news!" She spit the words out like rotten cherries. "Did he pay for this flight?"

"No, Bob didn't."

"Did the company pay for it?" She meant Greenblue; maybe it was a gift for a grief-stricken widow.

"Yes, it was a company, but that's all I can say."

"A company?" She figured it out fast. "It's Thunderrock, isn't it?"

"See that lodge down there? I'm beginning my descent now."

So it was Diane. But how would Diane know she wanted to fly anywhere? No way she could have known her plans. Then it occurred to her it was Diane who had first told her about Rainy River Lodge. Did she guess that Sonya would go see the place?

The Beaver glided down elegantly on a thickly wooded bay and made a semicircle in the water. A building that looked like a huge log cabin came into view; it was two stories high, with a pointed gable and large windows. The lodge was actually floating on the water, just as she'd seen on the Internet.

Sam docked and helped her get out. A number of fishermen with their fishing gear were just climbing into a boat. Sam took Sonya to the lodge, holding the glass door open for her to the nearly empty bar; it was paneled in dark wood and decorated with heavy mirrors. The fishermen were definitely capitalizing on the brightening weather to bring in their trophy fish.

"I'll wait here," Sam said, making a sign.

She gave him a quizzical look, and he grinned.

"Don't sweat it—I don't drink on the job, but there's somebody here I know," he said with a wink.

Sonya passed the bar, where a woman with upswept hair was lining up some glasses. She went to the main desk through a badly lit corridor. There were framed photographs on the walls, but looking closer, she didn't see fishermen and fish, but mountains and mountain climbers instead. Heavily muffled figures with white lips and dark sunglasses posed on snow-covered mountain ridges and peaks. Sonya tried to guess the countries where the pictures were taken. They seemed familiar. Tonio had transformed his own stairs and office into a picture gallery. His pictures were annotated with the place, date, and names of other climbers. Tonio mounted them to document the high points of his life. Not a single framed picture documented an event with Sonya.

"That was on the Mont Blanc massif. Do you know it?"

She turned around with a start. A tall, wiry man was standing behind the desk, looking her straight in the eye. He might have been in his midforties. She presumed he was one of the mountain climbers in the pictures, though she couldn't identify his face.

"Yes, I know it," she replied. "I was never on the peaks, but my husband climbed them often."

"Is he a mountain climber?"

"He was. He's dead."

The man came closer.

"I'm Carl Stephen, the manager of the lodge. I'm sorry about your husband. Mountains are a fascinating but perilous passion."

"He didn't die in the mountains, if that's what you mean. He died here, three years ago."

He took a step backward.

"Here? Whatever happened?"

"Were you the manager here three years ago?"

"Yes, but—"

"Can we talk in private?"

The manager didn't miss a beat.

"But of course. I'll let my assistant know at once."

He disappeared for a minute, and then he led her to a little room with a fireplace, where a wood fire flickered.

"We won't be disturbed here," he said.

They settled down in the shiny leather sofas. Before Sonya could begin, the manager spoke up.

"Your husband was Swiss, wasn't he?"

Sonya nodded. "So you remember him!"

"Yes, very well, actually. We chatted at length about all kinds of climbs. I spent many years in France, working in hotels and as a mountain guide."

He regarded her sympathetically.

"And you are his widow?"

"Yes. I've come here to . . . to see where it happened."

"He talked about you, I remember. He told me you wanted to breed dogs, and he wanted to help you. He said he was finished with risky climbs and wanted to spend more time with you—and with his son."

"He told you that?" She searched his face. Didn't he find it odd that she wasn't with Tonio on that trip?

"Yes, we were on the same page. My family is still my priority to this day."

"Do you know why my husband came here? He had no interest in fishing."

"I think he came with some guy he knew. Yes, that was it. Your husband wanted to stay longer, but the guy had urgent business back in Vancouver. That's why they took off so quickly. But the weather was very bad."

Sonya leaned forward.

"Shouldn't somebody have warned him? My husband wasn't familiar with the weather conditions around here."

The manager folded his arms over his chest.

"We talked about it. It didn't look so good, and I told your husband to go talk to Sam. He's an experienced pilot, he would give you his opinion for sure."

Had she heard right?

"Sam was here when my husband flew off?"

"Yes, Sam was picking up some guests, but he didn't chance it. We're very risk-averse in this lodge. We don't want to be sued for damages."

"You mean to say that Sam didn't fly because of the bad weather, but my husband—"

"Yes, he came back after talking to Sam and said he didn't see any problem with the weather."

"But that's strange."

She stared at the fire, trying to collect her thoughts. What did all this mean?

The manager cleared his throat.

"I think I remember . . ."

"Yes?"

"Your son, he didn't like it here. He was bored. Maybe that's why your husband decided . . ."

"I understand."

She stood up and looked out the window. She saw a big fishing boat anchored in the bay. Nicky definitely wouldn't have enjoyed killing fish.

The manager stood up as well.

"This lodge never showed up on my husband's credit card bill. Didn't he pay with his card?"

"His companion paid the bill. I remember that."

Sonya turned around.

"Who was his companion?"

"Unfortunately I can't tell you. That's a privacy issue, you understand."

"Did you know the fourth person in the plane?"

The manager pulled out a handkerchief and blew his nose.

"Did you inquire at the police station?"

"No," Sonya quickly added. "They haven't released any information."

"I'm not surprised."

Sonya noted a sharp undertone to his voice.

"But that would be OK with you. They were probably trying to protect tourism in the area."

He shook his head.

"They don't try to protect tourism, what are you thinking? If they want to protect anybody, it would be themselves. You can bet your bottom dollar on that."

He turned to the door.

"Excuse me, I have to take care of my guests. I hope I can help you clear up the matter. If you're staying longer, I'll be glad to be at your disposal later."

Sonya looked at her watch.

"My pilot's waiting for me. Thank you so much for taking the time."

She resisted the temptation to tell him the whole business didn't seem any clearer to her than it had before.

She found Sam at the bar. She waited discreetly behind the glass door until he'd said good-bye to the lady bartender.

"Sorry, I didn't mean to disturb you," she said as they walked down the landing steps. Still no trace of rain, though the air felt cool and damp.

"She's engaged," Sam said, "but not to me, unfortunately."

Sonya thought of Robert. She felt a slight pain near her heart. *Well, that's what you get*, she thought. *I should have been more careful.*

Sam stopped at the Beaver.

"Where to now?"

She told him straight. He could have asked questions, he could have shaken his head. Or come up with some excuse. He could have flatly refused. But he did nothing of the sort. He just looked at her in silence. Then he said, "No problem."

CHAPTER 49

They hardly spoke during the flight. What could she say? She was too tense, too wrapped up in her own feelings. The little pink pills couldn't help her. They were in her suitcase in Vancouver.

I've got to get through this. She said it to herself again and again. *I've got to get through this.*

The yellow seaplane glinted from a distance on the gray-green sea. Sonya's heart hammered. What if she was way off base? What if this was an exercise in futility?

"We're there," Sam's voice said in the headphones.

She nodded, unable to speak.

The Beaver made a gentle landing and headed leisurely for shore. Sonya looked out the window and saw nobody.

"He's there," Sam said. He tilted his head in the direction of two dogs leaping in huge bounds toward them. Now, with her headphones off, she could hear them barking. She let Sam go ahead on the dock and followed him, weak in the knees. A man's voice gave commands to the dogs, and the barking stopped. Since Sam's back blocked her view, she didn't see him until he was just a few steps away.

Sam greeted him and petted the dogs that were jumping up on him.

"This is Sonya," he said, nodding in her direction.

"Hello, I'm George," the man said.

George, of all the names to have! He was tall and heavily built, with hands like shovels. There was something Scandinavian about him; perhaps he was a descendent of the Oona River Norwegians. She couldn't say if he was forty or fifty. His face was lined, but he moved like a young man. He looked at her curiously, but didn't shake her hand. The dogs were sniffing her from every side.

"Did you bring me something?"

He asked Sam the question, but his eyes kept going from him to her.

"We're—" Sam started to say, but Sonya interrupted him.

"I've brought you something." She pulled out the mug from her backpack.

"I broke it the last time we were here. I took the pieces and glued them together."

If George was surprised, he didn't show it. Without a word, he took the cup and examined it closely. Sam gave her an inquiring look, but her eyes were fixed on George's powerful hands.

"Why don't you put it in the kitchen," George said, handing it back to her. "Sam, can you help me load my lathe onto the Cessna?"

The dogs tried to follow Sonya into the house, but George whistled them back. The steps to the front door creaked. The door was open, and Sonya closed it behind her. The kitchen seemed brighter than the first time—maybe because the light was on. On the table there were plates and glasses left over from a recent meal. A fire crackled in the fireplace. Through the window she saw the men go to the shed. She went into the living room, walking over the wooden floor where the mug had broken. The mug she held in her hand.

She opened the door to the next room. Where was that black cat? In the room, she saw a table next to the window. Sonya went closer. There were tubes of paint and brushes and the beginnings of a painting with a few lines sketched in. It smelled of oil and turpentine.

Both sides of the room had doors. Sonya chose the one on the left, and when she opened it, she knew instinctively she'd chosen the correct one. She just saw shadows and silhouettes at first. Blinds blocked off the light, so she paused, trying to orient herself. Her eyes fought the dark until it got grayer.

Then she saw the back of a chair. A head. Shoulder-length hair with bent ends like windswept grass.

"Odette?" It was almost a whisper.

The shape rose up slowly. Then a voice.

"I knew you'd find me."

Sonya's heart skipped a beat. Her legs trembled. She followed the figure's movements as it opened one of the blinds. The dark hair shone in the light now entering the room. The figure turned around.

Finally, Sonya could see with utmost clarity. The face wasn't one anymore: two eyes, oddly placed, had twisted outlines. There was a nose, but the mouth was split into two halves, one half completely normal and the other . . . a void—no lips, no beginnings of a cheek. Just a deep indentation.

The face changed shape into a bizarre expression.

"Was your trip worth it for *this*?" the figure asked.

There was something in that voice: a desperation, a pain that tore Sonya out of her shock. She put the mug on a little table and said just what happened to come to her mind.

"Can I turn on more lights so I can see properly? It's been a long, long time, you know."

She was calm all of a sudden. She had to be calm or else the two of them would go to pieces.

She slid the light switch on and then walked around Odette, who stayed on the same spot. She examined her face, the intact part of her forehead, the familiar arc of her eyebrow, the hazel irises, the right corner of the mouth that peaked slightly upward.

It was Odette. She felt Odette's eyes scanning her as well. Sonya took a step back.

"I see. Can we talk to each other now?" Sonya sat down on the sofa bed against the wall.

By way of an answer, Odette turned her armchair toward her. She tucked up her legs and leaned back against the cushion.

"I know it was a bear," Sonya said. "I found out."

"I can live with it. I deserved this punishment." Odette's voice seemed to have been picked up by a bad microphone.

"How did it happen?"

"I saw a shadow, then the bear was on top of me. I heard its teeth dig into my skull. I didn't feel pain—not at that moment."

"What did you do?"

"I screamed. And did I scream! They heard me . . . and drove the bear off."

"The fishermen, right?"

Odette's features shifted in a peculiar way.

"They told you that? Those guys saved my life. At the same time, I didn't want to live anymore. And afterward less than ever."

Her hair was full and beautiful as ever. The attack couldn't destroy that.

"Odette"—she heard herself saying the name from very far away—"they can do a lot with plastic surgery, there's—"

"Sonya, what you see is the end result of eleven operations. *Eleven* operations could only manage to do this." She spread her fingers, putting her hand to her face as if trying to flatten her nose.

"I was in the hospital for months. They took muscles from my legs and skin from my arms. All that is now in my face. My wounds kept getting inflamed. I took tons of pills . . . Now I just want peace and quiet. No more operations. Only peace."

"You were in Switzerland?"

"Yes. Only my parents knew. I didn't . . . I didn't want anybody to see me like this."

"Now you're in hiding here?"

"George is a good man. He's good to me."

"Were you also hiding from me?"

Odette drew her legs up even more closely.

"Tonio told you, didn't he?"

"No, he didn't tell me anything. He . . ."

She couldn't get it out. Her throat felt choked up, and suddenly the tears came. She wiped them away with both hands, but they kept on coming, like a dam bursting.

"You found the letters."

Again, a drawn-out murmur. Sonya nodded, pressing her hands to her face. She hadn't wanted to cry, but she was helpless now. She eventually found some tissues in her jacket and dried her eyes and nose. When she could focus again, she saw Odette's eyes were fixed on her. She couldn't say what Odette saw there. First she had to get used to those eyes.

Odette's voice betrayed her fears.

"I'm so sorry, Sonya, so terribly sorry . . ."

Neither of them uttered a word. Sonya gasped for air now and then, and it sounded like sobs.

"Tonio never faced me with it. He simply left, with Nicky. He wanted to put some distance between us."

Sonya didn't understand.

"Tonio wanted distance? You mean he wanted . . . to end it?"

"Of course. He wished it had never gone so far."

"So he went to Canada to . . ." Sonya couldn't finish the sentence.

"He just up and ran. He surely could have talked to me, but he simply took Nicky along. He probably thought that would jolt us back to our senses. But when Nicky told me, I panicked. I was terrified of losing him. That's why I followed them."

Sonya was still bewildered.

"Nicky told you? Why did *he* tell you? Did you two meet somewhere?"

"We met secretly, there was no other way. Nobody knew anything about it until . . . Nicky immediately agreed that I should follow them after they left. He thought it was a good thing."

"What did Nicky say about Tonio and you—"

"Like I said, there was never a confrontation between Tonio and me. He never talked to me about it. He simply took off."

Sonya was gripped by impatience.

"But how could you drag Nicky into it! He was just seventeen!"

"He was barely fifteen when it started. What can I say, Sonya? I know it was wrong. But I simply fell in love. I was head over heels in love. It felt like an earthquake. It was stronger than me. And it was the same for Nicky."

Sonya gaped at Odette.

"What . . . What do you mean, it was the same for Nicky?"

"Nicky loved me. He loved me pure and simple. He wanted to be with me."

A dark suspicion slowly crept through Sonya's brain, a thought so overwhelming that she tried with all her might to repress it.

"Nicky? I don't get it . . . You and Tonio, you had . . . an affair!"

A deathly silence. They looked at each other. Odette slowly brought her legs down to the floor.

"Tonio and me? An affair? No, Sonya, of course not! How could you think that? What are you talking about?"

"But the letters . . . your letters. You wrote Tonio love letters!"

"No, not to Tonio! I wrote them to Nicky! Tonio found them and kept them. He simply stole them from Nicky."

Sonya jumped to her feet.

"Odette, tell me the truth! You owe it to me. I saw those letters. '*Dearest Tonio.*' I saw them with my own eyes. 'Tonio' they said."

Silence. Then Odette's pained voice.

"'Tonio' was my intimate name for Nicky. You surely know he never liked his name. He thought it . . . wasn't a good one. He wanted to be called Tonio; it was, after all, his second name."

Sonya collapsed onto the sofa.

"'Tonio' was Nicky's second name?"

"Yes, but of course you knew that? Nicky was Niklaus Tonio Vonlanden. You must have . . ."

Sonya sat there, paralyzed, her mind racing.

"No, I didn't know, I . . . I . . ."

Her words trailed off.

Nicky and Odette.

The envelope of photographs—"*For Odette*"—were Nicky's photos.

Not Tonio's. Nicky's.

"You certainly didn't think"—now she heard Odette as if through a wall—"Sonya, you certainly didn't think that Tonio and I . . ."

Sonya made no reply. She couldn't even move her lips.

"Oh, my God, Sonya, that's . . . but that's . . . oh, my God!"

CHAPTER 50

Muffled barking. Men's voices. Shouts. Then quiet again.

Then a scratching from somewhere. The door was ajar and an invisible hand pushed it open. Sonya sensed movement in the room, and the black cat stalked toward her. It sniffed, turned its head, and mewed quietly. Then it landed on Odette's lap in a single bound.

Sonya broke her silence. *Talk, talk so you don't have to think the unthinkable. Keep on talking.*

"It's all because of the cat. I thought that someone must have opened the door for it, and afterward . . . the broken pieces from the mug. The umlauts first caught my eye. There's no umlaut in English, of course. Then I saw they were German words. *Kühe.* That's when I put two and two together."

Sonya stopped talking.

Odette stroked the cat's back slowly, looking for some kind of protection in that touch.

"I didn't want to see you, Sonya. I thought, *I just can't.* You'd never forgive me . . . because of Nicky. And then with this face . . . My parents knew you were going to Canada."

"They knew that? Who told them?"

"Inge. I mean, indirectly. She submitted your exhibition project to the Cultural Affairs Committee, and it was in the application. Inge wanted money for the project and also for the trip. My aunt's on the committee. It's as simple as that."

"Your aunt warned you about me?"

"She told my parents. I knew at once that you'd go and search for me. You would want to speak to me about Nicky. You're not like Tonio. You don't avoid a confrontation. You always had to fight his battles for him."

"You don't . . . didn't think much of Tonio?"

"Not in that regard. So how could you assume . . ."

Sonya didn't respond. Her inner turmoil was too great. Everything she'd believed, feared, fought against over the last three years had crumbled. More broken pieces.

The cat purred loudly at the human drama in the room. Sonya had never heard a cat purr so loudly. Odette raised her voice suddenly.

"I wanted to banish you from my life. I couldn't bear the truth!"

A strange sound escaped her. Maybe it was meant as a laugh, but it sounded like a cry.

"I literally couldn't bear my own face. And not yours either. That's why I sent for two friends out here. Gerti and Helmut."

"Gerti and Helmut! You know Gerti and Helmut?"

Odette said nothing.

"Don't tell me you got them to tail me?"

"Oh, yes, I did. I wanted to see what you were up to and where you were going. I know you very well, Sonya. You have a good nose. It's no coincidence that you're a historian. It was only a question of time before you tracked me down."

"It was purely by chance, Odette. We had to make an emergency landing here."

"Maybe it was chance. But somebody would eventually have told you about the Swiss woman who often flew to Kitkatla to participate in native purification ceremonies."

"No, I heard nothing like that, and I actually was in Kitkatla. They all kept their mouths shut."

"People in Kitkatla aren't afraid of me. They say I've got the power of a bear. They say the bear gave me its strength and courage. But I don't feel so courageous, Sonya. This face is my punishment."

Sonya shook her head. So many riddles, so many questions.

"Why Nicky? Of all the males around, why Nicky? You had plenty of admirers among those mountain climbers."

"I've often asked myself that. Very often. I didn't go looking for it, Sonya. I simply felt warm and happy in his company. I felt young again when I was with him."

"But you *are* young, Odette. You still are."

"But I never was a real kid, let alone a teenager. I was never really easygoing. I always had to achieve, to be better than others. 'Show you're tough,' my dad always said. Don't give up. Grit your teeth. Keep your eye on the ball. Keep going higher and higher. Was I ever allowed to play or drift along in life? Take each day as it comes? Make mischief? Never."

Odette's voice showed no emotion; it was a dispassionate monotone. Talking seemed to tax her strength. Sonya wondered for the first time whether Odette had chronic physical pain. But this wasn't the time to pursue it. She wanted to find out more about her ill-fated love.

"I'd noticed that Nicky liked you. But I never thought . . ."

"Me neither. But pretty soon I was smitten. Nicky was irresistible. He was so innocent, not weighed down by all the baggage grown men carry around. He didn't dissimulate; he wasn't a show-off; he didn't have to constantly prove himself. He was simply . . . Nicky. I thought he was a real man for all that."

"You seduced him? When?"

"Not long after his fifteenth birthday. I was never as happy as on that day. My guilty conscience came later."

"So that's why you stayed away from me."

"Yes. You'd have noticed. You'd have spotted the love in my eyes. What would you have done if you'd found out?"

Sonya took a deep breath. Odette and Nicky. Tonio had found the letters and not told her. Not her, his wife. He'd fled to Canada, thinking a holiday would take care of it. He wanted to spare her. Did he think she couldn't take the truth?

"Odette, just imagine you had a fifteen-year-old stepson and your best friend got into bed with him." She jumped up from the couch without warning, and the cat fled under the chair. "Look how it turned out!"

"I know," Odette croaked softly, her hands braced against the arms of the chair. "I ruined Nicky's life. I've ruined your life. Mine, too."

Sonya went to the door.

"I need some fresh air. I'm going outside."

She dashed out of the house. The dogs discovered her right away and darted toward her, yapping. George and Sam were just coming around the corner.

"Everything OK?" Sam inquired. Sonya knew that her tear-stained eyes would betray her. She didn't dare look George in the face.

"I need some fresh air," she answered. "When do we have to leave?"

George answered for Sam.

"You can spend the night if you wish. I know Odette would be delighted."

She gave Sam a startled look. Did he know about Odette? He didn't seem surprised. "Sure she can," he said. "I'll drop by tomorrow on my way back from Kitkatla and pick her up."

Sonya suspected for a split second that the two of them had somehow arranged all this. So what. She had to decide. She smelled the ocean, a wet, sluggish, single-minded beast. It held her fast. She simply couldn't go. She laid a hand on Sam's arm.

"I'll stay here."

"So tomorrow at two o'clock."

"I'll be ready."

She squeezed his arm and climbed up the rise behind the house. The dogs followed the men to the landing dock.

Sonya sat down on a tree stump. One of the windows of the back of the house must be Odette's room, but she couldn't see anyone. Now that she didn't have Odette's mutilated face before her eyes, now that she didn't hear her halting voice anymore—anger rose up within her.

Odette had always liked to take risks. On the ice, over an abyss, on an edge, in extreme cold, putting her life in danger. That was evidently the only way she felt she was alive. The only way she could sense herself.

Sonya shut her eyes; her breathing was shallow.

Nicky was just one more risk, giving Odette an adrenaline rush. She had always admired Odette—her courage, her cold-bloodedness, her contempt for mediocrity—but what a pathetic figure she seemed now! A pathetic failure. Hiding out! When the chips were down, she simply crept away, leaving her best friend alone with her grief, with her questions. She'd left her alone with everything. A single word could have cleared up this misunderstanding. A single word would have spared her despair and anger over Tonio's presumed unfaithfulness. But Odette didn't have the guts to tell her. She was a coward. A coward like Tonio, exactly like Tonio! He'd kept everything from her, never trusted her. He'd stuck his head in the sand once again. He couldn't admit his financial troubles, his company's downturn. As if the only challenge in life were to conquer a mountain peak. Cowards, the two of them! Scaredy-cats! Chickens! Leaving a trail of blood behind on their way to catch a thrill. Leaving dead bodies behind!

They had Nicky's blood on their hands.

A drone came from the bay, the engine of Sam's Beaver. She resisted the urge to rush down and fly away with him. But she couldn't run away either. Not like Tonio and Odette.

She heard frantic barking, and the dogs came galloping up the hill. Sonya climbed up higher on the tree stump.

"Get those dogs away from here right now!" she screamed. "Get those damn mutts off my back! You goddamn idiots! Call them off! Fucking animals!"

The dogs jumped up at her wooden pedestal. She screamed and screamed and couldn't stop. She was still screaming when George came to her aid. She was howling like a madwoman. George ran down to the house with the dogs in tow.

Not until Odette worked her way up the slope—Sonya could see that she was limping—did her screams give way to whimpering. She had slumped over.

"Sonya," Odette said. "Poor Sonya."

Very cautiously, Odette held out a hand to lead her down to the house.

George was in the kitchen, watching them.

"Maybe you'd like to lie down for a bit," Odette said, still holding her hand. "Come."

She took Sonya to the room with the sofa bed and covered her with a duvet.

Sonya watched Odette making bread that evening. That was another strange sight. Sonya asked questions about the flour and how the oven worked. Not a word about the tragedy that had ripped their lives apart.

Over supper, George recounted how he'd persuaded Odette to move in with him. He was one of the fishermen who rescued her on that fateful day by Kitsumkalum Lake. After a year of repeated operations in Switzerland, Odette had flown back to Canada to thank him personally. She'd had to fly over to his island because he couldn't leave it. One of his dogs was seriously ill. He had been undaunted by Odette's facial appearance; he'd seen her with blood all over and a gaping hole in her face. He told her he'd always have a room for her. Six months later, she decided to stay in Canada.

"Who flew you over here?" Sonya asked.

Odette looked at George.

"It was your friend, wasn't it?"

"Jack."

"Jack Gordon?" Sonya spoke his name as if it were a forbidden word.

"Exactly."

George wasn't so talkative all of a sudden.

"He died, in his boat, so I've heard," Sonya persisted.

George cast a glance at Odette.

"An accident. Goddamn booze. Jack was always a heavy drinker after . . ."

He didn't finish his sentence.

The black cat prowled around the table and jumped onto Sonya's lap, rubbing its head on her arms.

That night, Sonya dreamed a confused, disjointed dream about the cat.

At breakfast, George's chair was empty. He was already out on the ocean in his boat. Sonya and Odette ate some more crusty bread from the previous night.

"I'm unable to cry," Odette said. "It's my tear ducts. They have to be reconstructed, but it's a tricky operation. I have to moisten my eyes artificially."

"How did you learn about . . . about the crash and Nicky's death?" Sonya asked.

"Nicky phoned me from Rainy River Lodge shortly before takeoff. We planned to meet later in Prince Rupert. I waited for him at a hotel."

She took a deep breath.

"He didn't come. He simply didn't come. And I sensed—I knew that something very bad had happened."

Once again that noisy intake of air.

"I went to Seal Cove and asked around. The staff at Greenblue wouldn't tell me anything specific, but I could tell by the way they acted that Nicky's plane had gone down. The police were there already and sent all the passersby away. I phoned my father and asked him to inquire at the Swiss Consulate in Vancouver. I figured that as President of Parliament he'd obtain confidential information like that quickly. I waited in the hotel for two days. They were the worst days of my life, worse than anything that came . . . afterward. I knew Nicky was dead before my father finally called back. I just knew."

She pressed her hands to her cheeks, lowered her head.

"Why did you go off in that camper all alone?" Sonya asked softly.

"Insane, isn't it?" Her voice was almost sarcastic. "It's crazy what people will do in extreme situations. Nicky discovered that lake on a map of Canada. He liked the name, Kitsumkalum. We joked in Vancouver that we'd paddle a canoe around the lake. Nicky said he wanted his ashes scattered over it. All because he thought it had a great name."

Sonya caught her breath.

"Did you know he'd written his own obituary in advance? I found it in his room."

"Oh, that was Nicky all over. He liked to shock people. Just for effect. I think he needed that . . . safety valve. Where is it now?"

"What do you mean?" Sonya asked. Then she got it. She was asking about his body. "Well, he's buried in our cemetery."

Sonya wavered before asking her next question. "Will you come back to Switzerland?"

"Yes, but I don't know when. They can still improve on this"— she gestured vaguely at her face—"but I just need a break."

"You'll tell me this time, won't you, when you're coming?"

"Yes."

Odette took long sips of her café au lait and had difficulty swallowing. A brown trickle ran from where half her lip was missing. "But maybe you won't be there."

Sonya gazed at her in bewilderment.

Odette's crooked mouth grew even more crooked.

"This country doesn't let go of you so quickly."

Sonya was too startled to respond, though something rang a bell. The country. Else Seel's true love. That was what held her in spite of all her loneliness. Her love for this overpoweringly beautiful country. Else might have been able to leave her husband, but not this place.

Sonya was eager to talk to Odette about Else Seel, but she remembered that Odette knew absolutely nothing about her. Odette was ignorant about those three years in Sonya's life; there was a rift, a yawning void.

"Tonio loved you," Odette announced out of the blue. "There wasn't room for another woman." She brushed her hair back, revealing ugly scars.

Sonya's knife clattered onto her plate.

"No room! He was too busy scrambling up mountains and guiding glacier tours."

"He loved you in his imperfect way, as well as he could," Odette insisted calmly.

Sonya began to clear off the table.

"But I was never number one. That's how it really was, Odette. People like you and Tonio, you're on a perpetual campaign of conquest, and anybody else is . . . left behind."

"Dead bodies are left behind, is that what you're trying to say?"

"If you're just playing with your own life, that's one thing, but—"

Odette got to her feet.

"You married Tonio—and why? Didn't it fascinate you, the way he always swung over the abyss? You know, driving to work is just as life threatening."

Sonya didn't want to argue. That gap would always be between them. There was something more pressing to attend to.

"Nicky left some pictures for you at the Lions Gate Hotel."

She pushed the envelope across the table.

Odette wiped her hands on the dish towel and took the envelope awkwardly. She opened it, saw the note *"For Odette,"* and sat down. She went through the photos without a word, taking her time with each one. Her hands trembled slightly.

"Did he . . . did he write anything else?" she asked when she'd finished.

"No," Sonya replied.

"I . . . excuse me."

Odette dropped the pile onto the table and ran out of the kitchen. Sonya heard a door close. She stood there, at a loss, but didn't venture to follow her friend. She had to leave her to her pain, at least for a while. At that moment there was no consolation. Sonya had learned that from her own despair.

She collected the scattered photos. Then her eyes focused on one of them. She looked more closely. But that was a face she knew! Excited, she went through all the pictures again. This time something else caught her eye.

Two bicycles leaning against the quay's railing at Canada Place, where the large cruise ships took on passengers. And the bicycles showed up in the next picture beside the steam clock in Gastown. And again, beside the bronze statue in Stanley Park. And in front of the historic Marine Building on Burrard Street. Always the same two bicycles, except in the last picture.

She held it up to the light, studying it thoroughly. How could she have overlooked those two faces!

Sonya had to sit down. Why hadn't she realized it earlier?

She waited. Waited until the pieces of the puzzle in her head all came together. Then she put the last photograph in her backpack, washed the dishes, and wiped the table.

She found Odette lying on her bed, her disfigured face turned to the wall.

Sonya pulled a chair up to the bed and sat down.

"You were together in Vancouver, weren't you, you and Nicky?" she said quietly.

Silence.

"You rented bikes and went around the city."

More silence.

"Was that the last time you saw each other, Odette?"

The body on the bed moved. The other half of Odette's face slowly emerged. Sonya leaned over and gently stroked her devastated cheek. Odette took her hand, holding on to it tightly. Her mouth began to move.

"We actually wanted to meet in Prince Rupert, but . . ."

"Did Tonio know you'd come to Vancouver?"

"No," Odette replied.

"Where was Tonio when Nicky and you were together?"

"Nicky said Tonio was meeting somebody."

"Did he say who?"

"Some guy. A friend of a friend. Nicky didn't know exactly."

There were noises in the house. A racket on the stairs. Somebody called for Odette. George was back.

"Maybe he's brought some oysters," Odette said, rolling off the bed. "He knows a couple of good spots to get them."

As they were going out, she stopped at the table with the oil paints.

"Look. I painted those."

She took large sheaves of paper from a portfolio and placed them in front of Sonya. Abstract landscapes: mountains, islands, forests. Sonya took a long, close look at them while George and Odette's voices came from the kitchen. She took hope then and there that Odette would get over her trauma. The colors spurred on Sonya's confidence: strong, sparkling, bold, happy colors, slapped on with firm strokes—sunshine yellow, poppy red, parrot green, electric blue, saucy pink, glowing colors of orange and violet, all like those of an exotic fish.

Odette slipped through the door, and Sonya closed the portfolio, hugging her friend with tears in her eyes.

"You're marvelous," she murmured.

If there was hope for Odette, there was certainly hope for her. Odette moved away.

"You don't want to come into the kitchen. George is boiling lobsters."

"You mean . . . dead already?" Sonya asked.

"No, George is still alive." Odette tried to wink, but she couldn't manage it.

Sonya felt guilty eating lobster, but it tasted delicious. She berated herself for her lack of consistency, but she could see how proud George was of his feast.

Sam arrived in the afternoon, amazingly right on time. George and Odette waited with Sonya on the landing dock. They made their good-byes in just a few words. Odette embraced her tightly.

"You'll come back, won't you?"

"Definitely."

It was now clear to Sonya that she would be back. She'd go with George and Odette out to sea in his boat to the site of the plane crash. Then they'd scatter swan's down on the waves, like the Haida do, to appease the gods. And her inner demons. So that an ultimate peace might reach her soul.

"You should go," Sonya ordered, "or I'll start bawling in the plane."

She hugged Odette again, shook hands with George, and turned around to avoid seeing them walking slowly back to the house.

Sam held the door open for her.

"We've got another passenger."

CHAPTER 51

"He's a tourist from Montreal," Sam said. "He barely speaks English, so we can chatter away in peace."

"Sam, I have to go back to Rainy River Lodge."

"You're in luck. That's where this gentleman wants to go; he's going salmon fishing. There are scarcely any fish left back East anymore. The East has been completely overfished."

Sonya dove into the Beaver, greeting the passenger in French. The man was visibly delighted that someone could speak his native tongue. He wore a blue captain's hat and politely yielded his seat to her. She looked back at the house. Odette was already at the front door, covering the disfigured half of her face with one hand and waving with the other. George and his dogs were at the foot of the hill. Sonya tried to burn this image into her brain for the coming weeks and months. A huge lump stuck in her throat.

She wanted to ask Odette so many more questions, about the orange album, for instance, that she'd carried around on her trip three years ago, but there'd be a time for that later. Odette was back in her life, and she would not lose contact again.

The plane left the bay and hummed its way skyward.

"Sam, I've got to ask you something," Sonya piped up before she could get over the pain of her departure.

"Shoot."

"I know you were at Rainy River Lodge at the same time as my husband. Why didn't you tell me?"

Sam took his time answering. He threw a few switches beside and above him.

"I didn't want to dump it on you. It's sad enough as it is."

"But now I want to know. Tonio came to you and asked if he ought to fly that day, is that true?"

"Not true." He now looked serious. "Not true at all. That guy . . . he would never have come to me for advice. He was much too . . ." He paused. "When I saw him getting ready to take off, I went over to him. I told him the weather was too unstable. Only an experienced pilot who knew the area inside out would dare to fly under those conditions."

"How did he react?"

"He said he'd already gotten advice from some people who knew the area extremely well. He said he wasn't stupid."

"What? He said that?"

"I asked who. He said Carl."

"Carl, the manager?"

"Right. But I didn't believe a word of it. He was bluffing. He just didn't want to admit he was on the point of making a mistake. In the end he said . . ."

The roar of the engine drowned out the rest of Sam's sentence. She asked him to repeat it.

"In the end he said it was clear to him why I was trying to keep him from flying. If the pilots had their way, not a single foreigner would be allowed to fly anywhere around Prince Rupert."

Sonya was dumbstruck. It sounded incredible. Still, she couldn't exclude the possibility that it was just the way it happened.

Tonio always prided himself on being able to size up danger better than anyone else.

"What did you think of that?"

"At first I backed off. No sense trying to teach an idiot. But then . . . I went back to him. I said, 'At least leave the kid here. If you love your son, then leave him here.' I said, 'I'll get him to Prince Rupert safe and sound.'"

Sonya kept silent. Sam looked over at her as if not knowing whether to proceed. She returned his gaze.

"You know what he did? He smiled. I'll never forget it. I'm telling the guy that his son is in danger of losing his life—and the guy smiles. He says, 'You don't have to tell me to worry about my son. That's none of your business.'"

Sonya looked out the window. The grayish-white sky was blinding; the sun was managing to occasionally push through the clouds. She knew Sam was telling the truth. And she guessed he blamed himself for it, maybe to this very day. He blamed himself for not preventing Nicky's death. Tonio had surely seen Sam's urging as an irritating intrusion, not as a stranger's reasonable concern.

Not a word was spoken until they arrived at Rainy River Lodge. Sonya completely forgot the stranger from Montreal until the landing. He left the plane before she did. More boats were moored at the lodge than last time. The bar was packed with fishermen. Sonya navigated through the loud confusion of voices, which were muted somewhat at the reception desk. Carl, the manager, was dealing with a group of guests.

Sonya made another thorough perusal of the photographs on the wall, the hooded mountain climbers all virtually looked alike. She recognized Tonio in the second picture. His sweatband gave him away. It had been a Christmas present from twelve-year-old Nicky, his good-luck charm on many tours.

The crowd at the desk disappeared down the corridor, and Sonya strode up to the manager.

"I have to speak to you one more time."

The manager showed no emotion.

"But of course." He seemed to reflect for a minute. "Let's go to the deck out back."

Sonya followed him to the deck at the rear of the lodge. There were several washbasins and hoses for fishermen or their helpers to clean their fish. Sonya stepped carefully in her sneakers on the slippery boards.

"It's a little unappetizing out here, but at least we'll be undisturbed." The manager smiled. "You can put your backpack on the plastic pail there, it's clean."

Sonya came straight to the point.

"Why didn't you tell me you'd known Tonio for a long time? You climbed mountains in Europe with him many years ago."

"Whatever made you think a thing like that?" His smile vanished.

"I recognized my husband in a picture in the lobby."

"You must be mistaken; there's surely been a mix-up."

"Carl, you gave yourself away in our first conversation. You said Tonio told you his wife wanted to breed dogs. That wasn't me. That was his first wife, the woman he was married to when you first knew him in Europe years ago."

A surly expression flickered over the manager's face.

"I can only repeat: I met your husband for the first time in this lodge."

Sonya folded her arms over her chest.

"Strange—then how come you met Tonio in Vancouver?"

Something flashed in his eyes for a second. Then he composed himself.

"I don't know where you got these ideas, but . . ." Then he shook his head as if talking to a naughty child. "I can understand that your husband's death is a tragedy for you. It must have been an awful shock."

Sonya went for broke.

"There's a photograph of you and Tonio together in Vancouver. My stepson Nicky snapped it."

"A photograph?"

For the first time, she thought she glimpsed insecurity in his face. He glanced quickly at her backpack. Then he changed course.

"Be reasonable. Why should I keep from you the fact that I met your husband in Vancouver? Think about it, that would be . . . stupid, don't you think?"

He looked almost compassionate.

"That's exactly what I'm trying to find out. Maybe it was you who enticed Tonio to come to this place. Why? What were you planning to do with him?"

He made a parrying gesture, as if wanting to break off the conversation. But there was no stopping Sonya.

"You told me you'd advised Tonio to ask Sam about the weather conditions. But that's not the way it went. *I* think you told Tonio he shouldn't worry what Sam thought. You probably told him that pilots like Sam tried to intimidate foreign pilots. That's how it was, wasn't it?"

The manager stepped closer—much too close for her liking—and looked at her angrily.

"These are wild accusations! You hold your tongue! Tonio would have flown at all costs. He was a good pilot, and he was fearless. He said he was very experienced. You can't pin it on me."

Sonya took a couple of steps backward.

"I only want to know what went on. I want to know why you're hiding things from me."

"You're crazy, absolutely crazy. Get out of here, you and your crazy speculations!"

She felt rage mounting inside her.

"Maybe it was in your interest to have the plane crash. Maybe you were trying to get rid of somebody."

The manager came closer, his voice icy.

"Be happy that Tonio's dead. Or he'd have had a whopping big lawsuit on his hands."

She blew up.

"The police won't think I'm crazy when they see my picture from Vancouver! They'll be asking you some nasty questions! Then we'll see who's got a lawsuit on his hands!"

His face turned to stone. He pulled back his arm, and Sonya felt a blow, losing her balance and falling into the air. Then the shock of icy water. Sudden blackness.

CHAPTER 52

"How do you feel?" asked the man sitting at the end of her bed.

"All right," she said.

She looked down at herself. She was wrapped in a purple down jacket and gray men's sweatpants that were much too big. A hot water bottle on her stomach kept her warm.

She looked through the window and saw boats and people wandering around the deck. Rainy River Lodge.

"And how are you?" she asked.

"I just had a shot of hot rum; it works miracles," the man said with a grin. He looked younger without his captain's cap. Like an ambitious stockbroker. She'd learned already that he wasn't one. Nor was he a tourist from Montreal who only spoke French. He said in fluent English, "Our clothes are being washed and dried. Fishermen throw fish guts in the water at that spot. We don't want stuff like that on us."

Sonya knew he was joking, trying to calm her fears, but suddenly images flashed before her eyes. The manager. His arm. His shove. The slippery boards. The ice-cold water. The hard blows hitting the water beside her when she finally surfaced, which she'd dodged instinctively.

"Did he shoot at me?" she asked.

"No, he tried to hit you on the head with an oar. You were finally able to get to safety under the deck."

"But I can hardly swim, let alone dive under water." Her eyes suddenly filled with tears.

"You were fantastic considering how ice-cold the water was. When I dove in after you, I almost had heart failure."

"How did you know . . . ?"

"We caught Carl in flagrante delicto and overpowered him."

"*We* did?"

"Me and my partner, who was already here. I was his reinforcement. We've had Carl in our sights for a long time."

She cast her eye on the business card in her hand: Jean-Claude Lassière, Detective, Royal Canadian Mounted Police. So Canada's national police were after Carl. And maybe after her, too. They must have known from the start who she was, why she was here, and what had happened to the ill-fated Beaver. How could she have been so naive to think that the police weren't involved? They were certainly involved enough not to let her drown in the cold water. Detective Lassière had jumped in after her.

"I can't thank you enough for how fast you got me out," she said. "I'm such a lousy swimmer—I think I was so panicked. I must have thrashed around and bashed you on the head a couple of times."

"You were coughing and spitting water," Lassière said. "I got nothing like the beating the manager got."

"Was there a fight?"

"He took off and tried to hide on a boat, but my partner caught him. Carl fought like mad against the handcuffs. But resisting arrest—that doesn't look so good."

"You arrested him—because of me?"

The detective stretched his long back.

"We've had our eye on this lodge for a long time. It's a rendezvous for people of interest. Most of the guests are harmless tourists—they're camouflage for others who aren't so innocuous. The man who knocked you into the water provided those suspicious persons with a peaceful milieu so they could carry out their dubious transactions. Is there anything more innocent than a group of men from all corners of the earth just happening to meet while fishing on a boat? We'd dearly like to know how money changes hands here. Where it comes from and where it ultimately disappears."

She hesitated to ask a particular question, one that could compromise her. But this was her chance to finally get at the truth.

"What . . . part did my husband play in all this?"

"We found the photo in your backpack. We had to search it. Unavoidable."

"The picture of Carl and my husband in Vancouver, right?"

"Yes. We confiscated it as evidence."

"Did Carl try to get my husband involved?"

"Perhaps. But if he did, then something went wrong."

"What do you mean?"

"Well—he died too soon."

"Was it an accident or . . . ?"

"Our investigation until now hasn't turned up anything to indicate it wasn't an accident. That's all I can tell you."

"What's going to happen to the manager?"

"Now we've got grounds for taking him into custody. He's bound to sing once he's got a charge of attempted murder on his hands. He's withheld important information from us."

Lassière got up.

"We haven't been sitting on our hands all these years." He pursed his lips. "We don't make it all that easy for criminals." He offered her his hand. "All the best, Sonya. You'll be hearing from us. We're counting on your cooperation."

At the door, the detective looked back.

"I'm not very good at things like this, but . . . your stepson and husband's deaths—we were touched by them. We can empathize. You're a brave woman. We . . . we also had a dead man to mourn for. He was one of ours."

She didn't catch on right away.

"You mean . . . ?"

"Yeah, the fourth passenger."

Jean-Claude waved good-bye, gently closing the door behind him. Sonya sank back onto her pillows. The ominous "investor" had been an undercover police agent.

From:	yh6t9abeil@yahoo.com
Sent:	September 28, 12:42
To:	Inge Stollrath
Re:	I'm alive!!!!

Dear Inge,

Can you live with the consequences of what you've done? Have you ever considered what might come of my trip to Canada—the consequences for me *and* for you, for our future, for the museum? What if you can't get rid of the spirits you conjured up? The fact is, I have to appear as a witness in a trial. The museum will have to carry on without me for quite some time.

I'm certainly not the same person I was when I left Switzerland. Canada has me pretty much in its thrall—just as it did Else. It's a country that doesn't let go of you. I can't imagine yet what this will mean for my life.

But you should know about a few of my experiences here. I know you've heard from Diane, but I'll run through them quickly.

The plane crash wasn't a plot but an accident. A pilot error. Tonio really overestimated himself. An old mountain-climbing buddy lured him to a fisherman's lodge near Prince Rupert. This buddy, Carl, the lodge manager, introduced Tonio to Rudy, who probably tried to persuade him to make risky (not to say illegal) investments. Carl enticed Tonio with a rented seaplane, and Tonio couldn't resist the temptation to give proof of his flying prowess. That cost four people their lives, including Nicky.

I suspect Rudy had no great interest in Tonio. He had an investor on the hook, but he didn't know the investor was an undercover police agent. That agent risked his life. He surely knew that to fly in that weather was perilous. But he went along to stay on Rudy and Tonio's heels. And so as not to arouse suspicion. Maybe Carl entertained doubts about the undercover agent, but we'll probably never know. I've heard the police are charging Carl for assaulting me, as well as for money laundering and obstruction of justice. But that may be only a rumor. The police play their cards close to the vest.

I'm fine so far. I've actually survived the shock of my plunge into ice-cold water very well. Maybe I'm more hard-boiled than I thought.

I used to envy Tonio for the intense way he lived his life. But I have also felt very powerful these past few weeks; I've learned what it's like to live that intensely.

It could be addictive.

Cordially,

Sonya

PS I hope with all my heart that Wilfried gets healthy fast, and send him much positive energy!

From:	soneswunder@swifel.com
Sent:	September 29, 08:21
To:	Sonya Werner
Re:	So happy for you!

Dear Sonya,

The spirits I summoned up are newly awakened life spirits! Come what may: they won't bowl *me* over—and certainly not you.

Here's to your intense life!

Yours,

Inge

PS Wilfried's much better and sends his best wishes.

CHAPTER 53

The fog was impenetrable. The fir trees in front of the airport were barely visible. A group of worried waiting passengers peered through the windows. Somebody from the Eagle Air counter ran past Sonya repeatedly, a young agent trying to placate two angry men.

Sonya could guess that the agent was telling them what she herself had heard an hour ago: the Vancouver flight was delayed, and no one knew if it would take off that day.

Sonya had brought nothing to read. But for once she didn't care; she was too nervous to concentrate on reading. She had stage fright, like an actress in drama school before her Schiller monologue. What should she say to him? How should she begin? How would he react to gambits like these?

I've had enough of men who want their lives filled with danger . . .

Or: *I'm not going to reprise the biggest mistake of my life . . . We're worlds apart, oceans . . . I don't want to have to fear for the man in my life all the time . . . I want a quiet life. A quiet life.*

The fog cast a gloom over the waiting area. Sonya looked at her watch. It was just two. She jumped up impatiently. Suddenly she remembered that she did have something to read after all: her notes on Else Seel's diaries. They were at the bottom of her small suitcase. A lemon-green sticky note flagged a particularly moving passage: *"Why can I not just throw myself upon him, swamping him with my caresses?"*

Poor Else. Sonya couldn't read on. She felt a thick lump in her throat. Disconcerting feelings always turned up when you needed them least. Then she saw a pair of black boots and frayed hems on blue jeans. Then, higher up, an open jacket, as if it were springtime.

Sonya jumped up again.

"What are *you* doing here?"

"Forget your flight," Sam informed her. "Nobody's getting out of here today, you can bet on it."

He nodded toward the exit.

"I'll take you back to town."

To town? Sonya thought, shaking her head. She wanted to get to Vancouver as soon as possible. And then to Switzerland. Home.

"How did you know that today's flights—"

"I'm a pilot, remember?" He grinned, picking up her suitcase. "Let's go."

Sonya followed him as if in a trance. They crossed the room, pursued by curious eyes.

"I still have to change my ticket," she exclaimed.

Sam waved that idea off.

"You can do it tomorrow. It's routine here."

In the parking lot they got into a mud-splattered pickup and just made the ferry to the mainland.

"Where are you taking me?" she asked as they turned onto the Prince Rupert highway.

"I know some nice accommodations you're sure to like."

"The airline. They usually pay for this. We should've asked them about—"

"Sonya, stop it—you worry too much." He laughed.

The truck stopped in front of a little white chalet with blue-trimmed windows at the edge of town.

"Somebody's waiting for you in there," he said.

Sonya wavered. She had a slight premonition but got out and expressed her thanks.

"Good luck!" He grinned as he drove off.

The first thing she noticed was the fire in the fireplace. Then she stopped dead in her tracks. They looked at each other without saying a word. How good he looked—those regular, intelligent features, his relaxed mouth. She felt a sharp pain in the region of her heart.

"Sonya," Robert said. "Can't we sit down?"

He pointed to a wooden table by the window.

Sonya sat across from him. She still had her heavy jacket on. She was glad she did despite the heat.

"I drove up yesterday," he explained. "I really wanted to fly, but every seat was taken. I drove all night."

Only then did she notice the fatigue in his eyes.

Sam told him. Sam must have told him what had happened.

"I went to your hotel in Prince Rupert today, but you'd already left. You're always on the run."

He gave her such a penetrating look that she had to lower her eyes.

"Why do you run away from me, Sonya? Why must you keep putting distance between us?"

His voice gave her shivers.

"I know you've got a lot of questions, but you can only clear them up if we're with each other now and then, don't you see that?"

She hastily pushed a strand of hair away from her forehead.

"You never called me, Robert, not in the last few days. Shouldn't I be thinking *you* were keeping your distance?"

He nodded.

"Yes, that's right. I wanted to give you time for everything you . . . wanted to clear up. I didn't want to butt in. I found out yesterday what happened at the lodge and left at once. I couldn't get through to you."

"That's true. They wanted to give me a couple of days' rest and didn't put calls through. But you didn't leave a message, and Sam—"

"Sam is always true blue. He gave me the news, luckily."

He leaned back, stretching his back and his broad shoulders. How hard it was to resist him.

"You're constantly putting yourself under threat. Sometimes it seems you're just asking for it. As if you needed to."

"Who? Me!" Sonya looked at him, filled with indignation. "*You* are telling *me* that? You of all people?"

She was about to launch into a speech about not wanting to be afraid for men anymore, but Robert was quicker off the mark.

"My God, Sonya, are you blind? You almost drove me nuts with the risks you took all the time. I'm glad you're still alive!"

She was speechless. But only for a few beats of her heart.

"And what about the people who are after you? What about the drug in the tea? And that boat? Have you forgotten they tried to send you to the bottom of the sea? Who the hell's living danger- ously, Robert? I wasn't even sure I'd find you alive in Vancouver!"

Oh, no. No tears right now, please!

She stood up and hit the edge of the table with a bang. She couldn't see clearly now.

"And furthermore—all those secrets between everybody. I don't want any more of it! I can't stand it any longer!"

Done! The words were out.

Her cheeks were wet.

Robert got up slowly. Looking out the window, he said nothing. He came toward her and ran his thumb tenderly over her damp skin. He undid her jacket zipper. Slipped it off.

She let him do it.

"Yes, there is a secret between us," he said, stroking her arms gently. "This is it."

He drew her toward him. His body was warm and strong. Nothing could shield her from him. He softly rubbed his face on hers, and his mouth brushed her lips. The salty scent of the sea flowed from the curve of his neck. She lifted her hands up higher on his back.

He was right. This was it.

CHAPTER 54

He threw a stout log on the fire, and sparks flew. The dogs dozing before the fireplace got up, startled. He put the fire screen back and dropped heavily into his chair.

"She'll be back," he said. "She'll be back."

The woman stroked the cat's smooth fur.

"Yes, she will, but not just on account of me, if that's what you mean."

He turned, looking at her. The woman stared dreamily into the fire.

"I think she's in love," she said.

"Did she say anything?"

"No, but I could read it in her face." She tickled the cat behind the ears. "You can tell by her face."

The man rubbed his chin.

"But no way it's Sam?"

She knew him well enough to hear a wish in his voice.

"Why do you say that?"

The man said nothing.

"No," she continued, "I don't think it's Sam. I didn't see any love there when she was talking to him."

The man kept silent.

The dogs pricked up their ears. One of them began to growl.

"The bear's back!" the man exclaimed. "I saw its tracks a week ago."

"I don't want you to shoot it, you hear? It's OK, it's pretty much OK."

"And those nightmares?"

"I just wake up and take some pills. It's OK."

A rustling sound of wind in the trees washed around the house. She'd miss that when she was in Switzerland. But things weren't that far along yet.

The cat purred loudly. *She doesn't care how I look*, the woman thought, *she's satisfied if she gets warmth and cuddling.*

"Sam was involved in it," the man blurted out.

"Involved in what?"

"In recovering the bodies."

"You mean . . . ?"

She stopped petting the cat.

"Jack came here shortly afterward. That was before he . . . before he flew you here."

"Your friend Jack Gordon? Wasn't he part of the recovery, too?"

"Yes, he was. Then he moved to the Queen Charlottes and died there. Nobody rescued *him*."

"Didn't you say he drank too much?"

"I did, but it only started afterward, after they found the Beaver and the bodies."

"Did Jack tell you about the recovery operation?"

"Yes, he did. He told me Sam was involved."

"Oh? But she doesn't know that."

"She doesn't need to. Better she doesn't."

His voice sounded harsher than usual. She knew something significant was about to come out.

"Jack said one of them was still alive."

She flinched. The cat tensed its muscles.

"Who? The boy?"

"No, the father. The illustrious pilot."

"Oh, my God!"

"Jack's plane was the first on the scene. Sam came shortly after. Sam's the best pilot around here."

"And what did they do?"

"Jack said to Sam, 'Take that injured guy and get the hell out of here.' That's what they did. There was still hope, Jack told me. There was still hope."

It sounded like a conspiracy.

"Sam flew off with the injured guy. Nobody's as good as Sam. Even in the crappiest weather—if anybody can do it, he can."

He got up and poked at a log. More sparks. The dogs tucked in their heads.

"Jack said he didn't know what happened, but it took Sam forever to get back to Seal Cove. Hell knows what he was doing up there. As if he'd gotten lost. But Sam never gets lost."

She listened with her heart pounding. She didn't dare interrupt.

"When Sam finally came down, it was too late."

He was quiet for a long time.

"Jack . . . asked Sam later what took him so long. Sam didn't say anything at first, and Jack asked him again, 'What the fuck were you doing all that time?' Sam only said, 'You know yourself. You were up there, too.' Jack said it didn't make a damn bit of sense to him."

The man kept standing in front of the fire, his face turned away as if he couldn't look at her just then.

"All the others were back faster than Sam, understand? They flew out later but came back sooner. Sam told everybody he had problems with his Beaver, problems with his goddamn crate. But Jack said they'd never found anything wrong with the Beaver."

"You mean to say he tried to delay . . . ?" She didn't dare finish her sentence—as if by not saying the words, what she was thinking would go away; her shock would diminish.

He squatted before the fire, and she heard his words as if they were windblown.

"Jack told Sam they could've saved the guy. They could've saved at least one of them. Then Sam told him, 'Why should that motherfucker live, of all people? The kid died because of him. And that murderer's supposed to live?' Those were Sam's very words, says Jack."

"*Said* Jack."

"What?"

"'Said Jack.' He's dead, after all. Can't say anything."

He got up in a hurry. The same hard edge to his voice.

"He's dead. And we are not going to say one word."

She let the cat slink off her lap. She hauled herself out of her chair. She went up to him until she could see the fire reflected in his eyes.

"She must never find out. Never."

They gazed at each other. The pact was sealed.

ACKNOWLEDGMENTS

The Berlin poet Else Lübcke Seel (1894–1974) existed in real life. I have taken all my information about her life and work from extant documents, her book, and conversations with people who knew her. The chapter on her son, Rupert Seel, is based on a conversation, as was the chapter on Alan Blackwell and Alice Harrison, who both unfortunately died before the present book went into print. Their daughter and son, June and Ronald Harrison, gave me permission to use the conversation with their parents. All of them deserve my deepest gratitude.

All other persons and events in this book are purely fictitious. Any resemblance to actual persons living or dead is purely coincidental and unintended.

I wish to give warm thanks to everyone who contributed to the success of this book, first and foremost to Professor Rodney Symington, the official administrator of Else Seel's literary remains, and to the staff of the Special Collections archive at the University of Victoria. I am also deeply moved by the unwavering support from Professor Peter Stenberg of the University of British Columbia in the Department of Central, Eastern, and Northern European Studies and by his inspiring wife, Rosa Stenberg.

A very special debt of gratitude is owed to the German scholar and writer Professor Angelika Arend of the University of Victoria for her expert and moral support.

It is always an honor and a pleasure to work with Gerald Chapple, who translated this book so beautifully and with so much artistic enthusiasm. I bow my head in admiration. I am also very grateful to Gabriella Page-Fort and her persistent efforts in steering the book through from start to finish; to Declan Spring and Brittany Dowdle for their fine editing work; to Janice Lee for her sensitive proofreading; and to Nina Chapple as the translation's first sharp-eyed and supportive reader.

I acquired a huge amount of knowledge about seaplanes and flying from the experienced and friendly pilots Bruce MacDonald and David Norman at Inland Air in Prince Rupert and from the amateur pilots Heinz Tock and Rod Lizee. I had long talks with Brian Tough, a mining engineer, about his profession. Any errors in my presentation are solely my responsibility.

The traveling nurse Dolores Gwerder provided me with valuable information from her fascinating professional life in Canada. She deserves special thanks.

Last but not least, invaluable help came from the criticism and enthusiasm of my "test readers" Birgit Breuer, Gisela Dalvit, Peter Uhr, Brigitta Staehli, Fabian Fabian, Hartmut Scheffler, and Alexandra and Vaclav Elias, along with the impressive diligence and competence of my editor Dr. Ann-Catherine Geuder.

Bernadette Calonego

WORKS CONSULTED

Arend, Angelika. "'Es tut so gut zu lieben und ganz wieder Mensch zu sein!' Some Comments on Else's Love Poetry." *Yearbook of German-American Studies* 37 (2002).

Neering, Rosemary. *Wild West Women*. Vancouver: Whitecap Books, 2000.

Seel, Else. *Ausgewählte Werke: Lyrik und Prosa*. Edited by Rodney T. K. Symington. Toronto: German-Canadian Historical Association, 1979.

———. *Kanadisches Tagebuch*. Herrenalb: Horst Erdmann Verlag, 1964.

ABOUT THE AUTHOR

Bernadette Calonego was born in Switzerland and grew up on the shores of Lake Lucerne. A voracious reader from an early age, she fed her imagination with stories such as The Leatherstocking Tales, *Ivanhoe*, *Treasure Island*, and *The Adventures of Huckleberry Finn*. She was just eleven years old when she published her first story, a fairy tale, in a Swiss newspaper. She went on to earn a teaching degree from the University of Fribourg, which she put to good use in England and Switzerland before switching gears to be a journalist. After several years working with the Reuters news agency and a series of German newspapers, she moved to Canada and began writing fiction. She has published stories in *Vogue*, *GEO*, and *SZ Magazin* and is the author of three novels. She lives near Vancouver.

Visit her at www.bernadettecalonego.com.

ABOUT THE TRANSLATOR

Gerald Chapple is an award-winning translator of German literature. He received his doctorate at Harvard and went on to teach German and comparative literature at McMaster University in Hamilton, Ontario. He has been translating contemporary German-language authors for forty years. His recent prose work includes two books by the Austrian writer Barbara Frischmuth, *The Convent School* and *Chasing after the Wind*, completed with cotranslator James B. Lawson; Michael Mitterauer's probing history of Europe from 600 to 1600, *Why Europe? Medieval Origins of Its Special Path*; Anita Albus's wonderfully idiosyncratic book *On Rare Birds*; and Bernadette Calonego's English debut thriller *The Zurich Conspiracy*. After choosing early retirement, he lives in Dundas, Ontario, with his wife, Nina, an architectural historian. When not translating, he can usually be found studying birds, butterflies, and dragonflies; reading; or listening to classical music.